"You can hear everything . . . . . ." surprised.

Eden swallowed hard. "Of course I can."

"It's just that others . . . some haven't been able to hear me at all. And the ones who can don't hear everything."

She curled her hand around the baseball bat she kept under her desk. One could never be too careful. Triple-A wasn't exactly in the city's best neighborhood.

"What others?" she asked cautiously.

"My other . . . my other *hosts*. Look, I don't want you to be afraid—"

"It's getting a bit late for that, whoever you are." She gripped the bat tightly and stood up from the desk. Nobody else was going to sneak up on her. One serial killer a day was her limit.

She nudged open the door to the bathroom with her foot. The office was completely empty. She began to tremble. Even if someone had been hiding, their voice wouldn't be so loud in her ears. So loud that it sounded as if it was coming from—

Inside of me.

THE DEMON
IN ME

≫ Michelle Rowen ≪

BERKLEY SENSATION, NEW YORK

THE BERKLEY PUBLISHING GROUP
Published by the Penguin Group
Penguin Group (USA) Inc.
375 Hudson Street, New York, New York 10014, USA
Penguin Group (Canada), 90 Eglinton Avenue East, Suite 700, Toronto, Ontario M4P 2Y3, Canada
(a division of Pearson Penguin Canada Inc.)
Penguin Books Ltd., 80 Strand, London WC2R 0RL, England
Penguin Group Ireland, 25 St. Stephen's Green, Dublin 2, Ireland (a division of Penguin Books Ltd.)
Penguin Group (Australia), 250 Camberwell Road, Camberwell, Victoria 3124, Australia
(a division of Pearson Australia Group Pty. Ltd.)
Penguin Books India Pvt. Ltd., 11 Community Centre, Panchsheel Park, New Delhi—110 017, India
Penguin Group (NZ), 67 Apollo Drive, Rosedale, North Shore 0632, New Zealand
(a division of Pearson New Zealand Ltd.)
Penguin Books (South Africa) (Pty.) Ltd., 24 Sturdee Avenue, Rosebank, Johannesburg 2196,
South Africa

Penguin Books Ltd., Registered Offices: 80 Strand, London WC2R 0RL, England

This is a work of fiction. Names, characters, places, and incidents either are the product of the author's imagination or are used fictitiously, and any resemblance to actual persons, living or dead, business establishments, events, or locales is entirely coincidental. The publisher does not have any control over and does not assume any responsibility for author or third-party websites or their content.

THE DEMON IN ME

A Berkley Sensation Book / published by arrangement with the author

PRINTING HISTORY
Berkley Sensation mass-market edition / May 2010

Copyright © 2010 by Michelle Rouillard.
Excerpt from *Something Wicked* by Michelle Rowen copyright © by Michelle Rouillard.
Cover art by Craig White.
Cover design by Lesley Worrell.
Interior text design by Laura K. Corless.

ISBN: 978-0-425-23468-6

BERKLEY® SENSATION
Berkley Sensation Books are published by The Berkley Publishing Group,
a division of Penguin Group (USA) Inc.,
375 Hudson Street, New York, New York 10014.
BERKLEY® SENSATION and the "B" design are trademarks of Penguin Group (USA) Inc.

PRINTED IN THE UNITED STATES OF AMERICA

10 9 8 7 6 5 4 3 2 1

This one's for my mom!
xoxo

Acknowledgments

Thank you so much to my editor Cindy Hwang. It's an honor and a pleasure to be working with you!

Thanks to my agent Jim McCarthy for believing in this book from the very beginning when it looked absolutely nothing like this final version.

Thanks also to Bonnie Staring, Laurie Rauch, and Eve Silver for beta-reading and to Maureen Skinner for answering my police-related questions. You all rock!

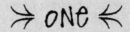 ONE

"You're Eden Riley, right? Wow, it's *so* exciting to meet a real psychic!"

Eden cringed and slowly turned to see a wide-eyed man with a receding hairline staring at her expectantly. She forced a smile. "That would be me."

He beamed back at her. "I'm Constable Santos. I was sent ahead to keep you company until Detective Hanson arrives. He's running a bit late."

Since she'd been waiting a half hour already, she kind of figured that.

"I should probably warn you that the detective's a bit of a skeptic. He's not that big on adding psychics to the investigation."

"Trust me, Constable, I'm used to that kind of attitude."

He waved a hand. "Don't let it bother you. You'll just show him how insightful you are and make a believer out of him."

Eden tried to hold on to her smile. "Fair enough."

"So how does this work?" he asked.

"How does what work?"

"The psychic thing to solve our unsolved cases. Everyone's still buzzing about what you did last month."

Eden's stomach twisted unpleasantly. Up until last month, and just before she'd moved to the city, she'd worked at Psychic Connexions, a phone-based service located two hours north of Toronto, meant for entertainment only—astrology readings, love life, and job advice. She had a talent for saying the right thing at the right time and keeping her customers happy enough to get them to be repeat callers.

She simply told people what they wanted to hear, helped by some mild insight and a knack for reading tarot cards. Everyone was happy.

But it didn't mean she was really, truly psychic.

Little did she know that one of her regulars was Meredith Holt, the wife of Toronto's current chief of police and a devout believer in All Things Mystical. She'd discovered Eden by accident (or *fate*, as she'd later relate the story) when her usual fortune-teller was away on vacation and she "got a hunch" to call the number advertised in the Entertainment section of the newspaper. Eden simply knew her as Merry, a lovely woman who always ended their daily twenty-minute sessions with a wish of "brightest blessings."

One day Merry called in crying and near hysterical. Her beloved Maltese terrier, Sunny, had gone missing and she was beside herself with worry.

There were . . . *moments* . . . when things just clicked psychically for Eden, even without consulting her deck of cards. As Merry poured out her emotions over the phone at $1.99 a minute, a very clear and precise image of a little white ball of fluff slammed into Eden's head with all the subtly of a Mack truck.

She knew that the dog was locked in Merry's neighbor's rarely used toolshed, living off birdseed and rainwater for two days, and was about to be adopted by a family of concerned raccoons.

She made up the last bit to soften the news.

Merry had thanked her profusely and Eden had gone back to her day, which included assuring a hysterical Aquarius that her Gemini boyfriend was going to pop the question soon. However, she didn't specify exactly what the question might be.

The next day, her boss got a phone call from the chief of police, who wanted to get in touch with Eden because of the grateful ravings of his dog-obsessed wife. He wanted to have Eden on the roster of psychic consultants for future police work.

The man would not take no for an answer.

Eden's boss at Psychic Connexions let her go later that week, explaining that his business, such as it was, would be better off without any close police scrutiny.

If she'd been able to psychically foresee that unfortunate outcome, she would have saved some money for a rainy day.

The first time she'd been called in to officially consult on a police case two weeks ago, it'd been a total bust. Even though she'd concentrated so hard it felt like her head would explode, she'd sensed absolutely nothing useful to do with the missing person. She hated disappointing people, especially when they looked at her with that too-familiar, hard-edged, cynical glare. Most people thought psychics, even mild ones like her, were major frauds, and failing to prove them wrong was even more annoying.

She had no guarantees this time would be any better. The house she presently stood in front of had recently been home to a serial killer and the police wanted to see if she could "sense something" about the killer's current whereabouts.

She wanted to help if she could, but maybe she was in way over her head.

In fact, she was quite sure of it.

Eden cleared her throat nervously. The mid-October air was getting cool enough that she regretted not bringing a light jacket along today. "So . . . how much longer do you think Detective Hanson will be?"

Santos seemed stumped by the question for a moment, but

then looked over to his left side. "Oh, here he comes now. But since you're psychic you probably knew he was nearly here, right?"

So very wrong. Eden took a deep breath, held it, and glanced over at the approaching figure.

Detective Ben Hanson was six foot two of *gorgeous* with a body like a Greek god and a face like a movie star. There was a reason that his last name sounded like "handsome." She'd noticed that women swooned—seriously *swooned*—when he walked past. And the fact that he was a cop, not to mention an *unmarried* cop, only added the proverbial fuel to the sexy-man fire. Eden had seen him twice before when she'd visited police headquarters at the chief's insistence. When she found out he was the one assigned to walk her through this case, she dropped everything and rushed over.

Did that make her seem completely sad and pathetic?

Yeah, well, Eden thought as she let her breath out in a long sigh. *The truth hurts.*

He approached and her heart did an annoying *ka-thunk-a-thunk.* It wasn't as though she expected them to get married and have lots of babies, but she did like checking him out.

He made her feel like a sixteen-year-old high schooler—geeky and pimply and drooling over the out-of-her-league football quarterback.

Eden was closing in on thirty now. She wasn't pimply anymore. However, the geeky thing was still up for debate. Gorgeous guys had a tendency to make her completely and embarrassingly tongue-tied.

"Is the psychic here yet, Santos?" he asked.

Hello? Had she suddenly become invisible?

Santos nodded at her. "This is Eden Riley."

That finally earned her a glance, but there was zero warmth or humor behind it. "Then let's get this over with."

Obviously, she thought wryly, *he's already fallen madly in love with me, but is having a hard time showing it.*

"Sounds super," Eden said, forcing enthusiasm past her nervousness. "Lead the way, Detective."

The sour-faced look that comment received from him confirmed it was official: She was still a geek.

She followed him to the average-looking house. The front door had some of that police-line-do-not-cross tape on it. He ripped it away and entered the front hallway that led to a small kitchen.

"Here's how this is going to go. The suspect vacated this location about six days ago. Our leads as to where he went have come up dry. The sergeant seems to think you might be able to"—he glanced at her—"work some mojo and tell us where he's hiding."

Eden raised her eyebrows. *"Mojo?"*

He waved his hand in a flippant manner. "Whatever it is you think you can do. Hocus-pocus. Mojo. You know."

He was lucky he was so hot or she might be annoyed by his rude and dismissive attitude. "For the record, Detective, I didn't ask to be here. It was requested of me." She cleared her throat. "If you'd prefer, I can take my, uh . . . *mojo* somewhere else."

"The chief thinks you can help."

"But you don't."

"No, actually I don't."

"Because you don't believe in psychics."

He raised his blue-eyed gaze steadily to hers. "That's right."

"Well, to tell you the truth, I'm not all that convinced, myself." She crossed her arms.

"Excuse me?"

She chewed her bottom lip and tried not to feel like a big, fat fraud. "I can't seem to control where and when I see stuff. It's not a tap I can turn on and get a big glass of sparkling psychic water. I just want you to know that up front so you're . . . you're not disappointed if nothing happens today."

"I won't be disappointed. I'm *expecting* nothing to happen." He tilted his head to the side. "Does the chief know how you feel about this?"

"He wouldn't listen to me." She had explained that it was doubtful she'd be much use to them, but he'd insisted—although Eden suspected it had a lot to do with appeasing his enthusiastic wife. "I figure if I don't turn out to be much help, he'll start to leave me alone. Maybe I only have a knack for finding lost dogs."

Ben looked confused. "So you're a psychic who doesn't believe in psychics?"

"I . . . I honestly don't know." It was the truth, at least. "Feel free to kick me out of here, you know, whenever you like."

Why was she sharing this information with him? She wasn't exactly sure, although sometimes it was better to admit one's weaknesses right away so there'd be no room for later misunderstandings. It might have also had a lot to do with Detective Hanson bringing out the schoolgirl babble inside of her. Once her mouth started spilling words, it was hard to stop the flood.

He studied her for at least thirty seconds before his frown turned into the first smile she'd seen on his face—and *wow*, he had one hell of a great smile. "I think you might be the only skeptical psychic I've ever met."

He scanned her then, from her long auburn ponytail draped over her right shoulder to her green peasant-style silk shirt to the tan leather ankle boots she'd bought only yesterday to go with the dark jeans she wore.

Whatever she'd said—well, *the truth*—was enough to make handsome Detective Hanson look at her a little differently. A *good* differently. She leaned against the kitchen counter and tried to look as alluring as humanly possible, but her elbow slipped so she straightened up. She was more than a little uncomfortable being in the house of a serial killer—although, by the looks of it, a very neat and organized one—but she pretended not to be as she felt Detective Hanson's gaze take her in.

"Huh. Interesting," he finally proclaimed.

She couldn't tell if he meant that in a good or bad way. "I'm sorry if you think I'm wasting your time."

He grinned. "Actually, I already thought this trip here today was a waste of time to begin with. You had nothing to do with it. But I appreciate you being honest with me."

"Honesty is a virtue, Detective Hanson."

"Please . . . call me Ben." He glanced at the clock on the wall that read almost five and then turned his attention back to Eden. "So do you need to be anywhere after this or would you like to grab some dinner?"

Remain calm, Eden, she commanded herself as a flush of pleasure heated her cheeks. Detective Handsome was asking her out. And he wanted her to call him Ben.

Her empty stomach growled its enthusiastic approval.

"That sounds like—" Then she froze as the strangest feeling came over her. A chill that made the hair stand up on her arms. *"Shit."*

Ben frowned. "What?"

She brought a hand to her head as a strange, fuzzy image flickered through her mind. *Damn it, not now.*

She was the "skeptical psychic," as Ben had just described her. But there it was—a feeling crawling down her spine that she couldn't ignore if she'd wanted to. She'd had the feeling many times before in her life, since she was a little girl, but it came and went and was never anything she could channel or control. An awareness that didn't rely on any of her usual five senses.

Suddenly the coat closet just beyond the kitchenette was all she could concentrate on. Something was in there—possibly a clue to help find the maniac the police were looking for.

"What exactly did this creep do?" she asked quietly.

His expression turned grim. "What he did was kill one woman a week by posing as a pizza delivery guy. Eight weeks and eight deaths. Then suddenly he stopped three weeks ago—

no more murders since then. It's strange because usually serial killers begin to escalate once they've established a pattern. We don't know when he'll start again, but it's only a matter of time."

A chill went down her spine. If she could do something, *anything*, then it would be worth it. She pushed away from the counter and walked directly toward the coat closet.

"I know what I said earlier about not really believing in my abilities," she began, "but I'm getting this weird vibe right now."

"Weird vibe?" The cool, cynical edge was back.

The impulse was too strong to ignore. "This will only take a second. It's probably nothing."

Hell, with her track record, maybe it was the guy's dog.

Eden wrapped her fingers around the handle. The hinges creaked as she slowly opened the door.

She blinked and stared with disbelief at what she saw.

She'd been right. There was a clue inside. A *big* clue.

A clue that was about six feet tall, 250 pounds, and held a large knife.

For a long, frozen second she stared, unable to move or speak with only one thought flitting through her head—

What were the damn odds that the very serial killer they were looking for would be in the house? Hiding in the freaking closet?

Good odds, obviously. *Very good odds.*

Eden shrieked as the large man thrust out his hand and grabbed her. He turned her around and held her firmly in place with one arm. The sharp tip of the knife grazed her throat.

"Shouldn't have done that," he growled. "I was trying to hide all quiet like a mouse."

"Drop your weapon!" Ben had his gun out and pointed at the friendly neighborhood serial killer currently pressed against Eden's back.

The sharp edge of the blade pushed closer against her skin. "I just came back to pick up a few things, not to have a show-down. You should have damn well left me alone."

Eden shot Ben a panicked look and then concentrated on not moving. "Please let go of me."

He dragged her roughly backward into the open archway leading to the living room. The curtains were drawn on the bay window, leaving them in shadows. "I need your help. I heard you talking. You're a psychic. That's how you sniffed me out."

Now that she was really close to him she could *literally* sniff him out. Considering how neat and tidy his house was, the man had obviously been away from deodorant or showers for several days. Her skin crawled and bile rose in her throat.

"How can I help you?" she managed.

"I'm possessed by a demon," he hissed into her ear. "And I want it out of me."

"A demon?" she repeated, trying to sound as if she believed him. "Is that what you think is making you kill people? The devil made you do it?"

She exchanged a fleeting look with Ben, who stood six feet in front of her. He'd be able to hear everything the freak was saying to her. The cop's expression was fierce but a distinct flicker of worry crossed his blue eyes. He was thinking what she was thinking. This guy was insane—even by serial killer standards.

"I can't concentrate." The killer shifted farther back with her. "Can't think with it in my head. I killed a homeless guy a couple weeks ago and the demon's been with me ever since."

"I'm warning you again," Ben snarled. "Let the woman go *right now*."

The guy tensed. "He's telling me to let you go."

"That's r-right," Eden said, her voice shaky. "Listen to the nice policeman. He wants to help you and so do I. Nobody has to get hurt here."

"No, not the cop, the *demon*. He wants me to let you go."

Okay. "Well, then listen to the nice d-demon. I can help you. I *am* psychic. Very powerful. That's me. I'll be able to talk to your demon and convince him to leave your body and go back to—to *Hell* . . . and then everything will be fine."

"You don't believe me. I can hear it in your voice."

Her stomach clenched with fear. "No, I do. I totally believe."

"The world is full of strange things and strange beings. They're among us. Walking around, eating, drinking, living side by side with humans. I couldn't see them before but now I can. They're everywhere. Do you see them, too?"

"Of course I do." It sounded like a lie. Mostly because it was. She could be this bastard's next murder victim. Her life might be crappy at the moment, but that didn't mean she wanted it to end. Her legs weakened, and if he hadn't been holding her tightly she would have fallen straight down to the beige-carpeted floor.

She gasped as the knife pressed closer.

"Maybe if I slit your throat the demon will leave," the killer growled into her ear. "He'll see that he doesn't have any power over me."

Eden met Ben's steady but worried gaze. He had his gun aimed at the serial killer's chest, but at the moment she was blocking the way.

"This is your last warning," Ben snapped. "I *will* shoot you."

Suddenly the killer let go of Eden and she spun around to see that he looked extremely upset.

"Shut up!" he yelled, and brought his hands up to his head. "I'm not listening to you, demon. I'll kill her."

His gaze tracked to where Eden stood, his eyes wide and crazed. He raised his knife and lunged at her.

She screamed, staggered back, and tripped over the edge of the carpet, landing hard on her butt.

A shot rang out, then another, and the serial killer crumpled to the ground.

He didn't move again.

"Eden, are you okay?" Ben asked sharply.

Okay? she thought, feeling stunned and shivery. Hell no, she wasn't okay. But at least she was still breathing.

"I'll be fine." Her hands shook so she clasped them in

front of her. She decided to stay seated on the floor since she was sure her legs were too shaky to stand on. A line of perspiration sped down her spine. "You wanted me to help find the s-serial killer—" She took a shuddery breath. "Mission accomplished."

Her stomach churned and she was afraid she would be sick right then and there. She tried to focus on something, anything until she could calm down. Her gaze moved cautiously toward the prone body of the dead man she knew she'd have nightmares about for weeks—possibly *years*—to come.

She frowned. "Hey, do you see that?"

"See what?"

"That." She pointed at what looked like a thin, dark shadow emerging from the serial killer's gaping mouth and trailing along the floor like a black scarf.

That is definitely *not normal*, she thought.

Ben shook his head. "All I see is a dead body. It's okay now, Eden. You're safe."

The shadow paused as it moved across the floor between her and Ben. Then, before she could do anything else or figure out what on earth it was, it shifted direction and, in a split second, flew through the air toward her. She shrieked and instinctively put her hands up to block whatever it was, but the moment the shadow touched her . . . it disappeared.

She looked at her hands.

What the hell just happened?

Had it only been her imagination?

Ben held out a hand to help her back up to her feet. "Are you sure you're okay?"

She swallowed hard. "I will be—you know—eventually."

He squeezed her hand in his. "Good."

She definitely needed a drink. A big one. Straight up.

She knew she should have stopped for some lunch earlier. A piece of toast and a glass of juice nine hours ago was not enough for proper mental alertness. She shook away the strange feeling and tried to relax while Ben got on his phone and called for backup.

Constable Santos ran in and swept the room with one look. "Eden! Damn, you sure work fast! You found the killer!"

That she did. And now the killer was killed.

But she still felt like she wanted to hurl. Missing dogs were much easier to deal with than serial killers. That was the lesson of the day.

At least it's over, she thought wearily. She'd be very happy to go back to her regular life now.

No more traumatic experiences for her, thank you very much.

⇉ TWO ⇇

Ben was too busy for that dinner date after all. In fact, other than a few concerned looks cast in Eden's general direction, he mostly ignored her once the rest of the cops got there.

He asked Constable Santos to give Eden a ride home, but she had him take her to her day job instead. Fifteen minutes later she arrived at Triple-A Investigations, a small, low-end detective agency.

Why Eden currently worked there was very simple.

Her mother, may she rest in peace, loved to play poker. And drink. And neglect her only daughter whenever possible, but that was another story. Recently, she'd won half the agency in a poker game with the owner, Andy McCoy. When she died last month she'd left her share of it to Eden, along with a pair of small diamond-stud earrings.

At least the earrings had some value.

When news reached Eden that half was hers, she'd just lost her job at Psychic Connexions—which meant she was officially looking for work again. She'd gone into Triple-A hoping what was behind the glass front door had more potential than the name of the place.

What she'd found was two desks. Overflowing garbage cans. Peeling wallpaper. The stench of cigar smoke permeated the air. All of this luxury was next door to a coffee bar, also owned by Andy, called Hot Stuff.

Andy wanted to buy Eden out, which was fine with her, but he didn't have any money, which *wasn't* fine by her. So, despite her gut instinct to walk away from the business completely, she moved to the city, rented a small apartment, and started to work there. She didn't have a PI license and had no intention of getting one, so she instead helped out with paperwork, filing, typing, and answering the phone. She'd tried to get the smell of cigars out of the air and walls; however, Febreze could only do so much.

She waited for Andy to get enough money together to pay for her half of the agency.

It had been almost a month. She was still waiting.

In the meantime, Andy did give her reasonable biweekly paychecks to help make ends meet. He wasn't a total tightwad.

"Eden," Andy greeted her when she walked through the glass front door. "I'm glad you're back."

"Trust me, after the day I've had, I'm glad to be back."

Andy was a man who'd definitely had the potential of being attractive and charming at one time, but life and circumstances had gotten in the way to make him pinched and squinty. An FBI agent until fifteen years ago, he was pushing fifty, still solidly built, pale blond hair and eyebrows, and warm and friendly green eyes.

"How did the thing go?" he asked. "With the cop?"

Well, he did ask. "I was attacked by a serial killer who said he was possessed by a demon. I almost died. A gorgeous cop who's a dead ringer for Brad Pitt asked me out for dinner but then reneged and I'm not sure if I should call him. Do you think that would make me look like a stalker?" She sighed. "I may actually throw up at any moment. Just a warning."

He stared at her. "Are you serious about the serial killer?"

"I'm not in a good enough mood right now to joke."

"But you're all right? You're not hurt at all, are you?"

It was sweet of him to care. "I'm okay."

"That's good to hear." He pursed his lips. "Listen, I'd stick around for moral support or whatever, but I have to split. Are you staying long?"

Well, maybe he didn't care that much. "For a while. I'm trying to take my mind off what happened, actually. This place is oddly soothing, despite the décor."

"Well, if you're looking for something to do . . . can you enter this all into the computer? I'd appreciate it."

Eden looked at the stack of files he had his hand on. Andy liked to handwrite everything. Eden was one of the only people in the world—she thought—who could decipher his penmanship. Typing was good mindless work and would definitely help her brain focus on something else before she went home. "Yeah, sure. No problem."

He grinned and actually patted her shoulder, placing the folders on top of her desk. "Super. You're a peach, especially after everything you've gone through. I'll see you bright and early tomorrow, okay?"

She nodded. "Sure. Have a good night."

He threw his coat over his shoulder and walked out the front door.

Eden watched him get into his leased red Porsche and drive away. The sky was turning pink and purple and orange as the sun slowly began to sink beneath the horizon.

She walked over to sit at her little desk, feeling oddly despondent about everything after her brush with death.

If she was really 100 percent psychic, would she be able to see into her own future? What would it hold? Excitement and romance? Or more of the same?

"Place your bets," she murmured. "My money's on more of the same. Bring it on."

She'd recently made a promise to look on the bright side of

things after reading *The Secret*. Five times. She owned the book, the audio book, and the DVD. If she believed that good things were going to happen, then they would. But the belief had to be complete. She had to clearly imagine what she wanted in life in order to make it happen.

Sure. It was possible.

I'd love more money so I could move out of my crappy apartment, she thought. *That would be super.*

She'd also love a great job that fulfilled her and would also help others in some way. All she knew was that she hadn't found it yet.

Finally, she'd love to find a wonderful man who loved her for who she was inside.

Believe it. Feel it. See it. Be it.

Her stomach still growled with hunger. And the universe provided an immediate solution. There was a big box of Hot Stuff donuts and pastries over on Andy's desk. There was also a pot of coffee that actually looked remotely fresh.

She picked up a Boston cream and devoured it in about five seconds, very glad there was no one there to witness it. She then grabbed an apple fritter, put it on a paper towel, and fixed her coffee—two creamers, two sugars. She tipped the mug back and swallowed a mouthful.

The warm liquid swished around in her stomach as she felt something else. A strange tingling sensation began to spread through her body and down to her arms and legs.

She put the mug down and held her palm over her stomach.

"Maybe that coffee wasn't as fresh as I thought," she said aloud.

"Hello? Can you hear me?"

The male voice made her turn around to see where it came from, but there was nobody in the office except for her.

"Hello?" she responded cautiously.

She felt a small lurch in her gut. *Indigestion so quickly?* Perhaps she should have had a salad. The nutrition gods were trying to tell her something.

"Who are you?" the voice spoke again.

Eden's gaze darted around the room. What was going on? Her body immediately tensed and her heart began to pound—hard. She was still feeling the effects from being grabbed by the serial killer earlier, and it was likely she'd do so for a while.

"Who are *you*?" she asked. "*Where* are you? Andy's gone for the day."

"You're a woman." Whoever this was sounded surprised by that.

"Good guess. Now you're going to have to tell me who you are and where you're hiding or we're going to have a problem. I'm not a big fan of hide-and-seek."

"You can hear everything I'm saying?" He sounded surprised.

She swallowed hard. "Of course I can."

"It's just that the others . . . well, most of them haven't been able to hear me at all. And the ones who could didn't hear everything clearly."

She curled her hand around the baseball bat she kept under her desk. One could never be too careful. Triple-A wasn't exactly in the city's best neighborhood.

"What others?" she asked.

"My other . . . my other *hosts*. Look, I don't want you to be afraid—"

"It's getting a bit late for that, whoever you are." She gripped the bat tightly and stood up from the desk. Nobody else was going to sneak up on her. One serial killer a day was her limit.

She nudged open the door to the small bathroom with her foot. The office was completely empty. She began to tremble. Even if someone had been hiding, their voice wouldn't be so loud in her ears. So loud that it sounded as if it was coming from—

Inside of me.

"You're the woman with the long, reddish hair, aren't you? He wanted to kill you. And then—" He paused. "Then I don't remember much—it's fuzzy right now. Was he killed? Of course, he had to be or this wouldn't have happened."

"How do you know about that?" she demanded, and began to shuffle backward into the far corner by Andy's bookshelf. "I'm going to call the cops if you don't leave me alone."

"There was a cop there. A tall man with blond hair. He had a gun."

"How do you know what happened?" She glanced under Andy's desk, which would have made a good hiding spot. But other than three balled-up pieces of paper that hadn't hit the trash can, there was nothing there. "I just want to be left alone. Honestly, I'm not really as psychic as people seem to think. Checking the coat closet was a lucky guess. It's called *coincidence* and it happens all the time."

"You're psychic?" he repeated. "Right, he mentioned that. He thought you might be able to help him get rid of me."

Eden frowned deeply. "Get rid of you? The killer said he was possessed by a demon he desperately wanted out of him."

Her head spun just thinking about it. Demons didn't exist. Of course they didn't. That was crazy.

Besides, a demon wouldn't sound like this, would it? Her newly discovered inner voice was deep, warm, and calm. She would have expected a demon to sound scary and, well, *demonic*. Her hands began to ache as she clutched the bat tighter.

"The important thing is not to panic," the voice said.

"What the hell is going on here?"

"Really, *demon* is a bit of a derogatory word, isn't it?" he continued conversationally. "I promise I mean you no harm at all. I did what I could to keep my former host from hurting you and luckily it all turned out okay. Well, sort of okay. Now if we can just talk about—"

"You . . . you're a d-demon?" she stuttered.

"Well . . . technically, yes I am. But just try to relax. I know this is a bit of a surprise, but everything's going to be fine."

No, it wasn't possible. Not a chance. Demons didn't exist. She must have had some kind of mental breakdown. Now, *that* was possible. It had been a very traumatic day. Something deep in her psyche must have cracked open wide enough for her to suddenly hear a voice in her head.

"Everything's going to be fine?" she repeated through clenched teeth. "I don't think so. I need to go to the hospital. I need a psych evaluation. I've obviously gone cuckoo for Cocoa Puffs."

"No, you haven't. I'm sorry, but I can't survive without a human host, otherwise I'll dissipate into the air like smoke. I had no choice. There were two of you there, you and the cop, and it was a fifty-fifty chance that I ended up with you—although, I've got to say, you're my first female host ever. This should be very interesting."

She licked her dry lips. Her muscles were so tight she thought they might snap like overused hair elastics. "Did you say smoke? Like *black* smoke?"

Black smoke had left the dead killer's body and flew through the air toward her. She'd since dismissed it as a figment of her traumatized imagination, but now . . .

"You're a *demon*," she said it so quietly even she had trouble hearing it.

"Yes."

"And you've possessed me."

"If you put it that way it sounds a bit ominous, doesn't it? I'd rather think of it as 'sharing living space.'"

It was true. She'd seen it with her own eyes when the serial killer had been killed. The black smoke hadn't just been smoke—it was *the demon* he'd claimed to be possessed with. The demon that was now *inside of her*.

For a moment she was positive she'd faint. The feeling passed, but the steadily growing fear that filled her remained.

"Get out of me," she said softly.

"That does sound like an excellent plan, but you need to understand, this isn't my choice. I haven't been able to exist outside of my host since—"

"Get out right now!" Eden clutched the baseball bat so

tightly she was sure she'd get splinters. She put every ounce of energy she could summon from the universe into those four words. She'd never felt so fierce or certain about anything in her entire twenty-nine years of life—and that included kicking her cheating jerk of a fiancé out six months ago. Although, it was still a close second.

She felt rather than heard the demon gasp inside of her—inside her head, her chest, her entire body. As if she'd been punched in the stomach she let out a wheezing breath and doubled over as the black smoke exited through her mouth in one dark, tasteless, odorless stream. She scrambled back from it until she hit the wall behind her and held the bat up as if that would be enough to protect her from Hell itself.

The smoke hung there like a small black rain cloud, unmoving, five feet in front of her, for a few more moments. Then something changed. She watched, stunned, as it began to take on a recognizable shape. The entire process took less than thirty seconds, but it was as if time itself had stopped. She couldn't move, couldn't breathe, couldn't think. All she could do was watch—waiting for a large, red, hulking, horned hell-beast to appear and devour her whole.

⇒ THREE ⇐

When he finished, he was tall, but not red or beastly—and he looked like a man, not the monster Eden was expecting.

He raised his wide-eyed gaze to hers and blinked. He looked as shocked as she felt. Then he looked down at his hands, holding them out in front of him, before reaching up to touch his face, mouth, cheeks, ears, and finally running his fingers through his black hair.

Full lips peeled back from straight white teeth and he began to laugh.

But it wasn't a demonically evil laugh. It sounded more like one of sheer joy.

"I can't believe this," he said after a moment. He stretched his arms over his head as if he'd just woken up from a long sleep and his muscles were stiff and needed stretching.

"That makes two of us." She was surprised she could even speak considering how beyond freaked-out she was. Her legs were too weak and rubbery to even consider running. She felt like the girl in Michael Jackson's "Thriller" video. The one who just stood there, frozen in place, screaming like a helpless twit while her date slowly turned into a werewolf.

Eden didn't think she had enough air to scream like a helpless twit.

He ran his hands down his sides and across his stomach and chest. He closed his eyes and sighed happily.

She eyed him with trepidation. "Do you want to be alone?"

His eyes snapped open and he looked directly at her. "More than you could ever possibly know."

The demon had ice blue eyes framed with dark lashes. The blue was a sharp contrast to the darkness of his shaggy hair that was almost long enough to brush his shoulders. He was pale, as if it had been a very long time since he'd felt the sun on his skin. He wore generic black clothes on his tall frame—pants, T-shirt, boots—however, if she'd seen him on the street she might have checked him out. He was inarguably attractive, but that little observation did nothing to help her relax. If anything, it made her tense up even more. His handsome exterior had to be a façade, a trap of some kind—like a Venus flytrap luring its prey to be consumed slowly and painfully.

She tried to see evidence of horns growing from his temples or black, leathery wings stretching out behind him, but visually there was nothing that alarming.

He pushed the unruly hair back from his eyes and smiled at her. "I haven't been able to take solid human form in over three hundred years. I can't tell you how much this—hey, watch it—"

He ducked out of the way just before her bat swung through the air where he'd been standing. When she swung again, he caught the bat and easily pulled it out of her grip. She stepped backward, scanning her immediate surroundings for another potential weapon.

His dark brows drew together. "What part of 'I mean you no harm' didn't you understand?"

"It's not every day I'm possessed by a demon. Sorry if I'm not reacting in the calm, collected way I'm supposed to." She grabbed a hardcover dictionary and whipped it at him. It made contact with his right shoulder and fell to the ground in front of him.

"Ouch," he said. Then he grinned again. "Hey, I can feel pain. Not something I thought I'd miss at all, but what do you know?" The grin vanished when she yanked the cord from the wall and threw a phone at him, but he was able to block it with his forearm. "That's enough pain for today, I think."

As she was desperately reaching for something else to hurl across the room, he was suddenly beside her.

He grabbed her wrists. "Don't do that."

"Let go of me." She struggled against him, but his strong grip was impossible to break free from.

"Will you stop throwing things at me?"

"Can't promise that."

He pulled her closer to him. "Then I'm afraid I can't let you go yet."

The demon was very warm and felt so human that if she hadn't seen with her own two eyes that he'd previously been a cloud of black smoke, she never would have believed it.

He shifted both of her wrists to one hand so he could slowly pull her hair free from its low ponytail and then stroked the length of it against her throat and collarbone.

"What the hell do you think you're doing?" she managed, shocked by his bizarre and unexpected behavior.

"Sorry." His gaze flicked back to hers and his smile widened. "All I've been able to do is observe for so long I'd forgotten how wonderful some things can feel. You don't mind, do you?"

"Yes, I do mind. I'm warning you, let go of me, or . . . *or else*."

"Is that a demand or a request?"

"It's a demanding request."

"You're a very beautiful woman."

"Uh . . . thanks. But I'm still thinking you should let go of me. Like, now."

It was unfortunate that she was no longer struggling against him. That kind of downplayed the force of her words a bit. But being so close to this strangely attractive demon was making her feel . . . well, *strange*.

The tingles she'd felt earlier had quickly gathered in one place now, low in her body. An intoxicating warmth began to fill her senses, and her fear was rapidly being replaced by something else—a strange and uncontrollable surge of desire, which was scarier and more dangerous since it was triggered by having a demon pressed against her.

"It's been three centuries since I've been able to touch anyone," he murmured.

"Sorry to hear that."

He focused on her mouth for a moment. "Or, for that matter, *kiss* anyone."

She cleared her throat nervously, certain that he was close enough to easily feel her racing heart rate. "Sucks to be you."

It actually felt about the same length of time for Eden, even though it was really only six months since she'd kicked ass-face— her pet name for her ex—out of her life. It was one of the many reasons she hadn't minded leaving her small town for life in the big city.

He leaned closer to her.

Her eyes widened as she realized what he was going to do. "Hold on a moment . . ."

She wasn't going to kiss a demon. It was absolutely not going to happen. Not a chance in—

The demon brushed his lips softly against hers.

Well, maybe I'm wrong, she thought.

She wasn't sure when he'd released her wrists, but his fingers now tangled in her long hair. For some reason her hands were closing in on the small of his back and rapidly heading farther south at about the same moment she opened her mouth to his knee-weakening kiss. In response, he groaned low in his throat as his tongue slid against hers and a lightning bolt of lust slammed through her.

What in the hell *am I doing*? she yelled at herself from what seemed like a far distance.

She wrenched her lips away from him and moved her hands up from a very firm demon-butt to his equally firm black T-shirt-clad chest to push him away.

A smile curled up the side of his mouth. "Now that wasn't so bad, was it?"

Eden's face felt like it was on fire. "I think I'm going to puke."

The smile held. "I don't think you really mean that."

"Get away from me," she said, only this time it sounded annoyingly breathless.

"Why? Are you going to throw something at me again?" He leaned toward her like a predator who'd cornered his prey.

"Not exactly." She brought her knee up sharply enough to let him know she was being serious and made contact with a sensitive area that demons seemed to have in common with human males.

"Okay . . . *ow*." Pain registered in his gaze. She slipped out of the demon trap she'd found herself in. He let out a long breath and studied her. "I don't know what you did to help me take solid form. I figure it has something to do with you being psychic—"

"I'm *not* psychic," she said, but didn't sound very convincing at all. "Well, not *really*."

"Keep telling yourself that. Your life will stay nice and orderly that way." He glanced at the door and at the rapidly setting sun. "I think I'm going to leave now."

"Don't let me stop you." Her voice shook. "Make sure to say hi to Satan when you get back home."

"Actually, he prefers to be called Lucifer, and he's not on my list of old friends to look up. However, I'll keep it in mind just in case our paths cross."

A chill coursed down her spine. "Go away now. Buh-bye."

He cautiously reached out to touch the handle and pushed the door open. "I can't believe it's this easy."

"Believe it. Now leave me the hell alone."

"Thank you for making this possible." The demon sounded incredibly sincere in his gratitude.

Eden pointed in the opposite direction. "Go away."

As if summoning something deep inside of himself, he finally swung the door all the way open and walked outside, pausing before he took a few tentative steps into the empty parking lot. Then a few more. Then a few more.

He stopped.

Eden rubbed her eyes, not really believing what she was seeing for a moment. With a shudder, his body seemed to turn darker and transparent.

He didn't move for a moment, but he suddenly took a shaky step backward, which was enough to solidify his frame again. Then he turned his entire tall, black-clad form around and quickly reentered the office. He leaned heavily against the glass door. There was sweat beaded on his forehead.

"Problem," he managed.

Every muscle in her body was tense. "Fix it."

"Not sure I can." He let out a long, shuddery breath and then his gaze moved to meet Eden's. "I got out there and couldn't maintain my solid form."

"Why the hell not?"

The demon shook his head. "You're psychic. This is just a guess, but my current ability to take human form must draw entirely from that energy. When I stray too far from your side, I can't maintain it."

A fresh line of panic raced through her. She *was* psychic— even if it was just a little bit. She couldn't deny it any longer.

But, hell, she could still try. "You're crazy."

His Adam's apple shifted as he swallowed hard. He looked even paler than he had before. "I had solid form until a witch cursed me. I've tried searching for her ever since to break the curse, but it's kind of hard to track somebody down when you have little or no control over your host."

"A *witch* cursed you?" she repeated with shock.

"I didn't think there was a chance to hope for anything else until today." He looked down at his hands again. "This is so amazing. But . . . I can't simply leave your side now."

"Try again," she suggested. "Try *harder*."

He shook his head. "I went outside and couldn't go any farther. I felt my energy draining away and then I was drawn back to you like a magnet. I have to stay close to you. You're my host now."

"Then you need to find another host," she said firmly.

"Can't do that. You're stuck with me until . . ." He trailed off.

"Until what?" The thought of being possessed by a demon—impossible to consider only an hour ago, but now the central concern of her existence—was too horrible to deal with.

"Until *your death*. Or until I find the witch who cursed me. But there is good news in this bleak scenario. I know she's in the area. I can sense her. It's why I directed my previous host here—the one before the killer. It was tough, but I could influence his behavior in small ways."

She'd only heard the first part. "Until *my death*?"

He nodded. "When you die, I'll be released and I'll have to find a new host."

"But you're released now. I release you." She flicked her hand at him. "You can leave any time you want to. Go."

"I can't." He glanced out through the glass doors. "I seem to be bound to your side whether I'm bodiless or not."

Eden's frustration welled inside her and threatened to spill over. "I didn't ask for this."

"I know." His brow lowered. "For what it's worth, I'm not a bad demon, if that's what you're thinking."

Actually, that was exactly what she was thinking. "There are *good* demons?"

"Before I was cursed it was my job to hunt down the bad ones that had escaped from Hell and bring them back. I made sure no humans got hurt." He grinned. "See? I'm one of the good guys."

She was far from convinced. "If you say so."

He let his gaze leisurely move down the length of her and then back up again, from her tight jeans up to where her arms crossed tightly over her green blouse. "My name is Darrak."

"I'm happy for you."

"What's your name?"

When she chose to bite her lip instead of answering him, he glanced around the room and moved toward her desk where there was a stack of business cards. He picked one up and looked at it. "I will assume you're Eden Riley?"

The fact that he knew her name made her feel even more ill than she had before. She didn't want him to know anything about her.

He put the card down and walked again to the door to look outside. "You know, it's been a very long time since I've seen a sunset with my own eyes."

Eden felt overwhelmed and on the verge of hysterical tears. She closed her eyes and prayed for the first time in forever for some divine intervention.

A few moments later, Darrak let out a harsh gasp and her eyes snapped back open. He held a hand to his abdomen, his expression darkening with obvious pain.

Divine intervention? She blinked with surprise. *Did it work?*

He braced his other hand against the wall. "The sun is gone."

She glanced outside. The sun had slipped completely beneath the horizon and darkness now spread across the sky.

"What are you talking about?" She grabbed her stapler as a potential weapon and held it tightly to her chest.

He braced his shoulder against the wall. "My form. I can't hold it much longer. It has to do with the . . . the darkness. In the human world, light sustains energy, darkness takes away. Even for me." He clenched his teeth. "I can't fight this."

Eden didn't care how normal this guy looked, how attractive, or how his kiss hadn't been completely disgusting—she wanted him *gone* and she didn't particularly care how that happened.

He clutched his stomach and gasped in pain before sliding a few inches down the wall.

She drew closer and reached out to touch him, but her shaking hand slipped right through his body as if he wasn't even there anymore.

His eyes raised to Eden's a moment before his solid form faded away completely and she was looking at the shadowy black smoke from earlier. That immediately reminded her that Darrak wasn't just a guy in pain that she might be able to help. He was a freaking *demon*.

She scrambled backward as the darkness began to swirl in front of her. She felt as if it was studying her movements—an evil rain cloud with a personality.

"Stay back," she warned it. "Or else."

Or else what? she thought. Or else she'd go get the vacuum cleaner? Or else she'd wave her hands really, really fast and hopefully stop it in its tracks?

It grew closer and closer until it had her cornered.

"Look"—she held her hands up in front of her as if that would be enough to ward it off—"there has to be another way. You don't need to do this."

If it heard her, it didn't pay any attention because the very next moment the darkness launched itself at her.

"Stop!" she yelled.

It didn't listen. The moment it made contact with her it disappeared. She'd expected to feel pain or cold fingers of death or something equally horrible, but there was only a warm sensation that slid through her body in a jarring and surprisingly sensual manner that made her gasp out loud. She pressed her hand against her stomach, breathing hard and fast as her heart rate slowly came back to normal.

It took a while.

"Darrak?" she whispered.

There was no answer.

She waited in breathless silence until he said something.

He didn't.

But she could feel him. The man she'd spoken to, the man who'd kissed her, the man who'd told her that he wouldn't be able to leave her unless she died . . .

He was deep inside of her.

She frowned. That sounded way sexier than it should have.

She was possessed by a demon—like that little girl in the movie with the pea soup puke and spinning head. But Eden was possessed by a self-proclaimed "good" demon who looked like a Calvin Klein underwear model.

What was she supposed to do now?

She yanked open the bottom drawer of her desk and pulled out the heavy Yellow Pages, thumbing through it so quickly she got a paper cut. Sucking on her injured finger, she continued to flip to the *E* section to see if reasonably priced exorcists were available in the local area.

⇒ FOUR ⇐

"Did he tell you his name?"

"Yes," Eden whispered into the receiver as if that would be enough to shield what she was doing in case "anyone" was listening. "It's . . . it's *Darrak.*"

"That's strange."

"This is all strange to me. Can you be more specific?"

"Demons rarely reveal their true name to a human. It allows one to have great control over them. I will assume he was lying, but I will still mark this information down." There was a pause, and the sound of Rosa, the exorcist from Specter-Stoppers, scribbling something about Eden's case. "Have you noticed any boils or other wounds appearing on your flesh?"

She quickly inspected her arms and felt down her jean-covered legs. "I don't think so."

"Has there been a noticeable increase of flies in your general area?"

"No. Everything actually seems quite normal. Other than the fact that I'm . . . *I'm possessed by a demon!*" She cleared her throat. "Sorry, uh . . . I'm having a hard time dealing with this."

"That is perfectly understandable, of course. The malevolent presence is allowing you to make this phone call? Has it tried to stop you in any way? Perhaps moving furniture about the room? Any levitating pens or pencils? Are the walls bleeding, by chance?"

"Bleeding walls? No, no . . . none of that." Eden concentrated, feeling around for the demon's presence. "I don't know why he's not talking right now. Maybe he's hurt."

Why did that thought bother her? Hurting a demon to get him to leave was the point of hiring an exorcist, wasn't it? But Darrak had seemed rather distressed when the sun set and he'd lost his solid form.

Rosa cleared her throat. "It will be a fee of fifteen hundred dollars to expel the evil from your body. Five hundred up front. The remainder once it has been permanently removed."

Eden's eyes bugged out at that. "Fifteen hundred dollars? That's a lot of money."

"Do you want this done properly, or not?"

She hissed out a breath. "How soon can you be here?"

"First I'll need your credit card number."

She grudgingly pulled her MasterCard out of her wallet and read the numbers off to Rosa.

"My assistant and I will be there as soon as we can," Rosa said. "I suggest not leaving the premises in case the demon influences you to wreak havoc upon all who cross your path."

"Wouldn't want that." She swallowed hard. "And what should I do in the meantime to . . . to . . ."

"Ward off the demon's evil power over you?"

She touched her stomach. The tingles that indicated Darrak's presence were barely noticeable now. "Yeah. That."

"I suggest, if you have one available, that you read aloud from the Bible. Perhaps wear a crucifix, although that might backfire and burn your own flesh, so make sure you have a glass of water—*not* holy water!—nearby to douse any potential flames. I would suggest the liberal use of salt, but since you're the one who's possessed that could also be detrimental to you. The Bible reading may be enough to keep the demon in a weakened state."

Eden glanced at the bookshelf next to Andy's desk. "Okay, I see one I can use."

"Very good. Bless you, dear. We will see you very soon."

She hung up and went to go grab the black, leather-bound book. Her stomach grumbled and she froze, listening for Darrak's voice, but it was only her previously eaten donuts settling down in her already upset stomach.

"Hey, Darrak, are you still . . . *here*?" she asked the empty room.

Nothing.

She waited with the Bible clutched to her chest, on edge and jumping at every sound.

The front door swung open ten minutes later, the bell above it jingling, and Eden sprang to her feet expecting it to be the exorcist. She'd had her eyes locked on the phone, wondering if she should call anyone else who might be able to help—no one came to mind—so she hadn't seen anyone approach.

It wasn't an exorcist.

Detective Ben Hanson stepped inside the office and smiled at her. "Just wanted to stop by and see how you're doing. Santos said he dropped you off here a little while ago."

She let out a long sigh of relief. "I'm so glad to see you."

He raised his eyebrows. "You are?"

Eden walked directly over to where he stood by the door and hugged him tightly. Then she realized what she'd done and backed away with embarrassment. "Um . . . sorry about that."

His lips quirked. "That's definitely not something you need to apologize for." He glanced at the Bible she tightly held onto. "Are you sure everything's okay?"

She shook her head. "That man earlier—the—the serial killer."

"I know that was a very traumatic experience for you. I'm

surprised that you decided to come back to your job today." He glanced around the embarrassingly shoddy office. "You should be taking it easy."

"It's not that. Well, it is. But . . . when he grabbed me he told me that he was possessed by a demon."

"Yeah, I heard him say that, too. He was completely crazy. Listen, if you want to talk to somebody qualified to handle post-traumatic stress, then I can easily arrange that for you. It's the least we can do for you after everything that happened."

"No . . . I . . ." What did she want to do? Tell him everything? That the killer had been serious and *was* possessed? And now she was, too?

"Eden . . ." Darrak said wearily from inside of her.

Oh shit.

"Can you hear that?" she asked Ben.

"Hear what?"

"It took me a while to recover from losing form," Darrak continued, "but I'm feeling better now."

Ben touched her shoulder. "Eden, it's going to be okay. He's dead. He's not going to hurt you again, I promise."

"I know that."

"Then why do you seem so scared?"

Scared didn't even begin to cover what she was feeling. "It's . . . it's the demon he was talking about."

"Demons don't exist," Ben said firmly.

"But—"

"Eden," Darrak interrupted her. "Are you trying to tell him about me?"

She stopped talking.

"But, what?" Ben prompted. He leaned against the small table next to the front door where they kept the coffeemaker. He unhooked a pair of dark sunglasses from the front of his shirt and placed them down next to him so he could cross his arms over his chest.

"Just look at him," Darrak continued. "Does he look like

the kind of person who would believe you? Or would you tell him that you're possessed by a demon and he might pat your head, say he understands, and then send for the doctors in white coats who deal with crazy people? Believe me, I've dealt with this situation many times before. Humans don't want to believe that this sort of thing is possible. It frightens them."

"I can see why it would," she whispered.

Ben looked confused. "Pardon me?"

"When humans are frightened or they don't understand, they'll subconsciously choose to ignore what they see," Darrak said. "They close their minds off to anything that isn't within their understanding of 'normal.' I guarantee if you tell the cop what's going on, he won't believe you and he will assume that you've lost your mind."

Of course he was right. Eden already knew Ben was a skeptic about the supernatural. This was about as supernatural as it got. What proof did she have that she was really possessed? The ravings of a lunatic—or at least that was how it would sound. Ben was already iffy about her psychic abilities. He'd dismissed it earlier as *mojo* and *hocus-pocus,* hadn't he?

She couldn't tell him. She'd have to handle the situation on her own.

"I'm fine," she finally replied and then forced a shaky smile onto her face. "Really. I just need a good night's sleep."

Ben studied her for a moment with concern. "Well, that's very good to hear."

The fake smile stretched Eden's cheeks uncomfortably. "Was there, uh . . . anything else you wanted?"

He cleared his throat. "Well, actually there was."

"See?" Darrak said. "That wasn't too bad, was it?"

"Shut up," she murmured.

Ben looked at her. "What did you say?"

"Uh—" Her gaze darted around the room, empty except for the two of them. "Would you care for a-a donut?"

He glanced at the box of pastries next to the coffeemaker

that she waved at as though she'd magically turned into Vanna White's awkward sister. "I thought you just told me to shut up."

"No!" She laughed lightly. It sounded just this side of hysterical. "I talk to myself sometimes. My inner voice seems to have a mind of its own."

Literally, she thought.

He moved toward the box of donuts and looked down at them. "I'm not all that hungry. Actually, that's why I'm here. I wanted to ask you something."

"You're romantically interested in the cop, aren't you?" Darrak prodded. "I can tell. But he's obviously not good enough for you. If he was you'd be able to tell him all about your problems and be certain he'd believe whatever you said."

She tried to ignore him. "What is it, Detective?"

"I thought I asked you to call me Ben?"

"Right . . . *Ben*." She felt incredibly angry that what should have been a kick-ass moment was tainted by Darrak's invisible but very audible presence.

"I know our dinner plans were ruined for tonight, but maybe if you're not doing anything later this week—"

"I think you should ask him to leave," Darrak said. "I don't like the way he's looking at you. It's very ungentlemanly."

Eden sighed with frustration. "Just *go away*, would you?"

Ben blinked. "Oh. Got it."

Her heart sank. He thought she was talking to him, dismissing him and his invitation completely. After all, why *wouldn't* he think that? There was no one else in the room.

He gave her a tight smile. "Hey, I can take a hint, don't worry about that. I won't bother you again."

"No, wait! Ben—" Eden held up a hand to stop him, but it was too late. Without a backward glance he slunk out of the office and went directly to his car.

She let out a long, exasperated sigh. "I hate you."

"Are you talking to me?" Darrak asked.

"Yes."

"Did I do something wrong?"

"I think you know what you did."

There was silence for so long she thought he'd vanished to the same place he'd been before when she couldn't hear him. But then, "You're right. I'm sorry for intruding. I guess I'm feeling a bit powerless at the moment."

"That makes two of us."

Another pause. "Like I said before, I've never been able to talk to a previous host so easily before. Maybe this is an opportunity to work together to find the witch so I, pardon the expression, get the hell out of your life."

She tensed at that. "How do you know she's close right now?"

"When she cursed me, the black magic she used left a residual trace that still remains after all this time. Think of it like a very weak, magical GPS. And right now it's signaling to me that she's not that far away."

Sure. That was as clear as scary, demonic mud.

Eden stared out of the window as Ben's black Chrysler LeBaron turned the corner and sped off into the distance. "I can't believe he asked me out and I insulted him."

"You like him."

"What's not to like? He's absolutely perfect." She pressed her lips together, frustration over this situation spreading over her again. "I want you to go away, Darrak. Please. I can't live like this."

"If you help me find the witch then I *will* go away. Gladly."

"What's her name?"

"I don't know."

"You don't know the name of the witch that cursed you? There are five million people in this city and the surrounding area."

"I'll find her. And as soon as I do, I promise that this will all be over."

"Not good enough."

Remembering what the exorcist said earlier, she clenched her jaw and cracked open the Bible.

"Be strong and of a good courage," she read aloud, "fear not, nor be afraid . . . for the Lord thy God—"

"What exactly do you think you're doing?" Darrak interrupted.

"I'm reading from the Bible."

"Do you do this a lot?"

"I like to read from my trusty Bible all day, every day. Do you have a problem with that? Does it sting a little?" She raised an eyebrow. "Does it make you want to leave and never come back?"

"I'm afraid it's not quite that easy. However, if you take requests, I always find Revelations quite soothing."

Damn. How could a demon not be affected by holy scripture? She hadn't gone to church since she was ten years old, but it should still work. What kind of a demon was he, anyhow?

A good demon, he'd told her.

Right.

"I don't know what I can tell you to set your mind at ease." He sounded weary. "I want this over with as much as you do. More, if that's possible. I've had to exist this way for so long I barely remember what it was like before. Please, Eden. I can't end this without you."

She put the Bible down. "I know how to end this."

"So, you'll help me?" he asked.

"In a way." She swallowed nervously. "Can you hear what I'm thinking?"

"No. You'll need to speak aloud for us to communicate."

That was a relief, because if he could read her mind then he'd know that the two people rapidly approaching the front door of Triple-A Investigations weren't potential clients—they were the exorcists she'd hired to take care of her little demonic problem.

Eden braced herself for whatever was going to happen next.

The walls weren't bleeding yet, but the night was still young.

⇒ Five ⇐

The bell on the door jingled as the two people entered the office. One was a small but round woman with short red hair and a—the only word for it was a *jolly* smile. She wore a loose, paisley-printed dress and carried a big, blue canvas tote bag. She also had a walking cane with a crystal set into the top of it.

The man with her was young—looked like a college kid— and he wore black pants and a white shirt. He *wasn't* smiling. His dark blond hair was a bit lank, but his face was very pleasant—almost *angelic*, actually—with heavy-lidded blue eyes, high cheekbones, and full lips. In school, he probably was called a pretty boy.

"Greetings to you, Eden Riley!" the woman said brightly.

"Uh . . . greetings," Eden replied awkwardly.

"I'm Rosa Devine," she said. "We already met on the phone, didn't we? And this is my son Malcolm. He'll be assisting me today."

Malcolm nodded curtly in Eden's direction, then took a moment to scan the office. "Are we alone?"

"Yes," she said.

"You were expecting these people?" Darrak asked from inside her.

"Yes," she said again.

"Friends of yours?"

"Mm-hmm."

Darrak was silent for a moment. "Do your friends normally make your heart gallop like an overcaffeinated racehorse?"

Eden didn't reply.

Rosa approached her, staring up into her face. Then she pressed her hands to Eden's cheeks and drew her closer until their eyeballs were only a couple inches away from each other. "We must begin immediately. Please sit down."

Malcolm moved toward the glass door and turned the lock. "Where do you need me, Mother?"

"By my side, dear."

"What's going on, Eden?" Darrak asked.

She sat down in her comfortable but ratty desk chair and tightly squeezed the armrests as if bracing herself for a root canal. "I'm helping you."

"Helping me?"

"Is the demonic presence speaking to you right now?" Rosa asked.

She nodded. "He is."

Rosa grabbed her chin and squeezed hard enough to make Eden's lips purse out unattractively. "Listen to me, demon. This is your last chance. Leave this woman of your own volition while you still can. If you refuse, then we will force you from her body."

Darrak sighed. "Exorcists? You've got to be kidding me."

"Speak, dark demon!" Rosa hissed, squeezing Eden's face even tighter. Eden tried her best not to bat the woman's hands away. "What is your reply?"

Another internal sigh. "Eden, let's talk about this."

"I'm rewwy shorry." Her words were distorted due to her current pursed-lip situation. "But you habben gibben me any udder choice here."

"So, you what? Called 411 to find the nearest Exorcists 'R' Us?"

Eden cleared her throat. "Akshlee, I just rooked in the phone book."

"I already told you I can't leave, but it's not because I don't want to. Believe me, I want to, but I can't."

"He says he can't leeb me," Eden said

"Liar!" Rosa snapped.

"You can tell this lady to bite me, though," Darrak added. "And she can take that holier-than-thou attitude of hers and shove it right under her granny panties."

"Does the demon show fear for my abilities?" Rosa asked.

"Not rewwy," Eden admitted, though she was finding it increasingly hard to talk while in the forcibly pursed position. Her cheeks began to ache. "You can let go of my faysh now. Preesh."

She finally released Eden, who sighed with relief and rubbed her sore cheeks.

"Right," Darrak said. "Actually, I'm *not* afraid because I've been faced with a lot of exorcists in the last three hundred years. Believe me, there have been a lot of yahoos who think they can get rid of me, but a true exorcist needs to completely believe in demons and the Netherworld—their faith needs to be absolute. And they have to use actual holy water—"

"Malcolm, pass me the holy water, please." Rosa held out her hand.

"Yes, Mother."

Darrak scoffed. "They say it's holy water, but that could just be from the tap for all we know."

"What's this *we* thing?" Eden said.

"Now, you must repeat after me," Rosa said. "I, Eden Riley—"

"I, Eden Riley."

"Commit to ridding my physical being of all things demonic—"

Eden repeated it.

"And renounce evil and all forms of black magic—"

Well, of course. "And renounce evil and all forms of black magic."

"And all lustful thoughts."

Eden frowned. "And all lustful thoughts?"

"Lust is a deadly sin. You may have been chosen as a vessel for the demon because of that sinful, cleavage-revealing blouse you're wearing right now. Shameful, really."

Eden held a hand to her chest. "I bought this at Sears last week. It's machine washable!"

"Lust is the most popular deadly sin, followed closely by vanity and greed." She gently patted Eden's cheek. "Speaking of money, I should let you know up front that the outstanding thousand dollars on this transaction applies whether or not I am able to dispel this evil spirit from you. It will be applied directly to the credit card number you provided earlier."

"There's no money-back guarantee?"

"I'm afraid not. We are working with Satan's darkest minions, here."

"Did she just call me a *minion*?" Darrak grumbled. "Talk about adding insult to potential injury."

"I also have a disclaimer for you to sign that absolves us of any responsibility should this exorcism lead to any property damage or, potentially, your death." Rosa placed a legal-sized document in front of Eden and handed her a pen.

Eden's eyes widened. "My *death*?"

"Much like a cosmetic liposuction procedure, it's a rare side effect, but one we should never gloss over. But wouldn't you rather be dead than be possessed by a demon?"

"Well . . ."

"Look, Eden," Darrak said. "I've tried to be patient, but you need to send these people away right now before this gets out of control."

"You think they'll be able to do it?" she asked out loud. Rosa and Malcolm would know she was chatting with her inner demon, so she saw no reason to whisper or try to otherwise hide it.

"No. But do you even know what an exorcism does?"

"Yeah, it'll get rid of the demon I'm possessed with."

"It will also damage your soul."

She tensed. "Really? Why would it do that?"

"Because that's what I'm going to grab onto when they try to get rid of me. I'm going to cling onto your sparkly silver soul like a lifeline. If she's really good, she'll eventually be able to rip me loose. Then my essence will be torn apart—we like to use the term *decimate*—I'll be cast into the void, a place of endless darkness and despair from which there's no escape—"

"Sounds like Hell to me."

He laughed humorlessly. "The void is the innermost ring of Hell—all of it, the rings of Hell, the void, and the Underworld make up the *Netherworld*. Actually the rest of Hell's a Las Vegas theme hotel compared to the void. When a demon is exorcised, it's not the same as simply being vanquished. If I was vanquished, I'd be sent on a one-way ticket back to Hell. I'd be damaged. It would take a long time, if ever, for me to recover, but I'd still exist. An exorcism is a bit more permanent than that. It'll be a few days of ultimate pain and suffering, and then it's all over."

Rosa continued to study Eden closely during Darrak's speech, taking down notes from what Eden said in reply in a small notebook she carried.

Eden swallowed. "Sounds like a root canal with no anesthetic."

"A trillion times worse than that."

"A *trillion*?"

"Well . . . *a lot*. I don't know the exact equation. I'm a demon, not a mathematician."

"Don't listen to whatever the demon is telling you right now," Rosa said in a commanding tone. "He'll try to convince you he is worthy of staying on this mortal level of existence. He may promise you great things—wealth, eternal beauty, or perhaps hours of evil, orgasmic sex—"

Eden's eyebrows went up at that. "Pardon me?"

"Well, now that she mentions it," Darrak said. "I do seem able to take corporeal form during daylight hours, don't I?"

"Where do I sign?" Eden asked. "Let's do this."

Rosa pointed to the right place on the form and Eden signed her name. Then the woman snatched the document away, rolled it up, and put it into her bag.

Darrak sighed. "I guess the thing about three whole days of torture leading to my complete decimation gave you no pause at all?"

"You're a demon," Eden said under her breath. "Demons lie."

"We don't have to have hours of so-called evil, orgasmic sex. I was just saying that because it's been so long for me. Vicarious sex through my hosts has been unfulfilling to say the least."

"I don't really care."

Would he really be in torturous pain for days before finally dying? Did demons *die*? She suddenly wished she'd paid more attention back in Sunday school. But that was a long time ago and, now that she thought about it, this hadn't been one of the topics. She remembered hearing about Noah and his ark of friendly animals, but the subject of what to do when one was possessed by a demon had not been covered, surprisingly enough.

"Aren't you scared?" Eden asked quietly. "Not even a little bit?"

"No. From what I've seen so far, I don't think this woman has enough power to get rid of me—she's weak. Even if that vial was filled with real holy water it wouldn't make any difference at all. And you already found out yourself what happens when you read from the Bible. Nothing. And you know why? Because I'm not evil. I mean you no harm. All I want is your help to solve this problem in a different and much more mutually beneficial way."

"You sure talk a lot."

"It's been three hundred years without somebody to talk to. So sue me. No, this lady is the one who's all talk. And, besides, how can I possibly be afraid of somebody wearing a dress that ugly?"

"*Darrak*—" Rosa began, "I say your true name in order to bind you."

"You told her my name?" Darrak asked with annoyance.

She frowned. "Aren't you supposed to be . . . binded, or whatever, now?"

"*Bound*. And no. Not so much."

Rosa's forehead creased. "Does the malevolent presence not acknowledge his true name?"

Eden shifted nervously in her seat. "Doesn't seem to."

"*Darrak*," Rosa said again. "I bind you, you filthy spirit."

"See, now she's just being a bitch about it," Darrak said.

Eden rolled her eyes. "This isn't working."

"He must have lied about his name," Rosa said emphatically. "If he'd given you his true name, this wouldn't be a problem."

"She's right," Darrak said. "One point for the lady in the muumuu."

"Darrak's not your real name?"

"More of a nickname. Sorry, I don't give out my real name to someone I've just met. I'd say you shouldn't be offended if you hadn't just tried to use it against me. Now can we end this while we all still have our dignity intact?"

"Mother, let me try," Malcolm stepped forward.

She nodded. "Very well."

The college kid, lanky and lean with that angelic face, approached Eden and leaned against her desk. He had a Bible in his hand. The vial of holy water rested on the desk next to him.

He leaned over and looked her directly in the eyes. "Demon,

I commit myself to casting ye from this innocent woman's body."

Darrak let out a small gasp inside of her. "Shit. This guy's the real deal."

He was? This college kid was a genuine exorcist—a true believer—when his mother wasn't?

"Unclean spirit—" Malcolm dipped his fingers into the bottle of holy water and brought it to Eden's forehead, before drawing a small cross there. There was a slight burning sensation as it dried.

Darrak must have felt more than a slight burn because he gasped again. "No—"

"Leave this place," Malcolm continued evenly. "Return to the eternal darkness from which you were spawned and never return."

Eden inhaled sharply. She felt something then. An unpleasant tightening deep inside of her. Whatever Malcolm was doing was working.

And that's what she wanted, right?

"Eden—" Darrak didn't sound happy. "Please, stop this. Don't let him exorcise me."

Malcolm then took the small black Bible in his hand and without any warning, pressed it firmly against Eden's forehead. She shrieked out loud as her chair skidded back a few feet on its wheels to crash against the wall.

"Leave her!" Malcolm raised his voice. "And do not return. I bind ye and cast ye into the pit forevermore."

The tearing and tightening sensation increased and Eden began to panic. Was this the right decision? Was she going to hurt somebody who—although their presence was more than a bit disconcerting to say the least—hadn't actually hurt her in any way? Were demons really capable of being good as Darrak claimed? And if so, was she the one being evil by essentially hiring somebody to tear him apart in order to get rid of him—as if she was simply cauterizing an unwanted wart?

"What is your true name, demon?" Malcolm's pressure on the Bible against her forehead increased. "Tell me. You now look into the face of justice and all that which is good in the world. You shall be incapable of lying to me now."

"My name . . ." Darrak began. "It's . . . it's . . . no. *No.* Please, Eden, stop this. I'll do anything. I promise we can fix this in another way!"

Eden gritted her teeth and grabbed Malcolm's wrist. "Okay, I think that's enough. Stop it."

"Mother, restrain her. The demon is forcing her to resist me."

Rosa moved quickly, placing her cane to the side, and kneeled beside Eden's chair to hold her wrists down against the armrests. Either she was really strong or Eden was suddenly really weak, but it was enough to keep her firmly pinned in place.

"It'll be okay, honey," she said. "Just think pleasant thoughts. Pure, *virginal* thoughts. We'll get rid of that demon for you just like you asked us to."

"I've changed my mind," Eden gritted out. "It's not really a demon."

Rosa tilted her head to the side. "It's not?"

"No . . . I . . . I had this spicy Mexican food last night. It's only a bad case of heartburn. I don't need an exorcism. I need some Pepto-Bismol!"

"Her tongue is forked with lies," Malcolm growled.

"You're the one who's forked." Eden glared at him. "Now, stop this right now or you're going to be in big trouble!"

Sure. That sounded insistent enough, didn't it?

"This exorcism won't stop until I'm finished." Malcolm pulled a notebook from his pocket and flipped forward a few pages. *"Sancte Michael Archangele, defende nos in praelio et colluctatione, quae nobis adversus principes et potestates . . ."*

"Eden!" Darrak had begun to sound panicked and the pitched tone of his voice, even though she only heard it internally, now held great pain.

"Stop this exorcism *right now*." Eden looked directly at Rosa, who was staring back at her with a confused expression.

"She is not entirely human," Rosa said in a soft voice. "She's touched with magic that gives this demon special strength. But I don't know what it is that makes her different. Be careful, Malcolm."

Could Rosa sense Eden's mild psychic abilities? Before she could ask for clarification, Malcolm roughly grabbed a handful of Eden's hair and pulled her head back around to look at him.

"So the demon is not the only unclean being in the room. Perhaps that's why he was attracted to your form. You are a minion of Satan as well."

"Get your hands off me," Eden growled.

"I can help you," he insisted. "But I need you lucid enough to break free of the demon's influence."

He let go of her hair only to backhand her hard across her face. The pain and shock was enough to knock any thoughts or protests out of her head.

"Malcolm," Rosa said sharply. "That wasn't necessary."

"Mother, please. Let me do my job here."

There was a knock on the door a moment before Malcolm struck the other side of her face, which left her ears ringing and pain reverberating through her skull as Rosa continued to hold her in place.

Eden looked over and was surprised to see that Ben had returned. He peered through the glass door at them, and his eyes met with Eden's.

He rattled the handle as he tried to get in, but the door was locked. Then he banged at the door hard with his closed fist.

This probably didn't look too good, Eden thought absently, both relieved and disturbed that her exorcism had another witness.

The next moment something shattered—it was the door. Ben had wrapped part of his leather jacket over his fist to break the glass, then he reached through to unlock it and let himself in.

"What the hell is going on here?" he demanded.

"Leave us," Malcolm growled over his shoulder.

"I don't think so. Let go of her"—Ben unsheathed his gun and pointed it at Malcolm—"*right now.*"

≫ SIX ≪

Malcolm put up his hands and took a few steps away from Eden. "You're making a grave mistake."

"I think *you're* the one making the mistake. And that goes for you, too, lady. Get the hell away from her." Ben's gaze moved to Eden. "Are you okay?"

She felt shaky and cold. She couldn't feel Darrak's presence anymore, which disturbed her. Was he gone? Had Malcolm been successful at exorcising him?

"Yes, I'm fine," she managed after a moment.

Ben narrowed his eyes as he looked at Malcolm and Rosa. "You're both under arrest for assault."

"No, wait," Eden said getting to her feet. "I'm not pressing charges."

She couldn't let Ben arrest them. She'd paid the exorcists to come here. They'd only done what she wanted them to do. That is, until she changed her mind.

It was a possessed woman's prerogative, after all.

"You're not . . ." Ben's forehead was furrowed. "What the hell do you mean? I saw this son of a bitch hit you."

Eden grimaced. "It wasn't what it looked like."

"Then what was it?"

"A misunderstanding, that's all," Rosa said evenly.

Ben's gun wavered. "Eden? Explain this."

She nodded. "It was a misunderstanding. No harm done." She glanced at the broken door. "Well, *almost* no harm done."

"But, I saw him hit you—"

She moved toward him and put a hand on his hard-muscled arm so he'd lower his weapon completely. "Seriously, Ben. Just let it go. Please. Let them leave."

It was obvious that Ben was torn about this decision. He searched her face for whatever answer he was looking for. Finally and reluctantly he holstered his gun. "Fine. Have it your way." There was no humor to the words.

Eden breathed out a sigh of relief and then looked at the exorcists. "You can leave now," she said firmly. "We're done here."

"You heard the lady," Ben growled. "Get out of here. *Now*. Before I change my mind."

Rosa quickly gathered her cane and the rest of her exorcism paraphernalia. "As I said earlier, Ms. Riley, the full price for this service stands. Thank you for your business and have a lovely day."

Malcolm moved toward Ben. "Do you have any idea what you've interrupted here?"

Ben glowered at him. "A piece of shit abusing a friend of mine?"

"Just the opposite, actually. Your *friend* is very dangerous right now and must be dealt with."

The cop clenched his fists at his sides. "You have no idea how dangerous *I* can be."

Malcolm nodded at the chain that held a small gold cross pendant Ben wore around his neck. "I see you're a believer in the difference between good and evil."

Ben's eyes narrowed. "It's how I live my life. What I've chosen to do as a career."

Malcolm cast a dark look back at Eden before returning his attention to the cop. "I'll remember that. Come, Mother."

He and Rosa left, their shoes crunching against the shards of glass from the broken door.

Eden got up and moved across the office toward the coffee machine. She poured a cup, black, and brought it shakily to her lips. She could have used a much stiffer drink, but it would have to do.

"Thanks for that," she said after a moment.

He just looked at her. "You want to tell me what that was all about?"

How must it have looked to Ben? She had no idea what to tell him. All she knew was that the truth was not an option. "Like I said before, a misunderstanding."

"So you know them?"

"Sort of."

"Who are they?" he pressed. "And what did that woman mean when she thanked you for your business?"

"Avon reps are really aggressive these days."

"Eden—"

She shook her head. "Just drop it. Please."

"Drop it?" His expression tensed. "I broke your door getting in here to save you and you won't even fill me in on what I saved you from?"

Despite what had happened, she couldn't help smiling at that. "My hero."

"I thought it was just the serial killer earlier, but you're obviously a magnet for trouble. Or maybe this is just your lucky day?"

"I forgot to check my horoscope. It probably said for me not to leave the house this morning. Or possibly ever again." She tried to make it sound light and almost succeeded.

He eyed her skeptically. "You're not going to tell me who they were, are you?"

"It really doesn't matter anymore. They're gone and they're not coming back." She took another sip of the strong, bitter liquid.

"How do you know that?"

She didn't. She looked at the door again. "Looks like I'm going to have to call a repairman."

"You're trying to change the subject." He rubbed his temples. "I should have arrested them."

"If I say pretty please let it go, will you?"

"I've always had a hard time letting things go. Even when I probably should." He actually laughed a little at that, then closed the distance between them, taking her face in his hands. He rubbed his thumb gently along her cheek. "He didn't even leave a mark when he hit you. That's one good thing."

"Like I said, it wasn't a big deal." She bit her bottom lip and looked up at him, feeling awkward at being this close to the gorgeous cop, especially after what he'd witnessed. "Uh . . . not that I'm complaining, of course, but why did you come back?"

His expression was still tense from having his questions unanswered. It probably wasn't something he was accustomed to. "I forgot my sunglasses." He nodded toward the table next to them that held the now unappetizing-looking donuts from earlier. Sure enough, his dark wraparound sunglasses were still there.

"You drove all the way back to get these?" Eden asked, surprised. "I could have dropped them in the mail for you."

"I know." He shrugged and a small grin twitched at his lips. "I guess I also had an urge to break a door. And here I am."

"Eden," Darrak said weakly from inside her head. "He's come back because he likes you."

She chewed on her bottom lip. "I'm glad you came back."

At the moment, she meant both of them. For a moment, she'd thought Malcolm had been successful in exorcising Darrak. An unexpected swell of relief filled her to hear her inner demon's voice again.

Ben's grin widened, finally breaking completely through the tense look he'd worn. "Oh, yeah?"

She nodded but found it difficult to speak again. What was

it about the cop that made her tongue-tied? Especially when she thought he might actually be interested in her.

"Look, I probably shouldn't have come back here, but I'm glad I did." Ben moved toward her to inspect her face again. "Did that bastard hurt you?"

She shook her head. "It—it stung a bit, but I think I'm okay now. Why? I thought you said there's no mark."

"There isn't." His warm touch moved along her jawline. "Looks perfectly fine to me."

"Oh. Uh . . . well, that's good." She cleared her throat and stepped back from him, then cursed herself for being a total, awkward wimp-girl.

"You like him," Darrak stated. "But you're shy, aren't you?"

She didn't reply. She wasn't shy. She was just . . . reserved. Yeah, that was a good word. *Reserved*.

"I have an idea," the demon said. "A good one. If you promise to help me find the witch who cursed me, I'll help you with the cop."

She really wanted to ask him how he intended to do that. In fact, she was curious enough to venture a "How?"

Ben frowned. "What?"

"Nothing." Just talking to herself, as usual. Nothing strange or remotely bizarre about that, was there?

"How will I help you?" Darrak replied. "I can tell you what to say and what to do to make yourself completely irresistible to this or any other man. It's obvious he likes you already, so that will definitely help. You just need to get over your fear. A little inner prodding will do the trick. I think it's a fair trade for what I want from you in return. What do you say?"

Darrak was offering to act as her Cyrano de Bergerac?

That was completely and utterly ludicrous.

She didn't need his help. She didn't want anything to do with the demon at all. He'd turned her life into a complete nightmare in only a few hours.

However, nightmare or not, after what had nearly happened

with the exorcists she'd hired, she was feeling very guilty. A few more minutes and she knew that Darrak would have been completely destroyed.

And he was right about one thing. She seriously needed some help in the romance department.

Was she actually considering his offer? She'd do whatever she could to find the witch and he'd help her not be a shrinking violet in front of Ben?

It was so crazy it just might work. A give-and-take partnership. With a demon.

"Okay, fine," she finally said.

Ben grabbed his sunglasses and put them in his pocket. "So I guess that's it. Do you need a ride home?"

She shook her head "My car's here."

It was a rusty old Toyota with over two hundred thousand miles on the odometer, but she still liked to use the word *car* to describe it, anyhow. She'd taken a cab into the heart of the city earlier for the police case so she could avoid driving on the busy highway.

He nodded. "And what about the door?"

She eyed the broken glass. "There's actually a guy around the corner I can call to patch it up right away."

"I can wait with you."

"No, really, it's not necessary."

He frowned. "You're sure?"

"I am."

Ben hesitated as if ready to argue with her, but then had second thoughts. He nodded firmly instead. "I'll send you a check to cover the damages."

"Not necessary. We could use a new door anyhow. Maybe a sturdier one this time. Obviously the old one was a bit flimsy. Not that I'm complaining or anything since its flimsiness came in real handy tonight."

Real sexy, come-hither talk if ever she'd heard any.

"Ask him to dinner tomorrow night," Darrak suggested.

She swallowed.

"*Ask him,*" Darrak said again.

"Good-bye, Eden." Ben smiled. "*Again.* And if those people come anywhere close to you again, give me . . . or the precinct . . . a call right away, okay?"

He reluctantly pushed the doorframe open.

"Do it," Darrak urged.

"Ben," she called just before he left.

He turned. "Yeah?"

She cleared her throat. "I know I kind of said no before, but listen, I want to change my mind."

"About what?"

"Um . . . I was . . . uh, kind of wondering if you had any dinner plans tomorrow night?"

A glint of surprise entered his dark blue eyes. "Dinner?"

"Yeah."

"With you?"

She faltered and felt her cheeks heat up. He was going to turn her down. This was Detective Ben Handsome, after all. She had no idea why he was single when any woman in the world would kill for the chance to date him. "Unless you don't want to. I totally understand."

Another smile touched his lips. "You'd understand, would you? Why, because I called you a troublemaker before? Or because that ass called you a dangerous woman?"

"Well . . . both. To start with."

"I'd love to have dinner with you."

She was honestly surprised by his answer. "Oh . . . well, good."

"Good."

Darrak groaned. "Sounds like you're definitely going to need my help."

She gritted her teeth.

"So I'll call you?" Ben asked. "Tomorrow afternoon? And we'll go from there?"

She grabbed a business card off her desk and gave it to him. "I'll be here."

He nodded and tucked the card into his jacket pocket. "Have a good night. And try to stay out of trouble, okay?"

She tried to think of a fantastically witty comeback for that, but came up blank. "Yeah, you, too."

He grinned at her and left the office.

"*Yeah, you, too?*" Darrak repeated. "That was smooth. Why do you have such a hard time talking to him? Are you like this with every man you meet? You're too attractive to be a spinster. Do you live alone with a great many cats?"

She pressed her lips together. "Shut up, please."

He went silent. She still couldn't feel him as much as she could earlier. Before, he'd been like a weight on her chest—not enough to hurt, but enough to be noticeable. Now there was nothing but his faint voice as if he was speaking from an adjoining room.

"Are you okay?" she asked.

"You mean, did I survive your attempt to exorcise me? Obviously, or I wouldn't be talking to you now, would I?"

"I didn't know it was going to be like that."

"Did you think they were going to lure me out with a bowl of warm milk and put a leash on me?"

"No. But I didn't know it would cause you so much pain." She swallowed, then crossed her arms and looked out of the broken door at the parking lot. "I'm sorry."

"I don't blame you. You didn't ask for this. You're going through the five stages of demonic possession. Denial, anger, bargaining, depression . . . eventually you'll finally reach acceptance."

"Aren't those the five stages of dying?"

"Same stages, different issue. Right now I think you're still dealing with the anger. But we've moved into the bargaining stage because you agreed to help me out."

She turned and went back to her desk, straightening her keyboard, which had detached from the computer during the attempted exorcism. "I look forward to my inevitable depression."

"I think you've done great so far."

"Great? I just spent fifteen hundred bucks on a crazy exorcist whose son slapped me around." She held her hand against her cheek.

"Some people pay much more than that. For the exorcism, that is. Although some people also pay to be slapped around. Humans are strange."

She concentrated on his voice. "You still don't sound too good."

"No, well . . . it was mostly from when he launched into the Latin. That part of an exorcism always tends to be a bit draining. Literally."

"I thought you said you've never been faced with a real exorcism before."

"I haven't. But I've seen them performed—from a safe distance, of course. It's not pretty. Another thirty seconds and I would have been only an unpleasant memory for you."

She sat on the edge of her desk. "Sure, now you tell me."

He was quiet for a moment. "So you really like that cop?"

She nodded. "That's an understatement."

"Fair enough. Tomorrow night we'll make sure you look extremely gorgeous. You'll go out for dinner with him. I'll guide you into not saying anything too embarrassing—"

She frowned at that.

"And he'll be eating out of your hand in under an hour. Guaranteed. Then we will focus on finding my witch. Deal?"

She still felt more than a little uncomfortable with the oddly helpful Darrak. "You're asking me to officially make a deal with a devil?"

"I'm not a devil. I'm a demon."

"There's a difference?"

"Vast. Devils are small, purple, angry, and tend to poke things with their pitchforks. And that's actually what they call their insanely pointy genitalia."

That was an image she'd prefer to lose as soon as possible. "And all demons look like you?"

"Tall, dark, and handsome?" There was humor in his voice as he said it.

"I meant *not* small, purple, angry, or particularly pointy."

"Demons . . . have varying appearances."

Her mouth went dry just thinking about it. "That's vague."

"It is, isn't it?" He was silent for a moment. "Now, unless you'd like to call Malcolm and his mom back . . ."

"I'll pass."

"Then I'm going to rest. I'm tired and my energy is very low right now."

"That's what happened when you lost form at sunset? You rested? I couldn't hear you for a while." Which is when she'd had the chance to consult the Yellow Pages and make the exorcism appointment.

"When I'm very weakened, I sink down to a deeper level of consciousness. To communicate with you like this I need a lot of energy to stay at the surface."

Eden twisted a finger nervously through her long hair. "Did you hear what that woman said about me not being completely human?"

"I did."

"What do you think she meant by that?" She leaned over to pick up a file folder that had fallen to the floor earlier. Then she spun her Rolodex to find the number of the door repairman.

"I'm not sure. I've never possessed a female before, so you do feel . . . *different* to me—even aside from your physical body. And I'm able to draw energy from you in order to take form as well as talk to you, unlike my relationships with any of my other hosts. Yet I don't sense anything overtly Otherworldly about you."

"She was probably just talking about my psychic ability." She thought back to working at Psychic Connexions. "I do shuffle a mean deck of tarot cards, I'll have you know."

"That must be it. Do psychic abilities run in your family?"

Eden thought about her mother. Other than an addiction to gambling, drinking, emotionally neglecting her daughter, and working her way through a long line of hairy men, she didn't recall anything unusual. Maybe her father had been psychic. She remembered one brief visit from him when she was a very little girl—a man with a big warm smile and hair the bright red color Eden's would be if she didn't make regular trips to the salon to keep it the darker auburn she preferred. But nothing like Ouija boards or crystal balls rang out in her memory.

"I don't think so. But I haven't exactly been all that close to my family over the years."

"Think about it. But I'm going now. I'll be back."

"Darrak," she began.

"Yeah?"

"What's your real name?"

There was a long moment of silence and then a tired sigh. "I understand your fear and misgivings about what is going on, Eden. And I also understand why you called the exorcists. But if I ever tell you my true name, that would give you a great deal of power over me, so it's something I must keep hidden from those who might do me harm."

The pleasant tone had gone out of his voice and was replaced with something much icier. He was pissed about what had nearly happened. She'd nearly destroyed him—it wasn't simply a matter of forgive and forget.

If someone had done the same thing to her, she'd have the same reaction. Darrak hadn't harmed her, and yet she'd tried to hurt him out of fear and confusion.

"I understand," she said softly.

"I'll return soon."

"Take your time."

With a soft chuckle, his presence faded away.

After making a quick call to the twenty-four-hour repair service to come and fix the door, she sat in the office in silence waiting for them to arrive. She hadn't even begun to work on the data input Andy wanted her to do, but she didn't give a rat's ass about that. She was exhausted. And she wanted to go home and fall into a big glass of red wine. Maybe when she woke up tomorrow morning she'd realize this had all been a bizarre dream.

The part about her and Ben going out for dinner tomorrow was the one good thing in this nightmare.

She'd nearly been stabbed by a serial killer. She was possessed by a demon. An exorcist had slapped her around. And to add insult to injury, she'd lost fifteen hundred hard-earned dollars.

She really should have checked her horoscope today. She made a mental note not to let that oversight happen again.

⇥ SEVEN ⇤

She'd just made a deal with a demon.

What in the hell had she been thinking?

It took until nearly eleven o'clock to get the door adequately fixed. Then Eden drove home, making a detour to the drive-through at McDonald's to grab a garden salad and a McChicken.

As she distractedly pulled up in front of her apartment complex, something darted out in front of her car. She slammed on the brakes and her car skidded to a halt.

She groaned. "Please tell me that was not a black cat."

But it was. The feline glared at her from the bushes at the side of the driveway as she continued on.

"Bad luck omen," Eden said under her breath. "You're about eight hours too late."

She parked in her assigned spot and got out of the car into the chilly October night, juggling her purse, takeout bag, and keys. Her leg bumped into something furry. She looked down.

The small black cat looked up. "Mrrroww?"

"Meow, yourself. Shoo. Go home."

After entering through the main doors, she went directly to the elevator and took it up to the fourteenth floor, her mind overflowing with replays of her day with a killer, a cop, and a demon. She worked her key into the lock of her apartment and opened it. Something dark moved along the floor and scooted into the apartment ahead of her. It was the cat.

Had she been too distracted to even notice it in the elevator with her? Tricky little thing.

"Oh, no you don't." Eden flicked on a light by nudging the wall switch with her elbow. The cat had made a beeline for her brown corduroy couch, jumped up, and curled into a ball.

"Great," she said, dropping her purse and bags on the coffee table. She pulled off her coat and threw it over the easy chair. "Sure. Make yourself comfortable. Same goes for your fleas. Fantastic, really. Just what I need."

The cat lifted its head, then put it back down on its paws and closed its eyes.

"You can stay for a couple minutes to warm up," Eden told it, "but then you need to go back to your home. I don't have pets—no matter how smart they think they are. I don't even have houseplants. Trust me, it's better that way for everyone involved."

She went into the kitchenette to pour herself a glass of wine—which she drained as she attempted to forget about her problems for thirty seconds—then sat down on her couch in the living room and pulled out her McChicken and forced herself to take a few bites before putting it down. The food sat heavily in her stomach. The cat raised its head, its attention fully on the sandwich.

"Mrrrow?"

She waved a hand. "Help yourself."

The cat got up, jumped over to the discarded sandwich on the coffee table, sniffed at it daintily, and then chowed down, sesame seed bun and all, as if it hadn't eaten in days. Then it returned to the couch and lay down next to Eden, resting its head against her leg. It began to purr.

So much for her plan to kick it out of the house. A quick glance out her balcony window showed it had started to rain outside. The cat didn't wear any tags, and its ears weren't tattooed with ID—she was pretty sure the Humane Society did that for strays.

"Fine, kitty." Eden scratched its head. "One night. Then you're out of here."

Eden liked living alone. She valued her privacy. She'd lived briefly—very briefly—with her ex-fiancé, but after that had ended, she realized how much she liked time and space to herself.

She hadn't even thought about having a pet. She'd had one when she was a kid—a turtle. Her mom had run over it with her Camaro and blamed Eden for leaving it on the driveway. Eden had cried for a week over Speedy's squishy demise.

Seemed that anyone or anything she loved always left her— either by death or simply . . . *going away*. It really was best not to get attached to anything. Eden even threw out her magazines after one week. No need for clutter—emotional or material.

"And I'm not a big fan of cat hair." Eden found that she was still scratching the feline's head. It was oddly soothing.

She was exhausted and the wine hadn't helped do anything but make her more tired. Her brain hurt from thinking too much.

The exorcism hadn't been draining for Darrak alone. She felt the effects of it as well—like a hangover.

Before bed, Eden poured some milk into a bowl and put it on the ground. As an afterthought, she also put down half a can of tuna.

"I know, I'm a sucker," she told the cat. "You saw me coming from a mile away, didn't you?"

She went to the bathroom to brush her teeth and wash her face. She looked long and hard at her reflection in the oversized mirror to see there were dark circles under her eyes. Stress circles.

Gee, I wonder what those are from? she thought. She

was lucky she didn't have a bruise from when Malcolm had struck her.

Jerk.

She pulled off her shirt and jeans, kicking them over onto her fuzzy pink bath mat, and then reached around to unhook her bra. She let it fall to the floor.

"I'm feeling much better now," Darrak said.

She stifled a scream and clamped her hands over her bare breasts. "Don't sneak up on me like that!"

"Did I interrupt something?" There was a short pause. "Oh, I see. Don't let me stop you from getting naked. Please, continue."

Eden scanned her reflection with wide eyes. Could she see the demon inside of her? Did she look possessed?

Nope. There was nothing noticeable. Other than the deep voice in her head only she could hear.

"This should be interesting." Darrak sounded amused. "As I said before, I've never shared living space with a woman before. I honestly never would have guessed black lace panties for you. But I do approve."

She glared at her reflection, feeling equal parts anger and embarrassment from being caught half naked by the demon. "I think we're going to need to set some boundaries."

"Then I suggest you don't look at yourself in the mirror when you're in a state of undress. It's the only way I can see you—*all* of you, at the moment."

She turned away from the mirror. "Fine."

"Isn't it a little early to have Christmas hand towels out? Or do you use those all year round?"

She looked at the floor instead. The last thing she needed was a demon critiquing her lousy decorating skills.

"Darrak"—she let out a shuddery breath—"I need my privacy."

"That's going to be difficult. For obvious reasons."

"I'm exhausted right now and I can't deal with this. Can't you just go wherever you've been for the last few hours?"

"Afraid not. I need to be much more drained in order to fade like I did earlier. I can stay quiet, if you'd prefer, and enjoy the view. I'm just happy to have somebody to talk to after so long. You have no idea what it's been like for the last three centuries."

She couldn't even imagine. "I'm sure it hasn't been fun for you."

"No, it definitely hasn't. There have only been four hosts over the years who could hear me—and none as clearly as you can. Two of them went insane. The other killed himself. You had the privilege of meeting the fourth earlier today. He figured out I was a demon, but he was already crazy to start with." He was quiet for a moment. "I tried to stop him. But my voice in his head only made him angrier."

Eden's eyebrows raised. "You really tried to stop him from killing people?"

"I tried. My influence on him wasn't going to last long, though." His voice sobered. "Luckily his death came early."

"I'd think a demon would be okay with murder and mayhem."

"Some are; I won't lie. But the rest of us . . . well, I think stomping out a human life is a waste."

She hadn't believed in demons until today. Well, not outside of the Hollywood ones. And they were all evil. Darrak said he wasn't. She didn't exactly have any choice other than accepting what was happening to her at the moment, did she? Until they found the witch who'd cursed Darrak, Eden was stuck having his voice in her head.

From her chest of drawers she grabbed the oversized red T-shirt she wore to bed and quickly slipped it over her head.

"Purple walls and framed movie posters," he observed. "Interesting choices for a woman of your age. Especially the *Goonies* one."

Her cheeks heated again. She had framed posters of her favorite movies. All of which seemed to be from the 1980s for some reason. *Goonies* was a very underrated flick. Some people decorated with an eye for chic design. She preferred choosing things that brought back happy memories.

"You're positive the witch who cursed you is in the area right now?" she asked after a moment, choosing to ignore his comment.

"I know she is. Or she will be." He hesitated. "But I don't know exactly where she is or how to find her."

She thought about that. "It should be fairly simple to find somebody who's over three hundred years old. Just look for the most dried-up old person in a seniors' home. She won't be able to move very fast."

"She won't look old. She's a black witch."

"What's that supposed to mean?"

He snorted softly at that. "I keep forgetting you're new at this. A black witch is one who practices powerful black magic. Even back when she cursed me, she was very vain and would undoubtedly have used some of that magic to keep herself as youthful as possible to go along with her immortality."

Learn something new every day. "We'll find her."

"You sound very certain."

"I have to be. I can't live like this." She yanked the edge of the T-shirt down as far as possible. She still felt nearly naked. She'd have to buy some full pajamas ASAP. "I can't have somebody lurking around in my head all the time. We'll find the witch, we'll break the curse, and then you'll go away and leave me alone."

"It sounds like the best plan I've heard for three hundred years."

"Now I'm going to bed."

"Lead the way."

She pulled the covers back and climbed in. "I thought I was exhausted, but now I just hope I can fall asleep."

"Do you want me to tell you a bedtime story?"

She refrained from rolling her eyes. "I'd prefer silence."

"I can do that, too."

She turned off the light, squeezed her eyes shut, and tried her best to forget she was sleeping with a demon.

The demon didn't say another word.

* * *

Smooth, warm skin. It felt so good.

She curled around the firm body next to her, sliding her hands over a muscled male chest and broad shoulders as she slowly woke with a contented sigh.

Her lashes fluttered as she opened her eyes.

"Good morning." Darrak smiled at her, his face only an inch away from hers.

Her eyes widened. *"You."*

She'd woken in the arms of the demon. He'd taken form again. Full and—by the looks of the rapidly slipping lavender sheets as she scrambled to move away from his embrace—completely *naked* form.

Darrak didn't seem to have a problem with his current state of undress. He reclined against an overstuffed pillow, casually put his arms behind his head, and raised an eyebrow at her. "What?"

Eden fell right off the side of the bed, but quickly jolted back up to her feet.

She cleared her throat and averted her eyes, then pointed in his general direction. "Don't you have any clothes?"

"Quite honestly, no I don't."

"Cover yourself up!"

"Fine." There was a rustling sound. "Okay, I'm covered. I had no idea you were such a prude."

"I'm not a prude." She glared at him to see he'd pulled the covers up to his waist.

"Sure you are. It's obvious."

"Yeah, well. You're an exhibitionist."

"Your point?"

She swallowed hard. "You—you were dressed yesterday."

"True. I'm currently very weak, but I had enough power to conjure those less than adequate clothes."

"Then conjure some more."

He studied her for a moment with amusement. "For the last

half hour you didn't seem to be having much of a problem with my current form."

Her cheeks began to blaze with heat. "You've been groping me for a half an hour?"

"More like the other way around. But don't worry, I didn't mind." He gave her a wicked grin.

She turned away from him and went into the bathroom, slammed the door, and locked it. Then she put her back up against it and tried to calm down.

This wasn't working. Not in any way, shape, or form. Maybe she hadn't been 100 percent perfect for the nearly thirty years of her life, but what had she done to deserve this?

She hated to sound whiny, but come on! Why her?

Luckily, Darrak didn't bother her or knock on the door. She decided to take the brief, precious moment of privacy to have a quick shower and wash and blow-dry her hair. When she cracked open the door and peered out, there was no sign of Darrak in bed or elsewhere in her bedroom. She breathed a sigh of relief and tiptoed out to get dressed as quickly as possible in black pants, a form-fitting but practical khaki tank top, and a black jacket.

She picked up the framed picture of her mother from her bookcase and looked down at the beautiful, smiling blond woman.

"This isn't funny," she told it firmly. Her mother would have been very amused by this situation. She'd always thought Eden was too uptight for her own good.

Men had fallen at Caroline Riley's feet all her life. Eden hadn't inherited her easy, breezy way with men at all. Even Andy had been head over heels in love with her mother. That was probably what had made it so easy for her to take him for half his business in the poker game.

She put the thoughts of her mother out of her head and left the bedroom. Her rented apartment was very small, and her bedroom was only a few steps away from the living room. The kitchenette was open concept and looked out at the living room over a breakfast bar.

Darrak, now clad in the same simple, magically conjured black outfit he'd had on yesterday, was peering into the fridge.

She felt a fresh swell of stress at the sight of him. However, she was happy he wasn't naked anymore.

"Coffee?" he asked.

She crossed her arms tightly and glanced at the coffeemaker. "You know how to make coffee?"

"I've been a keen observer of all things human."

Yesterday, she'd been way too freaked out to take a really good look at him, but today, in the daylight of her apartment, she'd never guess at first glance that he was a demon made of black smoke. Or second glance, for that matter. He just looked like a man. A tall, attractive one. Drinking coffee out of her favorite Snoopy mug.

Anxiety flowed over her. Coffee wasn't going to help the situation at all. The cat who'd conned her into letting it stay for the night rubbed against her leg.

Darrak nodded at it. "You don't seem to have any litter so I shredded some newspaper and put it in a shoe box. I'm very industrious."

She rubbed her temples. Cats and demons and makeshift litter boxes. Maybe she was still asleep and having a nightmare.

The toaster popped. Darrak grabbed the piece of toast and spread a thick layer of chunky peanut butter on it before taking a large bite.

"Do you know, this is the first thing I've tasted in three hundred years?" he asked. "It's fantastic."

"I hate peanut butter."

"Then why do you have it?"

She shrugged. "Because it's something people are supposed to have in their cupboards."

"Peanut butter is total ambrosia."

She grabbed the edge of her counter and squeezed. "Demons can eat?"

"Obviously."

"Learn something new every day." Her voice was tight. She glanced around the kitchenette to see the complete mess the demon had made in his quest for breakfast and grimaced.

Despite her questionable décor choices, she was a neat freak.

This was going to be yet another problem.

"We don't have to eat, but we can," he said and smiled at her. A glob of peanut butter fell off his piece of toast and splatted onto the floor. "Just like other things, it's more for pleasure than necessity."

Her cheeks burned again. "Just to make things perfectly clear between us, you can have my peanut butter, but my bed is off-limits."

He shrugged. "Sorry. I took form at sunrise and you grabbed on to me immediately. I didn't want to disturb your sleep or I would have moved."

She was about to debate the sheer unlikeliness of that when the cat rubbed against her leg again.

"So that's two unwanted guests I have to deal with," she said. "Great."

Darrak leaned back against the counter and took a sip from the coffee mug. "Other than the litter situation, I also fed your furry friend already and put down some water for her. You're welcome."

"Come on, kitty," Eden said, leaning over to grab the cat. "This hotel is officially overbooked. You're out of here."

The cat hissed at her, slipped out of her grip, and ran into the bedroom.

"Terrific." She sighed with frustration and looked at the clock. Her eyes bugged. "Is that really the time?"

She hadn't noticed it was nearly nine o'clock. Was she that distracted?

Well, yes, she was. Most definitely.

"No time for coffee?"

"My job is right next to a coffee bar. I think I'll manage."

"Come on, Eden. Turn that frown upside down. There's no reason for bad moods. It's a beautiful new day full of possibilities."

"Maybe for you." Eden turned toward the door. She grabbed her light coat from the closet and left the apartment. Before she could fit her key into the door to lock it, Darrak opened it and was at her side.

"Don't forget, I have to come with you."

For a moment she *had* forgotten that they were currently a two-for-one deal. How was she supposed to function like this? She locked the door behind her. "How close do we have to stay to each other?"

"I have no idea." He crammed the rest of the peanut butter on toast in his mouth and swallowed a mouthful of coffee from the mug he still held.

How could he be so blasé about something so important? If he had to follow her everywhere, then she wanted to know how close he had to be. She needed her space.

She walked down the hall to the elevator and pressed the button. A moment later it opened and she got in.

Darrak looked over his shoulder at the locked door of her apartment. "I need to put your mug back."

"No time."

"Okay, but if you—"

The doors on the elevator closed before he had a chance to get in. Eden jabbed at the ground floor button. She heard Darrak yell her name, and a bang as he pounded on the elevator door, and then a crash.

Had he dropped her Snoopy mug?

The elevator began to descend slowly and she stifled the immediate feeling of guilt that swelled inside of her.

She wanted to see how far apart they could be. The opportunity had just presented itself nicely.

By the eighth floor she began to feel a bit light-headed. She brought a hand to her forehead and inhaled shakily. She didn't remember feeling that way when Darrak tried to walk out of the office yesterday.

The impromptu experiment was working.

Six floors at approximately ten feet per floor? That was sixty feet.

Seventy feet.

Eighty.

A sharp pain wrenched through her stomach. She doubled over and staggered back until she hit the wall of the elevator. A moment later, thick black smoke slithered in through the crack at the top of the elevator door. It moved to pool on the floor, then slowly took form.

Just before the doors opened on ground level, Darrak had fully rematerialized. He crouched on the floor at her feet, his chest heaving. Sweat beaded his forehead. His current expression was anything but that of the pleasant and amiable Darrak she'd begun to expect. In fact, he looked furious.

She'd wanted to see what would happen—to test their boundaries and perhaps find out that they didn't actually have any, but now the guilt returned to replace the pain that she'd felt before.

"Don't do that again," he said darkly. *"Please."*

She swallowed hard. Well, at least he said please.

"I just wanted to see if we could—"

He rose to his feet, grabbed her upper arms firmly, and pushed her up against the mirrored elevator wall. In human form, he was very tall. And big. And strong. She suddenly felt extremely intimidated by him—especially by that angry look in his blue eyes that for a split second she swore changed to a strange, flickering amber.

"You want to get rid of me." Despite the fiery look in his gaze, the words were as sharp and cold as icicles. "I get it. We both want that. Do you think I want to put up with you every hour of the day, either? Think again. But right now we can't do anything but try to make this work."

"Let go of me."

"First I want to make sure you understand me." His eyes narrowed. "And just so you know, being forced to lose form like that hurts like hell. And I know what Hell feels like."

"I understand," she said through clenched teeth, before her own swell of anger faded. She'd only wanted to test a theory, not cause him any more pain. "I felt something unpleasant this time, too."

"Of course you did."

She frowned at his quick agreement. "But yesterday I didn't feel anything when you tried to leave the office. And even during the exorcism . . . I only felt a twinge. But today it was actually . . . *painful.*"

"Lucky you." A cold, humorless smile curled his lips. "It means we're bonding."

"Which means what?"

"Enough time has passed since I first possessed you that not only do I depend entirely on your physical and unusual psychic energy to exist, you've also begun to depend on me as well."

She blinked up at him. "I don't understand."

"Think of it like your morning cup of coffee. You get used to having it every day until one day you don't. Then you get a headache from the caffeine withdrawal. For now it's still mild. We haven't quite crossed the line into heroin territory yet."

Her eyes widened. "I'm becoming addicted to you?"

He raised an eyebrow. "You say it like it's a bad thing."

Darrak hadn't let go of her and still had her effortlessly pressed up against the elevator wall. The doors stayed open at ground level, but no one was in the lobby to see them.

"It *is* a bad thing," she said firmly.

"Then it's just one more reason why testing our limits shouldn't be on your daily to-do list. Just remember, Eden, I want this over infinitely more than you do."

Her jaw clenched. "I hate this."

"So do I. Bottom line, you don't have to like me and I

don't have to like you. But until we find the witch, we're stuck together."

"What if we can't find her?"

He looked at her for a long moment and any mild edge of humor left his expression completely. "Then a year from now I'll be looking for a new host."

"Why?"

"Because that's when you're going to die."

With that, he finally released her and left the elevator.

⇒ EIGHT ⇐

Eden caught up to the demon outside the building. "What the hell did you just say?"

His shoulders stiffened and he stopped walking. "None of my former hosts have lived more than a year from when I possessed them."

Her mouth felt dry. "I'm going to die in a *year*."

"Only if we haven't fixed this problem." Darrak turned so she could see his expression was stony.

Just when she thought this situation sucked as hard as it possibly could, it started sucking just a little bit more.

"So you've never possessed anyone for more than a year at a time?"

"That's what it means." Some of that angry expression left his face when he saw the reaction his latest newsflash had caused. "One year. And that's if they don't get themselves killed before that deadline. Pardon the expression."

Her breath caught and a wave of nausea rushed through her. She bent over and braced her hands on her knees. "Oh, my God. I think I'm going to be sick."

"We'll fix this. I promise. Don't puke."

She tried to breathe. "How many people have you killed?"

He looked confused. "What?"

"Some of them probably didn't even realize what was going on, right? You killed them just by using their bodies. Hundreds of them." She actually gagged at the horrible thought.

He opened his mouth as if to protest, but then closed it. "I know it doesn't look good. Being a demon, my first impulse is self-preservation—it's ingrained in me. I know it won't make much of a difference to you, but after I realized the problem, I tried very hard to find people the world wouldn't mind losing."

Eden took in a shaky breath. "What does that mean?"

He reached out as if he was going to touch her shoulder, but then pulled his hand back when she flinched away from him. "Like the serial killer from yesterday. The world is better off without him in it. I try to choose bad people whose souls are already black."

She blanched. "Is that what I have? A black soul?"

"No." He met her eyes. "Your soul is as bright as polished silver."

"You can see it?"

"I can sense it. Even right now as we stand here." His jaw clenched. "I think it's a big part of what gives me the strength to take form. I've never sensed a soul so . . . *shiny*."

She had a shiny soul. Like a stainless-steel refrigerator. That should be enough to save her from the forces of darkness, right?

"So why me?" It sounded like she was whining—mostly because she was. She didn't ask for this. And if she hadn't done anything to deserve it, then why was this happening to her?

"I didn't have any choice yesterday. If my host dies before I've had a chance to plan my jump, I need to possess the first human body I can get to. If I don't, then I'll . . ."

"You'll what?"

"I'll be sucked into the void as sure as if I'd been exorcised." His voice sounded thick and he raked his fingers through his dark hair. "It wouldn't take long. A few minutes at the most. That's why that irresistible self-protection force kicks in. I can't help it."

Eden frowned very hard at him. "Are you trying to make me feel sorry for you?"

"No. I'm just trying to make you understand."

"Black soul or shiny soul aside, just by your presence, you've killed over three hundred people since you were cursed. That's what you're telling me, right?"

His expression shadowed and he visibly swallowed. "I'm not trying to justify what has happened before. But it's different now. *You're* different. None of my previous hosts have ever been able to help me do this." He waved a hand at his physical body. "We can figure this out. I promise."

Figure it out. Which essentially came down to one thing, and one thing only. Find a witch who hadn't been seen or heard from in over three centuries.

And they had a year to do it or she was going to die.

Her heart was thudding wildly, but she forced herself to calm down and look at the demon.

Darrak looked so damned earnest. She'd already seen cocky and suave, and she'd definitely seen pissed off, but now he was all grave and sincere.

At that moment she wished he was totally, unrepentantly evil. If that was the case, then she wouldn't have tried to stop the exorcism and all of this would be a horrific but fading memory.

She started walking toward her parking spot. "So we basically need to find a missing person."

"The witch."

She nodded. "The man I work with, Andy, he used to work for the FBI before he moved up here and opened Triple-A. If there's somebody who might be able to help find a missing person, it's him."

Darrak's dark eyebrows raised. "Sounds like a start."

It did. A weak one, but still a start. Besides, despite Andy's stack of typing he needed done yesterday, the office hadn't been very busy since Eden had come onboard. Andy might welcome the chance to do a little pro bono digging. And if he didn't, she wasn't above begging and pleading.

She just had to make sure not to reveal that he was actually searching for a three-hundred-year-old witch. On behalf of a mass-murdering but self-proclaimed "good" demon. That might not go over so well.

If only her psychic abilities were more reliable and controllable. Sure, she'd found the serial killer yesterday, but that had been a total fluke. She couldn't simply find anyone, anywhere, at any time.

Unfortunately. Because that would be really helpful right about now.

Only a day ago she had no idea that demons even existed. Now that she did, she wanted to forget about that little chaotic piece of the paranormal universe she'd accidentally stumbled into and go back to her normal, orderly life where things were safer and controllable.

The sooner the better.

Andy waited for her outside Triple-A. His arms were crossed.

"Something you want to tell me?" he asked.

She froze. "Uh . . ."

He nodded at the entrance. "New door?"

"Oh . . . yes. It's a new door."

His eyes flicked to Darrak, who stood next to Eden. "Thanks for the heads-up. I don't have a key for it. I've been trying to call your cell phone for a half an hour."

Her cheeks flushed. "Sorry. I totally forgot. And my phone's off."

She grabbed her key, handed Andy the spare, and opened the shiny new door. It was symbolic, really. If a door could be fixed soon after it had been broken, then so could she. A positive attitude was all it took. She'd ask the universe for what she wanted—easy as that. The law of attraction would work to do her bidding.

I don't want to be possessed anymore. I want Darrak to go away and I never want to see him again. Ciao, demon.

There. That should be more than enough to get the universe working.

"Andy—" she said as they went inside the office. He was totally the key to getting the answers—she knew it.

"Are you going to tell me what the hell happened to the door?" He'd picked up the invoice she'd left on his desk.

"Uh . . . a little accident."

His pale brows drew together. "Rush service? Do you know what this cost?"

"Well, I figured it was better to fix it right away than leave a gaping hole there all night so anyone could just walk in and make themselves at home."

His attention moved to the tall man standing silently behind her and he thrust his chin in that direction. "Who's he? The reason why you're late this morning?"

In a word, yes, she thought. *He's my own personal demon. And he has to stay within approximately eighty feet of me at all times or it causes both of us excruciating pain. And he's going to inadvertently kill me in a year if I don't find a way to get rid of him. Also, FYI, he enjoys crunchy peanut butter and is comfortable with nudity.*

But she didn't say that out loud, of course. "This is . . . Darrak. He's . . . my *brother*."

Oh, sure. That sounded plausible enough, didn't it?

"Your brother?" Andy repeated. "I thought you were Caroline's only kid?"

Eden looked over her shoulder at Darrak, who had his arms crossed, and he raised a dark eyebrow at her to show his amusement.

"I'm her brother from a different mother," he offered.

Kill me, she thought.

She moistened her lips. "He's staying with me for a few—" *Hours? Days? Months?* Another wave of nausea surged through her. "For a little while."

"Really?" Andy seemed surprised. "I got the impression you were a total loner who hates company."

She forced a smile. That was his impression of her? Very accurate, actually. Uncomplimentary, but accurate. "For family it's different, of course."

Darrak snorted at that. "Sorry. I know . . . sis . . . likes her privacy, but she's been very accommodating so far. If you ignore the screaming. Ha. Just kidding, of course. Mostly."

"Good to meet you, Darrak. Any brother of Eden's is . . . well, you know." Andy stood up from his desk and thrust out his hand.

Darrak eyed it for a moment before tentatively shaking it. He looked at Eden with a half grin. "Having a body sure is hard to get used to, isn't it?"

She forced the smile to remain plastered on her lips. "It sure is."

Andy was looking at her strangely. "What does he mean by that?"

She coughed nervously. "Don't mind Darrak. He's a little . . . well"—she lowered her voice—"*slow* is a good word. He's not used to being out and about from the, uh . . . *special home* he normally lives in down south."

To say the least.

"Oh." Andy nodded. "I think I understand. I have a cousin like that, too." He punched Darrak playfully in the shoulder. "You have a very nice sister to let you stay with her and hang out at her job. It's fun being on vacation, isn't it, sport?"

Darrak looked at Eden dryly. "I just hope I don't hurt myself with my enthusiasm."

Eden pressed her lips together. The day had not started well.

"Andy, I need to ask a favor," she said.

He looked at her skeptically. "I don't have any money for a loan right now."

"You immediately assume I want money?"

He sat down in his chair, leaned back, and rubbed his temples. "Look, Eden, I have some bad news. I may as well tell you now and get it over with."

Her mouth went dry. *More bad news?* "What is it?"

"Triple-A is going out of business. I'm declaring bankruptcy." His voice broke and his face crumpled. "I'm such a pathetic failure."

"What are you talking about?" This was the first news she'd heard of this.

"I'm broke." He looked at Darrak. "That means that I have no money. Having no money makes it hard to be happy, chum."

"*Chum*?" Darrak repeated.

"Andy," Eden said. "It can't be that bad."

"Trust me, it is. The bills have been piling up for months now. I've been going to the racetrack to try to make some quick cash, but that's only sunk me in deeper. I haven't had a new client in forever. I've been keeping you busy just so you wouldn't figure out how much of a loser I am."

She let out a long breath. "We can figure this out."

He shook his head. "I've tried. Nothing has worked."

She didn't like seeing him so upset, but a fresh burst of annoyance filled her. "Well, you can't just make this decision by yourself. I own half this business."

"Actually, you own 49 percent of it. Check your papers. Which makes me the deciding partner. And I've decided to cut my losses." He looked over at a framed picture of a bikini-clad babe on a beautiful beach on the wall next to the bookcase. "And I'm moving to Hawaii. Even though I'm not really welcome in the U.S. anymore for reasons I'd rather not get into right now, I'll figure out a way to get to the glorious fiftieth state."

"Andy—"

"And I'll have to get rid of Rhonda," he said sadly.

"Who's Rhonda?"

He looked up and his face paled. "That's what I call my Porsche. I'm going to miss her so much." He exhaled shakily. "My beautiful Rhonda."

Eden had counted on Andy helping her find the witch. If he was busy feeling sorry for himself while getting a suntan in Hawaii, that wouldn't exactly help, would it?

Andy blinked slowly, rubbed at his eyes, and looked at her. "What was it you wanted to ask?"

She looked at Darrak. She couldn't talk. Her throat felt thick.

"I'm looking for somebody," Darrak said. "An old . . . friend. She's in the area, but I have no idea how to find her."

"I'd love to help you out, sport, but I don't think I can."

"I know you were in the FBI." Eden pushed the words out. "And it might be easy for you to locate somebody. A missing person case. My—my *brother* . . . he has his heart set on finding this woman. He doesn't take disappointment very well, especially when he's . . . um . . . off his medication. He might have a tantrum."

Darrak nodded gravely. "It's very likely, actually."

Andy frowned at her. "Did I tell you I was with the Bureau?"

"Not in so many words. But I'd have to be blind not to notice your Distinguished Service Award." She nodded at the framed document on the wall next to his Hawaiian beach fantasy.

He followed her gaze. "I got that a long time ago."

"So can you help Darrak?" *Help me*, she added internally.

Andy's bottom lip wobbled. "I can't even help myself."

"Andy, please—"

He held up a hand. "I'm sorry, Eden. Really, I am. But it's over. This whole façade of a business. I gave it my best shot."

"There's got to be a way," Eden said again and hated the tone of desperation in the words. She knew she sounded like a broken record, but at the moment stubbornness seemed to be the life preserver she was clinging onto as her life sank to the bottom of the proverbial ocean.

He sighed. "The only way I'd even consider staying open is if somebody walks through that door right now willing to pay big bucks for us to take on a new case."

He pointed at the door just as it opened and a woman entered the office.

"Excuse me," she asked. "There's no sign on the door, but I got your address from the phone book. Is this Triple-A Investigations?"

"It is."

She exhaled with relief, and Eden couldn't help but notice her eyes were brimming with tears. "I desperately need your help. And money's no object."

⇉ NINE ⇇

Eden exchanged a quick glance with Andy.

The universe at work. *Totally.*

Andy's chair scraped against the floor as he quickly got to his feet. He silently stared at the woman for a few moments longer than was comfortable.

She cleared her throat. "Perhaps I've come at a bad time."

"No," Eden said immediately as she began backing up toward the door. "Come in. Please. Andy would be happy to see you right away, wouldn't you, Andy?"

He was still pointing at the door. His hand dropped slackly to his side. "Well, of course. That timing just freaked me the hell out, is all."

The woman gave Andy a strange look and instead came toward Eden. She was a tall, willowy, sunny blonde and she wore an expensive Chanel suit. "I've never done this before, so I'm not sure how to begin."

Andy jostled in his desk drawer for a pad of paper. "Please, come sit over here, Miss—?"

"It's Mrs. Fay Morgan." She glanced over her shoulder and then back at Eden. "And if you don't mind, I want to speak to you. Only to you."

"Me?" Eden pointed to her chest.

"Yes."

"But, I'm not really . . ." She twisted a finger in her hair. "I mean, Andy's the one you need to talk to. He's got experience up the wazoo when it comes to investigating whatever you want. To be completely truthful, I just help out around here at the moment."

She shook her head. "I don't care. I'll only deal with you."

Eden opened her mouth to urge her to talk to Andy, when he spoke up.

"That's just fine. Eden, please take down Mrs. Morgan's case details. I'll go next door and get us all some fresh coffee. I haven't had a chance to make any yet this morning being that I was locked out of the office."

Before Eden could say anything, Andy pushed open the front door and went outside.

What did he think he was doing? Eden didn't know the first thing about how to handle new cases. She'd typed them up in the past month, but that wasn't remotely the same thing. She wasn't an investigator nor did she want to be one. Ever.

She glanced at Darrak. He was very quiet. His arms were crossed in front of him and he studied the woman with a narrowed, unfriendly gaze.

What was his problem?

"Sorry, Mrs. Morgan, I'm being rude." She held out her hand. "I'm Eden Riley."

"Please, call me Fay." Instead of shaking her hand Fay grabbed her into a tight embrace. "I knew I'd come to the right place."

The hug was so tight it actually hurt a little.

"Let go of her," Darrak said sharply.

Fay tensed and leaned back from Eden, her eyes wide. She

looked over her shoulder at the demon in the corner and drew in a sharp breath.

"I didn't sense anything . . ." she began, then shut her mouth. "I need to leave."

"No, wait," Eden said as Fay began moving toward the door. "Don't go."

If only so she could understand what the hell was going on. The air felt thick with tension all of a sudden.

Fay's expression was tight as she turned back to Eden. "I sensed that this was a welcoming place. But now I see that it is not."

"I'm not what you think," Darrak said.

"You're a demon."

He frowned. "Well, okay. Maybe I am what you think. But just relax. Unless you wish ill to Eden—and I don't think you do—then I mean you no harm in return. Seriously."

"And why would I believe that?"

"Because I guarantee it," Eden told her. "How do you know what he is?"

"I never would have come within a mile of this place if I'd sensed him"—she paused—"but his true essence seems to be somewhat weakened."

"You could say that," Darrak agreed. "Now, why don't you tell us why you came here today?"

She shifted her feet as her gaze darted back and forth between Eden and Darrak. "I suspect my—my husband is cheating on me. I want to hire you to follow him."

"What is your husband?" Darrak asked.

"*What* is he?" Eden shot him a look.

"He's human," the woman replied, as if it wasn't an odd question.

"So you think he's cheating on you?" Eden scribbled down the information as neatly as she could.

Fay sat down in a chair next to Eden's desk. "I think he might be enchanted in some way."

Eden dropped her pen. *"Enchanted?"*

"Yes. Manipulated by magic."

"I know what enchanted means." She swallowed hard. "I'm just not used to dealing with it on an everyday basis."

Fay glanced back at Darrak. "She's new to this?"

"You could say that."

She studied Eden for a moment and her brow lowered. "I thought you were different, but are you only human?"

Eden blinked. "Well, of course I am."

Fay dared another glance at the demon behind her. "I sensed this place was Other-friendly. In fact, when looking for a detective agency, I was compelled to choose this one in particular."

*"Other-*friendly?" Eden asked cautiously.

"Other than human."

"Oh." Eden felt the blood drain from her face. "Of course. Silly me."

"Eden is human," Darrak said. "She has some psychic abilities, but has no conscious control over them. And she has been touched by a magical presence recently. Perhaps that is all this is."

Touched by a magical presence. Demonic possession. Potato, potahto.

Eden exhaled slowly and tried to center herself. "We can have your husband followed, Fay. Believe me, I'm not trying to turn away your case just because it might have some *strangeness* associated with it that I'm not entirely comfortable with. This is a business, after all."

A business that was going to fold like a cheap suit without this woman's case. And if that happened, then Andy would never agree to help them find the witch.

If nothing else, it helped to make Eden's choices crystal clear.

Fay had been compelled to come to Triple-A? Eden could understand someone compelled to stay away from this flea-bitten office, but *compelled* to come here?

. "It makes me very uneasy knowing that you're involved with a demon," Fay said stiffly.

"I wouldn't really say we're involved per se," Eden said quickly. "It's really more of an unpleasant, temporary arrangement."

Fay shrugged. "I have a family prejudice against demons."

Darrak snorted. "Yeah, I figured."

"What does that mean?" Eden asked. She felt like she was constantly asking for clarification now, but it was the only way she was going to be able to keep things straight in her head. She liked order. Chaos and her brain did not get along.

"Fay is a fairy," Darrak explained. "From the Unseelie court if I'm not mistaken."

"A fairy?" Eden sputtered. "Like a happy little sparkly winged creature?"

"No." Darrak sighed. "Not happy or sparkly or, for that matter, *winged*. How have you managed without me all of these years, Eden? Unseelie fairies are malevolent little creatures of darkness—descended from demons, actually, eons ago; their Seelie counterparts are descended from angels—who like to play dress-up amongst the humans when they're not draining them of energy in order to keep up their power reserve in this world."

"I don't do that," Fay protested. "Well, not anymore. I'm a vegan now. I gave up my powers when I married my husband."

Darrak rolled his eyes. "Let me guess, you don't have a day job, either, do you? You just stay home and do laundry and cook meals for your cheating scumbag of a husband?"

"Darrak!" Eden exclaimed.

He looked at her guiltily. "Sorry. I have issues with fairies. Always have. Back in the day, pre-curse, a swarm of them tried to tear me apart."

Fay shrugged. "We hate demons. Foul creatures of darkness."

"Yeah, like your clan are any better."

She turned away from the demon to grab Eden's hand, which was very cold now. Going into total and complete shock made her chilly. "If my marriage fails, I'll have to go back to my family. I'll be tried as a deserter of my kingdom and if I'm found guilty I will be killed."

"Killed?" Eden gasped.

Fay nodded. "Fairy law is very strict. They see my marriage as disrespectful, especially when I refused an arranged marriage. Disowning me was my parents' only choice. If my marriage doesn't last I would have to return and face my punishment. Obviously, I don't want that. I want to stay here. I know my husband loves me. I never would have taken such a great risk if I didn't believe that. It's only very recently that he's been acting strangely. Please, you must follow him. Find out where he spends his days when he's not at the office."

Eden swallowed. Her mouth felt as dry as a room full of unbuttered popcorn. "Office?"

"He's an accountant. Here is Richard's picture." Fay pulled out a photo from her purse and slid it across the desk to Eden so she could see the handsome, dark-haired man smiling at the camera next to his wife.

"Does Richard know you're . . ." Eden cleared her throat. "That you're a *fairy*?"

She shook her head. "He doesn't know, and I'd like to keep it that way. I assume the woman he's seeing has enchanted him to get him to act this way. If that's so, then I need to know so she can be stopped and he can be released from her spell. But if he's truly been unfaithful"—she blinked very hard—"then it's important that I know that as well. Will you take my case?"

Eden thought about it. She didn't like it, not one little bit. She'd wanted to quickly and soundly back away from any paranormal elements, not welcome them into her life with open arms and a sloppy kiss. But she couldn't see any way to get what she wanted—for Andy to find the witch by using his fabulous missing person skills—if she let this fairy fly out of her net.

"Okay, fine," she said after a long moment of silence. "But

I'm going to have to figure out what kind of a deposit Andy normally charges for this sort of case, though."

"I've already written a check, which I imagine is plenty." She produced that as well and handed it to Eden.

It was made out for fifty thousand dollars. Eden blinked with surprise.

"I was able to leave the Underworld with a small fortune intact—"

"The Underworld?" Eden asked, with a look at Darrak.

He nodded. "That's where the Unseelie normally live. The outskirts of Hell itself. Not so sparkly now, are they?"

Fay looked at the demon with distaste, and turned her gaze back to Eden. "There will be another fifty when it's over—no matter the outcome, as long as it's resolved. My cell number and address are on the back of my husband's photo. He leaves the house promptly at eight every morning and gets a coffee at the Starbucks on the corner. Please contact me the moment you learn anything."

"I certainly will."

She stood up and gave Darrak another unfriendly look. "I will not judge you, Eden, on who you choose to spend time with."

"Who said I had a choice?" Eden replied, trying to make a joke. A weak one, but at least she was trying.

Fay met her gaze—with no humor. "Just please be careful." She left without another word.

"Fairies." Darrak shook his head. "Can't stand the freaks."

"She seemed normal enough to me."

"Hate to see her with her glamour down. That's when the sharp teeth and claws are noticeable."

"Excuse me?" she gasped.

He waved a hand. "Fairies look a little different when they're in their normal state. They use a glamour—a surface magic—to enhance their looks."

Eden decided to ignore the comment about "sharp teeth." And, for that matter, everything else Darrak said.

Andy swung through the door with a tray of coffee and donuts. "Where'd she go?"

"She left."

"Did you chase her away?" he asked with disappointment.

"Yeah, that's what I did. But she left a check first. It's for fifty Gs."

His mouth dropped open. "You're shitting me."

"No shit. It's a . . ." Eden swallowed. "A cheating husband case, believe it or not."

"Fifty grand for a cheater?" His eyes bugged. "Wow, she must be filthy rich."

"And another fifty when we're finished."

"Christ on a cracker! Seriously? Are we on *Candid Camera*?"

"Will that be enough money to keep us afloat?" She walked over and handed him the check. He looked at it with disbelief.

"If it clears, then yeah. It'll definitely help." He looked at her. "And it'll save Rhonda. It's like winning the lottery."

Eden leaned against his desk. "Now about Darrak's friend."

"Oh right. Missing person. Totally no problem." His voice and demeanor had brightened considerably. "I just need her name, last known address, physical description, and any other information you can provide."

Darrak grimaced. "That might be a problem. I don't know her name. And the last time I saw her was . . . well, let's just say it was a long time ago."

"It's very important that we find her," Eden told Andy. "I can't stress this enough."

"But you don't know her name?"

Her head throbbed. "No."

"How about a physical description?"

"I can help a little there," Darrak said.

"Not much to go on. But I've worked with less and come up with something." He grinned and punched Darrak in the shoulder again. "Sounds like a challenge, champ. I like challenges."

"Please don't call me champ."

Andy fixed his coffee. He seemed very happy now—the gloomy look from earlier had disappeared completely. "Why don't you tell me exactly how she looked the last time you saw her and we'll start from there. I can always run her profile through a facial recognition program. Donut?" He offered Darrak the box to choose from.

"Thank you."

"Eden, how much sugar is your brother allowed to have?"

"Uh . . ." The phone rang and Eden turned to answer it. "Triple-A."

"Eden." Ben's voice was immediately recognizable. "Good morning."

She inhaled sharply. "Morning."

"You doing okay today? Recovered from all the drama yesterday?"

Eden eyed Darrak as the demon enthusiastically tasted his first deep-fried chocolate-glazed pastry. "My recovery is an ongoing process."

"I was going to wait until this afternoon to call, but I had a free moment so I figured now was as good a time as any. It's good to hear your voice."

"You, too."

"Oh yeah?" He sounded pleased.

Her cheeks warmed. "Sure."

"Any sign of your friends from last night?"

She grimaced at the memory. "No. They're long gone."

"That's good to know." He was quiet for a moment. "It's strange, but it kind of feels like I've known you for weeks already."

"Is that a good thing or a bad thing?"

"A good thing, trust me. So . . . dinner tonight? We still on?"

It was on the tip of her tongue to cancel. How was she supposed to go on a date with a guy she really liked with everything that was happening all around her? Shouldn't she focus on getting rid of the problem that was Darrak the demon before even considering spending any time with Ben?

But who knew if she'd have the chance in the future?

"Yes, dinner's still on," she said firmly.

"How about I pick you up at your apartment at a quarter to seven?"

"Sounds perfect." Eden told him her address.

"Do you have a favorite restaurant? I can make reservations."

"Uh . . . no. Anything you pick is fine."

"You're putting a lot of faith in me."

"I trust you to make this very important decision."

"Okay," he said, and she could hear the smile in his voice. "Then I'll see you later."

"Bye."

She hung up. *Damn.* She really did need Darrak feeding her smoother, more confident lines. Was she always such a doofus when it came to talking to men? She had managed to get engaged to ass-face. But he'd been a friend of a friend who helped ease her into things with a lot of double dates. There wasn't this awkward "getting to know you" phase.

But she did want to get to know Ben. He was perfect. She needed a little bit of perfect in her life.

"Eden," Andy called. "You have to look at this! Hurry!"

Oh, God. Now what?

She crossed the room in five steps. Andy held out a piece of paper to her and she looked at a precisely detailed sketch of a beautiful woman with long dark hair drawn in blue ballpoint pen.

"That's her," Darrak said, pointing at the picture.

"He's an artist," Andy said. "This is really good. And the crazy thing is he says he's never drawn before. How is that possible?"

Eden gritted her teeth. "He's very special, Darrak is."

"Thanks, sis. You're the bestest." He grabbed another donut. "And so are these."

"It's not a lot to go on, but it's a start." Andy took the page.

"I can work on finding Darrak's old friend here and you can take care of the cheating husband case."

She pointed at herself. "Me?"

"Sure. She wanted you to do it. And I don't want to piss off a new client. Especially one who seems to be bleeding money. You can start on it tomorrow."

"Why wait until tomorrow?" she asked.

"Got to make sure this check is good." He grinned. "If you don't hear from me, don't even bother coming in here first. I'll call you if there are any emergencies."

"But I don't have a license."

He waved his hand. "Don't worry about that."

"Don't worry about that? It's the law. We could get in trouble."

"Honestly, Eden. Leave that sort of thing up to me."

She opened her mouth to protest some more, but closed it. Andy was going to search for the witch, and he seemed surprisingly positive about it. That was good. She wouldn't say anything to disrupt that. While she didn't feel comfortable with Fay's case, she'd do her best.

She was really a fairy? Other than the painfully tight hug there was nothing to indicate she was anything other than human. But she was a fairy who would be tried as a deserter of her people and possibly killed if her marriage was a failure. Talk about a good deterrent for divorce.

It was all very, very wrong.

"Fine. If you say so, then so be it," she finally said. "Cheating husband. No problem, right?"

"No problem," Andy agreed. "Grab my camera. Just jot down everything the husband does, who he's seen with. Take tons of pictures. Easy as pie. I've done a million of 'em. And I hate to say it, but 99 percent of the time the client is right about their husband or wife. The gut rarely lies. They just need us to confirm it so they can use the evidence in the divorce case. I say, keep it coming. Infidelity has always been Triple-A's bread and butter."

Eden's ex-fiancé cheated on her at a Valentine's Day party,

of all things. As far as she was concerned, 99 percent of all men were born to cheat. The challenge was finding that 1 percent that wouldn't.

However, searching for that elusive needle in the haystack usually resulted in finding a whole lot of other pricks.

Ben might be part of that tiny percentage. He was so perfect in every other way, from his looks to his job performance; he had to be the potential perfect husband as well.

Not that she was planning that far ahead. However, it did make for a nice mental image.

"Eden, why don't you take the rest of the day off? After talking to Mrs. Morgan and getting that nice juicy check you've totally earned it," Andy said. "Show your brother around the city. Have some fun."

She eyed him skeptically. "This is *so* unlike you."

"I'm feeling generous toward my favorite employee."

"Not that I'm looking the gift horse in the mouth, but you're actually not my boss. We're equal partners here."

"Oh, right. I keep forgetting that."

"Except he does own 1 percent more than you," Darrak added, now on his fourth donut. "So that does make him the controlling partner."

"That's right, sport." Andy nodded. "You're paying attention. You're totally awesome."

Darrak sighed. "I want to leave now, Eden. Please."

They left.

"I heard you on the phone with the cop," Darrak said in Eden's car as they pulled away from the office. "Everything's on for tonight?"

"It is."

"Thought you might cancel."

She eyed him sideways. "Well, I didn't."

He pressed back against the headrest. "I guess you really like him."

"I do."

"What's so great about him?"

"Everything. Now just try to stay quiet." She had to accept the fact that she had someone with her constantly until she figured out how to get rid of him. She'd never appreciated her now long-lost moments of silence before.

"You don't like me very much, do you?" Darrak asked, but he sounded amused.

"Do you blame me?"

"A little. You need to loosen up a bit."

"I'm loose enough."

"Oh, really?" He grinned. "I'll have to remember that."

She clutched the steering wheel tighter. "It's hard to think when you're around."

"Because you find me so devastatingly handsome?"

She refrained from rolling her eyes. "Were you always so vain, or is this a recent revelation for you?"

"No, I've always been this way. Don't hate me because I'm beautiful. Well, perhaps not as beautiful to you as your cop."

She jerked the wheel to the left and cut someone off, receiving a horn blast in return. "Leave Ben out of this."

"How is that possible? He's obviously your lifeline right now. You can deal with me as long as you have him as the big, dangling carrot urging you onward." He frowned. "Perhaps we shouldn't talk about the cop's big carrot. At least not until we see how the date goes."

Her knuckles whitened as a thought occurred to her. "And let's just say the date goes really, really well and I invite him back to my apartment. What then?"

"Is that something you'd do?" he asked. "On a first date?"

"Hypothetically speaking."

"Okay, continue. I'm all for hypothetical situations."

"What happens then? If you're inside my head, seeing what I see, hearing what I hear—"

"It means that I'd prefer if you wait to dent the sheets with him until after I'm gone."

Her face burned. Well, she'd asked. And he'd answered.

"Is that your natural hair color?" Darrak asked randomly.

"What?"

"This reddish shade."

She realized that he'd reached over and was stroking a lock of her hair, twisting it around his finger. The car swerved again before she managed to right it. More horns blared.

The demon was going to make her get into an accident.

"It's—it's dyed. I go to the salon regularly. Not that it's any of your business."

"I bet it's brighter in its natural state, right?"

She forced herself to focus on the road rather than the demon sliding his warm fingers through her hair. "I don't like my natural color."

"So you change it, make it duller. Less vibrant," he mused. "It's strange. If I concentrate, I can see past the façade to the real color. Normally a human female would have freckles with such red hair but your skin is like porcelain, isn't it?"

When he softly touched her face she almost ran the car right off the road.

She pushed his hand away from her cheek and put it back on his side of the car, but not before he entwined his fingers with hers.

"Let go of me." Her voice sounded breathless.

But he wasn't really holding her down or trapping her hand in any way. All she had to do was pull it away. Strangely, she seemed unable to do that. His skin was so hot, he had to be more than regular body temperature. She felt the warmth slide up her arm and flow into the rest of her body. It felt *really* good.

Eden finally forced herself to disentangle her hand from the demon's.

"Don't touch me," she told him as firmly as she could, looking at him out of the corner of her eye.

"I'm sorry. Couldn't help myself. I guess I'm a sucker for redheads." His lips curled.

She was sick of talking about herself. All of these personal issues out on the table for him to pick over. It was time to turn the tables.

"Fine," she said. "You want to talk? I have questions."

"Such as?"

"How old are you?"

"That's very personal. How old do I look?"

"You look like you're thirty. Or younger, even. But I know you're at least three hundred years old based on when you say the witch cursed you." The thought that he was that old made her shiver.

He noticed. "I know I'm very old. Probably a thousand in human years. Maybe more. But time doesn't really have the same value in the Netherworld."

That made another shiver run down her arms. "A thousand years old and you've never had a donut before?"

"I had no idea what I've been missing."

"Empty calories. You'll get fat."

"I don't have to worry about that. My body will remain the same no matter what I eat." He placed his palm over his flat stomach.

"Lucky." She wasn't going to consider the demon's body. Which she'd seen in all its glory first thing that morning, if only for a short time.

Bottom line, Darrak had every right to be vain about how he looked. He was just as gorgeous as Ben, but in an entirely different and much more darkly dangerous way. But she knew what he was and she knew what he could do. She wanted a normal man in her life. Ben was normal.

She had no interest in the demon in that way. After all, he was a *demon*. It didn't take a brainiac or a horror movie aficionado to see that was a bad idea.

However, sitting in her car, he didn't seem like a demon. He just seemed like a hot guy who knew how to easily push her buttons. *All* of them, apparently.

She cleared her throat. "We should probably get you some new clothes. There's a mall just up ahead."

"Clothes? You're thinking fashion at a time like this?"

"You said you couldn't . . . conjure . . . anything other than what you're wearing."

"I thought this was adequate. Isn't it?" He looked down at himself.

"It's getting really cold. It's supposed to warm up a bit but after that the temperature will be nose-diving to penguin climate. You need a coat."

"Temperature doesn't affect me."

"Yeah, but people will wonder why you're walking around in short sleeves."

He nodded. "Of course. Appearances are very important to you, aren't they?"

"I don't really care one way or the other." She was silent for a moment. It was frustrating talking to him. "Were you always a demon?"

"What? Oh, more questions?"

"I'm just getting warmed up."

"Some demons were once humans. Others were fallen angels. And others were created as demons from the energy of the Netherworld itself—hellfire, actually. I fit into the latter category."

He was created from hellfire? That was so strange she couldn't even begin to wrap her head around it. "You sound very human."

"From you, I'll take that as a compliment."

"You fit in. No one would ever guess what you really are."

"See, you're saying that with the thought that demons are completely different than humans. We're not all that different. You need to forget about everything you've ever believed."

"Easier said than done." She swallowed. "You have powers, though. Powers of conjuring up clothes that otherwise could be bought at Old Navy or the Gap. Anything else?"

"I used to have a few tricks up my sleeve. But maintaining form seems to currently take up all my energy."

"So what could you do?"

He didn't say anything for a moment. "Lots of fun things."

"Such as?"

He sighed. "Maybe some new clothes would be a good idea. We can pick you up some new hand towels while we're at it. You said there's a mall around here?"

Was he trying to change the subject? "Darrak, we need to—"

His body suddenly tensed and he inhaled sharply. "He's here."

She frowned. "Who's here?"

Darrak's eyes widened and he craned his head to the right. Another car was gaining on them, moving right up until it was only inches from her bumper.

"Who the hell is that?" she said out loud.

Darrak didn't answer, but he reached out to clutch her forearm hard enough to hurt.

The pursuing car swerved into the lane to her left and quickly gained until they were side by side. Eden struggled to keep the car on the road.

Palms sweating, she looked out the passenger side window past Darrak to see who the maniac driver was.

Her eyes locked with Malcolm's. The exorcist from last night.

⇉ TEN ⇇

Malcolm turned his angelic face toward Eden. His lips were moving but she couldn't make out what he was saying. Eden pressed the gas pedal down to the floor and sped up, taking the next right into the mall parking lot and stopped the car. She looked over her shoulder but couldn't see Malcolm anymore. He hadn't followed her any farther.

"Maybe he was just being friendly." She looked at Darrak. He was pale and there was a sheen of sweat on his forehead. His breath came shallow and rapid.

"Darrak!" She undid her seat belt so she could take him by his shoulders and shake him. "Are you okay?"

He wasn't talking. His blue eyes rolled back into his head.

"What did he do to you?"

Malcolm had already started the exorcism last night. Had he been trying to continue it, even at a distance? How was that even possible? Whatever he'd been doing, it was enough to hurt Darrak.

Darrak blinked after a moment and his eyes slowly regained focus. But he was still pale. "Eden . . ."

"What can I do?"

"I didn't realize how weak I am."

"It takes a real man to admit something like that." She tried to sound light.

"I'm stronger when I'm possessing you. When I have my own body I'm more susceptible. I can draw from your strength when I'm inside."

"So turn to smoke and possess me again." She couldn't believe she was actually suggesting it.

"I can't control that. Not when it's daylight. But I—I do need some of your energy."

"What?"

"The fairy . . . she hates demons because she knows how similar she is to us. Unseelie fairies must drain the energy from humans to survive and grow more powerful. They have to. They have no choice. A demon can survive just fine without doing this, but we can skim a little off the top if necessary."

"So skim, already."

He snorted softly. "So willing? And here I thought you hated me."

"I do. But you can take a little energy if it'll make you feel better. After all, I was the one to introduce you to Malcolm in the first place."

"Guilt is a powerful emotion." His dark brows drew together. "This wouldn't be enough to hurt you."

"Stop talking and do what you have to do. Just don't break the skin."

"That won't be necessary. I simply need an opening to that bright, shiny soul of yours." He brought his hands up to either side of her face and drew her closer to him.

She braced herself. "That sounds very—"

He kissed her. And not just any kiss. Open mouthed and, if she hadn't been sitting down, completely knee-weakening.

After a moment it started to make the rest of her feel weak as well.

But, she supposed, that was because he was purposefully

draining her energy. She moaned a little against his lips because the kiss felt surprisingly, well, *amazing*. If this is what being drained by a demon felt like, then she was seriously considering signing up as a regular donor.

Just when the kiss was deepening further, he broke it off.

"I think that's more than enough," he said.

"Oh. Well, good." She pressed her lips together and cleared her throat.

"Thank you. I feel much better now." He sounded tired. "Do you mind if we go back to your apartment so I can rest? That really took it out of me."

That made two of them. "Sure."

Darrak didn't seem as affected by the kiss as she was. Her cheeks felt hot. She was embarrassed by how easily she'd been ready to climb onto his lap just from a simple kiss. Then again, it wasn't a *real* kiss, was it? It was a dip into a lip-shaped donation box and she'd been feeling charitable.

She directed her Toyota back onto the road and drove to her apartment, parking in her designated spot outside. Darrak was still unsteady, but he didn't ask for any more help and got out of the car by himself. Which was fine. It would probably be safer if she didn't touch him at the moment.

What the hell was wrong with her? One little kiss and now she was swooning over him? *Hardly.*

Maybe she'd spend the rest of the day cleaning up her apartment. Even aside from the mess Darrak had left in the kitchen, it could use a good fall cleaning. Then she'd figure out what she was going to wear on her date with Ben. Maybe she should cancel it after all. Or reschedule it to a more opportune time.

There were too many other things to think about, including the unlicensed case she was going to start tomorrow. The thought of cheating husbands didn't put her in a very romantic mood, even if she wasn't dealing with her inner—sometimes outer—demon.

No. It would go on as scheduled. She wouldn't let the insanity she was dealing with mess with her chance at her shiny piece of happy.

Now *there* was a guy to swoon over—a human one, too. And swoon she would. It wasn't just the fact that he was gorgeous. She wasn't that superficial. He was charming and noble and brave and, well . . . normal. Dealing with a demon only made her realize how much she wanted stability.

She wanted Ben in her life if she had half a chance with him, and she wanted Darrak out of her life. Period. That should be simple enough to remember.

This time Eden didn't try to lose Darrak at the elevators. They got on together and went up to the fourteenth floor.

She didn't want to deal with the cat. Hopefully it hadn't shredded her curtains yet. Or peed on her carpet.

After unlocking the door and pushing it open, she looked at the very weary Darrak and suddenly realized how tired she also was. "Help yourself to the bed. Just don't get too used to it."

His lips curled. "So generous."

She cleared her throat nervously. "You think Malcolm has it in for you or was it just a coincidence he was pacing us on the road?"

"You introduced an eager young exorcist to a real demon. He's obviously intrigued."

She swallowed her lingering guilt from the exorcist experience. "So do you sleep? Is that how you recharge your batteries?"

"Something like that. It's . . . it's more like a deep meditation, really. I kind of zone out."

She waited for more of an explanation, but he didn't offer any. It seemed like something she should know. Knowledge was power, and all that. "Then go zone."

He was in a somber mood and entered her bedroom. She shut the door to give him some privacy. And herself. Privacy was good.

Her apartment was small enough that there was nowhere

she could be that was farther than sixty feet from her bed. No risk of forcing the demon to painfully dematerialize. She had a feeling testing those boundaries wasn't such a good idea at the moment.

Her date was in eight hours. She'd be able to do a clean sweep and then have a quick nap before getting as gorgeous as possible for Detective Hanson.

She turned to look at her messy apartment to gauge how much work she had in front of her.

It was spotless.

She rubbed her tired eyes and looked again. No, it was still spotless. Any mess in the kitchen from earlier had disappeared. The coffeepot sparkled. The counter was empty. She inhaled a whiff of lemon-scented cleanser in the air.

"Well, that's very strange," she said aloud.

She moved into her living room to see that the knitted afghan she'd had over her lap the night before was now folded neatly and placed strategically on the back of her sofa. The cushions were propped up in their designated places. Her small selection of current magazines was in a tidy stack on the coffee table.

The carpet even looked freshly vacuumed.

She turned around in a slow circle. Had her apartment been broken into by Molly Maid while she was gone?

Maybe Darrak had worked some sort of demon cleansing magic before he'd left the apartment to follow her earlier.

But, no. He said his powers—whatever they might be—were drained.

It didn't make any sense.

"Mrroww?" the black cat rubbed against her leg.

"Oh, there you are," she said out loud. "Who did this?"

The cat didn't answer her.

"Don't think I'm forgetting you," Eden said. "Come on, I'll put you out and you can go back to wherever you came from."

She reached down but the cat darted away from her and dove under the easy chair.

She put her hands on her hips. "Fine, be that way. Just don't get used to it."

Eden sat down on the sofa, suddenly more exhausted than she'd been in recent memory despite her bewilderment about the mystery tidiness of her apartment.

"I'll just have a five-minute nap," she said, pulling a beaded cushion under her head as she lay down. "And then I'll figure out what happened here."

Was she feeling this way because of donating energy to Darrak? Was a side effect an overwhelming need to fall into unconsciousness?

If so, she thought wearily as she closed her eyes, *that was very inconvenient . . .*

When she opened her eyes to see the view outside of her balcony the sun was low on the horizon. Considering it hadn't even been noon when she got back, that wasn't a good sign that she'd only fallen asleep for five minutes.

"Damn."

"Never thought you'd wake up," Darrak said.

She sat up so quickly she got a head rush. "What time is it?"

"A little after six."

Ben would be there at quarter to seven. She turned to see Darrak sitting in the easy chair next to the sofa. "And you've been watching me sleep for how long?"

"About two hours."

"That's really creepy."

"I do my best." He cocked his head to the side. "Do you know that you talk in your sleep?"

That was one of the things her ex-fiancé cited as an unattractive feature about her. "Is that right?"

"It is."

"Did I say anything interesting?"

"Something about wanting to donate regularly to some cause. What was that about?"

She thought back to their kiss. "I have no idea whatsoever. Anything else?"

"And then you prattled on about your date tonight. I know you're nervous about going out with your golden boy."

She got up from the couch. "I have to get ready."

"Maybe you should—"

"Should what? Cancel? No way." She shook her head emphatically. "I'm going. You said you'd help me. We had a binding agreement."

He gave her a slow smile. "I was going to say maybe you should let me help you pick out something to wear."

"Oh." She deflated. "What are you, a demonic fashion consultant?"

"I just have good taste."

She chewed her bottom lip and shook her head.

"What?" Darrak asked.

"Nothing. It's just . . ."

"Just what?" His brow was furrowed as he waited for her to finish the sentence.

"Are all demons like you?"

"Charming, handsome, and incredibly helpful?" He glanced down at her pile of magazines topped with *Entertainment Weekly*.

She pushed away the afghan she'd pulled over herself. "You just seem different than I would have thought a demon would be."

"I thought I explained that demons aren't what you think."

"I know, but it's still difficult to accept."

"You're not developing a soft spot for me, are you?" He grinned at her.

She blinked. "Not even remotely."

"Because the moment my curse is lifted, I'm out of here."

"I'm counting on it." She inhaled slowly and put her hand against the brown corduroy sofa to help herself stand up. "But Darrak . . . there isn't . . . I mean, you're not just putting on this front to get me to go along with what you want, are you? I've seen movies where demons do that. They have this nice fake exterior, but on the inside they're all scary fire and brimstone. And isn't Satan himself called the Prince of Lies? I know I heard that somewhere before."

His gaze was steady on her. "I am what you see. Nothing more, nothing less."

Well, if that was true then he was just a very good-looking man, not a demon. In her apartment. Who'd been watching her sleep. She supposed if he meant her any harm he would have had ample time to do something while she was unconscious.

"Okay," she said halfheartedly after a moment.

"I know this situation is difficult. And I am grateful for your patience, despite the few glitches we've already experienced. I know we'll figure this out and it won't take any time at all. And I'm going to make sure you and the cop hook up. I promised to play Cupid for you and that's exactly what I'll do." He smiled again. "I have to make sure there's someone around to take care of you after I disappear for good."

She relaxed slightly at his assurance. "Then I better go get ready."

"Actually, I must admit I already picked something for you to wear tonight and left it on your bed. It's been a long afternoon with you all unconscious."

"You . . ." she began and then sighed. "So you really are my demonic fashion consultant."

"Guilty as charged."

"Mrroww." The cat moved past them.

Eden grabbed it. "Can't forget about putting you back outside so you can finally go back home. I'm sure your family's been looking for you."

The cat started fighting her. She felt its sharp claws slice her forearm and she yelped in pain and dropped it.

Darrak was at her side in an instant.

She held her hand against the scratch, which stung badly. Blood welled on the wound. "I shouldn't have taken it by surprise. Totally my fault."

"Let me see."

"Ow. Okay." She peeled her fingers away.

His eyes narrowed. "I need to fix this before it's too late."

"Too late? Too late for what?"

"Shh." He held her arm in his then pressed his palm against the wound. "I need to concentrate. I keep a small amount of healing power in reserve and I think it'll be enough."

"What are you doing?"

"What part of 'shh' didn't you understand?"

The heat of his skin suddenly seared into her flesh and into the wound itself. Whatever she was going to say next was knocked out of her mouth with the overwhelming sensation.

Darrak grunted, his expression strained as he stared down at her arm. Again she could have sworn she saw an amber flicker come into his blue eyes. They appeared to glow with a strange inner light as he drew in a ragged breath.

Her arm felt as if it was literally on fire and she tried to pull away from him, but he was much too strong and easily held her in place.

"There. It's done." His grip on her finally decreased. "Damn. I need to sit down before I fall down."

He staggered, and she grabbed him. He wasn't kidding. She led him over to the sofa and he sat down heavily.

Then she looked down at her arm. The scratch had healed completely.

"What—" she began. "What did you do?"

"What does it look like?"

"You healed me?"

"That's right."

She was stunned. "But it was only a scratch. A nasty one, but it wasn't anything to get all worked up about."

The cat darted out from under the couch where it had hidden again and Darrak stopped it with his foot, pressing the feline down against the carpet.

"I tried to play along, kitty," he said. "I even gave you some cream this morning because I was trying to be nice."

It hissed at him.

"Tell it to someone who cares," Darrak continued. "Enough of this. Show yourself before I make you."

What the hell? Eden watched him with wide eyes as if he'd lost his demonic mind.

After another hiss, the cat went silent, glaring up at the demon through glittering eyes. Then, before Eden had a chance to say anything, the cat morphed into a woman with dark skin and long, shiny black hair who was wearing burgundy jogging pants and a white tank top. She lay on her side on the carpet with Darrak's foot still pressed against her shoulder.

"Let me up, demon," she growled.

Eden skittered back until she hit the kitchen counter. "What the hell is going on here?"

"Your cat is a shapeshifter," Darrak explained. "Although I would assume that is obvious now. But I wasn't sure if she was a born shifter or a made shifter. That's why I had to heal you. Otherwise, with a scratch like that, you might be looking for a groomer and a garden of catnip of your own in the next few days."

"I'm a born shifter," the woman said unpleasantly. "She would have been fine."

"Do you normally con your way into unsuspecting homes and then mooch off the kindhearted people who let you in?"

She smiled thinly. "Do you?"

"Touché." He removed his foot and she scrambled up to her feet. She looked over at Eden guiltily.

"Please don't make me leave."

Eden's mouth was open but no words came out for a moment. "I can't believe this. You . . . were a cat."

The woman's expression was tense. "I was. And I will be again. I promise if you let me stay I'll be very quiet. I won't make any trouble. I won't scratch you again—but just don't grab me when I'm not expecting it. That's not cool. I don't have any money right now but I can keep your apartment clean—"

"*You're* the one who cleaned up?" Eden asked, stunned.

She shrugged. "It was the least I could do. But don't go thinking I'm your maid and you can boss me around. That's not going to happen. This is just my way of bartering. I keep your place looking good . . . hell, I can even cook a bit . . . in return for you letting me crash here for a little while."

"No," Darrak said.

The woman glared at him. "I wasn't asking *you*, demon."

"The name's Darrak."

"My ass it is. And I'm watching you, hellspawn. Don't think I'm not." Her attention turned to Eden. "You need me. I can help protect you."

"Protect me?"

She nodded emphatically. "Demons are repelled by shifters."

"I thought I was just allergic to cat fur," Darrak said dryly.

"If he tries to hurt you or suck out your soul, or whatever, I can stop him."

"I'm not going to hurt Eden," Darrak said. "If I wanted her hurt then why would I have used any of my stored-up power to heal her?"

An excellent point. Eden looked at Catwoman, who regarded the demon with obvious distaste.

"Because if she'd been infected and was a shifter then you wouldn't be able to use her body anymore." The woman glared at him, then smiled. "You'd have to find a new home then, wouldn't you?"

Darrak's expression had turned stony. "I didn't even consider that."

"Sure you didn't."

"Is that true?" Eden asked.

Darrak met her eyes. "A shifter can't be possessed. It's true."

That was food for thought. Food she'd rather shove into the fridge until later when she could pick through the leftovers a bit more thoroughly.

A glance at the clock confirmed there was less than a half an hour before Ben arrived. It was one supernatural disaster after another today.

"What's your name?" she asked the woman.

"Kathleen Harris."

"And let me guess," Darrak said without any friendliness. "You go by the nickname *Kat*, right? That's almost as adorably predictable as a fairy named Fay."

"Sure. As much as you go by the nickname *asshole*. Actually, you can call me Leena." She turned back to Eden. "Please. *Please*. You have to let me stay here."

"Why here?" Eden asked helplessly, her mind drowning from the flood of information.

She wrung her hands and her eyes shifted nervously around the small apartment. "I'm hiding from somebody who wants to kill me. I've been wandering the streets for weeks and eating out of Dumpsters, which blows even more than it sounds like it would. I can't go home. I'm desperate. Then last night I sensed you—I felt you were different. That you'd be able to protect me."

"Me?" Eden pointed at herself. "Protect you from somebody who wants to kill you? That's ridiculous. You need to go to the police and explain this to them. They can help you."

She shook her head. "They can't. They won't believe me, anyhow. I just need to lay low for a while until all the shit I've been going through passes. Then I'll be out of your hair. A week or two tops. I promise."

"I don't know . . ."

"Please." Leena looked at her with such open desperation in her gold-flecked brown eyes that Eden knew she couldn't possibly kick her out. Not yet, anyhow.

She spread her hands. "I don't have any room. This apartment is barely big enough for one person."

"I can stay in my cat form." Leena's eyes lit up with hope. "I'm seven pounds that way. Tiny! And I don't eat much. I'll shift back to human form when you're out. Come on! I make a really amazing lasagna."

Well, Eden *was* a fan of homemade lasagna.

Ever since Darrak had come into her life it seemed as if

she was a magnet for paranormal beings—demons, fairies, and now . . . feline shapeshifters? And everyone seemed to be dealing with a life-or-death scenario. Including her.

And she'd thought working for Psychic Connexions had introduced her to strange, desperate people.

The least she could do was help out a bit. She would hope that somebody might help her in return. She was all about the karma. The universe looked kindly on that sort of thing.

"Fine. Two weeks," Eden said. "And that's it."

Leena smiled widely. "Thank you!"

"Just keep your claws to yourself."

"Well, you do seem to have a walking/talking first aid kit currently in residence." Leena shot an unfriendly glance at Darrak.

"That was only a scratch," he said, his arms now crossed in front of him. "Anything more serious could have drained me completely."

She looked at him skeptically. "Pretty weak for a demon, aren't you?"

"Luckily, I have a nice personality." He smiled thinly. "Didn't you say something about turning back into a furry, nontalking animal again? Any time would be good."

She pointed at her eyes and then at him. "I'm watching you, demon."

"I do enjoy an audience."

Leena grabbed Eden and gave her a big hug. "Thank you. You totally rock."

"Oh . . . okay."

"You'll have fun on your date. It will be nice for you to spend some time with a real man," she said pointedly. "Humans make for the safest lovers. Trust me on that."

Before Eden could reply to that, Leena shifted and shrank until she was a small black cat again that scooted into her bedroom.

Did that just happen? She turned to Darrak.

"Her clothes disappeared when she shifted," he said and shook his head. "Did you notice that? So convenient."

"I . . ." she began. "I . . . just . . . I don't know what to do right now."

"If you're taking suggestions, you really shouldn't think too much about the paranormal paradise of your life and instead go get dressed. Time is a fleeting thing."

He looked very pale, and he leaned against the wall by the wall unit her flat screen TV was on and a picture of her mom and her when Eden was ten years old.

"Are you drained again?" she asked.

"I'm at a level where I can recover on my own."

"Well, no matter what your intentions were, I appreciate you . . . uh . . . healing me. Thank you for that."

"My intentions were honorable, I assure you."

"Do you need to take a little energy from me again?" And no, she wasn't just looking for another earthmoving kiss from the demon. Because that would be wrong on too many levels to count. Especially when she had—she glanced at the clock—twenty-five minutes until Ben arrived.

"No. That's for emergency usage only." He crossed his arms. "It's not safe for you otherwise."

"Not safe?"

He shook his head. "Siphoning energy from a human is a tricky thing. If I were to take too much . . . well, I don't want that to happen."

"But I feel fine."

"Right. Other than your seven-hour nap, which you needed because of my draining your energy."

"Right, that." She frowned. "But I feel okay now. If you took just a little—"

Oh, God. She *was* trying to get him to kiss her again. How pathetic was she?

Very pathetic.

She forced herself to think about Ben, instead. Perfect,

courageous, wonderful. *Focus, Eden. Eyes on the prize. Not on Darrak's lips.*

"Seriously, Eden. I'm trying to be responsible here."

"And I'm trying to understand what is happening to me." She considered what he said. "What's so bad about taking energy from me?"

"Fine. You really want to know?" He paced to the other side of the living room, over by her neatly arranged bookshelf. He looked stressed. "If I'm not careful or if I get greedy, I can take too much of your energy. And it could hurt you badly. I don't want to do that."

"Could I be turned into a demon?"

"No. You could die."

She touched her mouth, thinking about when he'd kissed her in the car. It hadn't felt bad, that was for sure, but would it if it had gone on for much longer? "I'm glad you're against that, then."

He closed the distance between them and leaned against the sofa next to where she stood and studied the floor. "The problem is that the energy I've tasted of yours is very . . . what's a good word to use here?" His brow furrowed. "*Irresistible. Delicious. Addictive.* Any of those would do."

"My energy is tasty?"

"Yes. Very." He raised his gaze so that it seemed to burn into hers with an intensity she felt inside of her. Then his attention moved to her mouth. "So therefore I can't take too much or I might not be able to stop myself."

"You'd drain me completely."

He took another step closer to her, enough that she could feel the heat from his body as well as his gaze. Then he made a move as if to touch her face but seemed to stop himself before making contact. "That's what I'm saying. So maybe it's good that we have Pussy Galore in the apartment now as your fur-faced chaperone. Just in case I get a little too close for comfort."

She wasn't sure why the thought that Darrak found her delicious didn't freak her out. Okay, it freaked her out a bit, but not as much as she would have thought.

A demon admitting that he wanted to devour her totally? That was not a good thing.

But it was also strangely . . . exciting. And so was the look he'd just given her.

"So when you take the energy, it has to be through a kiss?" she asked, knowing that time was passing, but she still wanted more answers. "Is my mouth the only place you can get the energy from?"

"Actually, no. That was just personal preference."

Her eyes widened. "Personal preference?"

A slow smile spread across his handsome features. "It worked, didn't it? Unfortunately, it made your energy much more irresistible than it was to begin with. I'll have to remember your mouth is a serious danger zone for me." His gaze moved back to her mouth for a long moment before he met her eyes again. "You better go get ready quickly. The man you really want to swap spit with is probably already on his way here."

With a firm nod of her head, and not another word spoken, she walked into her bedroom and closed the door, pressing her back against it. Her heart had started pounding very fast during their conversation about her mouth and his preferences.

"The dress the demon picked out sucks." Leena, again in human form, held the red dress Darrak had picked out—coincidentally enough, Eden's favorite one—against the front of her as she gazed into the full-length mirror on the wall. "I can find you something way better. Red is so trashy for a first date."

"Okay," Eden said, not moving from where she was.

"By the way." Leena sat on the edge of Eden's bed and nodded at the wall by the small window. "*The Breakfast Club* is my all-time favorite movie. Great poster."

"Thanks."

"Molly Ringwald never got the credit she deserved as a great actress."

"I wholeheartedly agree."

When Eden finally emerged from the bedroom, Darrak inspected her from head to foot in the blue dress Leena had picked out.

"I preferred the other dress," he said. "But this one will do, I guess."

"Glad you approve."

His expression was grim. "Shifters are so annoying. Nearly as bad as fairies."

She tried not to smile. "Are there any life-forms that you don't dislike?"

"I'm fond of humans." His gaze slid down the front of her again. "Some of them are very tolerable."

She cleared her throat nervously and turned away from him, suddenly noticing how dark it was in her apartment. She flicked a glance out the balcony window to see the sun had slipped almost completely beneath the horizon.

She froze. The day had totally flown by. Now it was sunset.

And she knew all too well what was going to happen at sunset—other than Ben's arrival for their date.

Oh shit.

Darrak's breathing had suddenly grown more rapid and his expression tense. "It's time."

Those two words worked to kick her self-preservation instincts back into high gear. She took a step back from him. "You don't think there's another way?"

"There isn't."

"But what if you just try to resist?"

"If I could I would. Believe me, losing form isn't fun." He placed a hand over his stomach as a flash of pain went across his face. "Not good."

"Maybe some Tums might help."

"This isn't indigestion." He grimaced. "Maybe it only hurts when I fight it."

A wave of concern flowed through her. "So stop fighting it."

He looked at her and managed to smile a little. "Change your mind much?"

"I'm a Gemini, so sue me. But I don't like seeing somebody in pain."

"That makes two of us. Especially when the somebody is me."

At that moment, the buzzer to Eden's apartment sounded.

"That must be golden boy," Darrak managed. "Perfect timing. What a surprise."

She moved toward the intercom and pressed the button. "Hello?"

"Eden, I'm here," Ben said. "Are you ready?"

Panic moved through her as she watched Darrak gasp with pain. The next moment his body morphed into a six-foot-tall cloud of black smoke. "I'll . . . uh . . . be down in just a minute, okay?"

"Sure. Take your time."

She released the button and turned around to press against the wall. Leena exited the bedroom in cat form and hissed and arched her back as the swirling black smoke moved past her.

The smoke approached Eden almost tentatively, swirling on the ground like a sentient pool of thick smog. Darrak was waiting for something. He was holding back.

He was maybe waiting for . . . permission?

He didn't need it. He'd proven that yesterday by possessing her twice against her will. If he'd asked her then she would have answered with a big fat no.

But since then he'd shown that he meant her no harm.

Other than killing her in a year, that is. She assumed that had to do with him slowly draining her of her energy in order to survive.

He thought her energy was tasty.

This was so wrong.

"Fine," she said, attempting to control the instinctive fear she felt for the demon. "Just do it, already."

That was all it took. The smoke moved toward her and

swirled around her body. She inhaled sharply and braced her hand against the wall when she felt the strange, shuddering wave of pleasure as he disappeared—

—inside of her.

So wrong, she thought weakly. It was so, so incredibly wrong that being possessed by Darrak was unbelievably . . . *orgasmic*.

Andy *had* to find the witch so they could break Darrak's curse. She couldn't deal with this for much longer. It was going to drive her completely and totally insane.

"Darrak?" she said aloud. "Are you there?"

"Yes, I'm here." His deep voice flowing through her mind sounded worried. "I'm sorry if I hurt you."

Hurt her? Did he think it caused her pain?

"It's okay," she said. "I can handle it."

It was better that he didn't know. Better for both of them.

"Then let's get you your golden boy. Don't want to keep him waiting."

Right. *Golden boy.* To say she now felt torn about this date would be putting it mildly. She really liked Ben and thought this date was important to her future happiness. But dealing with Darrak and his addictive but energy-draining kiss, not to mention the fact that he didn't even realize he gave her mind-blowing pleasure whenever he possessed her body . . .

Despite all this, Eden sincerely hoped the date with Ben would go smoothly. The universe seriously owed her a big one.

⇢ ELEVEN ⇠

Ben had made reservations at a fancy, expensive seafood restaurant called Bella Bisque that had a great view of Lake Ontario and the Toronto skyline. Eden had never been there before, but she'd never met a lobster she didn't like.

"Did I mention how great you look tonight?" Ben asked as he held out her chair for her. "Blue is my favorite color."

She touched the blue dress that Leena had picked out for her. She'd already had second thoughts about wearing it, considering she'd agreed to let Darrak be the one to help her with Project Ben. "Thank you."

Darrak had been surprisingly quiet since they left the apartment, considering their mutually agreed-to deal. What was he waiting for? She knew she sounded awkward and nervous with Ben already—especially at such a fancy restaurant—but the demon hadn't offered her any help yet.

Was he okay? Maybe he was too weak to communicate with her. She tried not to worry. At least, not yet.

Ben looked divine in a navy blue suit and white shirt. She wondered if it was possible for him not to look good. He had a natural attractiveness about him that she was willing to bet he spent hardly any time on in the morning. He just got dressed, combed his hair, washed his face, and managed to look effortlessly hot.

There was a long silence as Eden looked at the menu.

"Why don't you ask golden boy if he's ever been here before?" Darrak suggested without much enthusiasm.

There he is, she thought with relief at hearing his voice. *Better late than never.*

"So . . . Ben, have you ever been here before?" she asked, feeling instantly more confident now that she had her internal backup in place.

He looked around. "No, but I got a great recommendation from a friend of mine. His wife thinks this place is the best restaurant in the city."

"It's not bad," Darrak said. "Nice décor. The waiters seem a bit snobby and the food's kind of pricy. And you really should have worn the red dress."

Comments like these were not particularly helpful.

They were seated in a crescent-shaped booth. The lighting was low and a candle was lit on the table. Ben ordered a bottle of pinot grigio and a few minutes later the wine steward brought it over and poured a glass for her.

"I'd like to make a toast," Ben said with a smile. "To Eden Riley. The most fascinating troublemaker I've ever met."

Her eyebrows went up. "Troublemaker, huh? Is that a compliment?"

"If you'd asked me a few days ago, I would have said no. But I think you've managed to single-handedly change my mind."

She smiled. "Then I'll definitely drink to that."

They clinked glasses.

She waited for Darrak to offer up any further bon mots, but there was nothing but silence in her head at the moment. She began to feel annoyed. What was he waiting for? A handwritten invitation?

"I have to ask," Ben said. "I know I was a bit of an ass yesterday when we first met about the psychic thing. I'm a bit of a cynic, I guess."

"You hide it so well."

"Yeah, right." He shook his head and grinned at her. "In my defense, you said you were skeptical, too."

"My beliefs in, um, *Otherworldly* things come and go." *Mostly they come*, she thought. *But I'd like them to go.*

Ben leaned back in his chair. "So how long have you been psychic? All your life?"

She waited for Darrak to suggest a response to this, but there was nothing from the demon in residence.

"It's off and on since I was a kid, actually. But it's really mild and usually completely nonuseful since I can't control it. I had to pay my way through college myself so a friend got me in at a psychic phone line she worked for."

"So your friend was psychic, too?"

Eden smiled at the memory. "Not especially. But she didn't get any complaints."

Ben actually seemed curious to know more about her past and he hadn't put on that skeptical expression yet at what she was saying. That was encouraging. "So what do you normally use? Crystal balls?"

Eden curled her fingers around the stem of her wineglass. "I prefer tarot cards, actually. They helped give a more detailed story to callers than a simple yes or no answer to their questions."

"That way you could keep them on the phone longer and make more money, right?" At her look, he held up his hands. "It's not a criticism, just an observation."

"Then you observe correctly." She took a sip of her wine. "I could read your cards if you like."

"How much will you charge me?" He played with the rim of his own wineglass.

She laughed. "I'd do it for free, of course."

"And what would a tarot card reading tell me?"

"It would give you a glimpse at your future."

Ben's smile stayed firmly in place. Which was a way better reaction than backing away from her in horror. "Knowing what lies ahead might be a scary prospect. I think I'd prefer my future to stay vague. So, is that what people want to see? What's going to happen to them?"

Eden nodded. "Mostly. They want to know if they're going to get a job they're after. Or if their love lives are going to pick up."

He raised an eyebrow. "So you could tell me how my love life is going to go? And if there might be a beautiful but troublemaking psychic in it?"

"Pardon me while I gag," Darrak said.

Her smile faded. What happened to his offer of helping her look good in front of Ben?

"I think you should tone it down a bit," her unhelpful inner demon said. "Play hard to get for a bit before you offer up any lap dances, okay?"

She gritted her teeth. That was an overreaction if ever she'd heard one. What was his problem?

The waiter finally came over after keeping them waiting for twenty minutes. He was a small, snooty-looking man with a tiny moustache, who wore a tuxedo with a white tie. He had a crisp white cloth draped over his arm.

"*Buena sera*. Welcome to Bella Bisque. I am your server, Antonio. Are you finding your wine satisfactory?"

Eden nodded. "Yes, absolutely."

He wasn't looking at her. He was looking at Ben.

"Oh," Ben said. "Yes, it's fine."

"I will tell you the specials now." He launched into a one-minute dissertation about all the creamy, high-calorie features.

"The salmon sounds delicious." Eden's stomach was growling and not just because of the demonic presence inside of her. She was starving. "Do you think I can get that with rice instead of pasta?"

Antonio wasn't looking at her. "It is the Bella Bisque tradition for the man at the table to make the dinner selections."

She blinked with surprise.

"I knew the waiters here were snotty," Darrak growled, "but this guy is a serious asshole. Kick him in the shins, Eden. Do it."

Kick him? "Not going to happen," she said aloud, then clamped a hand over her mouth.

"No, you're absolutely right, Eden." Ben looked at her, then at the waiter. "That's a bit of an outdated way of dealing with customers, don't you think?"

"*Outdated*?" Darrak said. "That's all he's going to say? If I had a body right now I'd punch him right in the face. Both of them."

She covered her mouth with her napkin. "Relax. It doesn't matter."

Ben frowned. "It does matter, Eden. I don't feel good about taking you to a place where you're treated like this."

The waiter shrugged with disinterest. "I meant no disrespect."

Ben looked at him. "Then we don't have a problem, do we?"

"No, sir." The waiter turned to Eden with a sour look on his face. "What can I get for the lady?"

She cleared her throat, stifling an urge to do as Darrak suggested and kick the condescending creep. "I still want the salmon. And I'd like to exchange the pasta with rice, if possible, like I just said."

The waiter looked at Ben again. "Please let your lady friend know that no substitutions are allowed at Bella Bisque."

"You've got to be kidding," Ben said with annoyance.

The waiter shrugged again. "It conflicts with the chef's vision for the cuisine."

Ben's jaw tightened. "I don't care what it conflicts with. Tell her that yourself." He looked at Eden. "I'm so sorry about this."

"As am I, sir," the waiter said. "But I can't help my desire for proper tradition."

Ben touched Eden's hand. "Do you want to go somewhere else?"

She didn't want to give the waiter the pleasure of knowing he'd annoyed her enough to leave. It was the principle of the thing. "No, it's fine. Really."

"You're sure?"

She nodded, and then looked at the food-toting Hitler. "Forget the substitution, then," Eden said grudgingly.

"As you wish," the waiter said with a thin, victorious smile.

"That smarmy son of a bitch," Darrak snarled.

She felt a growing surge of antagonism inside of her, which was odd since she wasn't outwardly angry with the mustached jerk, just annoyed. But the very next moment, as the waiter walked past, after taking Ben's order, her leg shot out and he tripped, almost crashing to the floor before righting himself with a grunt. He looked confused at what he'd tripped on and didn't seem to suspect it was her leg.

She hadn't extended it on her own.

What the hell?

"Okay, that was really cool," Darrak said. "I didn't know I could do that. But if I get all riled up enough I guess I can have some control over your body. What do you think about that?"

She didn't think much of it, actually. She pressed her lips together and forced a smile as she looked at Ben. Luckily, he hadn't noticed it was her leg that did the damage.

Ben looked a bit stricken. "You're sure you don't want to leave?"

Eden shook her head. "We'll extract our revenge when it comes time to tip him."

He nodded in agreement. "Vengeance is sweet."

"But promise me we won't come back here next time."

The grin returned to his face. "Next time?"

"Sure." She smiled, although it was forced. She didn't like the idea that Darrak had any kind of control over her bodily functions. The thought made her tense up. Darrak must have felt it, too.

"Just relax," the demon told her. "I'm not going to make you go all Linda Blair. I wouldn't want to strain that pretty neck of yours by twisting it around backward."

She forced her jaw to unclench.

Ben grabbed a French roll from the breadbasket and buttered it. "So, you work at a detective agency. Have you done the gumshoe routine for long?"

"I don't like the way he's belittling what you do," Darrak said.

She ignored the hypersensitive demon. Ben wasn't belittling her. "I recently inherited half the agency from my mother. It's the reason I moved to the city."

That and wanting to get away from her old small-town life, which included her ex-fiancé. Then again, her fresh new start hadn't exactly worked out the way she'd hoped it would so far.

"Inherited?" he repeated.

"My mother died last month."

Ben stopped buttering and his expression turned concerned. "I'm so sorry."

"It's okay." She got a strange twisting feeling in her stomach thinking about it. They'd never been close, but the thought that she was gone forever, with no chance for a reconciliation, was hard to swallow.

"It's rough to lose a parent. Is your dad still around?"

She shook her head. "Never knew him."

"Oh." He looked distraught again. "Sorry."

His reaction made her smile. "Don't be. And don't worry about me. I'm not going to have a breakdown here. I'm used to being on my own. In fact, I prefer it that way."

All on her own. No unwanted roommates. No one lurking at the corners of her mind primed to judge her dates. Those were the good old days.

"Is golden boy for real?" Darrak asked. "I thought you were

the awkward one. I stand mildly corrected. This guy might look *GQ* on the outside, but he's a total dork on the inside, isn't he?"

Actually, she found it oddly endearing to find a tiny bit of rust on that shiny suit of armor. The fact that Ben wasn't as perfect as she'd thought made him infinitely more likeable to her.

Ben's handsome face was now flushed. "I'm a bit out of practice at this."

"At what?" she asked.

"Dating. Conversation. At least, outside of work. But that's probably evident by now, isn't it?"

This surprised her. "Really? I would have thought you'd have women lined up."

"Oh, you thought that, did you?"

"I mean, not that I've thought about it that much, but . . ." She cleared her throat. "Well, I did hear some women talking when I was at the precinct a couple weeks ago."

That got his attention. "And what were they saying?"

"That you weren't dating anyone at the moment."

He shook his head and poured more wine for the both of them. "Well, yeah. I've been sort of out of the social scene for a little while."

"How long's a little while?"

He raked his fingers through his hair. "About five years. Give or take."

"Five years?" Handsome Ben Hanson had been out of the dating game for five years? That was very hard to believe.

He shook his head. "I shouldn't have said anything. It's just . . ." He blew out a shaky breath and took a sip of his wine.

"You don't have to tell me anything you don't want to."

Ben looked at her, his face tense. "No, it's okay. It's not a secret, anyhow. I was engaged for a while to . . . to someone. She . . . was murdered."

She swallowed hard. "Oh, my God. I'm so sorry."

"It was a long time ago. It's one of the reasons I'm so dedicated to my job. Sometimes too dedicated. I get in trouble for doing things my way instead of following the rules to the letter. But socially . . . I just haven't really gotten back on the horse, you know? I've been focusing completely on work and the time has just slipped through my fingers."

"I totally understand."

"I'm sure you're sorry you agreed to come out with me tonight, aren't you?"

She covered his hand with hers. "If you think that, then you really don't know me very well."

Ben smiled at her. "I'm glad you feel that way. But so much for light dinner conversation, huh?"

"Small talk's for wimps."

"Eden," Darrak said. "This guy is damaged goods. I wasn't sure what was off about him but now I know. He's not right for you. Too much baggage. You don't want that. Let's get out of here."

Not a chance.

"Hello? Are you listening to me?" Darrak asked after a moment.

"More wine?" Ben asked.

"Please." She held out her glass. "And let's toast to new beginnings."

He nodded. "Sounds good to me."

The waiter, now limping a little from his near fall, delivered the food soon after. Eden found that she was able to hold up her end of the conversation even without help from her inner demon.

Ben had been through a lot. It made her feel really lucky that she was the girl he wanted to go out with after all this time.

Damaged goods. Darrak was so unbelievably insensitive.

Considering the price of the food, the no-substitutions-allowed pasta was bland. So was the fish. Instead of complaining, she salted and peppered the food liberally.

"You probably shouldn't do that," Darrak said. "Too much sodium is unhealthy."

She added extra salt just to be contrary.

"Fine, ignore me. But just know that salt and demons don't go together so well. It's actually a well-known fact. You might feel strange if you try to eat that."

She tried not to roll her eyes and took a bite of her fish. It tasted much better now. But Darrak was right, the now salty food made her tongue tingle a little.

"Is there something wrong?" Ben asked.

"Wrong?"

"You're . . . um . . ." His brow lowered and he gestured toward his mouth. "You have a little something . . . uh . . ."

She brought her hand up to her mouth and felt something wet. And foamy.

Oh, my God, she thought. *I'm foaming at the mouth!*

She brought a cloth napkin up to her face and wiped, which took care of the foam and all of her lipstick. More foam immediately surged forward.

"I must be allergic to something in the pasta," she said, her voice muffled by the napkin and the continuing stream of disgusting foam pouring out of her mouth.

"Yeah," Darrak replied. "It was all the salt you put on it. Like I said, not a good combo. Now I'm feeling extremely dehydrated."

"Excuse me, Ben." She got up from the table and quickly made a beeline to the restroom. The mirror confirmed she looked like a rabid hound from Hell. She rinsed out her mouth with water until the foam stopped flowing freely. It took a while.

When it was taken care of she glared at her reflection. The restroom was otherwise empty. "That wasn't funny."

"Wasn't my fault. I warned you."

"You didn't tell me what would happen."

"Then consider this a lesson in what not to do when you're possessed by a demon. No salt, even out of a shaker. Bad. Very bad. Imagine what would happen with tons of the stuff."

"I don't understand."

"Salt is used to either trap a demon or keep the demon out of places."

"How does it work?"

"What do I look like, a walking encyclopedia? I don't know. It just does. I've never seen anyone possessed eat it and get that particular and oddly entertaining result though. I guess you're just special."

"So you didn't do that on purpose to make me look stupid?" she asked, feeling her anger quickly slipping away.

"Why would I want you to look stupid?"

"It's just . . ." Eden studied her reflection in the bank of mirrors set into the blue-tiled wall. "You said you'd help me out a lot more than you have. I feel like all you've been doing is sitting back tonight and heckling the performance. That wasn't exactly our deal, was it?"

There was a long silence. "You're absolutely right. And I'm sorry. I had every intention of helping, but . . ."

"But what?"

"I don't like golden boy."

"His name is Ben."

"Whatever. I don't like him so I am having a hard time helping because of that."

"What don't you like about him?"

"I don't like the way he looks at you."

She frowned. "The way he looks at me? How does he look at me?"

"Like he wants to have sex with you."

Her mouth dropped open. "Please tell me you're kidding."

"Don't you see it? He was undressing you with his eyes."

"I'm actually okay with that."

"Now I'm grateful you decided against the red dress. That was much more alluring than this blue abomination."

"Look, Darrak," she studied her reflection. "I like him. I like him a lot. And I really want tonight to go well. I want Ben to be a part of my future so I don't want to scare him off with any strange behavior. Please. I promised to help you and you promised to help me. And how can you be so cruel after everything he's been through?"

"Yeah. And the fact he'd bring up a dead fiancée during a first date doesn't strike you as a play to get the sympathy vote? Women love a good sob story. Five years without dating anyone. Sure. I believe it."

"Darrak!"

"Sorry," he said, sullenly. "I'll behave myself. It just won't be easy. And I'm still going to call him golden boy."

"You can call him whatever you want. Just try to be nice."

She heard a toilet flush and her back stiffened. She'd thought they were alone. Slowly the stall behind Eden opened up and a blond woman emerged. She looked confused.

"Oh, I thought maybe you were on your cell phone," she said. "But were you just talking to yourself?"

Eden gave her a frozen smile. "Bad habit."

"Okay." She cleared her throat nervously. "None of my business, of course, but I have a wonderful therapist. If you want her card, I have some extras in my purse."

"Not necessary. Really."

"If you say so." She washed her hands and then dried them on the pyramid-shaped stack of folded towels on the counter. "Have a nice evening."

"Yeah, you, too."

The woman left with a last concerned glance over her shoulder.

Eden looked into the mirror and shifted her purse to her other shoulder. "People think I'm insane."

"Maybe you are. Maybe I don't exist and I'm just a figment of your psychotic imagination."

"I wish."

She glanced at the stalls behind her. She hadn't used the bathroom yet while Darrak had been "present" in her mind.

"How do I get some privacy from you?" she asked.

"Why? Do you need to use the facilities?" His previously sullen tone turned amused.

"Maybe."

"Don't worry about me. I don't mind."

"Well, I do mind."

"Then I suggest you find a way to hold it until tomorrow morning."

"There has to be some way to block you . . . what's the term?"

"Dampen."

"Yeah, there has to be a way to dampen you out for a while."

He was quiet for a moment. "Afraid I can't help you."

Her brows drew together. "Why did you pause there? *Is* there a way?"

"If there was, it wouldn't really benefit me in any way, would it?"

She crossed her arms and peered at her reflection. "Tell me."

"Nope."

"This has to do with your instinct to protect yourself, right?"

"Can we talk about something else?"

"Is it anything like when I forced you out of my body yesterday? I was just all determined and single-minded about it. Can I dampen you, too, if I wanted to?"

"You'd better get back to golden boy. He's going to wonder if he should call the Humane Society to pick up his rabid date."

She gritted her teeth. "I'll figure it out."

"Good luck with that."

She left the bathroom and returned to the table. Ben looked up at her anxiously.

"Are you all right?"

That was a tricky question.

Her cheeks flushed. "I don't know what happened. I'm so embarrassed."

"Don't be." He stood up. "This restaurant is horrible. There must have been something in the food that you reacted to. I told the waiter and he was less than helpful, but I got the

impression this wasn't the first time. Maybe I should have
flashed my badge." He shook his head. "Forgive me."

"Forgive you? For what?"

"For being lousy at picking restaurants."

"It was fine, really. Besides, I've, uh . . . recovered."

"Let's go somewhere else. Your choice this time."

She waited for Darrak to say something to that. He didn't.

"Sounds good to me," she said.

"Great." He put a hand against the small of her back as they
left the restaurant and made their way to his car.

Then he turned to her. "I really wanted to make a good
impression on you tonight."

"You have."

"Do you think it was an allergic reaction? I can take you to
the hospital."

"Seriously, Ben. I've completely recovered." She couldn't
help but smile. "You wanted to make a good impression on
someone you consider a crazy psychic troublemaker?"

He laughed a little. "Did I use those exact words?"

"Not the crazy part. But I think it was implied."

He reached in his pocket for his keys as they stood by the trunk
of his LeBaron. "I'm so out of practice at this dating thing."

"You think you're out of practice? I was the one foaming at
the mouth."

He grinned. "I'm surprised you didn't psychically predict
you were going to do that."

"Like I said before, I really should have checked my horoscope this week. I'm sure it would have read: Gemini—stay
away from seafood restaurants unless you want to foam at the
mouth."

"That would have been very specific."

"Besides, my abilities, such as they are, seem to be only
applicable to tarot cards or sensing the location of people or
things."

"Clairvoyance without the ghost whispering."

She smiled. "You've done your research."

"I have indeed." He moved around to her side and leaned against his car door. "So, can you see ghosts?"

"Nope. No ghosts. Just little white dogs. And serial killers"—*and really good-looking but annoying and insensitive demons*—"and a friend once lost her keys and I was really helpful there, too."

"You know, you're different."

"I've heard that one before."

"I mean different in a good way. You seem so—I don't know. Like everything about you is right on the surface. Like you don't hide anything. You like to get it all out front and center."

She could have sworn she heard Darrak snicker inside of her. She ignored him.

"Well, thanks," she said. "I have been going through some stuff recently, but I'm going to do whatever it takes to fix it."

"You're all determined."

"I get that way about the things that matter to me." Eden studied the pavement for a moment. Then she looked up at him, realizing he was right next to her now. He brushed her long hair back over her right shoulder and brought his hand to her face. She forgot to breathe for a moment.

"I really want to kiss you right now," he said. "Is that wrong?"

Her breath caught and a shiver ran down her arms. "Aren't you afraid of catching my rabies?"

"Surprisingly, no." He grinned and lowered his mouth to hers.

A moment before his lips would have brushed against hers, she slapped him.

His eyes widened and he stepped back from her.

Wait . . . *no. She* hadn't slapped him. Her hand had acted all on its own. She had nothing to do with it.

Her eyes narrowed. *Darrak.*

"Huh. Just like your leg earlier," the demon in question murmured inside of her. "Didn't realize I could do that, but I really didn't want him to kiss you right now. Don't be mad."

A flash of white rage moved across her vision. He'd made her slap Ben before he kissed her. Because he didn't want him to?

She tried to contain her anger and not let it show on the outside. It was a struggle.

"Ben, I'm *so* sorry," she managed. "I don't know why I did that."

He still looked shocked. "Not much for kissing on the first date, I take it?"

"I don't know what to say."

No, she didn't. She was currently fighting being embarrassed, mortified, and furious. Her brain felt as if it was about to explode.

The man she really liked—who liked her in return despite her awkward and foamy ways—tried to kiss her and she'd just belted him.

She tried to summon up something inside of her to explain it away in an amusing and endearing way, but came up blank. Ben's gaze moved away from her and narrowed.

"Maybe you sensed someone else was nearby that you'd need to defend yourself against," he said. "I don't know how this psychic thing works exactly, but you never know."

She frowned. What was he talking about? She looked over her shoulder. Malcolm stood a dozen feet behind her.

"Ms. Riley," he said.

"Oh, great," Darrak said inwardly. "Just what I need right now."

Ben put his arm out and pushed Eden behind him. "What the hell do you want?"

"To talk."

"I think I witnessed what you consider 'talking' yesterday. And you were doing it with your fists."

Malcolm nodded. "I know what it must have looked like to you. But Eden herself knows there's more to the story."

"We need to get out of here now," Darrak said.

She shook her head. "Leave me alone, Malcolm."

"I can't do that. Please, listen to me. I only ask for a minute of your time."

It was strange. Malcolm didn't sound confrontational or dangerous. In fact, he just looked like a skinny college kid out for a walk, not an exorcist who could recite Latin as easily as if it was his first language.

"So talk," she said.

"I want to help you. Your situation is dire. Your life is in danger."

"What the hell is he talking about?" Ben growled.

"Doesn't your friend know?" Malcolm asked.

Eden tensed. "I have everything under control. I never should have hired you and your mother. Please, just go away and leave me in peace."

"You'll never be in peace now." Malcolm's jaw clenched. "You're in the grip of an evil being that needs to be destroyed. I don't just work with my mother; I've also been newly recruited into the Malleus. It's an organization that's been around for hundreds of years. We protect the world from that which is unseen and misunderstood. The dark forces that secretly lurk in our society."

Darrak swore under his breath. "The Malleus. There's a term I haven't heard in a long time."

What did that mean? Eden hadn't heard about anything like that before.

"You are talking nonsense," Ben said. "Get the hell away from us or I'm going to arrest you for harassment."

Malcolm's eyes narrowed. "If you knew the truth, you wouldn't stand in my way. In fact, you need to know all this so you can help protect Eden."

Ben looked at Eden. "Let's go."

That sounded like a very good idea.

But Malcolm continued undeterred. "You can't see the darkness that is corrupting her soul. If you care about her, you'll let me do what I have to do to save her."

"What are you, some kind of religious freak?"

"This is beyond religion. It's beyond anything you've ever faced before. You think you've seen evil in the human crimes you deal with day to day?"

"I know I have," Ben growled.

Malcolm shook his head. "You haven't looked into the face of true darkness."

"You are a kook from a cult and I want you to back the hell up right now." His hand tightened on Eden's waist as Malcolm drew nearer. "Eden wants nothing to do with you."

"You don't understand . . ."

Eden knew she had to get Ben away from Malcolm. Slapping him was one thing—something she might be forgiven for eventually. If he found out she was possessed by a demon, then all bets were off.

". . . Eden is possessed by a demon," Malcolm finished.

Well, *damn*.

⇒ TWELVE ⇐

"What the hell did you just say?" Ben snapped.

Malcolm stood under a streetlamp that lit up his young, angelic face. "Eden is possessed by a demon that will slowly but surely drain her life away in its single-minded need to survive on this realm of existence. It's part of what the Malleus fights against. Demons and witches—the army of Lucifer himself."

"She's possessed by a *demon*," Ben repeated incredulously. "I should lock you up right now so you don't hurt yourself or anyone else."

A flash of frustration came over Malcolm's face and he looked directly at Eden. "Do you refuse my help?"

She'd seen what he considered help. Even though she was furious with Darrak at the moment, she didn't want him to be exorcised. She'd get rid of the demon on her own terms. "Why can't you just leave me alone?"

"You would willingly assist a demon?" His expression darkened. "That makes you no better than the creature itself."

"You need to—" she began, but Malcolm grabbed her throat and effortlessly pulled her away from Ben's side.

What the hell? How strong was this kid?

"I will finish what I started with or without your help. I *will* save your soul."

"Let go of her!" Ben snapped, and grabbed his arm, although despite being larger than Malcolm, he wasn't able to budge the exorcist one inch.

Malcolm closed his eyes and began to speak in Latin again.

"Eden," Darrak gasped. "You have to stop him."

How was she supposed to stop him? His grip on her throat was so tight it was all she could focus on.

Then she gritted her teeth and glared at him, feeling a surge of anger fill her insides. She grabbed his arm and twisted it away from her. Malcolm yelped in pain and struck her with the back of his other hand, which hurt like hell but only helped the hot anger she was feeling burn away any other thought. Without thinking twice, she grabbed the front of his sweatshirt and shoved him as hard as she could.

He flew backward across the parking lot as if launched from a cannon and he hit a parked car, cracking the driver's side window. He slumped to the ground unconscious.

She looked at Ben, who had been fumbling for his gun but had stopped in midfumble. He'd just watched her toss a grown man fifteen feet away from her as if he was no more than a rag doll. The same man he'd been unable to move.

"What the hell just happened?" he asked.

Good question.

"You're stronger with me inside," Darrak said. "It's a protective measure in case someone tries to do us harm."

Great. She was like a demonically enhanced Wonder Woman now. And how exactly was she supposed to explain that to Ben?

She licked her dry lips. "Ben, I—I don't know how I managed to do that."

"You had good leverage," he replied. "That's all."

"Leave it to someone who's not a true believer to draw their own acceptable conclusions," Darrak said. "Despite that cross he wears around his neck, golden boy doesn't want to know any of this exists. Even when he sees it right in front of his own eyes."

"That makes two of us," she muttered under her breath.

"Well, you might not want to believe it, but he flat out refuses to. There's a difference."

"You need to go home now," Ben said. "We'll have to grab dinner some other night."

"What?" She was distracted, and she turned toward the cop.

"Go home, Eden. Get the restaurant to call you a taxi." He moved toward Malcolm and looked at her over his shoulder. "I'll take care of this."

"Are you going to arrest him?"

Ben cleared his throat. "No, but I sure as hell plan to tell him when he wakes up that if he comes near you again he's making a huge and regrettable mistake."

She felt completely powerless. It wasn't as if she really knew what to do in this situation. Malcolm knew that she was possessed. He wouldn't give up. She'd seen it now.

"Do what he says," Darrak said. "It's the first thing he's said tonight that I agree with."

"Okay," she said out loud. "And I'm . . . I'm sorry, Ben. For everything."

He shook his head. "There's nothing to be sorry for."

"Now you're just being nice."

"I don't do nice so well. But I do truthful great. I'll talk to you tomorrow, okay?"

She nodded. Ben didn't make any move to come near her again. After the slapping incident she couldn't very well blame him. Without another word, she left. The maître d' called her a cab, and she took it back to her apartment.

She was quiet the whole way there. For that matter, so was Darrak, who hadn't said a word since leaving the restaurant. But she knew he was still there. She could feel him.

Leena was curled up, in cat form, sleeping on the couch.

She raised her furry head, blinked once, and went back to sleep.

Eden threw her keys on the kitchen counter and went directly to her room. She shut the door.

"I can't deal with this," she said out loud.

"Which part?" the demon replied.

"All of it. I've been trying to be patient, but this isn't working." She sniffed and realized with a sinking feeling that she was crying.

"Hey." Darrak sounded disturbed by her outpouring of emotion. "It's going to be fine. Really."

She grabbed a tissue and blew her nose. "No, it's not. You're ruining my life."

"We'll fix this."

"Tell me how to dampen you."

"Pardon me?"

"Tell me how to get some privacy from you. It's the only thing that will help right now. I need to be alone."

"I can't do that."

"Please."

"Even if I wanted to tell you, I can't. It goes against my nature to give someone power over me, even something small like dampening."

She collapsed backward onto her bed. "I hate you."

"Harsh words, Eden. I think you should be focusing that hate toward Malcolm the exorcist. Not me."

"I hate both of you." She pushed the tears off her cheeks and sat up again, gathering a pillow against her chest and hugging it firmly. "What's the Malleus, anyhow?"

"A bunch of assholes who banded together to make the lives of Others complete torture. Sometimes literally. They took their name from the *Malleus Maleficarum*—that's Latin for 'the hammer of witches'—which was the book used to prosecute and punish witches back in the day."

"I thought you said you weren't a walking encyclopedia."

"Some things I know about firsthand without doing any

extra research. The Malleus has been a pain in the Netherworld's ass for ages—at least, for any of us who try hanging out on the human realm of existence for more than an hour or two."

Her head hurt just trying to wrap itself around what he was saying. "So they were around during the Salem witch trials?"

"Among other human atrocities. Because, of course, those weren't really witches they were executing. Not all of them, anyhow. They were regular women who pleaded for their lives right until their last breath. If the Malleus had come face-to-face with a powerful black witch *they* would have been the ones on fire. These men—because there are no women allowed in their exclusive gang—have no mercy for anyone they consider an enemy."

A chill went down her spine. "And now they know about me."

"Well, Malcolm does. Not sure if he's told his new buddies yet. I get the feeling he wants to take care of this little problem all on his own. He wants to save your immortal soul."

"Lucky me."

"No, you're definitely not lucky. I don't want you at risk because of me. This asshole won't leave you alone. I don't want you to get hurt."

She crossed her arms. Shouldn't he be more concerned with his own well-being? Darrak was what Malcolm was after. Not her.

She got up, walked into the bathroom, and started brushing her teeth. "Can't somebody talk to the . . . the Malleus organization? Explain that all . . . Others or whatever, aren't that bad?"

"A lot of Netherworld citizens are pretty bad, actually."

She spit out a mouthful of toothpaste and looked in the mirror. "Define 'pretty bad.'"

"Completely and unrepentantly evil."

She paled. "Oh." She'd started to believe that all demons might be like Darrak. But they weren't. He was obviously the exception to the rule.

"So," Darrak continued, "even if you did tell Malcolm that our situation is different, not to mention *temporary*, he'd never believe you. He's obsessed now."

He sounded disturbed by this again.

"Ben said he'd talk to him," Eden said.

"I don't have much confidence in that conversation." His voice turned sour.

She clenched her fists at her sides as her thoughts turned to the earlier festivities. "I still can't believe you slapped him."

"Believe it."

"You ruined everything."

"Are we going to go over this again? Yes, I slapped him. I couldn't help myself."

"Don't give me that. You *easily* could have helped yourself. It's things like that that make me want you to go away and never come back."

"I thought we were forging some sort of friendship here."

She took in a deep breath and let it out slowly. "We're not friends."

"But, Eden—"

"We're *not* friends," she said it louder. "And every time I forget about that little fact, you do something to remind me."

"If I say I'm sorry, will you forgive me? Pretty please?"

She turned away from the mirror and crossed her arms. "No."

"I know I wasn't much help tonight."

"I thought you wanted to help me get on Ben's good side."

"I thought I did."

"So what happened?"

"I think I . . ." His voice in her head trailed off.

"You think you *what*?"

"I think I got jealous."

"Jealous," she repeated. Darrak was jealous? Of Ben?

"You looked all gorgeous and then you went out with another man and expected me to help you get lucky with a guy who seemingly can do no wrong in your eyes. Plus he's got the dead girlfriend thing that makes him seem way more huggable or whatever. What can I say? I guess since we first met I've become a little . . . now I don't want to use the word *possessive*, because that would make it seem like I'm trying to make a joke. But, okay, I was feeling possessive. What can I say?"

"*Jealous*," she said again, still not believing her ears. "This is unbelievable."

"All I know is that I despise Ben and I don't think it's just because I think he's a bit of a trigger-happy meathead. I don't know. I've quickly grown fond of you. Despite the fact that you hate my guts and sometimes you're a bit of a bitch. I guess I find that oddly attractive."

Her mind was blank. Out of everything Darrak could have said, this wasn't it. And she had no idea how to react.

Wanting him to kiss her was one thing—something she knew was wrong. But now to find out he was fond of her? That he cared about her safety? That he worried about Malcolm coming after her?

She studied her reflection in the bathroom mirror. Her dark reddish hair over her left shoulder and her face very pale now. Paler than usual.

"Look, I know you hate me," Darrak said after a moment. "Your friend, the one who thinks I'm your brother who's escaped from a group home, is going to find the witch by tomorrow. I know he will. And then this will all be over."

She grabbed a brush and absently ran it through her hair. "And what happens then? You go away?"

"If that's what you want."

"It is." She said it as firmly as she could.

He was quiet for a moment. "I'll do you a favor right now. I'm feeling drained from our run-in with Malcolm. Enough to let me fade for a bit. You can have your privacy and finish your supersecret bathroom routine. I just don't know how long until I'm recharged and back."

"Good," she said quietly. "Don't let me stop you."

"Good night, Eden. And, just for the record, I'm not the least bit sorry for what happened earlier with golden boy. He's not the right man for you and he definitely doesn't deserve to kiss you."

She was about to say something in reply to that, but before she could she actually felt Darrak's presence fade away until there was nothing to indicate that the demon was still with her. It was like a weight had lifted. But it also left behind a chill when before she'd been warm inside.

"Good night," she murmured even though she knew he couldn't hear her anymore.

Stupid demon.

She *wasn't* growing fond of him.

Not a chance. Considering how much he'd messed up her life that would be totally crazy. She'd be so glad when he was out of her life forever.

Holding onto that thought made everything much simpler.

If she'd had a menu of men to dream about, she probably would have chosen Ben. But, instead, she dreamed about the demon.

She dreamed that she was kissing him. Very passionately. And clinging onto him as though if she didn't, he'd fade away to nothing but black smoke.

"Don't leave," she murmured against his mouth. "Stay with me."

"I'm here. I'm not going anywhere."

Wow. This dream felt really real.

Like, *really* real.

She slid her fingers through his hair as she explored his lips thoroughly. She felt his body, hard against hers.

"Eden . . ." he whispered and his lips moved to brush against her throat for a few moments before he kissed her again. "You feel so good."

He was wearing his black T-shirt and she wanted desperately to remove it so she could feel his hot skin against hers. She pulled it over his head, breaking off their kiss for a split second. His hands were under her nightshirt, sliding along her sides to grip the backs of her thighs. She wrapped her legs around his waist.

"I knew you didn't hate me," he said. "I knew I'm the only one you want to kiss."

Hate him? How could she hate somebody who made her feel like *this*? She wanted him inside of her. And she wasn't referring to being possessed.

Her alarm clock buzzed.

That's strange, she thought. *I can hear my alarm clock, but I'm still dreaming?*

Darrak slid his hand down between her legs and she let out a soft gasp, pressing herself closer against his touch. She wanted more of him. So much—

Wait a minute.

Her eyes snapped open.

This wasn't a dream, was it? she thought suddenly with a sinking feeling. *I'm totally and completely awake.*

And there's a demon in my bed.

Again.

"Darrak—"

"Yes?"

"Get off me."

"But—"

"Get off me *right now*."

He immediately removed both his lips and his hands from her body and rolled over onto his side. She glared at the demon who'd taken form again.

"You grabbed *me*," he said. "Don't even give me that accusatory look."

"I grabbed you," she repeated skeptically. Her face felt very warm.

"You made it very clear yesterday morning, okay? I took form when I had fully regained my energy a few minutes ago.

I even conjured clothes to protect your fragile PG world-view. See? I'm dressed. Well, I was until you ripped my shirt off. I was about to get up and make some coffee when you reached over and started molesting me." His lips twitched. "Not that I'm complaining, of course. I'm just trying to tell it like it is."

Her face grew warmer. She was sure she was red as a . . . well, a something really red and on fire. "I thought I was dreaming."

He looked pleased at that. "Dreaming about making out with me? I think I approve."

She cleared her throat. "Actually, I was dreaming about Ben."

That was enough to wipe the amusement off his face. "I see. You dream about golden boy a lot?"

"Constantly and obsessively."

"Well, I'm very sorry to have disturbed your private fantasy time."

She was surprised that the mere mention of golden boy . . . er, *Ben*, was enough to distract Darrak. She'd have to remember she had that weapon at her disposal.

The only problem was she *hadn't* been dreaming about Ben. She'd known all too well exactly who she'd been orally exploring.

She swallowed. Maybe that wasn't the best terminology for her to use, even if it was just in her head.

But it didn't change anything. She'd been kissing Darrak. Willingly. And she'd wanted to do a whole lot more than that. Whether she'd thought it was a dream or not, it was very disturbing considering how much she wanted him out of her life—since if he stayed she was going to die. Talk about a bucket of cold water thrown on her libido. Willfully groping him seemed contrary to that position.

It was a Lust thing. Capital *L*. That's all. Since it was one of the Deadly Sins it seemed demonically appropriate.

"You should get ready," Darrak said. "If we're going to follow your client's hubby we need to leave in fifteen minutes. Cheaters like early starts to their days."

"Is that something you're an expert on? Unfaithful men?"

"You'd be surprised just how many things I'm an expert on." His voice didn't hold a whole lot of friendliness at the moment. Which was fine with her. It made it much easier to concentrate on something other than the sight of his mouthwateringly perfect bare chest as he pulled his black shirt back on.

Snap the hell out of it, she commanded herself. *Nothing happened. You got off lucky.*

Getting off was also a bad turn of phrase at the moment.

Luckily she wouldn't have to think about it. They were going to follow Richard Morgan to see who his mistress was. Or even *if* he had a mistress. Eden would take some pictures to show his wife the proof. And then Eden planned on following the girlfriend and finding out if she was up to no good.

She wondered if Fay had been serious when she said she'd be taken back home and possibly killed for abandoning her fairy ways for the love of a human. What kind of fairies were these, anyhow?

Scary fairies.

Unlike yesterday, this morning when Eden had gotten showered and dressed, received a knowing look from Leena in cat form—which she ignored—and was ready to leave, she didn't try to sneak onto the elevator without Darrak. He accompanied her, although he was quiet. He sat silently on the passenger side of her car as she drove to a Starbucks, the one Fay said Richard always picked up coffee from each morning, and parked outside.

It was strange. Darrak was so different than Ben in more than the obvious ways. Ben made her nervous. But when she was with Darrak she felt like she could speak her mind. Easily. In fact, she'd been more open and honest with him than she'd been with . . . well, anyone. Probably ever. And that was all kinds of pathetic.

One of the many reasons why she wanted him gone.

Although, after seeing the real her, warts and all, it would surprise her if he'd even consider sticking around after their situation had been taken care of.

Which was good. She didn't like what she'd seen of the supernatural world so far. She was more than ready to get back to her blissful ignorance.

Also, she didn't want any obligations. Even working with Andy was beginning to have that permanent feel to it. Especially since it was doubtful that he'd be able to buy out her half—or rather, *49 percent*—any time soon.

But if she wanted to sell so damn bad, why had she felt ill at the prospect of him claiming bankruptcy yesterday?

Because she would have lost money. That's all it was.

Money that hadn't really been hers in the first place. Her mother was the one who'd won half the agency. Other than her name on a piece of paper, Eden had no claim to the business, or really any right to be there.

And then there was Ben.

When she'd first caught a glimpse of the cop, she'd never thought she would have a chance with him. It seemed safe to admire him from afar. Now things were different. So what happened if there was something between them? Not saying that he'd ever ask her out again, but what if he did? And what if she accepted?

There were a lot of big what-ifs in her life at the moment.

Another one was what if she didn't solve the Darrak problem and in a year she died because of him?

That one took up a lot of space in the what-if pile.

Her life sucked, but she didn't want it to end anytime soon.

See? That was a specific goal. She knew what she wanted and she knew what it took to get it. A chance at a happy and fulfilling future was dependent on her saying hasta la vista to Darrak as soon as humanly possible.

No matter how easy it was to talk to him. Or how much

she'd liked kissing him. Or how her unconscious self seemed to have extremely impure thoughts when it came to the demon.

None of that mattered.

Being possessed by Darrak would eventually kill her.

She didn't want to die.

He had to go. Simple as that.

⇒ THIRTEEN ⇐

"There he is," Darrak said after a moment.

Eden glanced down at the picture Fay had given her, and yes, that was Richard Morgan walking into the coffee shop. Right on time for his double espresso.

"So what should we do?" she asked.

"You're the fake private investigator in this car. Not me."

"Andy said to write down what he does and take pictures."

"Then that's exactly what you should do." Darrak leaned back in his seat and crossed his arms. "Have you thought about getting your license?"

"No." She held the camera up and snapped a shot of the back of Richard's head.

"Just no? Not a maybe?"

"I don't want to do this sort of thing on a regular basis. This is an exception to the rule."

"You sure have a lot of rules. You should think about breaking them sometime. You'd probably be a lot happier."

"I'm happy."

He eyed her sideways. "Sure you are."

"I'm ecstatic about life. I'm surprised it doesn't show."

"What do you want to do with your life?" he asked.

"Like a career?"

"Sure."

She shrugged a shoulder. "I considered flipping houses for a while but the economy's not so great anymore. Plus, my credit isn't fantastic either. So that's out."

"Flipping houses. I can't think of a career that has less permanence to it than buying a house, spending weeks making it better, and then selling it and moving onto something else. Is that really what you want?"

She tried not to glower at his appraisal of her career suggestion. "Maybe I'm not looking for any permanent responsibilities. I'm just like my mother that way."

"Your mother was a bit flaky?"

"You have no idea."

"You know what you need?"

That earned him a full-on wary glance. "What do I need?"

His lips curved. "Oh, you need a lot of things. But the first thing that comes to mind is passion."

Her cheeks heated. "Yeah, and let me guess. You're willing to provide it?"

His expression didn't change. "I'm not just talking sex. I'm talking meaning in your life. You need to figure out what you're passionate about and pursue that. You know, your dreams and hopes. Things that make life worth living."

"Is this self-help advice from a demon?"

"Guilty as charged."

"My life is fine just the way it is."

His smile faded. "I don't know that much about you, but I can tell by just looking in your eyes that you've been hurt in the past by people you've let into your life. You're very guarded. You don't let your hair down—"

"My hair's down right now."

"You know what I mean."

Darrak's gaze felt like it was burning a hole right though

her. She didn't like how perceptive he was. How it seemed like he knew her without her even offering up anything about herself. She didn't want him to know her. Frankly, she didn't want anyone to know her.

Great. She was even more screwed up than she even thought she was.

"So you're saying I need some sort of permanent, passionate outlet. Like a job I'm really into?" She snapped another photo just so she felt like she was doing something constructive.

"I think you might be good at this investigation thing," he said.

"That makes one of us."

"Not just the nitty-gritty details of surveillance and writing stuff down. I'm talking about helping people. The ones that come to you desperate and in need. That seems to be something that might suit you."

"I do tend to attract desperate, needy people. I'm like a magnet for losers. They recognize me as one of their own."

"I meant more that you're compassionate and seem to have a natural tendency to want to help people." He shook his head. "Just my opinion. Take it or leave it."

They went quiet again, but Eden's brain was working, turning over what Darrak said. He was right. She did need something in her life to make everything worthwhile. To give her a reason to wake up in the morning. Was it working with Andy at a low-end detective agency? Had fate handed her this opportunity and she wasn't taking advantage of it?

The universe did work in mysterious and somewhat annoying ways.

And if she applied the law of attraction to her life at the moment it would mean she'd attracted the job at Triple-A, as well as bringing Darrak into her life.

Maybe, down deep—way deep—there was something there she could learn and grow from and find a new path toward her bright, shiny future.

Or . . . not. Probably not.

Richard Morgan left the coffee shop and headed to work. Eden took a few more pictures, then followed at a fair distance until they got to his accounting office at the intersection of King and Bay. She parked and they waited.

For a long time.

Hours went by.

"This is boring," Darrak said while he taste-tested the food Eden had grabbed on the corner for their lunch. "I take it back. Maybe there isn't anything to be passionate about when it comes to investigation work. And this hot dog is disgusting. Do humans actually consider this food? It's no peanut butter or chocolate donut, that's for sure."

"I suppose I could march right up to him and ask if he's having an affair."

"That would be the direct approach."

"So you can't do any demon thing and probe his mind? Force him to tell the truth? Grow horns and a tail and scare it out of him?"

"Horns and a tail?" Darrak said dryly.

She shrugged. "I've seen pictures of demons before."

"Sounds more like a devil."

She fished in her purse for more change for the parking meter. "The ones with the pointy genitalia."

"See, I knew you were paying attention. There will be a pop quiz later."

She studied Darrak for a moment. He looked a bit on edge. "You didn't answer my question about the horns and a tail, though. You just diverted it."

"Did I do that?"

"Yes."

He gazed out of the window at the cement and glass sky-scrapers that surrounded them. "I can't believe we've been sitting here for so long. Talk about hell on earth."

His refusal to answer her question was starting to trouble her.

"You mentioned that Fay used some sort of a, what did you call it, a glamour? To hide her fairy appearance and look more human."

"I did say that, didn't I? Well, fairies don't look much different than humans. Just a little bit scarier."

"You never really answered me before." She swallowed. "But, is that what you do, too? Is this what you normally look like or is this a glamour so you won't scare me?"

He turned to look at her and she studied his now-familiar handsome face, his square jaw and lips she had been exploring up close and personal only a couple hours ago. His dark hair, slightly messy and slightly too long. His ice blue eyes that she'd seen shine with good humor or burn with anger or pain. It was hard to remember that he actually was a demon, and sometimes she had to admit that she forgot.

But she did remember her first impression of his physical appearance when he'd taken form. That it was too perfect, too appealing, to be real. That it was some sort of a trap to lure her closer so he could devour her whole.

She shivered.

"There are some things about me," Darrak began, a bit tentatively, "that it is best you don't know."

The fear that had disappeared toward the demon came slithering back. "What's that supposed to mean?"

He looked at her sharply. "I tell you that there are things about me you shouldn't know, and you still want to know?"

"I'm curious." *And terrified*, she amended internally.

"Don't be. This is who I am, Eden. The man you see in front of you. Nothing more, nothing less."

"You're a demon, not a man. Men don't turn into black smoke at sunset and have to possess people in order to survive. Men aren't afraid of draining others of too much energy."

"And a full demon wouldn't care who he drained."

"So if you're not a full demon, then what are you?"

His face was blank of expression, but his brows had drawn together as if he was concentrating very hard. "I wish I knew.

Three hundred years of living inside of humans . . . it's changed me, Eden."

She was about to ask how it had changed him when his eyes narrowed as he looked out the windshield. "Your cheater is on the move."

Richard left through the front doors of his office building at just after two o'clock. She shifted into drive and followed his car as he seemed to go through a list of chores. Drugstore, liquor store, even the library.

She tried very hard not to think about what Darrak had said. Or rather, what he *hadn't* said. She almost wished he'd lied—said he wasn't using any kind of glamour. But he hadn't said that. And what did that mean? Did he look different underneath his handsome exterior? More demonic? More scary and dangerous? Not somebody she could feel relaxed about sitting in a car with for more than a second?

She gripped the steering wheel. She really didn't know who Darrak was at all. All she knew was what he'd told her. She was going on faith alone. Faith in a demon who'd been cursed to lose his former body—whatever it had looked like then—over three centuries ago by a black witch.

Which sounded completely insane when she actually thought about it.

"Relax," he said, noting her tense form. "Nothing's changed. I'm not going to hurt you, if that's what you're worried about."

"No, of course not. You're too weak." She cleared her throat. "But if you weren't, then maybe I'd be in trouble."

"I could have taken way more energy from you yesterday. Or even when you were sleeping and dreaming about your golden boy. But I didn't."

"You said you might not be able to stop."

"But I did stop. I'm not saying it was easy, but I did. We might not get along that well, but I mean you no harm. I'm grateful for everything you've done for me so far."

Eden pulled the car to the side of the road as Richard stopped in front of another Starbucks. "I haven't done anything."

"Sure you have. You've accepted something into your life that would make a whole hell of a lot of humans run for the hills screaming. You didn't know any of this was real until just a couple days ago. And you've handled it so well. You're very strong."

"Is that the impression I'm giving you?" she said. "Because I'm shaking like a leaf on the inside."

"Can I do anything to make you feel more comfortable with me again?"

"Again? Did I feel comfortable with you *before*?"

His lips twitched. "Well, you know what I mean."

She thought about that. "Tell me your true name."

He turned his attention to their left as Richard left the coffee shop. "Can't do that."

"Then I guess we've reached an impasse."

"I guess so." His jaw clenched.

They continued to follow Richard's car as he got onto the highway headed west and after twenty minutes stopped in front of a motel by the Toronto airport. The booming sound of planes departing and arriving overhead filled Eden's ears. Eden parked at the curb and quickly wrote down the address in her notebook.

"Get the camera ready again," Darrak said. "I think we've got something here."

Eden fumbled with the digital camera and raised it up so she could look at the viewscreen. She zoomed in on Richard getting out of his car and walking up to a motel room door. He knocked. The door opened and a blond woman stepped outside, embracing and kissing him passionately.

She snapped a few pictures, her heart sinking.

"I guess Fay was right," she said. "There's the mistress."

Fay herself was a beautiful woman, but this girl—and she couldn't have been too far into her twenties—had a blatantly sexy appearance. *Bimbo* might be a good word to use. Tight clothes, short skirt. Long bleached blond hair. Big red lips. Big boobs that Eden could tell, even from thirty feet away, were fake.

"See, humans use glamours as well," Darrak said pointedly. "It's used to improve on what's already there."

"You think that's an improvement?"

"It's certainly . . . eye-catching. But even you use glamours. Your hair color for one, your makeup. When you wear high heels. It's an unnatural way to enhance your undeniable natural beauty."

She rolled her eyes. "If you're trying to get on my good side again, just know you were never on that side to begin with."

"Can't say I didn't try." His gaze moved down from her face. "Your breasts, however, unlike this woman's, are completely and flawlessly natural."

She'd had a feeling that her shirt was too low cut for a Thursday. "Thanks for the newsflash."

"My pleasure. Really."

Eden expected Richard to disappear into the fake-breasted woman's motel room, but instead she got in the car with him. Eden followed as they drove a mile down the street to a strip club called Kristoff's. The car stopped at the front doors, the girl got out, and Richard drove away.

"Taxi service?" Eden said out loud. "That was unexpected."

"I tried to sense any magical essence coming from the girl but didn't get anything. I'm not at full strength so I could be wrong. You should go in there and talk to her. Find out who she is."

"You make it sound so easy."

"All we need to know is if he's cheating on his wife against his will by being magically coerced. It happens more often than you think. Needy witches and their spells." His expression turned sour. "They won't take no for an answer."

"Sounds like a really bad date."

"You have no idea."

She scribbled down her location in the spiral-bound notebook she'd kept beside her all day. "And what if she is a witch?"

His jaw tensed. "Then you get your cute little ass out of there as quickly as possible."

"You're not coming with me?"

"No. I'll have to stay close, but not too close. If she's really a witch she might be able to sense what I am. And it's doubtful she'll be happy to see a demon."

"Don't go too far."

"Couldn't even if I wanted to."

"Wish me luck."

Before she got all the way out of the car, Darrak grabbed her hand and squeezed it in his before bringing it to his lips. She turned to look at him with surprise at his heated touch.

"Be careful," he said.

"I'll do my best."

She walked up to the strip club and opened the front door. It was dark and empty inside, but a big, broad-shouldered bartender was behind the bar, wiping the counter with a wet cloth.

"Hey," he said.

"Hey yourself."

"Can I help you?"

"I was just . . ." She cleared her throat nervously. "The girl who just came in here a minute ago—"

"You mean Vanessa?"

"That's the one."

"I'll get her for you. No problem." He disappeared from behind the counter before she could say another word.

A minute later the bleached blonde in question came out of the back room through a beaded curtain. She teetered on black patent leather stilettos as she walked toward Eden with a big smile on her face. She wore a short red miniskirt, fishnet stockings, and a sparkly black tank top.

"I'm glad you got here early," Vanessa said. "Please, have a seat and we can do the interview right away."

"Interview?" Eden's eyebrows shot up. "But, I'm not—" She shut her mouth before she said anything else. "That's great. I really appreciate it."

She'd been mistaken as somebody coming in to apply for a job at the club. Did she really look like she could work as a stripper?

It didn't matter. The opportunity had nicely presented itself to get a sense of who this Vanessa person was and if she was corrupting Fay's husband into having an affair with her as if she was using a magical roofie.

She took a seat on a precariously high stool at the table Vanessa indicated. The blonde had a piece of paper in front of her.

"You have lots of experience," Vanessa said. "That's fantastic."

"Totally," Eden agreed, although she wasn't sure what kind of experience she was claiming.

"Was this two-year gig at the Eager Beaver in Dallas all-nude?"

"Yes, yes it was. Completely."

"Good stuff. We like the girls here to be completely comfortable with their bodies."

Okay, so she was a stripper looking for a job. She had to get into character. "You are looking at somebody who feels exactly that way. I'm ready to get completely and totally naked."

Perhaps the less she got into character, the better.

"Your thoughts on lap dancing?" Vanessa asked pointedly.

"I'm . . ." Eden bit her bottom lip. "All for it? Provided the, uh, customer follows the . . . rules of the club?"

"We have bouncers to protect you. Don't worry. If somebody gets frisky, they are so out of here. Like other places, you're allowed to touch the customer, but he, or she, isn't allowed to touch you."

"Awesome," Eden said weakly. She was definitely not a natural at this. Plus, as Darrak liked to remind her, she was a bit of a prude. "So, you're . . . you're a dancer here?"

"I am. And I'm also the brand-new owner of this club."

Vanessa grinned, showing off very white teeth. "It's so exciting having all this responsibility."

Eden struggled to stay on the high stool. "You're so young, too. It's quite an accomplishment to be a business owner at your age."

"I'm twenty-five. That's not too young. But I have to admit, this was a gift from my boyfriend. He bought me the club last week when they were going to shut it down. We're closed right now to hire some new girls and to do some renovations."

"That's the man I saw drop you off outside?" Eden asked, then added, "I was parking my car at the time and couldn't help but notice you and him."

Her smile only grew. "Yes, that's Richard. He's so wonderful."

Wonderful. Well, that was debatable. Fay said he was an accountant. Eden was sure he would make a decent salary, but enough to buy his mistress her own strip club? She didn't need a PI license to notice that smelled a bit funny.

"Generous," she said.

"He is."

Eden glanced over at the T-shaped stage with three strategically placed poles. "Have you been dating him long?"

"Three weeks tomorrow." Vanessa cocked her head to the side. "Hey, you're supposed to be the one being interviewed here, not me."

"Sorry, I can't help it. I'm naturally curious." Eden focused very hard and tried to sense something Otherworldly emanating from the girl. Was she a witch? Or was something else going on here?

And would a witch willingly put up pink neon wall art that looked like ten-foot-wide breasts?

A witch with bad taste might.

"It's okay," Vanessa said. "Actually, I love talking about Richard. I've never been so happy."

"And he feels the same?"

"I hope so." She sighed. "He's so totally intense. Like when he looks in your eyes it feels like you're being taken over completely, body and soul. Actually, that freaked me out a bit when we first met. I normally prefer guys who are way more casual. But Richard wanted me. And he didn't take no for an answer."

"Sounds a bit like a stalker."

Vanessa laughed it off. "It does, doesn't it? But I'm fine with it now. He likes to pick me up and drive me places. And he's kind of jealous, which, considering my career, is not easy to deal with. But right now I'm so in love with him that it doesn't matter."

Despite her light tone, Eden could sense there was something unsaid there. A strange edge of desperation caused by more than her torturous choice of footwear.

"Do you know anything about him? Like where he works? Who his friends are?"

Vanessa's smile faded. "I don't need to know anything except what he tells me." Her thin, arched brows drew together. "Let's get back on your interview, okay? And keep the personal stuff out of this."

"Yeah, of course. No problem."

But it was a problem. Eden could tell, without any psychic skills at all, that this girl was in trouble. And she needed to keep her talking.

Eden shifted a bit on the stool and tried not to fall off. "You know, what you've told me about Richard reminds me of a boyfriend I had back in college."

"Oh yeah?"

"He was really good-looking and friendly and everybody liked him. Including me. I was head over heels for the guy. But when we were alone he was completely different. A real jerk, actually."

"Did he hurt you?"

Eden gripped the edge of the table. *Damn.* Why was she talking about this? There were parts of her life she really would prefer to keep in the past. *Way* in the past. But if it might help right now, then it was worth it.

"He wasn't nice. Let's just put it that way. But I'd convinced myself that he was so wonderful in other areas that it made up for the bad stuff."

"So what happened?"

Eden cringed at the memories she normally kept tightly locked up and hidden away. "I ended up in the hospital for a while with a few broken bones, which was when I finally clued in that he wasn't any good for me. And I'm not saying it wasn't hard. There was a part of me that really did love him—he was the last guy I really felt that way about, actually. So ever since then I guess I've built up a bit of a brick wall when it comes to men so I don't get hurt again. Nobody's even come close to breaking through."

Awesome. Eden Riley's past mistakes and lousy relationships used as a way to bond with the mistress of a client's husband. Those were some dark times and one of the many reasons she hadn't finished her college degree.

Thank God for the superglue of time and distance. The broken bones only took a couple of months to mend and she was sure it wouldn't take much longer for the rest of her to be completely repaired as well.

It was a goal.

"What was his name?" Vanessa asked.

"Zack. He was a fraternity guy. Lots of money, big future. I'm sure he's somewhere doing something important right now."

Vanessa looked angry on Eden's behalf. "Sounds like an asshole."

"Oh, he was. But that money helped him buy me lots of nice things when he wanted to get back on my good side. And it almost always worked, I'm sorry to admit. It's definitely two years of my life I'd like to have back if I had the choice."

Vanessa glanced around the empty club and then down at the paper in front of her that held the stripping resume of whomever Eden was impersonating. "Sounds familiar, actually."

This girl wasn't a witch casting spells to get some supernatural attention. This was a twenty-five-year-old exotic dancer who was in over her head and was playing along so she wouldn't get any bones broken. Or worse.

Did Fay know what kind of a man she'd married? If she had, she probably wouldn't have given up so much to be with him.

"Vanessa, if you want to talk—"

"Not a good idea." She slipped off the stool she sat on. "I think this interview is over. Thanks for coming in. I really appreciate it. I have some other girls coming in, but I'll let you know by next week, okay?"

This interview *was* over. Time to get to the important stuff. "Okay, full disclosure. I'm not who you think I am."

Vanessa frowned. "You're not Sugar LaCroix?"

"Uh . . . definitely not. No, I work for a private investigation agency." Eden produced a Triple-A business card from her purse and handed it to her.

"This is about Richard?"

"Yes."

A shadow of anger came over her pretty face. "So you were just making all that up about your ex-boyfriend to trick me into talking about him?"

"I wanted you to talk about him, but I didn't make anything up. Unfortunately, it was all the ugly truth."

"Who hired you?"

"His wife."

Vanessa swore under her breath. "I *knew* he was married." She blinked and looked up from the card. "You know, there's something really not right about him. I thought it was just my imagination, but now I'm starting to believe there's more to it than meets the eye."

Eden was about to ask for more details when she was startled by a painful lurch in her stomach.

What was happening?

It was the same feeling she'd had in the elevator when she and Darrak had been separated too much. Where was he? And why wasn't he staying close? Eden hadn't moved at all since she'd entered the club, so that meant that Darrak was wandering away from the car. But where? And why?

"I have to go," she said. "But please call me."

Vanessa tucked the card into her cleavage. "I'll think about it."

Eden turned and left the club without a backward glance. The feeling in her stomach had already lessened.

So that meant he was close again. But she couldn't see him anywhere.

He wasn't in her Toyota parked just to the left of the front doors.

"Darrak?" she called, looking to her right and left.

She wandered to the side of the building. The sound of the traffic on Dixon Road next to the club was loud. She turned the corner to the rest of the currently empty parking lot.

She wanted to tell him what happened with Vanessa. Eden was no expert on the subject, but she was convinced that the girl had nothing to do with anything other than being involved with the wrong man.

But was Richard simply a man who lived a double life? Or *was* there more to him than met the eye?

"Darrak!" she called again. "Where the hell are—?"

A hand came around her throat and she was dragged around the corner of the strip club. Before she could register what was going on, someone slammed her up against the brick wall, knocking the wind out of her.

⇒ FOURTEEN ⇐

Richard Morgan glared at Eden, his hand fisted in the front of the V-neck sweater she wore under her thin black wool coat.

"Who are you?" he demanded. "Why are you spying on me?"

Eden gasped for breath. "Spying on you? I was here for an interview."

"To be a stripper?"

"I prefer the term *exotic dancer*. And, yeah. I'm Sugar La-Croix. Nice to meet you."

"Bullshit."

"It's true. I have my feathers and sequins in my trunk ready to go."

His eyes narrowed. "You've been following me since I was at Starbucks this morning."

"What? A girl can't indulge in a morning caffeine infusion without being accused of spying?"

"Stop lying to me."

She grabbed hold of his arm to try to push him away from her. "Let go of me right now."

"Maybe after you tell me the truth." He bashed her head against the wall, which made her feel like a woozy rag doll. "What the hell do you know about me?"

"Other than the fact you're obviously a complete asshole, nothing at all."

She looked into his eyes to see that the irises were as black as the pupils—unnaturally black as if he was wearing contacts. And there wasn't the slightest bit of friendliness there. It took all her strength to hold him back from her at arm's length.

He still managed to lean closer. "You don't want to know anything about me. It would be hazardous to your health as well as your ability to sleep soundly at night. Got it?"

She tried to knee him but he twisted her around so she was facing the wall, bringing her arms up sharply and painfully behind her back.

"Will you leave me alone?"

"Yes," she hissed, feeling like a fool to have allowed this cheating bastard to get the upper hand.

"I don't believe you. You don't sound very sincere."

"I'm the definition of *sincere* right now."

"I don't think so. I think you like sticking your nose into other people's business a bit too much. You need to be taught a lesson."

She gasped as she felt the sharp tip of a knife trace down the side of her face and she flashed back to being at the serial killer's mercy the day before yesterday. She didn't like knives.

"Let go of me," she snapped again, sounding much braver than she currently felt.

"You don't need this nosy little nose of yours, do you? It might be a nice reminder for you to lose it."

Who was this guy? Was he just making threats or was he really going to hurt her just for following him? She felt pathetically helpless at the moment. It didn't feel good. She struggled against the tight hold he had on her.

And where was Darrak?

The moment she thought his name, Richard let go of her. The demon in question had grabbed him and pulled him off her. Darrak stood in front of Richard, his eyes a bright, flickering amber as if he was burning with fire from the inside. He grabbed Richard by the lapel of his jacket, and with his other hand on Richard's wrist, Darrak bashed it against the wall hard enough to make him drop the knife.

"Don't you dare touch her," Darrak snarled.

Richard cocked his head to the side. "Interesting. Didn't expect to meet up with a real live demon today. I would have worn my Sunday best if I had."

Darrak narrowed his fiery gaze and studied the man for a moment. "You're a drifter. That explains everything, actually."

"Good guess." Richard smiled thinly at him. "Obviously we have tons in common. So why don't I leave and we can forget about this little incident."

"We have nothing in common." Darrak's eyes flicked to Eden. "You okay?"

"Fabulous. Really." Although she'd come very close to being sliced. Eden tried to keep her teeth from chattering. "Thank you for the intervention."

"Sorry it took me so long. I was observing."

Her eyebrows raised. "Observing?"

"I was trying to figure out what this guy is. Now I know."

She glanced at Richard with distaste, then back at the demon. "What is he?"

"Drifters are disembodied earthbound spirits. They travel from human to human to survive."

"Possessing them, you mean."

Darrak's attention was still focused on Richard, whom he held prone against the wall. "They don't have to wait until their host dies before they can move, but that's right."

Sounded chillingly familiar, actually. No wonder the *drifter* thought he had something in common with Darrak.

She glanced around to see if anyone could spot them, but this side of the strip club was shielded from the road and there was a high fence to their left blocking off the sight line from other local businesses.

"Is the real Richard still in there?" She peered at the drifter warily. She and Darrak were able to talk to each other when he possessed her. Was Richard okay with this? Or was he fighting to get his life back?

"No," Darrak replied. "Drifters are able to put the consciousness of their hosts into a psychic coma so they can take over completely. That way, if they want to, they can take over the human's entire life."

"Uh . . . what exactly are you doing?" Richard's expression had turned bemused during Darrak's explanation. "Helping a human? Educating her on Netherworld factoids? Must say, it's the first time I've ever witnessed something like that. You sure you're okay, friend?"

"I'm not your friend." Darrak didn't loosen his hold.

The drifter's black eyes moved toward Eden, taking a moment to leisurely inspect her from head to toe.

Darrak bashed him against the wall. "Don't look at her."

"Sorry, can't help myself. She's kind of hot. Is she yours?"

"You need to leave this shell today."

Richard shrugged noncommittally. "But I like this body. This guy's got a lot going on. Good job, pretty fairy wife . . . and she's filthy rich, too. My current host probably didn't even know he had access to her bank account or the secrets she's been keeping from him."

"That's her business."

"Maybe." Richard grinned. "Have you seen my new girlfriend? She's so hot it burns. Who made the rule you're only allowed one woman these days? Not fair at all."

Eden watched their exchange cautiously. She didn't like this guy's attitude, and not just because he threatened to cut off her nose. She was very fond of her nose exactly where it was, but even aside from the violence she now sensed something else. Something . . . *Other* about this guy. Was it only because she knew there was more than meets the eye about him or was she starting to get more sensitive about that sort of thing?

"You're in way over your head," Darrak told him. "If you don't release this human's body it will not end well for you, I can promise you that."

Richard's brow creased. "Why are you so pissed off about this? I'm playing with a few humans. So what?"

Darrak clenched his jaw but didn't respond to that.

"I was about to carve some sense into this one"—he jutted his chin in Eden's direction—"until you stopped me. Humans need to know they're inferior to us."

Darrak tightened his grip, and his fiery gaze flicked toward Eden for a split second. "You're damn lucky you didn't hurt her."

Richard snorted. "Oh? And what would have happened if I had?"

"I would have torn your arms off."

He didn't sound like he was kidding. In fact, Eden had never heard him sound more serious about anything since they'd met, even during the "don't take the elevator without me" conversation. The violent edge to his voice made a shiver race down her spine.

"It would suck to be armless," Richard agreed. "Then I'd have to shift into a brand-new body when I'm perfectly happy with this one. But, no arms? Definitely a deal breaker."

"This isn't funny."

Richard didn't look terribly concerned, but his expression turned curious. "There's something different about you, demon. Didn't sense it until just now, but you're weaker than you should be, aren't you?"

"What part of 'leave this body now' are you having trouble understanding?"

"All of it." Richard broke Darrak's hold easily and shoved him back. "It's been a while since I saw my last demon face-to-face, but I'm sure hellspawn are way more fun than you're being right now. Does this bitch have your balls in a knot? I've never seen a demon so whipped before. I almost feel sorry for you."

"Darrak . . ." Eden said cautiously, remembering how strong the drifter was when he held her against the wall. "Maybe we should go."

He didn't look at her. "Not yet."

Richard shook his head, looking at Eden and Darrak each in turn. "You both need to stay out of my business."

"Or what?" Darrak growled.

Despite the smile on his face, Richard's expression was chillingly unfriendly. "Or I'm going to find your little human girlfriend when you're not around and have some fun with her. Before and after she's dead."

Darrak's fist moved too fast to register as he punched Richard squarely in the face. The drifter staggered backward and whacked his head against the side of the building. Blood gushed from his nose as he slumped to the ground. Darrak's eyes were ablaze, his arms flexing, and he moved forward to grab Richard's throat and lurched him back up to his feet.

"I'm going to kill you." The words were coated with fury.

Eden grabbed his arm, which felt like a steel bar. "Whoa. Hold on, Darrak. Stop. Don't hurt his body. If what you're saying is true, you'll be hurting the real Richard, not the demon inside him."

"He's not important enough to be a true demon," Darrak hissed through clenched teeth. "A drifter is nothing more than a migrant spirit. Worthless troublemakers, that's all they are. More garbage for the rest of Hell to clean up in our spare time."

"Forget about him."

"He threatened you. Right in front of me."

His body shook with anger and Eden grabbed his shoulders and then touched his face to force him to look at her. Finally, he let go of Richard.

"Hey," she said. "Come on. You're starting to scare me."

His chest heaved and he blinked those fiery eyes. "He was going to hurt you."

"But he didn't. You hurt him, instead. I'm okay with that, really. But I don't want you to kill him."

Richard took the small window of opportunity, scrambling to his feet and running away from them without saying another word.

Darrak tensed as if ready to pursue the fleeing drifter.

Eden tightened her grip on him. "Where do you think you're going?"

He looked at her with confusion. "I need to go after him."

"No, you don't. My shoes were meant for a surveillance duty today, not for running, and we have to stay close to each other, remember? We've figured out what the problem is. And it's a big, really freaky one. But, case solved. Not too shabby, if I do say so myself. I'll let Fay know."

He swallowed and seemed to relax the longer they stood there. "You'll tell her that her husband's possessed by an evil spirit?"

She forced a smile. "I had no idea how much we had in common. Maybe we'll become best friends."

"I'm not evil."

"So you keep telling me."

He looked at her. "Do you finally believe me?"

"Aside from the threats of death and arm removal I just witnessed . . . I'm . . ." She swallowed. "I'm starting to. Yeah."

"You are?" He looked surprised.

She nodded. Her hand now rested on his chest and she could feel his heart beating. It was reassuring that he had an actual heart somewhere in that very human-looking body of his. "How can you be evil? You're totally my guardian angel."

He snorted at that. "Now let's not start using the A-word. That's just insulting."

"It's just an expression, not a full-out accusation of having wings and a halo."

His eyes slowly shifted back from the scary swirling amber flames to their normal cool blue color. He blinked. "I'm sorry I reacted like that."

She stroked his dark hair back from his forehead. "I'm okay with it, actually. That freak was going to cut my nose off. How am I supposed to make a living as an exotic dancer without a nose?"

He traced a line down the nose in question with his index finger. "It would be difficult, but I have a feeling you could make it work."

"Yeah, sure." She exhaled shakily. She was putting on a good front but the run-in with the drifter had scared her deeply. "I wasn't so thrilled with the death threat, either."

"Drifters are tricksters and opportunists but they're rarely murderers. I think this asshole was just saying that to scare you and get a rise out of me."

She felt a small bit of relief. "He got it."

"He did." He scowled. "He's probably laughing at me right now."

"And bleeding."

"That, too."

It helped ease her mind a little bit to learn this additional fact about drifters. She wondered if she should start keeping notes on all of the Others she was meeting. It might be a good idea.

She suddenly realized that she and Darrak were so close they were practically embracing. Even though he was a demon, and a weakened one at that, she felt safe with him, especially when his arms were around her.

"Uh . . ." She forced herself to move away from him. He broke his hold on her with no argument. "Let's go back to Triple-A. I can call Fay and give her the news. Actually, I'm surprised that since she's Otherworldly herself she wasn't able to tell there was something up with her husband."

He leaned against the brick wall. "Drifters are hard to detect. They're like con men, easily able to adapt and thrive in their human camouflage. But the good news is that as a fairy she'll have the right contacts to exorcise the drifter right out of him—even if she doesn't want to dip into her own magic to do it."

"So you're saying I shouldn't recommend Malcolm and Rosa's services to her?"

He shook his head. "That's a bad idea."

"I was kidding."

His lips twitched into a half smile. "I figured."

She fished into her purse for her cell phone. She had a text message from Andy asking her to come back to the office as soon as possible. He'd left it two hours ago.

"Maybe Andy has some news on your elusive witch," she said, tucking the phone back into her purse.

"I hope so."

She put a hand on her hip, waiting for the remnants of her afternoon fear-fest to leave her. "Then again, if everyone is possessed these days, maybe it's the latest fashion. Maybe I should keep you as an accessory."

He eyed her. "Kidding again?"

"Oh, yes. Completely."

She drove back to the office, struggling to keep her attention on the road. She was still shaken by the events of the long day. Between figuring out what Darrak was trying to hide from her to being attacked by another possessed person, it was a bit too much to process. So she focused exclusively on the demon.

He'd protected her. Fiercely. Did he do that because he was defending his current host? Or for other reasons? Last night he'd admitted to being fond of her. Was that the truth?

She hadn't been lying when she told him she believed he wasn't evil. He'd been a pain in her ass so far, but he hadn't done anything to make her feel overly threatened. And he was her guardian angel, although she agreed there was probably a better term for it.

Eden didn't think he was evil, but he still scared her. The

last time she'd had this much drama in her life was when she'd gone out with Zack in college. She'd repressed most of those memories but they'd all come flooding back when talking to Vanessa about her situation.

If there was one guy in the world who had the ability to hurt her in more ways than one, it was Darrak. Good or not, he was a literal demon, while Zack had only been one in theory.

Was he fond of her? Maybe.

Was she growing fond of him in return?

She couldn't help it—she was.

But no matter how much he tried to protect her, at the end of the day she knew he was using her. How could he not? This was his chance after so many years to finally break his curse. If she was in his position, she'd do whatever it took to find the answers she needed.

And how much did he trust her in return? He wouldn't tell her his real name because that would give her power over him. He wouldn't tell her how to dampen his presence because ditto on the power. He wouldn't admit to using any kind of glamour to make himself more attractive and disarming, but she had a strange and chilling feeling that he did.

So what did that leave her with?

The man she'd been passionately kissing and attempting to undress that morning so they could do more than just kiss? Or an energy-draining creature of darkness who was using her to get what he wanted?

Place your bets, she thought.

They arrived back at Triple-A and Eden was surprised to see that the small parking lot outside of the Hot Stuff coffee bar and the detective agency was busier than she'd ever seen it before. Two people brushed past her as she entered through the front door with Darrak right behind her.

"Hi there," a balding man said. "It's so wonderful to know you're here for us. We appreciate it more than you can imagine."

Before she knew what was happening, he grabbed her into a tight hug. She didn't hug him back, instead opting for feeling awkward and confused.

"Uh . . . great," she managed when he released her. "Thanks, I guess."

Before she could ask who he was, or who the beaming woman next to him who gave her a big thumbs-up was, he left and they made their way to the VW Beetle parked next to Eden's Toyota.

She looked at Darrak, who was frowning deeply.

"What?" she asked.

"That's strange."

"What?" she repeated.

"Nothing." He shook his head. "I'm sure I'm just imagining things, but . . ."

"But what?"

"I could have sworn those were a couple of werewolves."

"*Were*—?" She clamped a hand over her mouth to keep from shouting. Then she whispered, "Werewolves don't exist."

He raised an eyebrow. "You're not slipping into denial all of a sudden, are you?"

"No, I wish. But *werewolves*?"

He waved a hand. "They're just shifters like your werecat. Only I sensed wolf in those two." He grinned. "You are so lucky I'm around. I'm like your guide, or something."

"Or something." Her stomach felt queasy. Could she not just have a couple hours of normal to help balance out the not-so-normal? Was that too much to ask for?

"Andy?" she said, tentatively, hoping that he wasn't freaked out or terrified by being visited by Others. Maybe he had no idea. Come to think of it, if they were all over the place and looked human, it was very possible she herself, back in her blissfully ignorant days, had met more than her share of them and never been the wiser.

The good old days.

There were a couple of people standing in front of Andy's

desk, and he shook their hands. "That's Eden right there," he said. "Speak of the devil."

There was an expression that wasn't as innocent as it used to be.

They turned to look at her with smiles on their faces. "Wonderful," a woman with short brown hair said. "Then I take it my case is in good hands."

"The best," Andy assured her.

"You'll be in touch?" she asked.

"In a few days at the most. Thank you for choosing Triple-A."

She smiled. "It's as if it chose me, not the other way around. I was compelled to come here."

"Our ad in the Yellow Pages is eye-catching."

"Yes." Her smile held. "I'm sure that's what it was. Come, darling."

She and her companion left the agency.

Darrak leaned toward her. "That was a white witch and her shifter lover."

She tensed. "Please stop."

"White witches are all nature- and animal-loving vegetarians. Don't worry."

"I'm not worried, I just want you to stop talking."

They were alone in the agency. Andy looked at her with a huge smile on his face. "You are not going to believe my day. I texted you! I wish you'd been here!"

She cleared her throat nervously. "What happened?"

"A phoenix has risen from the flames."

Her eyes widened. "Literally?"

He looked at her strangely. "Uh, no. But my business—well, *our* business—has been revitalized by a ton of new cases. It's been nonstop since I got here this morning. I might even have to hire an assistant."

"Really?"

He nodded. "And the strangest thing is what that woman,

Mrs. Larenby, just said. They all were compelled"—he made air quotes—"to choose Triple-A."

Darrak leaned over to whisper in her ear. "I think I figured it out. The reason why Others are attracted to you and this place."

"Do tell," she whispered back.

"This is where you forced me to take form the first time. The amount of psychic energy you expelled, added to what I am, was enough to create a hot spot. I've heard of that sort of thing happening before. Works like a magnet for Others. Now they think this is the go-to agency for paranormal clientele."

Shit. That wasn't good. Was it?

"That's great," she said then to Andy, smiling though her face felt very tight. "And the cases are . . . uh, is there anything unusual about them?"

"Unusual? No. The usual stuff. Surveillance, another potential cheating spouse, white-collar crime, background checks."

Only for werewolves and fairies and witches, Eden thought. *Oh my.*

"Great," she said, not liking the pitched, slightly hysterical tone of her voice.

"We should celebrate. I need a cigar. Why don't I keep champagne on hand around here?"

"No idea."

"I ordered some fresh coffee from next door. Nancy is going to bring it over."

"Sit down." Darrak had rolled her chair closer for her. She sat down. That felt much better.

"Such a nice, helpful young man you are." Andy clipped the end of the celebration cigar he'd retrieved from his top desk drawer and pointed at Darrak with it. "So good to your sister. Aren't you, sport? Did you have a nice day today? Did you do some sightseeing around the city? Did you go to the top of the CN Tower? That's fun."

Darrak sighed. "Make him stop, Eden."

She coughed nervously. "Andy, did you have any luck looking for the wi . . . er, I mean, the woman Darrak's looking for in the city?"

Andy shook his head. "Didn't even get a chance to start. And now I'm up to my neck with these new cases. How did the cheating husband stakeout go?"

"Really good," she said, brushing aside her morning trauma and immediate disappointment that Andy hadn't solved her problem yet. "You really can't find any time to look into that?"

"Wish I could. I'm sure it can wait a week or two."

"A week or two?" Her heart sank. "I really wanted this taken care of right away."

"To tell you the truth, Eden, if the woman in question doesn't have any prior convictions or anything to get her into the system, there's not much chance of finding her based purely on a sketch. I'm sorry. I should have mentioned that yesterday."

Darrak's brow was lowered. "That's too bad."

"I know. Look, you could always do it the old-fashioned way."

"And how's that?"

"If you think she's in the city, print up a bunch of flyers and paste them up around town."

"But, Andy—" she began.

"No, Eden," Darrak stopped her. "It's fine. We'll find another way."

She could see the disappointment in his eyes. He was counting on this. Hell, so was she.

"Fine." They'd find another way. Another way to locate a witch who might or might not still be in the area. By now she could have taken a plane—or, hell, her *broomstick*—to Tahiti.

She rolled her chair over to her desk and reached into the bottom drawer to pull out her worn deck of tarot cards. She hadn't used them since she was let go from Psychic Connexions. But desperate times called for desperate measures.

The phone rang and Andy grabbed it and started chatting to

someone in a happy, animated manner. His problems were solved. Hers were only beginning.

"What are you doing?" Darrak asked, his voice tense.

"I'm grasping at straws."

"Looks like a deck of tarot cards to me."

"I'm going to see if I can figure out what direction to go from here. It's not my love life or job prospects, but it's worth a shot."

"You don't think you can just concentrate very hard and pull the witch's location out of thin air? I know you've done that before."

"One thing at a time." She closed her eyes, focused on what she wanted, and flipped over one card. That was usually all she needed.

It was the Strength card, inverted.

"Well, that's not good," she said.

He'd moved to stand behind her and looked over her shoulder. "What does that mean?"

"The pathetic defeat of losers?"

"That's the literal meaning?"

"No. But that's what I'm seeing." She flipped another card. The Devil.

Well, that was not too surprising.

Darrak glanced down. "Okay. And what does that mean? Let me guess, true evil?"

"Not in its upright position." She cleared her throat. "No, I find that it usually means . . . uh, sexual obsession. Sometimes. And, you know, lust. And stuff like that."

"The Devil card represents lust?"

She waved a hand. "Among many, many other interpretations."

"And yet that's how you interpreted it. You, who are an insightful psychically gifted expert in this sort of thing."

"I never called myself an expert. I'm an enthusiastic amateur. I can also do some really cool card tricks if I'm so inclined."

Despite his disappointment that their road to finding the

witch was not going smoothly, he looked slightly amused. "Lust, huh?"

"Possibly lust for money. Material possessions."

"Or?"

She refused to think about waking up in Darrak's arms that morning and feeling more than a healthy dose of lustfulness. "I'm going to try to concentrate and pinpoint your witch's position now. No more talking."

"Take all the time you need."

She closed her eyes—pushed all thoughts of a naked Darrak out of her mind—and tried to do her thing. Whatever that thing was. Damn, she wished she could control it better. It was like playing roulette. Sometimes her number came up, but usually she just lost time and money trying.

The door jingled and her eyes snapped open to see Nancy, the assistant manager of Hot Stuff, enter with a tray full of coffee and pastries. Andy waved her over to his desk.

Eden closed her eyes and tried to think "witch."

Instead, she smelled coffee and cinnamon.

Mmm. Freshly baked cinnamon buns. It made her stomach growl loudly.

"Hey!" Nancy exclaimed. "*Oh, my God.* I love her so much. I can't wait to see her at the reading tonight. Are you going?"

Eden's eyes snapped open.

Andy frowned at her. "What are you talking about?"

Nancy grabbed the sketch of the witch that Darrak did yesterday. "Selina Shaw, of course. She *so* rocks."

⇒ FIFTEEN ⇐

Eden was on her feet and over on the other side of the room so fast it could have been some kind of a record.

"You know who this woman is?" she asked.

Nancy nodded. "Of course I do. Doesn't everyone?"

"Well, I don't. Who is she?"

"Selina Shaw."

"Who is Selina Shaw?"

"Only the coolest writer on the planet."

"She's a writer? Like a novelist?"

"No, no. She writes books that empower women and help them find their inner strength and harmony."

"She writes self-help books?" Eden asked carefully, thinking she might be misunderstanding.

"Not self-help," Nancy said as if it was an insult. "Her books *transcend* self-help. Selina Shaw is the Love Witch. I heard she even trademarked the phrase."

"*Love Witch*," Darrak repeated dryly.

Nancy turned to him and her eyes widened. "Well, hello there. I don't think we've met."

"I'm Darrak. Eden's . . . brother." He extended his hand.

She gripped it tightly. "Wow. Okay, hi. I'm Nancy. It's really great to meet you. I mean, *really* great. I didn't know Eden had a brother. Do you live in the city? I haven't seen you around before."

"I'm just . . . visiting."

"That's great. With your . . . wife? Your girlfriend, maybe?"

"Uh . . ." He disengaged his hand from her grasp. "Neither, actually."

"Oh, that's *very* interesting."

"Nancy," Eden interrupted. "Tell me more about this love witch."

She reluctantly moved her appreciative gaze away from Darrak. "She's not a real witch, of course. But she may as well be. She's worked her magic on me whenever I read one of her books. I left my lousy husband thanks to her advice. It's like she's speaking directly to me through her books." She smiled and her eyes flicked back to the demon. "And yes, I'm still single. I'm just saying."

Eden could barely breathe. She went back to her desk and computer keyboard where she typed *Selina Shaw* into Google search.

It yielded 1.5 million hits. The first one being her official website.

Click.

And there she was. A sexy woman, smiling wickedly out at her. Dark flowing hair, perfectly styled. Black-ringed vividly green eyes. Full pink lips. She looked like a movie star, only she wasn't. She was a self-help guru, and her moniker the Love Witch was there as a flourishly designed logo, along with her two most recent releases, *Curse That Creep Right Out of Your Life*, and *Hocus-Pocus Is the New Black*.

Both of which featured Selina's perfect, smiling face and ample cleavage on the cover.

"So are you going, or what?" Nancy asked.

"Going where?" Eden replied, feeling stunned. One moment she felt that she'd never find this woman, and the next . . . she couldn't believe she'd never heard of her. She was a number one *New York Times* best-selling author, for Pete's sake.

"To the reading tonight."

"I . . . uh," Eden blinked rapidly. "Where is she going to be?"

"At the World's Biggest Bookstore on Edward Street."

"What time?"

"Seven thirty. I'm going earlier so I can get a seat. So exciting. I can barely wait."

Eden just stared at her, stunned.

Nancy shifted her feet in a nervous manner. "Anyhow, I guess I'll go now. You know, I have some banana muffins in the oven. I might see you tonight?"

"Yeah, sure. See you."

"Great!"

Nancy left the office, giving Darrak an appraising look as she went.

Andy finally hung up the phone. He hadn't paid any attention to this exchange.

"Darrak," Eden said, clicking through the website. "Selina Shaw's even been on *Oprah*. And you didn't even know her name?"

He shrugged. "My hosts haven't been big TV watchers." He paused. "I shouldn't say that, actually. One was heavily into soap operas. And another had a very unhealthy love of clown porn. But I've tried to block that out."

She cringed at that. "But this *is* her?"

He came to stand next to her and leaned over so she could feel the heat from his extra hot body. "That's her," he said grimly.

"Why aren't you excited?" Eden had gone from stunned to relieved in thirty seconds or less. "This is it. She's here, just like you said she was. And we know where she's going to be tonight."

"Is it really the world's biggest bookstore?"

"That's the name of it."

"But is it? And is that determined by square footage or by the number of books they keep in stock?"

"Stock, I think. But who cares? It's a big-ass bookstore and she's going to be there. This is exactly what you've been looking for for over three hundred years and I'm not seeing even the slightest glimmer of excitement in your eyes. Your curse is going to be broken. You're going to be free to go wherever you want. And I'm not going to die in a year. So obviously I'm ready to celebrate."

He turned to look at her and their faces were very close. He tucked a strand of auburn hair behind her ear and kept his hand against the side of her face. Just his touch was enough to chase away the chill she now constantly felt during daylight hours.

"I'm happy. Of course I am."

"But?"

"But maybe I'm going to miss you a little. Can't help it." He ran his thumb lightly over her bottom lip and she felt a sudden, unbidden surge of desire for him right then and there.

"Uh," Andy said. "What the hell are you two talking about? And um . . . does your brother usually touch you like that, Eden? Because it's making me very uncomfortable."

She pulled away from the demon. "We're a very affectionate family."

"I think there's another word for affection like that."

Sheesh. It wasn't as if they were actually making out, or anything.

That damn Devil tarot card and its lustful implications.

She began piling the mess of paper that had accumulated on her desk into a tidy pile. "Forget it, Andy. Just bask in the fact that you're the 51 percent owner of a newly thriving business."

"Good point. Strange and awkward sibling love forgotten. How long is Darrak going to be staying with you?" he asked. "Maybe I can put him to work for us."

"I'm standing right here," Darrak said. "And the last time I checked I was capable of speaking for myself."

"He won't be around much longer." Eden was surprised by the strange sensation of loss she felt when she said that.

Andy leaned back in his chair and finally lit up his cigar, puffing it slowly. "He's going back to his, um . . . home?"

"Yes. It's almost time."

Darrak's home back in the Netherworld. Or Hell itself. Where did he live? Did he have a house? Was it hot there? What about that river of fire she'd always heard about? Was it a completely different existence there than here? How did that even work?

So many questions she wasn't sure she really wanted answers for.

The phone rang again and Andy grabbed it, pressing it to his ear. "It's a beautiful day at Triple-A."

"Long past time for me to go home," Darrak agreed. "Maybe that's why I'm not jumping for joy. I've accepted how things are for so long that I can hardly believe they might change."

"We'll go tonight and talk to her."

"Then you'll be going by yourself, won't you?" he said. "Or, at least that's what it'll look like."

"Right. Well, you can let me know what to say to her."

"I think it's better if we just go to the signing and get a feel for her. Like I said before, she's dangerous. She might not take kindly to unwelcome blasts from her past suddenly coming out of the woodwork."

"Even if I buy a couple of her books?" Eden clicked through to the excerpt pages. "They actually look pretty interesting."

Curse That Creep Right Out of Your Life

Is your man unfaithful? A big, fat, cheating creep? Does he look at other women right in front of you? Do you think you deserve much, much better? Selina Shaw, bestselling author of A Million Little Witches *takes you, step-by-step, on a journey of magical self-discovery. Get immediate results! You'll either have your former Mr. Right eating out of the palm of your hand, or you will find it easier than ever before to show him and his fabulous new, magically inspired case of hives the door.*

"Selina helped show me the magic
inside myself that I can use to punish my
cheating ex-husband. It's fabulous!"

–Kathy Kilborne,
best-selling author of *Hexual Healing*

Darrak blinked. "We'll go. We'll observe. And then we'll decide how best to approach her. Sound okay?"

"Sure." The appearance page said that Selina had been in Toronto since last week taking a short vacation in the middle of her book tour, culminating with the signings tonight and tomorrow. Darrak had been right. He'd sensed she was in the area, and here she was.

The witch looked nice enough. She also looked really young—younger even than Eden herself. All of those years, all of what she would have experienced.

What would it be like to be beautiful, powerful, and have the chance to live forever?

Without wasting another minute, Eden called Fay and let her know what had happened with her husband and what they'd discovered. While upset and shocked by the fact that Richard's body was currently possessed by a drifter, after a minute she sounded extremely relieved.

"Of course," she said. "Why didn't I see it before?"

"Apparently drifters are really sneaky."

"I do know that. And what about the woman?"

"She's involved with him. But since it's not really him, I don't know if I'd call it cheating."

"No, I agree. To say you've literally saved my life wouldn't be an exaggeration. And you worked so quickly, too."

"Just be careful. He wasn't happy with me. He might be dangerous."

"I can handle him now that I know what's going on."

"Still. Humor me and be careful."

"I'll forward my check to you immediately. A weight has been lifted off of me." Her voice cracked with emotion. "I knew my husband loved me. I shouldn't have doubted him. Thank you, Eden. So much."

"You're very welcome."

A happy customer. It felt really good to know that she'd helped somebody. Maybe Darrak was right. Maybe she could do this "helping others" thing for a while to give her life some meaning. Especially when it worked out really well in the end.

She just had to get over the fact that their clientele at Triple-A were Others.

And just because Darrak would be leaving didn't mean that she'd automatically forget everything she'd seen in the last couple of days. She didn't think she'd be able to forget even if she tried. But when Darrak left, would the clients go as well? Would Triple-A still be a paranormal hot spot, as the demon had said it was?

Well, whatever was going to happen, her personal life would be back to normal.

It was a good thing. She had to embrace it. But it didn't mean she'd ever forget.

The phone rang again. She'd never realized how few times the phone normally rang until now that she heard it every couple of minutes. Andy picked it up to give his oddly cheery, singsong greeting.

"Eden. It's for you."

She picked up. "Eden Riley here."

"Eden, hi. Sorry I didn't call earlier."

She immediately recognized Ben's voice. She bit her bottom lip. "I figured you probably wouldn't call me at all after what happened last night."

"Why? Did something out of the ordinary happen?"

She could hear the smile in his voice and was surprised by it. "Only a couple of things."

"Are you busy right now? I wanted to see you again."

"Me, busy?" She twisted the phone cord around her finger and leaned back in her chair. "Later yes, but not too bad right at the moment."

"Good."

She heard the jingle and looked up. Ben entered the office with his cell phone pressed against his ear. He pulled it away and closed it, then slid it into his pocket.

"The question is," he said, "do you want to see *me* again."

She smiled and stood up from behind her desk after hanging up the phone. "Of course I do. But last night . . . I'm so sorry."

"Are we talking about the slapping me thing?"

She forced herself not to look at Darrak, who stood by the window to her left. "Among other embarrassing issues."

Ben tilted his head. "So you didn't really mean to slap me?"

"Of course I didn't."

"Because I was thinking I shouldn't have tried to kiss you."

"Then that would have been a drastically wrong assumption." She moved out from behind her desk. "Although I understand why you'd feel that way. With the physical violence and all."

He nodded, studied her intently for a moment, and then closed the distance between them, ignoring both Andy and Darrak. "Then I think it's best to get this out of the way right now so it doesn't become an ongoing issue between us."

"What are you talking about?"

He captured her face between his hands and kissed her very

firmly on her mouth. Her eyes widened at the feel of his lips against hers before he let go of her.

He grinned. "See, I feel much better now."

"Uh . . . wow, I didn't expect that."

"Less time for you to build up a defensive tactic." His grin disappeared. "Does that mean I shouldn't do it again?"

"No, I'm definitely not saying that. You have my full permission to do that again." She cleared her throat. The cop could kiss very, very well. And he looked extremely pleased with himself considering the fact he had a fiery-eyed demon now standing directly behind him with fists clenched at his sides.

"If I wasn't so busy," Andy said from across the room, "I'd be very curious to know everything that's been going on with you lately, Eden. Okay, maybe I'm a little curious. Who's this guy?"

"Oh, uh . . . this is Ben Hanson. Or, rather, *Detective* Ben Hanson. Ben, this is my partner here at the agency, Andy McCoy."

Andy drew closer and extended his hand. Ben shook it. "Good to meet you. Nice to see that somebody's willing to give our little recluse Eden a good time."

"Andy!" Eden's face flushed.

"Well, you know what I mean. You can't always depend on your brother, especially considering his special condition."

"I didn't know you had a brother," Ben said.

"Right." She cleared her throat again. It helped to give her a moment to think. "Uh . . . this is Darrak."

Ben turned slowly to see the demon. Eden breathed a sigh of relief to see he'd changed his eyes back to their normal blue color. Flame-filled eyes might be hard to explain away.

They were exactly the same height. She hadn't realized that until seeing them side by side. Ben had short blond hair, while Darrak's was dark and unruly. Ben wore faded jeans and a white shirt under a dark brown leather jacket. Darrak wore head-to-toe black. They had similar builds to go with their similarity in height. Hard, lean muscle. Broad shoulders and chests.

Ben was smiling. Darrak was not.

"Hey there." Ben extended his hand in greeting. "Good to meet you."

Darrak didn't shake it. "You go around kissing a lot of women without their permission?"

Ben's smile faded at the edges. "I guess that might not have looked very good to you, did it?"

"No, it didn't."

"It's fine," Eden interjected. "Really."

"You're interested romantically in my . . . sister?" Darrak asked.

Ben let out a small laugh. "Didn't know I'd be meeting the family today. But, uh . . . sure. I'll play along. Yeah, I like Eden. A lot, actually.".

"But you don't like psychics. You're turned off by the supernatural."

"Well, I wouldn't say turned off, exactly. But I am a skeptic. Besides, Eden herself doesn't claim to be able to bend spoons with her mind or anything crazy."

Darrak crossed his arms. "Crazy, huh? Bending spoons is serious business. If you ever come face-to-face with a true spoon-bending telekinetic, I hope for your sake you don't piss them off."

Ben's eyes shifted back and forth. "Are you being serious with me right now?"

"Deadly." Darrak eyed the cop distastefully. "Do you normally abandon the women you like at restaurants so they can find their own way home?"

Ben glanced at Eden then back at Darrak. "I can tell we're not getting off on the right foot here. Last night was hard to explain. There were some issues I had to take care of."

Yeah, and one of them was Malcolm. Eden was very curious to know what had happened there.

"Did everything turn out okay last night?" she asked.

He nodded. "It's taken care of. He says he won't bother you again."

She had a hard time believing it was that simple. "Well, thanks for talking to him."

"Maybe the three of us should go out for drinks some time." Ben looked at Darrak. "It would give you the chance to get to know me a bit better and see I'm not a bad guy."

"I'm going to be leaving town very soon," Darrak said. "So that won't be possible. All I want to make sure of is that Eden is safe and in good hands when I'm gone."

"She is," he grinned, with a flick of his eyes to Eden. "My hands have never gotten any complaints before."

She almost smiled at that but it was chased off when she saw the fire return to Darrak's eyes at the casual innuendo.

"I think you should leave now," Darrak suggested firmly.

"Oh, do you?" A less than friendly tone had gathered in Ben's voice as well. "Look, man. I know you care about your sister, but I don't understand this attitude. We just met. You don't know me. So I would prefer if you keep that judgmental tone out of your voice. I might not be perfect, but Eden could do a hell of a lot worse than me."

"Or, much, much better," Darrak said dryly.

Ben took a step closer to Darrak, his eyes narrowed, and he cocked his head to the side. "Oh, yeah?"

Darrak pressed his palm against Ben's chest and shoved him back a step. "Yeah."

"Okay," Andy said, "I think that's good enough. We've had one broken door this week. Let's not make it a double. If you two are going to go to fisticuffs, then you should leave right now."

"*Fisticuffs?*" Darrak repeated.

"Besides," Andy continued, "Darrak is very special and I would assume sometimes he doesn't realize what he's saying. He's just very protective of his sister."

"Special, huh? That's debatable." Ben glowered. "Eden? Tell your brother to get away from me. He doesn't know who he's dealing with."

That made two of them, actually.

"Darrak," she said with a warning tone to her voice. "Back the hell off. Right now."

A slow smile crept onto Darrak's handsome face. He raised his hands and stepped back from the cop. "Of course, sis. Anything you say."

"Maybe I should take off," Ben said.

"That's a great idea," Darrak agreed.

Ben's eyes narrowed. "Eden, I'll be in touch soon. Maybe we can continue from where we left off. When there are fewer people in the room."

She walked with him to the door. "That sounds really good. And, I'm sorry about Darrak. He's very protective of me."

"I can see that."

"I'll see you soon."

Ben was focused now only on Eden. "Count on it." He leaned over and brushed his lips against hers again. "Bye."

He left with another look over his shoulder at her before he got into his car.

The phone rang and Andy picked it up.

Eden turned and cast a very unfriendly glare in the demon's direction. "Could you have been any less friendly to him?"

He shrugged. "I could have killed him. That would have been much less friendly."

"Darrak—"

"I can't help it."

"Sure you can. You just don't even try."

He focused on her completely, his jaw tense, and then he blew out a long breath. "I don't want to see you get hurt."

"And I appreciate that, but I'd prefer if you stay out of my business."

"The cop's intentions are not pure. He wants to have sex with you. I can tell."

"I'm actually counting on that."

"You like him?"

"Isn't it obvious?"

"Are you in love with him?"

"Love?" she repeated. "Let's not go overboard. I like him a lot and I want to go out with him again to see if there might be something between us in the future."

A couple of days ago she was practically picking out her and Ben's china pattern and now, even though Ben seemed to like her in return, her feelings had cooled toward him a bit. Why was that?

Damn. It was Darrak, wasn't it? He'd gotten under her skin—literally—even though she tried to fight it. And he was totally ruining her mental wedding registry with Ben.

Darrak looked at Andy when he hung up the phone. "What do you think about the cop?"

"Me?" Andy pointed at himself. "I don't know. He seems nice enough. I have to agree with your sister, sport. You're overreacting. Ben seems like a perfectly nice guy with a good job and I'd be willing to bet he doesn't have three wives and a dozen kids hiding somewhere. Eden will be fine. And when you go back to your normal home I promise to keep an eye on her for you, okay?"

Darrak closed his eyes for a moment. "I am overreacting. What the hell is wrong with me? I don't normally get this way. Like, ever."

"You're not taking your medication. It's rough sometimes, kiddo."

His eyes snapped open. "Let's get something straight. I'm not slow. I don't live in a special home. And if you call me *sport*, *buddy*, *chum*, or *kiddo* one more time you're going to have to retrieve your Porsche from the bottom of Lake Ontario."

Andy shot Eden a surprised look.

She gulped. A glance out the glass door showed that the sun was getting very low on the horizon. "Uh . . . we need to leave now. I have some things to take care of."

"That sounds like a good idea," Andy said. "Uh . . . bye Darrak. Sorry for any, um, misunderstandings. If I don't see you again, it was very nice to have met you."

Darrak's face was tight but he managed a smile. "Likewise."

Eden grabbed her purse, and the demon, and they left the office. She was furious with him so she didn't say anything as they got into her car and she pulled away from the parking lot.

"I'm sorry," Darrak said after a few minutes had passed.

"No, you're not."

"I actually am. I don't mean to hurt you. I can't help the fact that I'm an asshole sometimes."

"You're not an asshole," she said.

"I'm not?"

She sighed. "I know on some level you're just trying to be helpful. I think your heart is in the right place." She eyed him sideways. "You do have a heart, right? I felt it beating earlier."

He hesitated. "Demon anatomy is a bit complicated."

That was not the answer she'd hoped for. "Can I ask what's the deal with the fire eyes?"

He frowned at her. "What?"

"Sometimes your eyes look as though they're filled with flames. Usually when you're mad or upset."

"They do?"

"Yes. It's kind of freaky."

He blinked a couple of times. "It has to do with what I am, of course, and where I'm from. I'm not human and never was. My eyes—and every other part of me—were created in the Netherworld. Sometimes when I lose my concentration, it shows. Luckily I don't lose all of my concentration when I get pissed off."

"What would happen then?" She chewed her bottom lip as she waited for his response.

"It's probably best you don't think about it at all. Seriously."

"Wouldn't want to give myself nightmares, would I?"

"No, wouldn't want that." He cleared his throat. "I know having me and my eyeballs of fire suddenly thrust into your life is difficult for you. If I was human and you were the demon I'm sure I wouldn't have handled it half as well."

"I appreciate the vote of confidence." Her anger was quickly fading away. "So you hate Ben because you don't want me to get hurt."

"Essentially."

Also the fact he'd admitted to the cop making him jealous. This was getting complicated. She flicked on the radio and then flicked it off before whatever song was playing even registered. "Would it be different if it was anyone else? What if I was dating Andy?"

"He's too old for you."

"He's not even fifty yet."

"Still."

"You said you're a thousand years old. Or more."

He looked out the passenger side window. "I'm too old for you as well."

That made her shut up for a moment. A long moment. And then, "Are you worried about seeing the witch tonight?"

"Yes."

"Why?"

He turned to look at her. "The last time I saw her she destroyed my original body in a fit of rage. I would assume she thinks that she destroyed the rest of me as well. She won't be happy to know that wasn't the case."

"What did you do to piss her off?" She couldn't believe she hadn't asked the question yet. It was kind of important.

"Did I have to do anything? She's a black witch. They're very mentally unstable. Every time they increase their power level or use their magic they lose more of their souls to the darkness."

"I'd think as a demon you'd be all for that."

He raised an eyebrow at her. "Is that what you still think about me?"

She clutched the steering wheel tighter as she made a left at a set of traffic lights. "I keep forgetting. You're a *good* demon. You used to come here and find those nasties that had escaped Hell and bring them back. Did that happen a lot?"

He raked his hand through his dark hair. "More than you'd probably like to know about."

"How do they escape?"

"There are gateways. Mystical back doors and cracks in the walls between worlds. There are beings who sense this and it's their job to patch things up. Other beings are the gatekeepers and they keep watch in front of the largest openings."

She swallowed hard. "*Beings?*"

"Do you really want to know all about this?"

"I'm not sure."

"Your head might explode."

"It feels like it already has. But who are the beings who are the gatekeepers?"

He leaned back in his seat. "They're usually angels who have volunteered to temporarily fall from their realm to protect humans from the things that go bump in the night. Some demons were assigned to work in a similar capacity, only from the other team."

"Angels," she said flatly.

"Yes."

"I think I'm going to throw up."

"You have a very sensitive stomach I've noticed. See? This is why I didn't want to go into details. I've completely messed up your vision of the world around you."

"Not messed it up so much as completely changed it forever. Did you work with the . . . the *angels*?"

He laughed out loud at that. "No. Angels have prejudices toward demons, for obvious reasons. They aren't quite as open-minded as you might think."

"They don't believe a demon can be good?"

"To admit that would mean they'd have to believe an angel can be bad."

A shiver went down her spine. "I guess that makes sense."

"Now, when I say I was a good demon, I'm not saying I was a Boy Scout. I wasn't all sunshine and rainbows."

"I wouldn't believe you if you said you were."

She felt his attention firmly on her but didn't look at him. Taking her attention off the road would be a bad thing, and the demon was so distracting in more ways than one.

"But you believe I'm not that bad?"

"Yes," she said it without hesitation, then jumped a little when she felt his very warm hand take hers.

"Thank you," he said. "That means more to me than you know."

He didn't let go of her hand and she didn't try to pull away.

"You'd better pull over," Darrak suggested.

"Why?"

"Because it's almost time."

The streetlights flickered on as the sun continued to sink swiftly behind the horizon. She pulled the car off to the side of the road, shifting into park. He entwined his fingers with hers and it felt really good to be touching him. Too good.

"I know this part isn't fun for either of us," he said.

It was scary, sure, but the sensation of actually being possessed by Darrak was anything but unpleasant.

"Don't fight it this time," she said. "And maybe it won't hurt you."

"But—"

"Trust me. I can take it."

To say the least.

He nodded and looked into her eyes. "I'll be with you tonight, of course, but I want you to know right now—now that I'm still here solidly beside you—that you need to be careful around Selina."

"I will."

"She's dangerous."

"Understood. I will be careful. I don't want to be turned into a toad."

"Well . . . you'd make a very cute toad."

Toads weren't cute. She waited for him to possess her, but nothing happened. "What are you waiting for?"

"I'm not waiting. I'm thinking."

"About what?"

He was looking at her strangely. He reached over to twist a long piece of her hair between his fingers. She didn't stop him even though she knew she probably should.

"Darrak—" she began, although she wasn't sure what she was going to say next.

"I think I know why I hate golden boy so much."

"Why's that?"

"Because he gets to do this in the future."

Darrak leaned forward and kissed her.

She hadn't realized how much she wanted him to do that until he did it. She should want to kiss Ben, want to be with Ben. He liked her. He was normal and wonderful. He represented a solid future filled with potential happiness. But Darrak was . . . he was different. And so was his kiss, which was entirely too addictive.

When she went to touch him, though, her hands went right through his body that had turned to black smoke. She opened her eyes just as that smoke gathered over her and disappeared inside. It was a sudden reminder that he wasn't a man . . . he was a demon.

She kept forgetting that important little fact.

⇾ SIXTEEN ⇽

An hour later, Eden stepped through the front doors of the bookstore. The first person she spotted was Nancy. The coffee shop barista was in the front row of an audience a few dozen strong. There was standing room only available in the area that had been cleared in the "Hot New Releases" section.

She also saw another familiar face. Vanessa the exotic dancer with bad taste in accountant boyfriends sat on the side opposite Nancy. She looked over at Eden and waved.

Eden waved back, feeling uncomfortable at having so many people there to see a dangerous curse-spewing three-hundred-year-old witch—even if the makeup in her headshots was spectacular.

She made a mental note to speak to Vanessa about the drifter otherwise known as Richard. By now, she figured that Fay had already taken care of her spousal issues. The fairy had sounded very determined on the phone.

"Are you nervous?" she asked. She sensed Darrak was. He hadn't said much since he'd possessed her at sunset, but she felt his presence like an anxiety-filled weight on her chest.

"Yes," he replied.

"It'll be okay."

"Of course it will. No worries at all."

He didn't sound convinced.

Eden joined the crowd and waited, listening to the mostly female audience chatting amongst themselves about how much they were looking forward to seeing Selina in person and how much her books had helped change their lives for the better.

There was no mention of black magic, eyes of newt, puppy dog tails, or anything else overtly malevolent.

That was a good sign.

A store employee approached the podium set up in front of the audience. "It's our great pleasure to introduce internationally best-selling author Selina Shaw, the Love Witch. Please give her a warm welcome!"

The crowd burst into applause and Eden began to feel a growing nervousness as the woman in question appeared, dressed in a sparkly white, skintight dress. She had a white feather boa draped over her shoulders. The white of her outfit contrasted sharply with her black hair and green eyes. She looked exactly the same as she had on her website.

"Is that really her?" Eden asked breathlessly.

"It is." Darrak's voice was tight.

"Was she always that beautiful?"

"Yes."

The one word answer brought forth an unexpected emotion from Eden. Was that jealousy she felt?

Jealousy at Darrak confirming that the witch who'd tried to destroy him three centuries ago was beautiful? How did that make any sense?

"Good evening, everyone." Selina spoke into the microphone, smiling broadly at her audience. "Thank you so much for coming out tonight to see me."

The applause swelled again.

"This is my latest book, *Curse That Creep Right Out of Your Life*. Anyone read it yet?"

More applause along with some enthusiastic "woo-hoos."

"I'm impressed! That's almost all of you and it only came out last week."

"You're the best, Selina!" a woman in the second row shouted out.

She pointed at the shouter. "So are you. Thank you. Really! This is great. Why don't we start with some questions? Then I'll roll into a short reading and then we can sign some copies of these for you all. Sound okay?"

The audience appeared to approve as a dozen hands shot up.

"Yes." Selina pointed at a woman in the front row.

"Oh, this is so exciting," the woman said, standing up. "I am a huge fan. A *huge* fan."

Selina pulled the microphone off its stand. "I appreciate that more than you know. What's your question?"

"What I want to know is if there's a man in your life right now and if your books about female empowerment were inspired by somebody in your past."

"Excellent questions. Yes, I am dating someone right now." She smiled, showing off perfect white teeth. "Actually, scratch that. I'm dating a couple of guys. Why limit ourselves to just one?"

The audience howled with laughter.

"Do they know each other?" the question-asker asked.

"They do and frankly, I think sometimes they might like each other more than they like me if you know what I mean." She winked as the crowd laughed again. "I try not to take my love life too seriously. There are so many other things in our lives that are important. I don't believe the focus of anyone's life should be a man. I mean, are we the focus of their lives?"

"Hell, no," the woman replied firmly.

"There are some exceptions, of course," Selina continued. "Very, very, very few exceptions. But all in all, what should we do with most men?"

She held the microphone out to the audience.

"*Curse that creep!*" was the unified reply.

"This may be the scariest thing I've ever seen in my existence," Darrak said. "And trust me, that's saying something."

Eden raised her eyebrows. It was like a cult. A white, sparkly, man-hating cult.

"As far as my past—" Selina smiled like the Cheshire Cat. "Has my heart been broken into a million pieces? Of course it has. Such heartbreak has made me the woman you see before you today. I've lived. I've loved. I've worked my magic on many men."

"That's an understatement," Darrak said unpleasantly.

"One cannot come out of such a romantic history unscathed. But now I know what to do to protect my heart for all eternity and to help you do the same. A little white magic sprinkled through our lives today can save us picking up the pieces of our broken hearts in the future."

"White magic?" Darrak scoffed. "If that's what she thinks she does she's living in a dream world."

"Maybe she's changed," Eden countered quietly so no one other than Darrak could hear her.

"Not possible."

But the longer Eden listened to what Selina Shaw had to say, the more she became a believer. And it wasn't all about magic. Sure there were some cute little spells involving candles and flowers and meditative walks through nature, but there didn't seem to be anything particularly evil about what the Love Witch was selling.

After the Q&A, Selina launched into a reading that only cemented Eden's feelings about the author.

"She's kind of awesome," Eden said quietly, her arms crossed. "I don't know what she was like in the past but I think she's changed. She'll help us if we ask her to."

"Is that your psychic read at the moment?" He sounded sarcastic.

"I don't need psychic abilities to tell me she's changed. Don't you think it's possible at all?"

"She—" Darrak began and then was quiet for a moment.

"I don't know. It's possible, I guess. But unlikely. When I knew her—"

"That was a long time ago. I'm going to get her books. Just relax and let me talk to her."

Despite Eden's attempt to talk quietly to herself, a woman holding a stack of books gave her a strange look.

"I don't think that's a good idea," Darrak said. "Maybe we should leave."

Eden got in the line. "No. Not yet. Just relax and let me handle this."

"Fine. But don't say I didn't warn you."

She ignored the sensation of unease that flowed through her mostly from the demon. The line shuffled forward slowly. Selina sat behind a table draped in red fabric, piles of her books on either side of her. As readers reached her she spent a few moments talking to them, grasping their hands in hers and squeezing, a broad, friendly smile on her face. There wasn't one moment when her friendly exterior slipped. Was it the real her? Or was she just a really good actress?

Finally Eden reached her. Selina looked up.

"Hi," Eden squeaked. She hadn't realized how nervous she was until she spoke.

"Hi there." Selina reached forward and took her hand. She wore many rings on her fingers as well as a large gray-stoned pendant on a long gold chain that fell between her ample cleavage. "Thank you for coming to see me tonight."

Eden searched for something casual to say in response. "I wish I'd known about you six months ago."

Selina studied her. "When your fiancé was unfaithful to you?"

Eden's eyes widened. "Wow, you're good. How did you know that?"

"I'm the Love Witch, of course. I can tell these things just by touching your hand." Then she frowned slightly and cocked her head to the side. "That's strange . . ."

"Eden—" Darrak said quietly. "I think it's time to go. Right now."

"Silentium!" Selina's voice rose and her grip on Eden's hand grew very painful. She rose to her feet. "You dare bring that thing anywhere near me?"

Eden could barely breathe. "I don't know what you're talking about."

She looked around to see if somebody might help her but no one even looked in their direction. The lineup behind her continued to wait patiently. Browsers in other parts of the store kept browsing. People entered and left through the front doors by the cashier area.

She couldn't feel Darrak's presence anymore.

Selina stormed around to the other side of the table and grasped Eden's upper arms before she could back away from the witch.

"Why can't anyone see what's going on?" Eden looked around again, panic welling in her chest. "Why can't I feel . . ." Her voice trailed off. She didn't want to say it out loud.

Darrak was right. She was dangerous. Evil. And Eden had gotten too close.

"Why can't you feel the demon inside of you anymore?" Selina finished for her. "Because I just dampened his sorry ass."

Eden opened her mouth to say something in reply, but nothing came out.

"I can't believe this," Selina said, starting to pace the small area in front of her signing table. "This is horrible. Absolutely horrible. All these years and he's still existed? I should have known." She turned to Eden and grabbed her shoulders to shake her. "Are you okay?"

"Am I okay?" Eden managed.

"Yes!" She shook her head. "You poor, poor thing. I'm sorry if I scared you. You've obviously been through so much. But I've been able to dampen him. We have some time. I can get rid of him right now."

"Wait a minute. What are you talking about?"

Selina exhaled shakily. "You're possessed by a demon."

"I know that."

"I tried to destroy him three hundred years ago."

Eden backed away from her a few steps. "I know that, too. You destroyed the body he had back then but not the rest of him. It's why I'm here to see you tonight. You need to break the curse you put on him so he doesn't have to possess me anymore."

Selina's mouth gaped open. "Break the curse."

"That's right."

She touched her gray-stoned pendant. "I'm not breaking any curses. Don't you understand? You're possessed by a demon. From Hell. Why aren't you more upset about that?"

"I finished freaking out the other day." Eden wrung her hands. "You need to help us."

"Help . . . *us*?" Selina repeated with shock and took a step forward. "You don't seriously think that demon is your friend, do you?"

Eden took a step back. "Yes. He's my friend."

The witch looked very confused but then a slow clarity came into her eyes. "I think I see what's going on here. You're yet another woman who has been seduced and manipulated by a man. And not just any man—a *demon*."

"You don't know Darrak."

"Darrak?" Selina rolled her eyes. "This is worse than I thought it was. And this was supposed to be a nice, relaxing signing. Okay, listen to me and I'll take it really slow so you understand me. Demons are *not* the friends of humans. Ever. I don't care what he's told you. What's your name, honey?"

Eden shook her head. This had gone badly enough as it was, she didn't need this crazy witch knowing her name.

Selina sighed with exasperation, then closed her eyes, reaching out to touch Eden's arm for a moment, before opening her eyes again. "Okay, Eden, let's chat."

"How—?" Eden shut her mouth. She knew how the witch knew her name. Because she was a *witch*. She might have been able to reach right down into Eden's brain and scoop out the information.

"That's right," Selina said with a slight smile. "I can retrieve the info I'm looking for telepathically with a little effort. One of the bonuses of being me. And I couldn't help but notice that you've got some interesting skills, yourself. A little bit psychic, are you?"

"A little bit. A very little bit."

Selina studied her cautiously. "You remind me of myself when I was fully human. I could sense changes in the weather and tell when there would be a storm even if the skies were still blue. It was an ability one kept to themselves in my time for fear of repercussions."

Eden glanced around at the lineup who continued to wait patiently as if there was nothing more interesting to pay attention to at the moment than the easy-listening music piping through the store's audio system.

"I can imagine."

Selina shook her head. "I don't think you can. You have no idea what it was like back then. Now a woman can walk into a bookstore and buy a book about witchcraft or demonology and no one raises an eyebrow. But back then, if you were sexually active before marriage you might be considered one of Lucifer's concubines."

"But you became a black witch. You must have accepted it."

Her expression went from wary to frigid. "The demon tells you many things, doesn't he?"

"He . . ." Eden's mouth was dry. "Can we just try to calm down. I don't want any trouble here."

"Then you shouldn't have brought him here. Did he tell you why I became a black witch?"

"The subject hadn't come up."

"My abilities to predict the weather caught the attentions of men in my village. They decided I was a witch. Before I could be tried, I ran away and fell in with new friends who recognized my abilities before I even said a word about them. They taught me how to develop them and how to gain more. They had books of magic that I poured through, eager to learn everything I could. However, after I left, my sister was captured in my place, tried as a witch, and executed after weeks of torture. She didn't have any special abilities at all. Her only crime was trying to protect me after I'd run away from home." Her voice caught. "Try having that on your conscience for three centuries."

It sounded so horrible that Eden could barely believe it. "I'm so sorry."

"Don't be. It made me realize that men are the source of all evil and the only way to fight evil is with more of the same. Using the books of magic I learned how to summon a demon to give me the strength and power I wanted."

Eden's mouth was dry. She touched her chest. "This demon?"

"That's right. I summoned the demon you call 'Darrak' and he helped turn me into a black witch. The rest, as they say, is history."

"So he helped you," Eden tried to reason.

Selina laughed. "Oh, that's a very naïve way to put what he did to me, but I think it's kind of cute, actually. *Helped me.* Sure. Let me guess . . . he's told you things about himself, hasn't he? Maybe that he's harmless? That he's decent and respectful to humans? An all-around wonderful guy?"

Eden really didn't like the condescending way she said it. "It was his job to hunt down those who escaped from Hell and bring them back so they wouldn't hurt anyone."

That earned another humorless laugh. "Oh, that's priceless. Yes, there are demons who are given such assignments, but trust me, your Darrak wasn't one of them."

Eden felt weak and light-headed as if she was about to faint at any moment and fall to the floor, taking a pyramid of *Curse That Creep* hardcovers with her.

"I'm not trying to be cruel," Selina continued, noting her stricken expression. "Not too much, anyhow. And I'm not evil like I'm sure he's told you I am. I want to help you. You're in a bad place right now. I'd have to be blind not to see that."

"You have to break the curse and free him."

She shook her head. "He's too dangerous."

"That's funny. He said the same thing about you."

Selina's lips twisted. "Yeah, I bet he did. Poor thing. I know he can be very charming when he wants to be, can't he? Did he happen to tell you how he has to break the curse if I won't do it of my own free will?"

"No."

Selina's cheek twitched. "He would have to kill me with his bare hands and tear out my heart. Not exactly a walk in the park, is it? Although, since he's incorporeal I don't know how he plans to do that."

"I need to sit down."

Selina helped Eden back behind the table where she sat down on the chair. "I would understand if you don't believe me right away, but what I'm telling you is the truth. Darrak's an *archdemon*. Do you know what that is?"

Eden shook her head. "It doesn't sound good."

"It's a demon of high rank and great power who answers to Lucifer himself. The archdemons gain their power from one of the four elements: earth, wind, fire, or water."

"Isn't that an R&B band from the 1970s?"

"Trust me. Not the same thing."

"Fire," Eden said then. "His eyes . . . when he's mad they seem to be made of fire."

"His eyes?" Selina repeated with confusion. "How can you see him? I destroyed his body."

She looked up at the witch. "He . . . he can take solid form during the day."

"That's not good." Selina slumped down in a spare chair next to Eden as if her own legs had given out. "And he looks like a man? Dark hair, blue eyes, tall, and . . ."

"Really hot?"

"That's him."

Eden nodded. "I asked him if that was his true form or if he used a glamour, but he wouldn't answer me."

"That should have been your tip-off that he was hiding a lot."

"His first impulse is self-protection. He can't control that."

Selina shook her head. "He can control whatever he wants to. But he doesn't want to. He's selfish. All demons are."

"An *archdemon*." Eden rolled the word over in her mouth. It tasted as bad as it sounded.

Selina nodded. "Before he was promoted to archdemon, he was a lower-ranking demon—an incubus. That's one of the reasons I chose to summon him. Incubi prey on women, stealing their energy to increase their own power. With a spell I cast, I was able to have him give me power instead. That's what made me into a black witch."

Eden didn't want to hear anything else. She didn't want to believe it, but she couldn't block it out. Everything the witch said felt like the truth.

Darrak was a demon. And he was a bad one.

Because, *duh*, there weren't any good demons, of course.

No. She still didn't want to believe it. Selina could be lying to her. Even though it felt like the truth, it could still be lies.

"Darrak . . ." Eden managed after a minute. "He said if we don't break the curse that keeps him bound to me then in a year I'm going to die."

Selina's eyebrows went up. "What do you know? He told you one truth. That's got to be a record. You have a year—at the very most. He will drain your energy slowly but surely. That's what demons do and why they need to be destroyed when they get too close to humans."

Eden's head was stuck in a cloud of confusion and denial. "But I don't understand. If you summoned him and you got what you wanted, then why would you try to destroy him?"

Selina pulled one of her books off the pile and clutched it tightly as if it was a life preserver. "Defending myself against a dangerous demon who wanted me dead, mostly. Also because I realized what I did was wrong. That nothing I did, magical or not, would bring back my sister. Destroying an archdemon who'd stepped foot on human soil was to be my self-appointed penance. I tried. I failed." She blinked. "And now you're here with him during my signing. It's been such a great week up until now."

"Sorry to ruin it for you."

Selina touched Eden's hand. She tried not to flinch away. "You must let me destroy him for you. Since I'm the one who cursed him, I can do it while he's dampened. There's no other way."

Eden moved away from her. "No."

The witch's eyes widened. "No? Haven't I convinced you that I want to help you?"

Eden exhaled shakily. "You've given me a lot to think about. But . . . I'm not ready. Not right now. Not like this."

"Then when?"

"I need to think."

"Fine. But think fast." Selina opened the book she'd been clutching and scribbled down a phone number on the title page. "I can't force you to let him go. You need to do it of your own free will, otherwise it will probably kill you as well. I don't want to hurt anyone who doesn't deserve it." She touched her gray pendant. "Black magic isn't my thing anymore. At all. And killing humans with magic would turn my soul completely black. Call me tomorrow. If not, I'm leaving and I won't be returning."

She pushed the book toward Eden. She took it.

"I don't know . . ."

"You said he wouldn't tell you the truth about his appearance," Selina said.

"That's right. And he wouldn't tell me his true name, either."

"Just like a man. Wouldn't want to give his power to someone else. Might come back to bite him in the ass." Selina smiled thinly. "It's Darrakayiis."

Eden was surprised. "What?"

"His true name. And a further reason to trust me because I'm sensing that you're fighting that. I'm giving you this as a favor to show that I want to help you."

It sounded like Dare-ah-KAI-iss.

She memorized it and tucked it away in her head. "Can I dampen him with this name?"

"Yes, but that would be overkill. Using his name will give you power over him, especially if he's weakened. With the amount of psychic energy I feel from you, and his ties to you, you should be able to dampen his presence with a well-placed commanding thought. It's really not that hard." Selina ran her hands over her hair as if to neaten it. "I can't hold this camouflage spell much longer. I'm a bit rusty using any higher level magic. So if you'll excuse me."

"What about . . ." Eden touched her chest. "When will he be back?"

She shrugged. "I dampened him really good. He's gone for a while and won't know what hit him. Call me tomorrow if you want my help. If not, good luck. You're sure as hell going to need it."

"Thanks."

"And that book's not a freebie. You'll have to pay for it before you leave."

She looked down at the hardcover. "I was going to get it anyhow."

"It's helped a lot of women even more clueless than you are when it comes to lying, cheating men." Selina pressed her palms down on the table. *"Susciatatio humanus."*

There wasn't a major shift in the crowd's behavior, but now they could look directly at Eden instead of her being invisible to them. Selina began signing again as if nothing had happened. Eden shakily made her way to the cashiers, paid for the book, and left the store. The cool night air swept over her.

What in the hell just happened?

A sob welled up in her chest but she forced it back down.

Having a breakdown was not going to be very helpful at the moment. But she couldn't concentrate. It felt as if her entire life had just imploded.

Selina said that Darrak was evil. An archdemon. And that everything he'd told her about himself had been a lie.

Was it the truth? If so, she should have let Selina get rid of him. Why would she want to delay it another minute?

But there was a small part of her that remained strongly skeptical. The witch could be the one who was lying. It was a good story with a great delivery, but did that make it true?

It felt true. That was the worst part. It felt as if Selina had just filled in the blanks in a really difficult, demonic crossword puzzle.

Had Darrak really lied to her? This realization made her more angry than hurt or sad or afraid. How many men had to disappoint her before she realized they were all creeps who deserved to be cursed? And Darrak wasn't just a normal, run-of-the-mill creep. He was a demonic one.

So what was preventing her from marching right back into the bookstore and asking Selina to get rid of him tonight?

Why would she even want to defend him or give him the benefit of the doubt after everything Selina told her? Darrak wasn't her friend, and he was just using her.

But she'd spent a lot of time with him over the last few days—more time than with anyone else in recent memory. And the more she was with him the more she . . . liked him.

More than liked him.

Is that what this was about? She'd developed a strange, warped infatuation with an evil entity from Hell?

Yes, that was exactly it.

She was so completely screwed.

"Hey, Eden! Wait up!"

She looked tentatively over her shoulder. It was Vanessa with a bag of purchased books in hand.

Pull it together, she told herself. *We have an audience.*

"Hey," she managed weakly.

"I wanted to thank you."

"Thank me?" She'd completely forgotten about the girl in her rush to leave the store.

Vanessa grinned. "Yeah. I knew I needed a change, but you helped put everything into perspective. I was going to call you tomorrow—you gave me your card, remember?"

"I remember. So, your boyfriend?"

She huffed out a breath. "Gone. Literally. I tried to contact him a few hours ago to break things off with him, but couldn't find him anywhere. I don't care if I lose the club. I'd rather be in control of my life than dependent on any man. That's what Selina always says."

"Right. Selina." Eden glanced back at the bookstore. "She's . . . she's great, isn't she?"

"She's like a goddess of good advice." Vanessa studied her. "You don't look so good. You okay?"

"I've been better."

Vanessa nodded knowingly. "Man trouble?"

Eden sniffed. "You have no idea."

"That bad, huh?"

"Worse."

Vanessa shifted her book bag to her other hand. "Are you headed to your car?"

She'd parked in the underground parking lot across the street from the bookstore. "I am."

"Would it be terrible if I mooched a ride off you?" Vanessa asked tentatively. "If you don't mind, that is."

Eden nodded. "I don't mind."

Of course she didn't. Despite her current traumas, she'd rather know that Vanessa got home okay—since Eden still didn't know how everything had worked out with Fay and her husband—than leave her to wander the streets at night alone. Besides, it would give her something else to think about for an hour before she had to deal with her own issues again.

Eden led her into the parking garage and down the elevator to the level where she'd parked the Toyota.

"Maybe you're overthinking things," Vanessa said.

"What things?"

"With your boyfriend. The reason why you're upset."

"He's not my boyfriend. He's just . . ." She had no idea who or what he really was. "Let's just say he's somebody who's managed to get under my skin and now I can't figure out the best way to get rid of him."

"Come on, nobody gets this upset unless there's some romance involved."

"I'm not upset. And there's no romance."

"Yeah, right."

Eden wiped a hand under her nose while she dug into her purse for her keys. "It's complicated."

"It always is. It's kind of funny, though."

"What is?"

"I didn't think he ever let you out of his sight."

Eden placed her purse down on the trunk of her car so she could find the keys that seemed to have slipped down to the bottom. Then she frowned at Vanessa. "Did you meet him? He didn't come in the club with me earlier today."

"We met. Never guess he was a demon at first glance, that's for sure."

Eden froze and looked at the blonde. "A . . . demon?"

"Yup."

"Not sure I know what you're talking about." She was getting used to denying certain things. This was one of them. "Are you sure you met him?"

"I am, indeed." Vanessa smiled and Eden suddenly noticed that her eyes were very dark. Black, in fact. "He threatened to rip my arms off if I hurt you, remember? However, I was in a different body at the time. I'll forgive you for not being so clear on the details."

Eden's stomach sank. "You know, now that I think about it, he's going to meet me here any moment."

"I think you're lying." Vanessa's smile turned cold. "I knew you were a nosy little bitch earlier today, but you had to go and ruin everything for me, didn't you?"

The drifter. His dirty little secret had been found out and he'd had to switch over to a different body. And he'd chosen his girlfriend's.

"My business card," Eden said flatly, but feeling the panic begin to swirl inside her. "That's how you found me?"

"Called your office earlier. A man told me where he thought you'd be tonight. He sounded really cheery, actually. Funny. You really don't strike me as the private investigator type."

Andy had been in a good mood with all their newfound business. He'd probably thought Vanessa was just a friend who wanted to meet up for drinks tonight.

"You need to leave me alone," Eden said. "And we won't have any problems."

Vanessa laughed. "Not so fast there, sweetheart. I think I need to settle up with you for ruining a good thing I had going on. Now I need to start all over again."

She drew a knife out of her handbag. Eden eyed it with growing alarm.

"Drifters aren't murderous," she said.

"I guess you must be special, then." Vanessa smiled. "Because I've decided to make an exception for you."

⇻ SEVENTEEN ↤

"Wait a minute." Eden staggered back a few steps and hit a cement support beam. She looked around for someone within screaming distance, but the parking garage appeared empty. "Let's talk about this."

Vanessa raised a thin eyebrow. "What do you want to talk about?"

"You don't want to kill me."

"I don't?"

She shook her head. "No, you absolutely don't."

The drifter laughed. "Humans are so entertaining. You walk around like you own this world, but you're actually not the top of the food chain. You don't have any idea how many things are out there lurking in the darkness with a taste for human flesh. Then again, I'm sure you know that now since you're dating a demon."

"I'm not dating him."

Vanessa eyed her curiously. "Is it a spell you're using to bind him to you?"

"No spells."

"Then why did he protect you earlier today? That wasn't normal demon behavior."

"He's different." Her answer even surprised herself. But it was true. He'd seemed different. He'd acted different. Was it all just pretend?

She tried reaching inside to find the dormant demon, kind of like how she'd reached into her purse trying to find her car keys. She couldn't find him, either.

Would he bother to help her now that she might know the truth about him?

"He's different? Yeah, I bet." Vanessa held the knife tightly and threw her purse and bag of books over toward the Toyota's front tire. "It's strange, that's all. The only time I've ever known a demon to be interested in the well-being of a human is when they were after something. Has he bound himself to you? Must have. That would act as protection for him. Can't be dragged back to Hell without the human's permission then." She shook her head. "For such weak sacks of meat, you have a certain level of power in the universe."

"Why are you telling me this?"

She shrugged. "Maybe I'm cherishing the moment before I take the life of a human a demon was in love with."

The thought was completely ludicrous. "He's not in love with me."

"He seemed kind of into you, if you ask me."

"I'm not asking." She glared at the drifter. "Besides, he's evil."

"Evil's a lot like the color black. There are many shades."

"Black's not a color."

"Let's not get technical."

She came toward Eden with the knife. Eden grabbed her arm but found her just as strong as the drifter had been when he'd possessed Richard.

"Don't bother trying to fight," Vanessa said. "You'll lose."

Eden fought anyhow. She attempted to squirm out of the drifter's grip and almost made it, but Vanessa maneuvered her around and trapped Eden's hands. She thought of Darrak then.

What would happen to him when she died? Even though he was currently dampened, would he be able to find someone else to possess before it was too late?

Why did she even care what happened to the demon?

The blonde raised the knife high in the air. But then she froze. "What the hell?"

"What?"

"I can't move my arm."

"You can't?"

"No. And I was seconds away from plunging this into your chest. Or slashing your throat. I hadn't decided yet."

Eden stared at her with shock. "And now you can't move at all?"

"No. It's very strange." Strain showed on the drifter's stolen face. "What's causing this?"

"I am." Malcolm stepped out from behind a beam near the stairway exit.

Eden stopped breathing for a moment at the sight of the exorcist. She was happy to see a familiar face at a time like this. Even if it was his.

"Who the hell are you?" the drifter snapped.

"One whose sole focus in life is to destroy things like you." Malcolm approached and, without even glancing at Eden, plucked the knife from the girl's prone hand.

"Go ahead," the drifter said without any fear in her voice, glancing at her knife. "Kill me, then."

"Why would I want to do something like that? So you can escape? You're trapped at the moment, but you should probably know that I'm immune to being possessed."

The drifter narrowed her heavily made-up eyes.

"That's right," Malcolm continued. "I know what you are. Although, it did help that I've been listening in on your conversation."

"Please. Give me a break. What are you, eighteen years old?"

Malcolm scowled. "I'm twenty-one."

"You're just a child. Do you have any idea how long I've existed? I strongly suggest you leave me to my business right now or you're going to regret it."

Malcolm's gaze finally flicked to Eden's. "This woman is under my protection. So that makes this my business."

Eden was surprised at this news. When did this happen? Not that she was complaining.

"Your protection?" Eden said aloud.

"Unless you'd prefer to deal with this creature on your own."

She shook her head violently. "No, no. A little help would be fantastic, actually."

"Can you please hold this for a moment?"

He handed Eden the knife and she stared at it with surprise before curling her fingers around the hilt.

Malcolm had given her a weapon? Had she missed a memo? Since when was he so trusting and helpful when it came to her?

Maybe Rosa had had a talk with him recently about his manners.

"No knife?" the drifter asked, almost bored. "Then whatever are you going to do with me, child?"

"Like I said before, I'm not a child." Malcolm pulled a chain out from underneath his shirt. On the end of it was a rough, thumb-sized colorless crystal.

The drifter's eyes widened. "Don't even think about it."

"I'm going to do more than think about it."

The drifter looked frantically to her left and right, her blond hair tossing about. "Let's talk about this."

"Let's not."

"You son of a bitch—"

"My mother has nothing to do with this." Malcolm smiled thinly. "Not today, anyway." He began to speak Latin.

Eden clutched the knife and took a few steps back from him. Latin made her nervous. She knew what it could do.

Nothing happened for a full minute, but the drifter's expression continued to get more and more distraught, her breathing erratic. Vanessa began to shake.

He really was an exorcist. Rosa would be very proud.

"No," the drifter managed. "Please stop!"

But Malcolm didn't stop. He looked so determined that Eden was sure an earthquake wouldn't stop him.

The drifter screamed, but it wasn't any ordinary scream. It was high-pitched and inhuman. The sound reverberated around them and a stream of dark blue smoke exited from the girl's mouth. Malcolm held up the crystal at arm's length and the smoke went directly toward it as if it was a magnet and disappeared. The crystal turned blue and appeared to swirl and glow with energy.

The former host for the drifter staggered forward.

"What in the hell just happened?" she said, before she clutched at a support beam. The next moment she collapsed to her knees and passed out completely.

Eden held a hand to her mouth. "Is she—"

"She'll be fine."

"But she's—"

"She'll be fine," he said again, firmly.

She turned her attention toward the crystal. "Is the drifter in there now?"

"Yes."

"Can it escape?"

He nodded. "It can. This is a very weak prison. It wouldn't take very long for it to figure out how."

Leaning against her car was the only thing currently keeping her upright. "So what are you going to do?"

"This." Malcolm bent over and placed the crystal on the ground. Then, without another word, he brought his thick-soled black boot down on it, crushing the shard into dust. There was a blinding flash of blue light. "It can be destroyed when it's inside of a crystal by whomever trapped it. However, if the crystal is destroyed by someone else, the drifter or demon could still escape." He turned to her and she noticed that his brow was now covered in sweat. He smiled. "Although, I suggest you never use a diamond. They're nearly impossible to smash. This was a sodium chloride crystal. Or, in other words, a big piece of rock salt. Are you okay?"

She was finding it hard to breathe. "I'm . . . I'm okay now. Thank you for stopping her. Or him. Or whatever it was."

"You're very welcome." He moved toward her but she held the knife up in front of her.

"Don't come any closer."

Malcolm stopped in his tracks. "I know you won't believe this, but I mean you no harm."

"Sure you don't."

"Why would I have just saved you if I wanted to hurt you?" He tilted his head to the side and frowned. "I don't sense the demon anymore. Where is he?"

"He's gone."

"Where did he go?"

"Maybe I had him exorcised."

He shook his head, any humor leaving his expression. "You're in way over your head, Eden. Please let me help you."

Help her? Why did she find that extremely hard to believe? But it had to be true. He'd just saved her life.

A rush of emotion came over her. "I think I do need help."

He nodded. "The demon must be destroyed. Do you see that now?"

"I . . . I don't know."

Was he right? Did she need to let him help her get rid of Darrak once and for all? Even though Selina had offered to help, she didn't trust the witch. Did that mean she trusted Malcolm? He did seem rather . . . earnest. He felt he was doing the right thing. That's why he helped Rosa with her exorcisms. That's why he was a member of the Malleus.

"Can you get rid of him right now?" she asked. The words actually hurt to speak.

He shook his head. "With my skill level, he's too deep for

me to touch him, even with your permission. Drifters are much easier to destroy than demons. For my exorcism ritual to work, the demon must be conscious and present. You have to be completely willing to rid yourself of him. You can't fight me once it begins or you'll be risking your own safety. Are you ready to do that?"

Eden clenched her jaw. Was she ready? She didn't know. Which probably meant she wasn't ready.

"You'll be glad once this evil is finally removed from your body." Malcolm's words were firm.

"You can sense he's evil? And you're absolutely sure?"

He frowned. "I don't know what you mean."

She shook her head. "I . . . I was told there were good demons. That it's possible for them to not all be evil."

"Yes, that's true."

She felt a wave of shock and a smidgen of hope at that unexpected confirmation. "It is?"

He nodded. "Some demons were once human and sold their souls for some agreed upon price. They become demons when they die, but there is the humanity that remains within them that occasionally compels them to seek redemption. Is the demon you're possessed with a former human?"

Her heart sank. "No. He told me he was created in the Netherworld. He was an archdemon."

Malcolm's lips thinned. "An *archdemon*?"

She nodded.

"I had no idea he was that powerful." His voice sounded hollow and she could hear fear there now. "We're lucky he hasn't done any more harm to you. An archdemon—they don't travel to the human world often. But when they do it usually ends very badly for anyone or anything that crosses their path." He exhaled shakily. "Has the demon told you his true name yet? That might be helpful."

"He . . ." she began, but then closed her mouth. "He refuses to tell me."

It wasn't a lie. Darrak hadn't told her. She'd found out his true name from Selina. So why wasn't she telling Malcolm?

She still needed time to sort through everything in her head. And now that Malcolm couldn't exorcise him right away, she'd have that time.

"I need to consult with my mentor in the Malleus. Now that I know we're dealing with an archdemon, that might change how we proceed." Malcolm shoved his hand into his coat pocket before pulling something out. "Take this. You can reach me at that number at all hours."

The card had Malcolm's name and a phone number in simple black type.

"What's this?" she asked, pointing to a small emblem of a fleur-de-lis.

"It's the mark of the Malleus." He rolled up his left sleeve to show her his forearm that bore a similar symbol. "It's a brand. When we're accepted into the Malleus, it's given to us—and with this mark and the ritual that accompanies it, we're given insight to be able to sense demonic activity and the presence of evil."

The wound looked fresh still. Pink. It was the fleur-de-lis enclosed in a circle, about three inches in diameter.

"Did it hurt?" she asked.

"Like hell." He grinned at her. "But it was a cleansing pain."

"If you say so."

"Take this as well." He pressed another crystal in her hand. "It will help protect you from your demon. Call me if there are any problems at all. I will contact you once I speak to my mentor and learn how best to deal with an archdemon. Is that acceptable?"

Was it acceptable? That was a very good question.

She nodded. "Okay."

"Then, good night. And be safe." He turned and walked swiftly out of the parking lot.

After a moment went by, Vanessa stirred on the ground before blinking her blue eyes open. She sat up and rubbed her
forehead. "Where am I?"

"You fell and hit your head," Eden said, gripping the
piece of salt in her hand before slipping it in her pocket
and Malcolm's card into her purse. "But it's going to be all
right now."

Yeah, right.

By the time Eden dropped Vanessa off at her place and
returned to her apartment she was kicking herself for not asking Malcolm to come back with her. Not that she had a habit
of luring twenty-one-year-old boys back to her home, but it
might have been a good idea tonight for safety reasons.

It felt completely insane for her to be thinking she needed
to be afraid of Darrak. After all, he'd been nothing but protective of her so far. That was the most difficult thing about this.
She couldn't rationalize how he could be one way with her and
yet be something she had to be afraid of.

But he was a demon. There was no doubt about that. And
demons, according to both Selina and Malcolm, were evil. Full
stop.

Was there another explanation? Or did she need to get rid
of him by any means possible as soon as she could?

After all, the piece of salt in her pocket definitely wasn't for
making margaritas.

She closed the door, locked it, and pressed up against it, her
fearful gaze moving through her small apartment as if looking
for a definite sign of what she should do next.

Leena, in cat form, jumped down off the couch and came
over toward her, batting Eden's leg with her head. "Mrroww?"

The concerned-sounding meow helped the rush of emotion
she'd been holding back for hours surge forward. Eden burst
into tears.

It only took a couple of moments for Leena to morph into

human form and Eden felt her hand on her shoulder. "Let me guess. Bad night?"

Eden continued to blubber uncontrollably. "The worst."

"You need something to eat?"

"I don't think that's going to help very much." She sat down heavily on a dinette chair.

"What's the problem?"

Eden took in a shaky breath. "I'm possessed by a demon."

"No shit. Didn't we already know that?"

Eden chewed on her thumbnail—a nervous habit she thought she'd given up long ago. "He'd convinced me that he was a good demon—"

"There are no good demons."

"Sure. Now you tell me."

Leena sat down across the small table from her. "Didn't know you had to be told. Everything that comes out of the Netherworld is some form of evil. That's the way it's always been and it gives balance to the universe. There can't be good without evil. There can't be day without night. There can't be chocolate without vanilla. Et cetera."

Eden blinked at her and rubbed her tears away. "You know about this sort of thing?"

She nodded. "I know more about a lot of things than I wish I did, to tell you the truth. I knew the moment I saw that demon that he was no good."

"How did you know that?"

"Mostly because he's a demon."

"But he healed me when you scratched me. And he's been really helpful. And he's a pain in the ass but he hasn't done anything really horrible. And he . . . he doesn't *seem* evil to me."

Leena frowned. "Are you in love with him?"

Eden's eyebrows went up. "What?"

"I can't think of any reason why you'd be defending him like this if there weren't feelings involved. And just before you say yes or no, just know that demons are well-known for manipulating the feelings of humans and using them against the human in question to get them to do what they want."

"I know that."

"Then if you know that and you're still defending this dude, then you're seriously screwed."

"Tell me something I don't know." Eden tried very hard not to think about the times when she'd felt close to Darrak, despite what he was. When she'd woken up in his arms. When they'd kissed. When she'd called him her guardian angel. "I'm going to have him exorcised."

"Where is he right now?"

"He's been dampened." She quickly told Leena about what happened with Selina.

Her eyes widened. "The Love Witch is a real witch? That is so cool."

"You think she was telling me the truth?"

"She's the Love Witch. Of course she was. Summoning an incubus to make her into a black witch back in the Salem witch trial days . . . that's pretty powerful stuff. She should sell the movie rights for that. I'd go see it."

Eden twisted a finger absently through her long hair. "It's got to be powerful. I mean, even with proper instructions, summoning an archdemon sounds dangerous."

"Summoning a *what*?" The pleasant, curious look fell from Leena's face.

"An archdemon. It's apparently a really powerful demon who answers only to Lucifer and—"

"Oh, I *know* what an archdemon is. And you're saying that tall, dark, and gruesome is an arch?"

Eden nodded.

Leena gave her a frozen smile. "And I am out of here."

"What?"

She stood up. "It's been fun. I made a lasagna like I said I would. It's in the fridge. Help yourself. Well, since I used your ingredients it's legally yours anyhow. There's a Caesar salad in there, too. And you might get your cable bill later and find out that I've been watching a lot of pay-per-view movies. Like, *a lot* of them. I'll send you a check . . . some time soon. Thanks for letting me stay here."

She walked to the door.

Eden blocked her. "Wait. You can't leave."

"Oh, but I can."

The panic that had subsided a little rose again. "I need you here."

"Why? You don't even know me. And you didn't want me to be here in the first place."

"I thought you were hiding from some people."

Leena physically pushed past Eden to get to the door. "I am. And I can hide somewhere else that doesn't have an arch-demon in residence. In fact, I think I'd prefer it that way."

"Don't go."

Leena laughed short and bitterly. "You have no damn idea how much trouble you're in, do you? And I'm sorry if it seems like I'm being selfish. Well, I am. But if I found out a nuclear bomb was about to go off in the town I was living in, I wouldn't think twice about getting the hell out of there as fast as I could."

"You're exaggerating."

"Wish I was." She shivered. "I've seen demons, Eden. I've seen them in their demon form—none of this human-looking pretty exterior."

"So he does look different," Eden breathed. "I knew it."

"Oh hell yeah, he looks different. Demons have two . . . the word used is *visages*. A human visage and their demon one they have to wear like a uniform when they go see the big boss downstairs. And the demon visage can be pretty goddamned scary. I had nightmares for weeks after I ran into my last one who wasn't wearing his human visage at the time. Like something out of a horror movie. There was slime involved."

"Slime?" Eden yelped.

Leena crossed her arms tightly, her expression one of disgust. "Yeah. Not pleasant, believe me. Sure he was hot as hell in his human form, but that didn't exactly erase the other form from my mind. And he wasn't even an archdemon."

Eden's mind reeled, trying to process this latest influx of info. "So what's the difference?"

"Power. An archdemon can level an entire city if they have a mind to with so-called natural disasters like floods, earthquakes, fires, or tornados. These things aren't always caused by archs, but they've had a hand in some of the worst things to ever hit humans in the past—mostly for their own amusement. And they try to one-up each other. They want to be closer to Lucifer—closer to the top. They hunger for power. It's all they want."

Eden chewed her bottom lip so hard she thought she might break the skin. "But there are demons who can be redeemed—ones who used to be human."

"Never heard of that before." Leena studied Eden's face. "Are you seriously coming to his defense right now? You need to send him back to Hell."

"I'm going to." She was. Malcolm would contact her tomorrow, she was sure of it.

"I'm outie. Bye, now!" Leena grabbed the doorknob.

"Please don't leave." Eden hated the pleading tone in her voice.

"I'm sorry. I need to protect myself first." Leena did have the grace to look guilty about her decision as she looked over her shoulder at Eden. "I'll check back in a few days to see if you're still alive. Good luck!"

She opened the door and walked out of the apartment. The door closed behind her.

Eden was in shock. She's just been abandoned. She was all on her own.

Well, not totally on her own. She had a sleeping demon inside of her. One she was going to have exorcised tomorrow even though the thought of it made her feel queasy.

Leena was gone.

Eden blinked.

Well, if there was a bright side to all of this, at least there wouldn't be a cat hair problem anymore. That stuff was getting everywhere.

⇒ EIGHTEEN ⇐

Eden couldn't sleep. She didn't even try. She sat at her tiny dinette table all alone, waiting and watching the hours tick by.

The shapeshifter didn't come back.

"Hey Darrak? Are you still here?" she whispered. She still couldn't feel him. Maybe Selina had permanently dampened him. Maybe he was gone and wouldn't come back.

Or maybe the piece of salt in her pocket that Malcolm had given her was enough to hold back his presence.

As long as she didn't start foaming at the mouth again, it was a good thing to hold on to. Tightly.

She tried to stay awake, but despite the fact that she was worked up and stressed out . . . not to mention, scared to death . . . it was a lost cause. She was exhausted. The moment she rested her head on her folded arms a few hours later, she fell asleep.

When she woke, she opened up one eye and saw daylight. She swore out loud and tried to straighten up but she was so stiff from her sleeping position it took a moment.

"Ow." She rubbed her sore neck.

The phone rang and she jumped with surprise, her heart thudding violently. Then she reached forward to grab the cordless phone on the table in front of her and held it to her ear.

"Yeah?"

"Eden?" Andy asked. "Why are you still at home?"

"Still?" She glanced at the clock. It was nearly eleven o'clock. "I didn't realize the time. I'm . . . I'm not feeling so good. To put it extremely mildly. I don't think I'll be in today. Is that a problem?"

"I guess not. I need you healthy for our new caseload, so rest up while you still can. Should I bring over some chicken soup?"

"No soup required." She rubbed the sleep out of her eyes and stifled a yawn. "You do remember I'm not a licensed private investigator, right?"

"We can work around that."

"But the law—"

"Eden, don't be so literal. We'll have you as my assistant for now and I'll get the license for you. I know people."

"But what about classes and tests and—"

"You are really nothing like your mother, are you?"

She sighed. "I'll take that as a compliment, actually."

"You've got Caroline's looks, but not her taste for adventure. You need to open up to the idea of putting some danger and intrigue in your life. Shake things up a bit."

Things were shaky enough as it is. "I'll work on that."

"I'm going to close shop early today and turn on the voice mail. I'm starting a case for a guy—wants me to look into somebody he feels is spying on his pack and interested in becoming . . . and I quote, 'alpha.' Weird way to put it, isn't it?"

She blanched. Was this the werewolf client? "Just be careful."

"Always. Now you take it easy today and get yourself healthy again, okay?"

"I'll try my hardest."

She hung up.

"So what happened last night?" Darrak asked wearily.

She froze and slowly turned to her right. Darrak sat on the couch ten feet away. His shoulders were hunched over.

"Last night . . ." It came out as a barely audible squeak. She cleared her throat. "Uh . . . Selina dampened you."

"And then what happened? I don't remember a damned thing." He raked a hand through his dark hair, his expression alternately confused and concerned.

She wrung her hands nervously. "Then—then I got the hell out of there."

"She didn't try to stop you?"

"No."

He leaned back and exhaled with relief. "Well, that's good. I was worried."

"About what she might tell me?"

"Actually, I was worried she might hurt you."

This wasn't good. She hadn't been prepared to face the demon yet. She needed preparation time—to figure out what to say, how to act, what to do. Why did she have to fall asleep?

Eden got up from the table and went around to the fridge in the kitchenette and pulled out a bottle of water. She uncapped it and took a shaky swig.

"So you came back here?" Darrak asked.

"Uh-huh."

He got up from the sofa but it seemed as if it took some effort.

She eyed him uneasily. "Not feeling so good?"

"I've felt better. Selina is just as powerful as she ever was. Her dampening ability is very admirable—witches are good at that sort of thing. I didn't even come to until an hour ago. That's way after sunrise." He gave her a weak grin. "I notice that you weren't in bed ready to molest me again. I won't take it personally, really."

That earned a vivid flashback to yesterday morning and the "dream" she'd said was about Ben. But it had been about Darrak. Fully and completely. And she'd wanted him badly.

But that was then and this was now.

She tried to look at him with her new eyes, her new information, but he seemed the same to her. He wasn't acting any differently. He didn't look any different.

But he was.

"Will you be okay?" She tried to sound as normal as possible.

"I'll be fine. I think." He was quiet for a moment, but then frowned. "You know, you're acting very strangely right now."

"Am I?"

He came into the kitchenette. She took a quick step back from him.

His frown deepened. "Yes, you are. What's the problem?"

"Oh, there are a lot of problems. And Leena left. She . . . decided she didn't want to stay here anymore."

"Can't say I'm sorry to hear that." He grinned and took another step toward her, then braced a hand against the refrigerator. "So it's just the two of us now?"

She staggered back from him, hitting the stove behind her and bit her bottom lip, refusing to meet his eyes. "So . . . how do you plan to convince Selina to break your curse if the moment she senses you, she dampens you? Doesn't exactly seem like she's all that open to discussion on the topic."

Eden originally believed that Darrak meant to reason with the witch to get her to agree to help. But now she knew Darrak had probably planned to kill her to get what he wanted.

"You're shivering," Darrak said, his brows drawing together. "Eden, what the hell is going on? Something bad happened last night. What was it?"

"Nothing. Nothing at all. Everything's super. Fabulous, really."

"You're lying. Tell me what's wrong."

"Don't come any closer." Her hand curled around the crystal of salt in her pocket.

He didn't listen to her and came within two feet before he stopped in his tracks. His forehead creased. Then he swore under his breath. "Who gave you that?"

"Who gave me what?" she asked innocently.

"The big-ass piece of salt you have there."

"You mean this?" She pulled it out of her pocket and thrust it at him.

Darrak stumbled back a foot, his eyes narrowing. "That would be the big-ass piece of salt I was referring to, yes."

Eden watched him carefully. "No foaming at your mouth."

"The day is young. Also, I'm not sucking on it, so that makes the situation much less foamy." His eyes narrowed further. "What's going on, Eden?"

"Just trying to protect myself. You know, with a big piece of salt."

He pointed at his chest. "Protect yourself from me?"

"No, from the ice monster who moved in next door."

"Okay, so let me take a wild guess here. You were lying before about what happened with Selina."

"Me, lying?" She let out a short humorless laugh at that. "Interesting. I guess it takes a liar to know a liar, doesn't it?"

He sighed. "Are we going to play word games, or are you going to tell me what the hell is going on?"

"I'm okay with word games. Scrabble, crosswords, Boggle. You name it."

"Did Selina give you that?" He nodded at the salt.

"No. Malcolm did."

"What?" His jaw clenched. "Did he try to hurt you again?"

Not the reaction she'd expected. "No, just the opposite actually. The drifter you threatened to tear apart yesterday jumped into another body and tried to kill me. Malcolm saved me."

"Kill you?" he repeated harshly. His brow was lowered over his blue eyes. "Are you okay?"

"I'm standing here in one piece, aren't I?"

"Something's different, though. Very different." He studied her face with a growing distress in his expression. "Please. Tell me what happened last night. What did that evil bitch say about me?"

She was breathing so fast now that she felt ready to hyperventilate. "Actually, she said that you're an evil, powerful, ex-incubus archdemon and to break the curse you need to kill her and tear out her heart and that everything you've told me has been lies so you could get me to do what you want. In a nutshell."

He stared at her stonily. "What else did she say?"

"That she tried to destroy you out of self-defense and also to redeem herself. But she failed."

"Oh, she failed, all right."

She searched his face, which looked more upset than pissed off at her fast-forward recount of last night's events. "Tell me she's the one who's lying."

He let out a long exhale. "Is that all it would take? Would you believe me again then?" His jaw clenched. "I knew you shouldn't have gotten too close to her."

"You're not denying anything."

"No, I'm not, am I?"

Her chest hitched. "You said you were a good demon dispatched to get the bad things that escaped the Netherworld. That you protected humans. That was a lie?"

He swallowed hard, then shook his head. "Busted."

"What?"

"I lied to you," he said softly. "Selina told you the truth. I am an archdemon. Or, at least, I *was*."

Chills broke out down her arms. She wasn't sure what she expected him to say. At the very least, she expected him to deny it.

She could barely breathe now. "The fire I see in your eyes . . . that's part of your demon visage."

"Yes."

"The only type of demon who can be good is a former human."

His jaw clenched. "Somebody's been doing their homework, haven't they?" He swore again and looked away. When he turned his gaze to hers again his eyes were fiery. "I know how this looks. It's bad. But I'm not going to lie to you anymore. I only lied in the beginning because I didn't want you to be afraid of me."

Her back hurt from pressing up against the stove edge, but her kitchen was so small, and she didn't want to move any closer to him.

"No, you lied so I wouldn't exorcise you."

"Well, yeah. That, too. But I am not going to hurt you. I swear it."

"You swear it?" she repeated incredulously. "You *swear* it? On what? A Bible?"

He sighed heavily. "I don't know what to say to make you believe."

"You don't have to say anything. You know what the craziest thing is? Even after Selina told me all of that, I still didn't believe her. Not really. But now . . . it's over, Darrak. It's *over*."

"Which means what?"

Her throat was tight. "Exactly what it sounds like."

Darrak nodded. "Normally if you're planning on exorcising a demon, it's best not to give him a heads-up about it first. The surprise factor works best." He swallowed and raised his gaze from the floor to hers again. His eyes had returned again to their ice blue shade. "I know you won't believe anything that comes out of my mouth anymore, but I'm going to try anyhow."

"Try what?"

"I was a very powerful demon, and I did what I wanted to do for a very long time. But do you want to hear the real truth and nothing but?"

"More than you know."

"I've changed."

"Bullshit."

He shook his head. "For three hundred years I've been trapped inside a succession of humans. Do you know what that's done to me?"

"Made you into a lying, evil sack of shit?"

He huffed out a small laugh. "Other than that."

"What, then?"

"It's changed me. The humanity has infused me."

"Humanity?" She held onto the piece of salt so hard she was sure it would leave a permanent mark.

"That's right. I didn't know what it meant to feel like a human back then—to love and fear and want things that weren't totally selfish. That has bled into me from the humans I've possessed. Now I feel *everything*. Even the things I don't want to feel."

She didn't think she could be any more confused by Darrak than she already was. She'd been wrong. "But . . . you said you possessed bad people. Was that a lie, too? How can you claim to have absorbed their humanity if they were scumbags like you said they were?"

"I wasn't lying about that. But it didn't matter if the humans were good or bad, they were still human. That alone has given me some of that intrinsic humanity."

She brought a hand up to her aching head. There was not enough aspirin in her medicine cabinet—or, possibly, the entire world—to deal with her current headache. "But you were an archdemon. Why would you even care if you chose a bad or good human?"

"In the beginning I didn't. As an archdemon I thought of humans as insects—less than worthy of life. Pests to be played with or squashed." He actually winced at whatever horrified expression moved across her face at that statement. "But I'm different now. It was slow, but it happened. My former existence as an archdemon has been permanently dampened for me."

She shook her head. "Dampened?"

"I remember well enough what I was like and what all I was responsible for, but it's as if I'm watching from afar, seeing the horrible things I considered fun and games as if they happened to someone else. I wasn't a very nice guy back then. Selina wasn't the only one over the centuries to summon me and have me do her unpleasant bidding—but she was the only one to escape my wrath."

"You killed the others?" Her voice was very quiet.

"Yes," he replied without hesitation. His jaw tensed and he looked down at the ground again. "Even after I changed, my single goal has been survival. I've only been able to observe." He went silent for a moment. "But when you could hear me, and when you were able to help give me form, that gave me so much hope for the future. That I even had a future." A smile stretched his lips, but it didn't seem like a happy one. "*Hope*. There's another human emotion I never would have felt as a full-strength archdemon. It would have amused me then to see myself now. See how weak I've become. How *human*."

So Darrak was saying he was all kinds of evil in the past but ever since the curse he'd become steadily more like a human? More lies? Or was he finally telling her the truth? Part of her was still desperate to believe he had changed.

"You've been using me," she said.

"Of course I have." His lips curled with an unpleasantness that seemed directed toward himself rather than her. "My first chance in three centuries to fix this mess I'd gotten myself into? How could I possibly resist?"

"And then what would you do? Go back to the Netherworld?"

His brows drew together. "No. They're not very open to change in Hell—especially when that change includes lessening the so-called evil inside of their high-ranking demons. Good is the one thing that scares them—it's very unpredictable. If I didn't go back to the way I was before I'd probably be destroyed. In fact, I'm sure of it."

She repressed a shudder as well as a sliver of concern for him. "So what would you do?"

"I'd try to stay here in the human world for as long as I could. But as soon as my presence was detected they would send agents after me."

Further confusion only caused the fog in her brain to

thicken. "Then why try to break the curse at all? It might be a prison, being stuck inside a human, but at least you're relatively safe."

He swallowed and then met her eyes. "If I don't break the curse, you'll die."

Her mouth dropped open. "So you were planning on becoming the hunted, on the run from the hordes of Hell on your ass, so you wouldn't kill me?"

"Basically."

"What happened to your pledge of self-protection?"

"It's still very much intact. I don't want to be exorcised. Being on the run is different from being destroyed all at once. At least I have a chance—even if it's not a very good one." He inhaled deeply. "So there you have it, Eden. The ugly truth about yours truly."

She tried to process everything Darrak had told her. It was difficult. But what Selina had told her last night had rung really true for her. She'd felt in her gut that the witch had been honest with her. She had a similar feeling right now.

It was the truth. The bad parts and the good parts.

She'd opened up the can of worms and she still wanted to pick around at the gruesome contents. "I still don't know what you really look like."

His jaw tensed. "This is what I look like."

"Maybe part of the time."

"I never have to look any different from this if I don't want to."

"Show me," she said firmly.

He shook his head. "I don't want to scare you."

"Way too freaking late for that."

"You're afraid of me."

That much would be obvious even if she was trying to hide it. And she wasn't. "You're a demon. How can I *not* be afraid of you?"

The very next moment he stormed toward her and knocked the salt out of her hand. It skittered across the kitchen counter.

She gasped as he pressed up against her and held her wrists firmly against the counter on either side of the stove.

"If I wanted to harm you," he breathed against the side of her face, "I would have already done it. I don't want you hurt because of me. Ever."

Her heart slammed against her chest. "Let me go."

He brought her hands up to touch his face. "I'm the same man you knew yesterday. The one you said you trusted. Nothing's changed."

"You're not a man."

But he did feel like one. The rasp of his slight growth of beard, the hard edge of his jaw, his full lips. The silk of his hair slipping through her fingers. His skin against her skin. So real. So human.

"I'd do anything to prove myself to you." His mouth was very close to hers and she didn't turn her head or pull away from him. "What can I do?"

"Tell me your true name," she replied without missing a beat. It was a chance for him to be completely truthful with her.

He tensed. "Eden . . . you don't know what you're asking me."

"Sure I do. If I knew your true name I could make you tell me everything. I could make you show me what you really look like when you're a demon, right?"

"You could also make me eviscerate someone you didn't like. Or . . . juggle. Or sing karaoke. Or throw myself off a cliff. If you knew my true name you could make me your puppet."

Karaoke? Normally, that might sound like fun. "But what if I promised not to do any of that?"

His jaw tensed. "I can't. I'm sorry."

"How does someone find out your true name?"

He finally let go of her and stepped backward. "They have to be very determined. And very deceitful, and willing to face the consequences when I'm finished doing what they've forced me to do."

She studied him. "Is that really why Selina tried to destroy you? Because you were pissed off that she summoned you and forced you to make her into a black witch?"

His expression closed off. "What did she tell you about that specifically?"

She crossed her arms again. "Not much, actually. She used some sort of a spell to have you give power to her instead of you taking power from her. That was around the same time my head blew up."

"I can imagine." He walked to the other side of the kitchenette, which was only a few feet away, and clutched the side of the laminate countertop over the dishwasher. "Selina received too much power from me on multiple occasions because of that little spell of hers. It nearly destroyed her. She had to learn how to curb it so the black magic didn't corrupt her soul completely." He raised his troubled gaze to hers. "So what's next, Eden?"

Where were they supposed to go from here? She was torn. He'd admitted that he was a liar, an archdemon, a total nightmarepalooza, and yet she still wasn't running away from him while screaming her head off. She couldn't get away even if she wanted to. Evil or not, he was still supernaturally superglued to her at the moment.

And there was more than that. A deep sense of wanting to trust him again, despite everything she now knew to be the truth.

Before she could say anything else, there was a knock on the door and Eden's shoulders tensed.

"Expecting somebody?" Darrak asked.

Eden shook her head. He didn't look as if he believed her. He walked toward the door and glanced out through the peephole. After a moment, he surprised her by unlocking the door.

"What is it?" he asked unpleasantly.

"You're still here?" It was Ben. A breath caught in her throat.

"Obviously."

"Is Eden in?"

"She is." Darrak turned with a frozen smile on his face. "Great timing, by the way. If I didn't know better, I'd say you were psychic."

Ben entered the apartment. "I called the office and Andy said you weren't in yet. I was in the area anyhow, so I thought I'd try my luck and see if you were still at home."

"Oh," she said. "Uh . . . great. Here I am."

He grinned at her. "Somebody let me in the door downstairs so I came right up."

There was a long moment of uncomfortable silence.

"Listen, Darrak," Ben said. "Do you think I can talk to your sister alone for a moment?"

Darrak laughed hollowly. "My sister, huh?"

"That's right."

He cocked his head to the side. "And what would you say if I told you that I'm not really her brother?"

Eden looked at the demon sharply but his full attention was on the cop.

Ben frowned. "I'd probably wonder why you would have told me that in the first place. And why you're staying with her."

"That's very complicated, actually."

"Can you go somewhere else so I can talk to her in private?"

"Afraid not. I need to stay close to her."

"You're very stubborn."

"You could say that." Darrak glanced at her. "Eden?"

Eden's stomach churned. She didn't want to involve Ben in this. "Ben, this isn't really a good time. Can we talk later?"

Confusion was plain on the cop's face. "No, we can't. I want to know what the hell is going on here. Why did you tell me Darrak's your brother when he's not?"

"She was trying to protect you from the truth, of course," Darrak said.

Eden clenched her fists. "Darrak. Stop."

"And what truth is that?" Ben's eyes narrowed on the demon. "That you're her lover? Her ex? Her overprotective gay roommate? Stop me any time I'm getting close here."

"The other night at the restaurant," Darrak said. "When you stayed to chat with young Malcolm, what did he tell you? I'm curious."

"How do you even know about that?" Ben rubbed his temples as if they had started to ache.

"I know a lot of things."

"I guess Eden told you, right? Well, that little deluded freak filled me in a bit more about a group he's in. Same thing he was yapping about to you, Eden. Something called the Malleus. Says they fight against evil. Demons and witches and evil spirits."

"Among other things," Darrak confirmed.

Ben eyed him. "Actually, Malcolm gave me a card. Told me to call if I ever wanted to join up. He thought I had potential, can you believe that?" He snorted and his gaze flicked to Eden. "The freak insists that you're possessed by a demon. That's why he's been stalking you. He wants to help. Totally crazy. Just like that serial killer the other day. He said he was possessed, too, didn't he? What the hell is going on in this city? All of a sudden everyone has the same paranoid delusion?"

"Why? Don't you believe in demons?" Darrak asked. "That cross around your neck makes me think you believe in angels. Is it that big of a stretch to think there's more out there unseen by the average human eye?"

"*Darrak*," Eden warned again.

He laughed and it wasn't hard to hear the bitterness there. "Wouldn't want to corrupt your cop's pure mind, huh? Keep him nice and squeaky clean. That's how you like the men in your life, isn't it? Forgot about that for a moment."

Her eyes narrowed. He was baiting her. "Okay, fine. You want to play this game? I'll do it. I don't care how crazy it makes me look."

"Game on," he replied dryly.

She gathered her thoughts as best she could. She hadn't planned on this but she might as well make it good. "Ben . . . the other day, that serial killer. When you shot him, the demon he was possessed with left his body and entered mine. I've been possessed ever since."

Ben stared at her blankly. "What?"

"Literally possessed. But because I have some sort of psychic ability—the same thing that helped me sense the killer was in that closet in the first place—the demon's able to talk to me. He's also able to leave my body and take human form during the day."

"Come on, Eden. This isn't funny."

She clasped her hands together tightly and summoned up the courage to tell him the whole truth. "Darrak's that demon. That's why he needs to stay near me. He's bound to me until I die or I exorcise him."

Ben stared at her for a very long time. Then he laughed nervously. "Okay, I get it. This is some kind of joke. Did the guys at the precinct put you up to this?"

She had to keep trying. It suddenly felt incredibly important for him to believe her. "It's not a joke. It's very real. The other day when you saw Malcolm hitting me at Triple-A he and his mother, Rosa, were trying to perform an exorcism. I tried to stop him before you arrived."

"And why would you want to stop something like that?"

Her eyes flicked to Darrak's.

"Good question," Darrak said. "Yes, Eden, why would you want to stop something like that? Share with the class."

"I—I didn't want to hurt him," she replied. It was the truth, after all. At the time. "He'd convinced me he was a nice demon."

She met and held Darrak's troubled gaze. He didn't say anything.

"Okay, let me get this straight." Ben rubbed his temples. "Darrak here's a demon. He possessed you. You had a chance to get rid of him and you didn't because you didn't want to hurt him because at the time you thought he was . . . nice?"

"That's right."

Ben stared at her for a long moment as if waiting for the punch line. When there wasn't one he shook his head. "I think you're right. I'm going to go now. Leave you two to whatever twisted fantasy you're role-playing." He turned back to the door but Eden was right behind him.

"Wait, I can prove it." She couldn't let him leave like this, thinking she was playing him for some kind of fool. She looked over her shoulder at Darrak, who cocked his head to the side. He had the audacity to look amused at her frenzied explanations.

So much for a future with Ben. She was kissing her chance at a normal relationship with a nice, normal guy good-bye. At least, *this* nice, normal guy.

Ben turned around. "So prove it."

"Yeah, Eden," Darrak said. "Prove it."

He didn't think she could. She wasn't so sure either, but it was worth a try. If only to wipe that smug look off the demon's face.

"I know your true name," she said. "Selina told me."

The smug look was officially history. "No. Eden, don't do it—"

"Darrakayiis." She said it slowly so as to pronounce it perfectly.

Darrak went rigid, his arms straight at his sides. He looked like a soldier awaiting instruction from his drill sergeant. Everything about him was still except his eyes, which focused on her, pleadingly. Begging her not to say anything else.

Eden felt surprised by the immediate reaction a few simple syllables had caused. The power of a name. Selina sure hadn't lied about that.

"I'm waiting," Ben said dryly. He hadn't noticed the change in the room as the power shifted to Eden.

She nervously approached the unmoving demon, his gaze following her every step. She touched his shoulder and upper arm. It felt like stone, his muscles were so tense. She couldn't decide if she felt guilty or pleased by having found out something he'd kept a closely guarded secret.

But now she wanted to find out even more.

"Show me your demon visage," Eden said simply and couldn't help but hear the fear coating every word.

The very next moment, Darrak burst into flame.

➢ NINETEEN ➣

Eden shrieked and leapt back from him. Amber flames coated his entire body, which grew to seven feet tall and broadened to twice his human width. Long, black, curved horns emerged from either side of his now-hairless head and almost touched the ceiling. His eyes were the only thing vaguely recognizable and not covered in the fire.

She clamped a hand over her mouth to prevent herself from screaming.

"The hellfire won't burn you." His voice was deeper, raspier, and a whole lot more frightening now to match his exterior.

"It's really you?" she ventured.

"You wished to see my demon visage, Eden. Here it is."

It took her a moment, but she tentatively stepped closer and couldn't feel any heat coming from him.

"How is it possible?" she asked.

"The fire is part of me—I won't burn you. I promise."

She shakily touched the surface of the golden fire. It felt very warm and dry, as if she was touching sand on a hot beach. It didn't hurt at all. She forced herself to press closer until she felt his hot skin underneath—now hard and rough to the touch, but solid and real.

"Get away from her!" Ben yelled from behind. "Don't hurt her!"

"Eden, you need to let me go back to my human form," Darrak said. "Please."

"H-how?" she stuttered.

"Give me permission."

She looked up at him, this demon who stood in front of her in all his hellish glory. He looked nothing like the Darrak she'd gotten to know over the last few days. He sounded nothing like him. But it was Darrak. They were the same.

"Okay, fine. You have my p-permission to return to human form."

Immediately the flames extinguished and he returned to his normal size—still over six feet and muscular, but much smaller and less intimidating than as a full demon.

His handsome face was filled with pain, but she wasn't sure if it was emotional or physical. "I really didn't want you to see me like that. I can imagine it was a bit . . . jarring and terrifying."

Her hand still rested on his chest, now clad in his usual black T-shirt.

"Jarring, yes." She nodded. "But . . . surprisingly enough, I wasn't all that terrified."

He raised an eyebrow. "Now you're the one who's lying."

She shook her head. "No lie."

He studied her with disbelief. "Were you drinking heavily this morning when I wasn't looking?"

"Maybe that would explain it."

"Step the hell away from her now," Ben growled.

Eden turned and her breath caught when she saw that Ben, who still stood over by the door, had his gun out and aimed at Darrak. "Ben, no. Put the gun down."

"You convinced me that he's a demon. Funny how seeing is believing."

"Ben, it's okay."

"That—that *thing* almost killed you."

"He didn't. It's fine."

"Fine? No, it's not fine. Not in any sense of the word."

Darrak held his hands out to either side of himself. "I mean Eden no harm."

"Shut up." Ben swore under his breath, his brow was furrowed with stress. He lowered the weapon a little. "He was right. Malcolm—he was right about everything. You're a demon."

Darrak pushed Eden away from him and took a step toward the cop. "Put down the gun before you hurt somebody."

"You're dangerous. I saw it with my own eyes. I need to stop you."

Ben raised his gun.

"No, Ben—" Eden lurched forward to try to stop him before this got out of control, but it was too late. He'd already pulled the trigger.

Eden gasped as the bullet tore through her chest. It felt as if she'd been hit with a baseball bat. Pain exploded inside of her.

The force of the bullet made her stagger backward into Darrak's arms. She gasped for breath, but every inhale felt like a red-hot knife slicing through her lungs. Her vision began to whiten at the edges.

"Damn it!" Ben moved forward, horror etched on his face. "Eden! Oh, my God. Why did you get in the way?"

"Stay back!" Darrak hissed at him. "You've done enough."

She looked up at Darrak's strained face. He'd placed her gently down on the floor and he pressed his hands over her wound.

Her breathing was ragged and it hurt with every inhale. "Darrak . . . if I d-die . . . what will you . . . what will you do?"

"You're not going to die."

"I'm sorry . . ."

His brows knitted together. "For what?"

"For not trusting you."

He actually laughed shallowly at that, but there was no humor in it. "Can't say I've given you much of a reason to up until now."

"But . . . you're . . . you're my . . . guardian angel . . . I shouldn't have forgotten that."

"This is no time for insults. Shh, Eden. It's going to be okay."

She touched his hands he held over the wound. She didn't have much longer. She knew she was going to die.

Would she see her mom? Caroline Riley had never seemed like somebody who'd want to hang out in Heaven if she was given any choice in the matter. But maybe . . .

Suddenly, she felt an unusual warmth where Darrak's hands were. "What are you d-doing?"

His jaw was tight, his forehead creased in concentration. "This isn't a simple cat scratch, but I'll give it everything I have left."

A wave of heat flooded into her chest. For a moment it hurt even more than the gunshot wound itself—a sensation of all her internal organs lighting on fire—and she cried out in pain, but then the pain lessened and she felt her chest begin to tingle as Darrak healed her, mending and knitting her wound.

His breathing became more erratic and his hands began to shake.

"Okay," he said after a minute had passed. "That does it for my reserve of power. And then some."

She propped herself up on her elbows and looked down at her chest. There was a large patch of blood on her shirt and she touched it tentatively. There was no pain anymore. Surprisingly, she felt even better than she had before and strangely energized. A quick glance underneath her shirt showed undamaged skin. She looked up at Darrak with wide eyes. He'd healed her.

But he wasn't looking at her anymore. He was looking at the cop, and there were now amber flames behind his furious gaze. Before she could say another word, he'd rushed over to

Ben and slammed him into the wall. The mirror on one side of the door fell to the floor and shattered.

"You almost killed her," Darrak snarled. "Give me one good reason why I shouldn't tear your head off right now and shove it down the garbage disposal."

Ben didn't reply. He simply looked from the furious demon over to Eden, who scrambled up from the floor as fast as she could.

"Darrak, stop it! Let go of him."

Darrak finally pushed away from Ben and staggered back a few feet. His pale face was shiny with sweat and he looked ill and weak. He covered his stomach with his hand and leaned over as if wracked with pain, his chest heaving.

"Eden—" Ben turned to her, shock and grief in his gaze. "I'm so sorry that happened. I—I can't believe what I'm seeing here—but it's true. You're in danger. You have to come with me. Away from that—that *monster*."

She shook her head. "You need to go."

"Eden—"

"Ben, listen to me. You need to forget what you saw here. It's better for you that way."

He frowned as if he didn't understand what she was saying. "He's a demon."

"I know that."

"Come with me. Please."

"I can't."

"You want to stay with him even . . . knowing what he is?" His dark blue eyes clearly showed his shock.

She swallowed hard. "Yes. And I want you to leave now."

He stared at her for a full minute, perhaps waiting for her to change her mind, before he shakily holstered his gun under his leather jacket. He cast a last glance at Darrak, who was now hunched over against the wall by the coat closet.

"Fine." He nodded with one jerk of his head. He absently ran his fingers over the cross he wore. "But don't say I didn't offer to help you."

He turned, opened the door, and left the apartment. Eden rushed to Darrak's side. He was slowly sinking to the ground.

He'd grown even paler. His eyes were glazing over.

"What's happening to you right now?" she demanded. "What happens if you lose all your energy?"

"You get . . . your wish." He forced a weak smile. "I'll . . . vanish into thin air and be . . . out of your life forever. Won't take long now."

That's what she wanted. That's what she planned to get Malcolm to do for her tomorrow.

"Take some of my energy," she said.

He shook his head. "No, Eden . . . I need too much right now."

"I don't care."

"You don't know what you're saying."

"Sure I do." She crouched in front of him.

"Let me fade. I'm . . . close now. Only another minute and—"

She grabbed hold of his face and kissed him hard on his mouth.

It served two purposes. It shut him the hell up, and it opened herself up for him to dip into her newly restored energy.

It was like an endlessly rotating circle. He healed her. She healed him. Rinse and repeat.

He didn't resist for very long. He pressed his mouth against hers and began to absorb her energy. After a few moments, she started to feel light-headed. She opened her mouth to the kiss, knowing full well that this was the same demon who minutes ago had horns and was covered in gold flames in the middle of her apartment. An *archdemon*. A title that made people who knew what that meant shudder in fear like Malcolm had, or hightail it right out of town like Leena.

But Eden wasn't afraid of him. She thought she would be— she had every damn reason to be—but she wasn't afraid. At least not at the moment.

She could have gotten rid of him once and for all. The opportunity had presented itself, and she hadn't taken it. Instead she was metaphysically making out with the demon on the linoleum floor of her kitchenette. And it felt way too good.

Maybe she *had* been drinking heavily that morning. At least that would be a reasonable explanation for her current behavior.

The longer the kiss went on, the weaker she felt, and it wasn't just because Darrak was an amazing kisser.

She remembered what he'd told her the last time he'd taken some of her energy.

"The problem is that the energy I've tasted of yours is very . . . what's a good word to use here? Irresistible. Delicious. Addictive. *Any of those would do."*

"My energy is tasty?" she'd asked.

"Yes. Very. Therefore I can't take too much or I might not be able to stop myself."

But he did stop himself. After another minute Darrak finally broke off their kiss. He looked totally renewed and alive. He smiled at her for a split second until he saw the expression on her face. She was the one who was fading now.

And fading fast.

"Eden . . ."

"I'm okay." She shakily rose to her feet. A wave of dizziness came over her and she braced her hand against the wall.

"I took too much, didn't I?"

"Maybe just a smidge," she replied, just as her legs gave out completely. She felt his firm arms come around her a moment before she would have hit the floor.

Everything went black.

When Eden woke up, she smelled lasagna.

She raised her head from the sofa where she currently lay to look over at the kitchenette. Darrak was removing a piece of lasagna—courtesy of the departed Leena—from the microwave oven.

"Are you hungry?" she asked.

His shoulders tensed. "This is for you. I sensed you were about to wake up and thought you should have something waiting when you did."

He brought it over to her with a fork and placed the plate on the coffee table in front of her. Then he took a few steps back to give her space.

She felt nervous with him standing there watching her after everything that had happened, but reached forward to have a few bites of the pasta dish. Leena hadn't been kidding. She really knew how to cook.

A glance at the clock on her wall unit told her it was almost four o'clock. "Guess I've been out for a while, huh?"

"I took too much energy from you. I couldn't control myself."

"It's understandable."

He barked out a laugh. "Is it?"

"You were in rough shape." She pushed the plate away from her. Then she started folding the afghan that Darrak had covered her with while she slept. The demon stood with his back against the breakfast bar. Even though he looked strong and energized, his face was still as pale as it had been when he'd almost faded away to nothing. "You still don't look so great."

"I've made a decision."

"Oh, yeah?"

He nodded and pulled a business card out of his pocket. "I found this in your purse. Malcolm gave you his phone number when you saw him last night?"

She stood up from the sofa, moved toward him, and snatched the card out of his hand. "You went through my purse when I was unconscious?"

"I went through your closets yesterday. It was only a matter of time before I got to your purse. I'm eyeing your medicine cabinet and lingerie drawer next." There was a momentary spark of humor in his blue eyes at her outraged expression. "You need to call him."

"And why would I want to do that?"

"You already intimated you'd scheduled my exorcism. I assume it's through the boy wonder."

When she didn't say anything he must have taken that to be a confirmation.

"Why didn't he already do it?" he asked.

Eden tried to think of a reasonable explanation for everything but decided that the truth was the best idea, all things considered. Otherwise, she'd be a bit of a hypocrite, wouldn't she? "He couldn't do it when you were dampened. And then when he found out you're an archdemon he had to go ask his superiors how to . . ."

"How best to squash me like a cockroach from Hell?" he finished.

"He didn't put it that way, but that was the general idea."

"Call him and tell him he doesn't have to ask anybody anything. I won't fight him. He can come over right now and we can finish this. I'm sure he'll be thrilled to bag an archdemon. He might get a medal or something for his efforts."

She exhaled. "I'm so glad to hear you feel that way. Could you please be a doll and bring me the phone?"

He stiffened, then walked over to the dinette table, grabbed the cordless phone, and brought it over to her.

She took it from him. "Thanks so much. I wonder if he'd mind picking me up a coffee on his way over?"

Darrak shrugged. "I don't know. You should ask him."

She glared at the demon. "You don't really think I'm going to call him right now, do you?"

His jaw was tight and there was no humor in his expression. "I can't think of a single reason why you *wouldn't* call him. Don't you want to be free of me?"

"To say it's been a goal of mine would be putting it mildly."

"So do it, already. This is your chance."

She placed the phone down on the dinette table and put her hand on her hip. "You saved my life."

"Then I almost sucked it out through your mouth. And I'm draining you of energy every single day you're possessed with me. Everything I am, everything I do, is killing you."

She cringed. "We'll figure out another way."

"There is no other way. Call Malcolm. He wants to help you. He *can* help you. Even though I'm corporeal right now, I'm still bound to you, so don't fight him. You need to open yourself up to him the same way you opened yourself up to me earlier."

She looked down at the phone. "Are you saying I need to make out with him? He's a little too young for me."

He grabbed the receiver and pointed at her with it. "This isn't funny."

"Darrak, let's talk about this."

He sighed with frustration. "What's there to talk about? I lied to you over and over. Shamelessly. I'm an evil archdemon from the belly of Hell who turns nice girls into black witches. And I'm killing you, little by little, even without trying just by my very existence. What's the problem here?" He thrust the phone out to her.

She didn't take it from him. "What happened to your self-protective instinct?"

"I'm fighting it as we speak. I might start crying like a baby in a moment if you don't take this phone from me. But I know this is the right thing to do. Just do it, would you?"

That made her actually laugh out loud. It was a small burst of hysteria that surprised even her. "The badass, evil archdemon is demanding that I call somebody to exorcise him so he doesn't hurt me anymore. Is that it?"

He glowered. "That's pretty much it."

"What happened to the whole 'I've been infused with humanity and I've changed to be a good boy now' story?"

His face was expressionless. "All lies, of course. I'm evil

incarnate. You saw what I look like in demon form. Did that look like a fluffy, helpful bunny to you?"

"No, it certainly did not. Bunnies don't have horns or hell-fire going on."

"Then . . . there you go."

"There's one problem with what you're saying, though," she said.

He sighed again. "And what's that?"

"I believe that you've changed." She stepped closer to him and put her hand on his chest and looked up at his tense face. "Because you have. I don't know what you were really like before, but you're not evil anymore. And the fact that you'd be willing to sacrifice yourself to save my pathetic little life is all the proof I need."

He swore. "Fine. I'm going to have to call him myself."

"I'm not giving you Malcolm's card."

He smiled thinly at her. "You don't have to. I memorized the number."

He started dialing.

"I can stop you if I use your real name, can't I?" she said.

He looked at her. "You can. But just remember I've killed all but one human who ever had that sort of power over me."

"I already used your name earlier, remember?"

"You did."

"So kill me."

He jabbed his index finger at her. "You're crazy. I think I get it now. You've gone completely nutty as a fruitcake. I'm surprised it took this long, actually. There have been humans who've seen my demon visage and gone insane with fear at my greatness."

She rolled her eyes. "Okay, you're obviously very full of yourself. It was impressive, sure. But let's not get carried away."

"Crazy." He shook his head and started dialing again. "So are you going to use my real name to stop me?"

"No."

"Then you're going to let me do this?"

"No."

"Then what are you—?"

She kissed him.

⇒ TWENTY ⇐

Darrak dropped the phone.

It had been the reaction she'd hoped for.

He grabbed her shoulders and pushed her back from him, his expression filled with confusion at her strange behavior. "What the hell was that for?"

"I had to stop you from making a serious mistake."

"A mistake?" he repeated, eyeing her warily. "Maybe I'll drain you of the rest of your energy. That would be a mistake. For *you*."

"I don't think you will."

"Then you're very naïve. And you're asking for trouble."

She tried to touch him but he grabbed her wrists firmly, pushing her easily back up against the wall, effectively trapping her in place.

"You're playing a dangerous game, Eden," he whispered in her ear. "Now that you know the truth about me. Now that you know what I'm capable of. Are you feeling reckless all of a sudden? The brush with death wasn't enough for you?"

She inhaled sharply at the feel of his extremely warm body pressed against hers. It made it difficult to think straight.

This was the same demon who'd been seven feet of horns and fire only hours ago. The one who had, admittedly, nearly drained her of all of her energy. Sure, he might have changed somewhat since his archdemon days, he might be charming and handsome and easy to talk to in human form, but he was still dangerous. She knew it.

He could hurt her so easily if he wanted to.

But she truly believed he didn't want to.

There was one way to find out for sure.

"Darrak . . ." Her mouth was only inches from his.

"Why did you have to start this?" His voice sounded strained. "I gave you the chance to end this. You really are crazy."

She nodded. "Maybe you're right."

He'd released her, but hadn't stepped back. She brought her hands up to his face and looked into his eyes.

Then, without another word, he kissed her hard enough to make her gasp against his lips. She slid her fingers into his dark hair, and his hands moved down to the small of her back and over the curve of her butt, pulling her even closer to him.

"Eden, please," he managed after a moment. "This is a mistake. You shouldn't be with me. You should be with your golden boy. He won't hurt you."

"He shot me."

Darrak blinked. "Well, other than the near-fatal gunshot wound and his tendency to use violence to solve problems, he only wants what's best for you. I see that now."

She nodded. "You're right. But there's only one problem."

"What?"

"I don't want him. I want you."

"You want me," he repeated with disbelief. "But don't you—"

She pulled his face down to meet hers again and kissed him. After a moment, he effortlessly picked her up without breaking the kiss for a moment.

The next thing she felt other than Darrak's lips against hers was the softness of her mattress against her back. He'd taken her to her bedroom—all of fifteen feet away.

Okay, so her big plan of kissing him to get him to forget about calling Malcolm had worked.

Like, *really* well.

"Tell me to stop and I will," Darrak said, looking down at her and bracing himself on his forearms.

Instead, she pulled the black T-shirt off, over his head, and ran her hands over the hard, muscled planes of his chest and abdomen before her hand drifted lower.

He sucked in a breath. *"Eden."*

She smiled up at him. "Very human right now, aren't you?"

"At this very moment, excruciatingly so." His gaze burned into hers. "You're playing with danger."

"Is that what I'm playing with?" Her smile grew. "Thanks for the clarification."

He groaned, then crushed his mouth against hers. She felt strangely victorious to have broken through all of his annoying protests.

Ten points to her.

And then, as he stripped her clothes off piece by piece and slowly kissed every inch of her body, she was reminded of the previous morning when she'd stopped herself, embarrassed at the extent of her need for this man she barely knew.

This *demon*.

But she did know him. Even though it had only been a few days, she knew him better than anyone else she'd known in her entire life.

And this time when he finally entered her, it wasn't because he'd turned to black smoke first.

"Eden . . . you feel so good . . ." he breathed as their bodies moved together. "But I don't want to hurt you."

His dark hair felt so soft sliding through her fingers. "You're not. Believe me."

She thought he wanted to say something else, but he didn't. His blue eyes bore into hers. There was none of the cocky, smart-ass flirtation from when she'd woken to find him in her bed before. He was serious. He desperately didn't want to hurt her. Was he afraid of being so swept away with passion that he couldn't control himself with her?

That was as hot as it was scary.

But despite his multiple warnings, she trusted him more than he trusted himself. And she now knew she wanted this—wanted *him*—since nearly the first moment she saw him.

Maybe she *was* crazy.

She'd been closed off before, afraid of trusting, afraid of being hurt after everything that had happened in her life—abusive boyfriends, cheating fiancés, unreliable mothers, bad and unfulfilling jobs—but Darrak was different.

In more than the obvious ways.

Despite being a demon—an archdemon—he was also her guardian angel, her friend, and somebody she cared about despite herself. He was a part of her.

And now he was her lover.

Even though he didn't realize it, when he possessed her it actually felt really good. But that was nothing compared to the real deal.

She let herself open up to Darrak completely, body and soul, in a way she'd never opened up to anyone before. She ran her hands over his beautiful body. Smooth, hot—very hot—skin over hard muscle. She kissed him over and over to show him that she wasn't afraid of him hurting her. Because he wouldn't.

She moaned his name—well, his nickname, anyhow.

And then something really strange happened as Darrak cried out her name, his breath hot against her lips.

A glow of amber light moved from Darrak to her, and it surrounded her body like a golden aura. It burned into her—as hot as Darrak's skin, as hot as his mouth as he took hers again. He didn't seem to notice the light.

Then suddenly the light entered Eden and disappeared completely.

What the hell?

"Eden," Darrak murmured against her lips as he kissed her for a long time and stroked her auburn hair back from her face. She wrapped her arms around him and promptly forgot about the light.

"That is my name," she said with a smile.

He brushed his lips against hers and grinned. "The garden of paradise."

"My mother had an interesting sense of humor."

"I think it's fairly appropriate."

"You do, do you?"

He lay, breathing hard, wrapped in her arms for a moment more before she felt him suddenly tense up. Then he pushed up from the bed and looked down at her.

"Something wrong?" she asked tentatively.

His expression was suddenly grim. "Eden . . . this . . . shouldn't have happened between us."

She frowned. "Not something I really want to hear at this very moment."

"Sorry. You're right." He kissed her softly, and then sat up and grabbed for his clothes.

"Then what do you mean?"

"It's just . . . my history." His jaw clenched. "You said Selina told you I was an incubus, right?"

"She did," she said cautiously. "She said incubi drained their victims of power. But you're not an incubus anymore, and you didn't drain me at all that time, so if that's what you're worried about, don't be."

"You're okay?"

She shook her head. "I feel fine."

"Good." He nodded firmly, then pulled his T-shirt on over his head. "When I was exclusively an incubus, I did drain women's energy after seducing them to increase my own power level."

She raised an eyebrow and pulled the sheets up over herself. "Do I really want to know this right now?"

"Probably not. But you should. After the first step was over, I'd pick and choose the best souls to bring down to Hell to be part of Lucifer's harem. He has a very large harem of women. And men. About the size of New York City, actually."

She felt herself pale, then she sat up and drew her knees up to her chest. "That doesn't sound like much fun."

"Oh, but it was." He didn't sound happy about it. He sat stiffly on the edge of her bed. "I had a completely different idea of fun back then."

"Why are you telling me this?"

"Let's just say that I've never . . . been with anyone . . . just for the sake of being with them before and without any ulterior motives. Sex was my duty and a lot of women came to regret their decision to be with me. I figure it's only a matter of time before you join those ranks."

"You think I'm going to regret this?"

He swallowed. "Yes, I do."

"You obviously don't know anything about my ex-boyfriends."

"This is different."

She tried to figure out what the hell he was trying to say. He didn't want to hurt her. She got that. "Okay, so you were an incubus. Not exactly a normal sexual history, I'll give you that. But again, that was then and this is now."

His jaw remained tight. "The last woman I had sex with became a black witch."

"You slept with Selina?" She wasn't sure why that took her by surprise. Also, there was that strange jab of jealousy again when it came to the beautiful witch.

"I did. At her command."

"Okay. So you're saying we should have used a condom considering your skanky sexual history?"

That almost earned her a smile breaking through his now rigid expression. "Believe it or not, that's one thing you don't have to fear from me. Demons are immune to all human diseases."

Well, that was good news, at least.

"So you wish that hadn't happened," she began.

He took her hands in his. "I'm—I'm just worried something bad's going to happen to you. It's like a gut instinct."

She touched his face and slid her fingers into his dark hair. "Don't worry about me."

"I can't help it. It seems to be my new job."

"I'm going to call her," Eden said firmly. She wanted to steer this conversation into a different direction. A practical one.

His brows drew together. "Who? Selina? You know how to contact her?"

She nodded. "We're going to go talk to her face-to-face."

He studied her warily. "You think that's a good idea?"

"You're not the only one who's changed. So has she. I think we can reason with her."

"If you say so."

"I do." Holding the bedsheet to her chest she leaned over and grabbed the phone from the side of her bed. She had Darrak retrieve the book she'd purchased last night with Selina's phone number inside. Darrak, now fully dressed, sat silently next to her as she dialed.

After three rings, the witch picked up.

"Selina Shaw here."

"Selina . . . it's Eden. We met last night at your signing."

"I remember. Where can I meet you?"

"I do want to meet, but not for the reason you think."

"I can destroy the demon for you, Eden. You'll be much better off."

"We want to talk to you."

"We?" Selina repeated. "Don't tell me he's been filling your head with more of his lies."

"No. But we need to—"

"You need to read my books, Eden. That's what you need to do. They will change the way you allow men to treat you by finding your inner power. No more manipulations. We don't need men at all. We can rely on ourselves for everything. My website has my entire backlist. Everything is also available in electronic and audio versions."

Eden tried to remain patient and calm. It wasn't easy. "I appreciate your concern. Really. But you're wrong about him. You had a change of heart about giving yourself over to black magic. Darrak . . ." She looked at him. "Darrak's that way, too. He's different than you remember. Meet with us and find out that it's the truth."

"You want me to break his curse."

"Give us five minutes of your time, then make your decision."

"And if my decision is that he's still a monster and not worthy of your charity?"

"Then that's your decision."

It was quiet on Selina's end of the line for so long Eden thought she'd hung up. "I'll meet you somewhere populated. But if there's any funny business then I'll reduce both of you into a pile of ashes. Got it?"

There was no humor in the witch's voice. She wasn't kidding.

"I got it." Eden gave her the address for the Hot Stuff coffee bar.

"I'll be there in one hour," Selina said tightly. "And you have five minutes to convince me the archdemon's become a Boy Scout. And then, maybe, I'll consider breaking the curse if only to be done with the both of you once and for all."

"Thank you so much. I have to say, I'm surprised you agreed to this."

"I'm feeling charitable today. I just got booked on *Oprah* again."

"Totally understandable. I haven't started reading it yet, but the book looks really fantastic."

"Don't suck up. It's not attractive. I'll see you in an hour." She hung up.

It took a moment for Eden's heart to come back to a regular pace as she switched off the phone. "Did you hear that?"

"Half of it." Darrak exhaled. "I can't believe it."

"Believe it." Eden said, placing a hand on his firm chest. "She's going to hear us out. Prepare to be on your best behavior. And it would probably be best if you don't try to kill her and tear out her heart."

"Noted."

He should have looked elated at this news, but instead he looked worried.

That made two of them.

What would happen if Selina decided to break the curse? Darrak would have to leave. And that's what she wanted all along, wasn't it?

Of course it was. She didn't want to die.

It didn't matter what had happened between them, there was no place in Eden's life for a demon . . . reformed or otherwise.

And that's just the way it was.

An hour later, Eden watched a taxi pull up in front of Hot Stuff and Selina get out of the back, staring at the exterior of the café warily before she entered.

There was a buzz of activity in there—it seemed busier than usual. There were probably fifteen other patrons enjoying a late afternoon refreshment. The pastries and sandwiches were kept under a glass cabinet by the cashier. Stools were set up along the main coffee bar itself, and that was where most people were seated. The espresso machine whistled and gurgled as it coughed up caffeinated beverages at stiff prices.

Eden and Darrak sat at a table in the farthest corner in the back. The more privacy they could get, the better. For some reason, Darrak hadn't even made eye contact with her since they'd left the apartment.

He felt guilty about what happened between them. And even though she understood why he felt that way, it didn't exactly make her feel like a million bucks.

A strange sensation crackled over Eden's arms as Selina tentatively approached. What was that? Electricity?

Selina played with the gray-stoned pendant around her neck as she eyed them each in turn with anything but friendliness in her green eyes. Darrak stood and held his hands, palms up, in a disarming manner.

"I mean you no harm."

Selina eyed him suspiciously. "Why do I find that incredibly hard to believe?"

He sat back down in his seat. "I'm just here to talk to you."

Selina remained standing. "Funny, I could have sworn you wanted a great deal more from me today than just talk."

Her distrustful gaze moved to Eden and a moment later it changed to something else. Something unreadable.

"What have you done?" she asked quietly.

Eden's eyes widened and that electric feeling again crackled along her skin. "What?"

"Something's changed since last night. I sensed it the moment I entered this place. But . . ." She looked around as if trying to pinpoint the source of her distress before her attention returned to Eden. "It's you."

"Me?"

Selina's red lips curled back from her teeth with disgust. "You allowed yourself to be physically seduced by a member of Lucifer's court?"

Eden stared at her blankly. "I—I . . . uh . . ."

"You fornicated with this demon," Selina snarled under her breath.

Fornicated? That was such an unpleasant word.

Eden cleared her throat and felt her cheeks flush. *Terrific.* Had a magical memo gone out that she'd jumped Darrak's bones? She looked around at the coffee bar, but no one was paying any attention to them. Despite the subject matter, their voices were hushed.

"That's actually none of your business," she said.

Selina laughed humorlessly. "I wish that was true." She glared at Darrak. "You should be ashamed of yourself. She's just a human."

His expression didn't change. "Eden's right. This is none of your business."

She shook her head. "You're as deceptive as ever, aren't you, demon?"

"I never deceived you, Selina," he said evenly. "You're the one who summoned me and forced me to give you the power you so desired."

"And I've regretted it every day since."

He curled his fingers around the mug of hot coffee in front of him. "Doesn't look like you've suffered much over the years."

"Doesn't it?" She touched her pendant. "My soul is black."

"Looks more like a middling gray to me."

Eden looked at the jewelry as well. "What are you talking about?"

Selina let out a shaky breath. "I wear this special amulet—it tells when the wearer's soul is in danger. The blacker it is the more I must control my magic or else lose myself to the darkness completely."

"So it's kind of like a mood ring?" Eden asked.

Selina fisted the stone and squeezed. "Oh, absolutely. The gauge of my damaged soul is exactly like a mood ring. My, aren't you smart?"

Darrak's knuckles whitened on the edge of the table. "Eden has only started to learn that there is more to the world than meets the eye."

"Her ignorance is obvious. Especially when it comes to you, demon. I guess she's been charmed by your handsome face and hasn't seen your demon visage yet."

"You still think I'm handsome after all this time?" Darrak asked dryly. "Please stop. I'm blushing."

"I've seen him," Eden said. "The demon him."

The witch looked surprised. "I don't believe you."

Eden nodded. "He's a lot larger, he has these big-ass horns, and he's covered in hellfire. Not exactly male model material." She glanced at Darrak. "No offense."

"None taken."

Selina blinked. "I stand corrected. But I can't believe you have accepted him. That you . . . fornicated with him."

There was that word again. Eden winced.

"Let's stay on topic," Eden suggested.

The witch crossed her arms. "My life is perfect right now. I don't want to do anything to risk that. I destroyed you, demon."

"Well, you gave it your best shot." Darrak didn't sound friendly.

"I was such a newbie back then. I should have made sure that the job was done correctly."

"Water under the bridge."

"It is?"

He shifted in his seat. "I'm trying to be diplomatic. But being incorporeal and voiceless for three hundred years has a tendency to weigh heavily on one's mind."

"And yet you have a body right now. A very fine one."

"Are you coming on to me? I think that's a bit inappropriate at the moment, Selina. Given our history."

She scowled at him. "I don't even know how it's possible for you to have a body. I destroyed your previous one."

He visibly tensed. "Haven't forgotten that. Believe me."

"So, what's changed? Is it her?" Selina nodded at Eden.

"I believe so."

"There's something about Eden's psychic energy that makes it possible for you to draw enough strength from her to take corporeal form during the day. But at night you have to possess her body."

"Insightful as ever, Selina."

Eden kept her attention on the mug of hot chocolate in front of her.

Selina smiled thinly. "You're trying to resist the urge to strangle me with my purse strap right now, aren't you?"

"I was eyeing my coffee stir stick as the weapon, actually. It could do a great deal of damage in the right hands." He looked at Eden. "Despite Selina's ability to work magic and her . . . well, moldy Swiss cheese soul, a black witch is still essentially human. Despite her potential for immortality, her body is vulnerable to all kinds of damage."

Eden didn't like how he said that. There was the threat of true violence behind it. She wondered then, and not for the first time, if it had been a mistake to bring these two back together after all this time.

Oh well. Too late now.

"Yes, the only way to break his curse is if I do it willingly or he kills me with his own hands," Selina said. "So excuse me if I'm not terribly comfortable at the moment."

"Selina, please sit down," Eden said.

"I'd rather stand."

"It looks a bit conspicuous."

"Like I care. I thought I told you that you had five minutes. I believe that time is nearly up." Her eyes narrowed. "I feel your weakness, demon. Not quite the same as you were all those years ago, are you?"

"No, I've changed. I'm much more pathetic and needy now. I believe that's the point of this meeting."

"Then I'll give you another minute to convince me to break your curse. Beg if you like."

Darrak nodded grimly. "I can do that if I have to."

"Oh. My. God." A voice from Eden's right exclaimed. It was Nancy, the barista, who must have just come on shift. "Selina Shaw. *Here* at Hot Stuff. I can't believe this."

"Wonderful," Selina said sarcastically under her breath. "A fan. Just what I need right now. I should have done a camouflage spell on this table the moment I walked in here."

Nancy rushed over. "Can I get you a coffee, Ms. Shaw? A biscotti?"

"No, thank you."

"Perhaps a blueberry scone? I can heat it in the microwave for you and put some butter on it. Are you lactose intolerant at all?"

Selina sighed. "I'm going to decline. But I appreciate the offer."

She beamed at the writer and then looked at Eden. "And look at you, talking to Selina Shaw herself. If it wasn't for me you would never have found her in the first place. And now you're friends!"

"Found me?" Selina asked. "You're the one who helped them locate me?"

"Yes! Can you believe they'd never heard of your books before? Eden never would have known about your signing last night if I hadn't told her."

Selina smiled. "Go now. Before I tear out your intestines and stomp on them with my new Ferragamo pumps."

"Sure thing. If you do decide you need anything to eat or drink, just holler." She sauntered away, happily oblivious to the threat of evisceration she'd just received.

Selina turned to leave. "I shouldn't have come here."

"No. Please, stay," Eden said. "Darrak's changed. Just like you."

She froze. "He's nothing like me."

"Having to possess humans all of these years has infused him with humanity."

Her eyebrows raised. "Is that what you think has happened?"

"It is," Darrak confirmed.

She raised an eyebrow. "I thought I sensed something oddly human about you. For a moment I thought it was simply residue from your recent and ill-advised horizontal romp with this girl."

"What makes you think we were horizontal?" Darrak's lips twitched.

She glared at him. "Do not make light of this."

Darrak's grin widened at her outrage. "Don't be jealous. It's not becoming to a woman of your age."

"Jealous is the last thing I am right now."

"Look, Selina. Here it is. You summoned me years ago. You sucked all the energy out of me you could possibly get and left me an empty husk. Then you tried to destroy me completely."

"You were going to kill me. Do you deny that, demon?"

His smile vanished. "Not for a moment. I don't take kindly to being summoned and forced to do things against my will."

She put her hands on her hips. "Forced? You didn't seem to mind my attentions at the time. In fact, you welcomed my body like the horny little ex-incubus you are."

Eden considered getting up to grab one of those blueberry scones Nancy mentioned. Anywhere to escape this extra-uncomfortable part of the conversation.

Darrak's blue eyes narrowed. "That was a long time ago, *witch*."

"If you hadn't tried to kill me I wouldn't have had to destroy you."

"You should have released me when you had the chance."

"But I didn't. And here we are reliving the good old times in a place that serves pastries and cappuccino. Now what?"

"Now you break my curse. You've changed. I've changed. We can both have a future here."

She eyed him for a moment. "Have you convinced this foolish woman that you're in love with her?"

He flicked a momentary glance at Eden, who was now anxiously watching their conversation like it was a supernatural-infused tennis game. "She has nothing to do with what happened between us."

"You honestly think that?" Selina sighed. "Eden, be very careful with him. I thought he loved me, too, once. But he didn't."

"Can we please try to stay on subject here?" Eden said tightly, disturbed equally by the talk about love and destruction.

His jaw was tight. "If you don't break my curse, I will eventually drain the life completely out of Eden and she will die."

"Well aware of that. But why I should care?"

"Because if you're the nice self-help-book-writing witch you say you are, then you should care if someone lives or dies."

"I never said I was nice." Selina touched her pendant. "I said I didn't want to lose my soul completely to the darkness. And I would hate for someone else to have the same struggles

I've had all these years. I would have warned you last night, Eden. But now it's too late, isn't it?"

"What are you talking about?" Eden asked.

Her eyes widened. "You really don't know, do you?"

"Know what?" She didn't like the look on the witch's face. Especially since it was directed at her.

Selina turned to Darrak. "Can't you even sense it? Are you that much of a fool?"

Darrak frowned at her, confusion crossing his expression. He looked at Eden and searched her face until a glimmer of clarity came into his widening eyes. "It's not possible."

"I sensed it the moment I got here," she said matter-of-factly.

"Damn you, Selina." His jaw clenched. "This is all your fault, isn't it?"

The witch crossed her arms. "You only have yourself to blame."

Darrak's expression looked like it might shatter. "I knew something bad would come of it because of what I am . . . but . . . I didn't know what. Eden . . . I'm so sorry."

Eden felt so confused by whatever they were saying, it was like she'd walked into a foreign movie halfway through. "Can somebody please explain what the hell you're talking about?"

Selina finally sat down next to her. She took Eden's hand in hers and squeezed it. "Last night when you spoke with me, I told you that I'd summoned the demon and done a spell so that he would give me enough power to become a black witch."

"I remember."

"That spell was never broken."

"And what does that mean?"

"With this spell, a woman must willingly have sex with a demon in order to gain that power—the same dark magic I try not to use so I don't destroy my soul completely. I summoned the demon specifically so I could have sex with him and become a black witch."

Every word burrowed into Eden's brain. Everything Selina

said started to connect and make sense—and then it hit her like a thunderbolt of clarity.

Eden had willingly had sex with Darrak. *Very* willingly.

"So this means . . ." she began.

"You're now a black witch as well." Selina smiled without humor. "Welcome to the family."

⇛ TWENTY-ONE ⇚

There was silence at the table. The coffee bar around them continued to buzz with activity. The warm smell of baked goods still pleasantly hung in the air. The cash register dinged as someone made a purchase.

And Eden's entire existence took a graceful swan dive into a swimming pool full of crap.

"So, demon," Selina continued, "if you've really changed as much as you're trying to make me believe, it goes without saying that unless you decide you want to corrupt more of this poor woman's soul, you can never touch her sexually again. Hope that won't be a problem for you."

"Break the spell, Selina," Darrak said darkly.

"What about your curse?"

"One thing at a time."

The amber glow she'd all but forgotten about when she and Darrak had been together physically . . .

It was the magic settling over her, entering her, changing her. Making her into something different.

Eden was a black witch because she'd had sex with Darrak.

If Hell had created an STD, this would definitely be it.

"What do I do now?" she asked, stunned.

"Can you feel it?" Selina asked, searching her face. "The magic inside you now?"

Eden shook her head. "I don't feel anything."

"Concentrate."

She did. And she sensed a bit of that electricity she'd felt earlier. A warm flush of power permeating her skin. "I think I can feel it. And it feels kind of . . . good?"

Darrak swore, gripped the edge of the table, and looked ready to tear it apart with his bare hands. "It's not good. Nothing about this is good."

Selina looked at him skeptically. "You mean you had no idea this might happen?"

"I—I didn't know *this* would happen."

"But you thought something bad would happen, right? And yet you did it anyhow." Selina shook her head. "*Men*. Always thinking about pleasure before practicality."

Eden looked blankly at the both of them.

Selina laughed. "I can barely believe you're the same archdemon I summoned. I'd think you'd be thrilled to have corrupted yet another human soul."

Flames entered his gaze. "You need to fix this."

Her smile disappeared. "I can't. What's happened to Eden isn't a spell I can break. It's the *result* of a spell. Just like what happened to me."

Eden's brain was flailing about, attempting to piece everything together and also trying very hard not to freak out over this life-altering avalanche of news. "So anyone Darrak would have—would have *been with* would become a black witch?"

"My spell was specific to someone with my level of psychic ability." Selina gave another one of those humorless smiles. "I guess we have more in common than I thought we did."

"Only I didn't ask for the ability to do black magic. It really wasn't on my list of must-haves this year." There was an edge of barely restrained hysteria in her voice.

Selina squeezed Eden's numb hands tighter. "You haven't used the magic inside of you yet. If you never use it, maybe that will keep your soul from any damage."

Eden tried to stay calm, but it was a losing battle. "I'm seriously going to be sick right now. Right here."

Selina curled her hand around her wrist and Eden felt a strange calming sensation move through her that helped settle her stomach.

"Try to breathe," the witch suggested. "I'll put my book tour on hold for a few days and stay here in the city to help you. I feel a sisterly bond with you now."

A weak glimmer of hope moved through her in this otherwise hellish scenario. "You'd do that?"

She nodded. "Just try to be in control of your emotions as much as you can. I do yoga daily and take frequent meditation breaks. Scented candles are also very soothing. Anger will automatically bring the dark magic to the surface where it becomes very tempting to use." She touched her pendant. "As a black witch, our magic is at our fingertips in a way that makes it much easier to use than through books or verbally cast spells. It's a lot like being a drug addict, actually. The only way to defeat the desire to use the black magic is to ignore it."

That didn't sound very good at all. "And there's no way for me to get rid of it?"

"No. I'm sorry."

Eden gulped. "Are there *any* perks at all to this condition?"

"Well, there is the chance to live forever." Selina smiled. "Just make sure you move and change your name every ten years so people don't realize you're not aging. Botox can only account for so much, you know."

Eden looked at Darrak to see the demon was furious. Selina turned to him as well.

"You're upset over this," she observed.

"You're brilliant."

"At me or at yourself?"

"Both. This never should have happened. I should have known. Should have predicted it."

Selina cocked her head to the side. "Are you playing games, demon?"

"I wish. Games are fun. This? Not so much."

She studied him for a moment longer. "The archdemon I summoned would never blame himself for something like this. You really have changed, haven't you?"

"Yes, I have."

Selina's expression remained skeptical. "But that doesn't mean it will last. You're weakened right now. If you were to regain your power, these feelings will slip away and you'll return to how you were before."

He shook his head. "I won't."

"How do you know that?"

"I just do."

She pursed her full red lips. "If you were human once I might believe it. But you weren't. So you need to stop acting so naïve."

Eden shakily took a sip of her now lukewarm hot chocolate. It slithered unpleasantly down her throat. "I don't think he's being naïve. I believe Darrak's telling the truth."

"You think so, do you? After everything he's done to you?" Selina's green eyes flashed. "You need to see something. Now that we share this power inside us, I can share other things as well." Her grip tightened on Eden's wrist.

"Wait, what are you—" But the next moment the words were ripped out of Eden's mouth. The coffee shop shimmered away before her very eyes, and suddenly she was standing in the middle of a small grassy meadow surrounded by trees. It was night and a full moon hung heavily in the dark skies above.

A cool breeze moved past her. She could smell pine needles and wildflowers.

Where was she? What the hell was going on?

"Release me," a dark voice said from behind her. She spun around and gasped at what she saw.

It was Darrak, in demon form. Tall, huge, and horned. Golden flames licked at the surface of his entire body, lighting the darkness around him, and he stood in the middle of a ring of white powder. His voice was harsh, raspy, and pissed off.

"Release you? Why would I do that?" The words left her lips and she sounded like Selina. She *was* Selina. It was Selina's memory she was currently sharing.

"I've given you what you want." Beneath the flames, she could see the demon's lips curl. Inside the magic circle he couldn't tempt her by shifting to his human form—a form she did find very tempting indeed. As a human she could pretend that he was only handsome and charming and irresistible, but he wasn't. It was only an illusion. In the binding circle there was no hiding from what he truly was.

"Release me, witch," he said again. "Before I lose my patience with you completely."

She felt the magic simmering inside her. She'd taken everything she could from him and knew he was greatly weakened. But a weakened archdemon was still more powerful than a hundred regular humans. "I want revenge on the men who killed my sister. I command you to destroy them. Make them know a demon stripped the flesh from their bones."

He nodded once. "I will do as you say."

"You're mine," she reminded him. "Body and soul."

"I have no soul. But my body is yours to command."

"Do you love me?" she asked, surprised at the pathetically needy words spewing from her mouth. What happened to being strong and taking control of her life? It was why she wanted to become a black witch in the first place. But she had to know.

He'd been quick to respond to her seduction. Each time they'd coupled during the days since his summoning her magic grew stronger—the dark power inside of her growing until she felt as if it would burst through her very skin. She was ashamed at how quickly she'd fallen in love with him, knowing what he was. It was so hard to remember his dark nature when he was in his appealing human form.

"Do I love you?" he repeated. "You don't want the answer to that."

But she did. "Tell me the truth. I command you to, Darrakayiis."

He flinched as she used the power of his true name against him. He squeezed his eyes shut for a moment before opening them again. It felt as if his fathomless gaze bore right into her very soul.

"I am a demon, created from hellfire," he said. "I bring pain and death to those who cross me. So, do I love you, witch, who has trapped me, forced me to give you Hell's power, and commanded me to kill your enemies? *Do I love you*?" Those soulless eyes narrowed. "An archdemon cannot love anyone or anything. I will kill you the moment I'm able and you will feel my wrath much more acutely than you felt my body. I will taste your blood on my lips as I retrieve the power you've stolen from me from your darkening soul. And then I will leave you in pieces for the winds to scatter."

The cool breeze whipped the long dark hair back from her face as she stifled her fear at his cold threat. "A simple no would have been just fine."

"Then, no. I don't love you." His lips curled again. "However, I'm very fond of the weather tonight."

She looked down to see that the wind had blown some of her salt away, breaking the circle. Which meant that the archdemon was no longer trapped.

Darrakayiis stepped out of the magic circle and he smiled, showing off razor-sharp teeth as black as the thick obsidian horns extending from his temples. "About that arrangement we had? And the tearing-you-apart thing I mentioned a moment ago? Let's take care of that right now."

She scrambled backward, but not before his talons sliced shallowly into her throat and she felt the ooze of her warm blood.

Darrakayiis's terrifying smile widened. "I don't mind a bit of a chase. Makes it more interesting, actually."

There was no reasoning with him now. She knew what he meant to do to her.

Without another thought, she unleashed everything inside of her, every ounce of her new black magic. It was a power that scared her deeply, but she needed it and the destruction curse was at her fingertips in an instant. She watched the inky blackness wrap itself around the demon, pulling him away from her, dousing the hellfire that protected him, and trapping him in place as effectively as the circle of salt had.

She focused that destructive magic—magic she knew was damaging her soul as well—and opened up to it completely. The archdemon screamed in pain as she decimated him, his body literally exploding into a ball of fire.

And then it was all over.

She collapsed on the ground, gasping for breath, but alive. Ashes fell like snow all around her. It was all that remained from the demon's body.

But she'd paid dearly for her victory. The power inside her had only grown stronger from being used, and it was still ready at her fingertips. She was putting her soul in danger.

But what was done couldn't be undone.

She touched the shallow wound at her throat and her hand came away bloody. It reminded her of what was important. There were still men with the blood of her sister on their hands who had to be dealt with—human, but as evil as any demon.

She no longer had the archdemon to do her bidding, so she'd have to take care of them herself.

It would be worth another piece of her soul to avenge her sister's murder.

Eden gasped as her consciousness slammed back into the café after her vision, and she looked at Selina with wide eyes.

"Did you kill them?" she asked, breathlessly. "The men who killed your sister?"

Her expression was unreadable. "Would you believe me if I said no?"

"Probably not."

"What did you show her, witch?" Darrak asked harshly.

Eden slowly turned to look at him. She hadn't seen that side of Darrak before and it was everything she'd been afraid of. A living, breathing nightmare.

But what she'd seen was very unlike the man who looked across the table at her with concern etched into his handsome features.

"I saw when she cursed you," she said quietly.

"I'm sorry you had to see that." His jaw tightened. "Enough of this, Selina. Will you break my curse or won't you?"

Selina was quiet for a very long time just studying Darrak as if trying to figure him out like a particularly difficult riddle. And then, "Okay, fine."

His eyebrows went up. "Wow. Really?"

"I'll do it."

"I can't believe you're actually saying yes."

She glared at him. "Don't give me enough time to second-guess myself here."

He cleared his throat. "When can it be done?"

"Now."

"Now?" Eden said, still attempting to get over the frightening vision of the archdemon sitting across from her. "Right here?"

Selina stood up and slid her purse strap over her shoulder. "No. Somewhere private and outdoors, preferably similar to where the curse was originally cast."

"There's a little wooded area near my apartment," Eden suggested.

Selina nodded firmly. "Fine. And just a warning. Breaking the curse will send him back to the original location where his body was decimated."

"It will?" Eden looked at Darrak.

"Yes. So his ass is going on a one-way trip back to Salem,

Massachusetts. Hopefully they didn't build anything on that specific location or it might be a bit of a hard landing. Is that a problem, demon?"

He shook his head. "No. In fact, I'm glad to hear it."

Eden swallowed. He was glad to hear it? Break the curse and, poof, Darrak was gone. And after everything that had happened, he wouldn't be taking a plane directly back to Toronto. He'd be on the run from Hell's agents who wanted to drag him back to the mother ship.

"I'll also break the black witch spell I put on him while I'm at it. A bit like closing the gate after the horse has run off, but it's the least I can do. And when the demon is finally out of our hair, we can begin your education." Selina smiled a little. "I had to learn all this on my own. Believe me, it hasn't been easy. You're lucky I'm willing to help you."

She *was* lucky. All things considered, her brush with demons, witches, and the supernatural could have turned out much worse. At least she was still breathing.

The power of positive thinking. Maybe she should subscribe to that philosophy. The law of attraction sure hadn't helped too much lately. The universe had one hell of a strange sense of humor.

Something caught her eye as they stood up from the table to leave. A familiar woman walking out front of the coffee bar and peering in through the bank of windows. She made eye contact with Eden and then rushed in through the doors a moment later.

Darrak swore. "Thought we'd seen the last of her."

Eden thought so, too. It was Rosa, the exorcist she'd hired the other day—the mother of Malcolm. She wondered if the woman had any idea how knowledgeable her son really was about demons and exorcisms.

"Ms. Riley," Rosa said, approaching her.

"I don't want any trouble," Eden replied. That was putting it mildly. Her current mountain of worries was so high that she couldn't even see over the top.

Rosa anxiously clasped her hands on top of her walking cane. She wore a bright yellow floral dress covered by a thin red coat that looked handmade. "I think we made a mistake the other night. I feel horrible that an officer of the law had to intervene. I've had a few complaints lodged with the police as it is. I wanted to come by today to apologize to you personally and check in on how you're feeling. Was it really only indigestion?"

"Yes." Eden smiled tightly and glanced at Darrak. "Uh . . . trust me, I won't be having Mexican food again for a long time. Those refried beans are a killer."

"I didn't put through the other half of the payment on your credit card and I've refunded your deposit. I'm very much hoping you won't submit an official complaint against me."

"Let's just forget it," she replied.

Finally some good news. Maybe the universe hadn't given her the finger as much as she'd thought it had.

"Do you get a lot of calls for exorcisms?" Darrak asked her.

"You'd be surprised," Rosa said. She glanced at him and Selina as if noticing them for the first time. "I'm sorry. I didn't meant to interrupt. I just wanted to have my say. I hope there are no hard feelings toward me or my son."

Darrak laughed a little at that.

"Do you know my Malcolm?" she asked.

"We've met. Sort of. He's very dedicated to his work."

"Yes, he certainly is. I'd hoped he would consider going back to the university. He has a scholarship waiting for him, you know. But he wants to pursue other interests. He's a stubborn boy." She looked at Selina. "You're that author lady, aren't you?"

Selina eyed her coolly. "I have written a couple of books."

"What is it that you call yourself . . . love guru . . . love something."

She smiled thinly. "Something like that."

Rosa scanned Selina's expensive suit and jewelry, stopping briefly on the gray stone pendant. "That's lovely."

"Thank you." Selina touched it. "It was a gift from an acquaintance a long time ago."

Yeah, Eden thought. *A long* time ago.

"Thank you for talking to me and for the refund, Rosa," Eden said. "And there are no hard feelings. Toward you or Malcolm."

"I'm so glad."

They all began to leave the café at the same time.

"Bye Ms. Shaw. Your books have changed my life! Like, *seriously*!" Nancy called from behind the counter. "And bye, Darrak. *So* great seeing you again."

Rosa turned with a frown to look at him directly. "Did she just call you Darrak? Ms. Riley, wasn't that the name of your demon?"

"No," Eden said immediately. "That was . . . uh . . . *Eric*. And it wasn't a demon at all. It was Mexican food. Indigestion. Ugh. Not pleasant."

Rosa frowned. "Mexican food named Eric?"

Eden clenched her jaw. "I have one heck of a crazy imagination."

"Oh." She shook her head and laughed a little, resting her weight on her crystal-topped cane. "Don't we all. And my memory isn't what it used to be, anyhow. No surprise. At my age everything is starting to fail me."

"Right." Eden forced a smile, but her sudden swell of fresh anxiety had made strange electric tingles course up and down her arms. Was that the black magic inside her sensing a change in her mood?

"I don't like that woman," Darrak said under his breath as they parted ways outside. "And not just because of her unfortunate fashion sense."

"We need to go now," Selina suggested firmly. "While we still have daylight. That is, if you still want me to break this curse."

Eden nodded. "Of course we do."

She thought back to what had happened between her and Darrak earlier. His mouth on hers. How it felt when they'd made love. She'd wanted him so badly, it had blinded her to everything else.

"This shouldn't have happened." Darrak's words echoed in her head.

No, it shouldn't have.

Sex with a bad boy usually left one with a broken heart.

Sex with a demon left you with a broken soul.

She'd have to remember that important little fact for future reference.

Eden drove Selina and Darrak back to the apartment com-plex, although truthfully her attention was not on the road as much as it should have been. Luckily she didn't get them into an accident. Even though she was a black witch—*Oh, my God*, she thought—she knew from what Darrak had told her previously that despite her new immortality—*Oh, my God* again—she was still fragile and as easily killed as a regular, nonmagically infused human.

Oh. My. God.

So she kept her hands at ten and two on the steering wheel and tried not to think about everything that had gone horribly, horribly wrong. It wasn't easy.

She entered the outdoor lot and parked with an unhealthy lurching gearshift sound. She might be about to live forever, but her rusty Toyota was another story altogether.

With a nod of her head, Eden indicated the wooded area. "Over there."

Selina inspected it with a sweeping glance. "That will do. We still have some time before sunset, but we should get to work right away."

"And you're sure the curse can be broken?" Darrak asked. Eden jumped. She hadn't noticed he'd come up behind her after leaving the backseat.

Selina nodded. "You get your wish, demon. Your freedom. Although I'm still not convinced you deserve it."

"Then why are you doing this?"

"To help Eden, of course." Selina looked at her with strange affection. But then again, she felt like they were sisters now, didn't she? It wouldn't be long before they were magically braiding each other's hair. "She's got enough to deal with now without you further complicating matters. She'll be lucky to be rid of you and never see you again. Ten minutes and this will be over."

"Good," he replied.

Yes, he was getting his freedom. Just like he wanted. And Eden would live to see another year without the risk of death by demonic possession.

The perfect happy ending for everyone involved.

If that was so, then why was her throat thick and emotion stinging her eyes? She exhaled shakily and tried to compose herself. Ten minutes and this would be over. He'd be gone. And she'd try to forge some sort of normalcy in her life again. If that was even remotely possible.

She'd found a newfound interest in working with Andy at Triple-A. She wanted to help people. Funny how helping others was useful in forgetting other troubles. It was a good lesson to learn. So, black witch or not, that's what Eden would be doing.

All by herself.

Well, with Andy, too, but suddenly after days of having Darrak with her it still felt oddly alone.

And that was a good thing, she reminded herself firmly. And it was how she wanted her life to be. Independent. Private. Solitary. Much easier that way. Nobody around to let her down or abandon her when she got too used to having them in her life.

"Can I talk to you for a moment before we begin, Eden?" Darrak asked. "In private?"

She swallowed past the stupid and inconvenient lump in her throat. "Of course."

"Don't take long," Selina said tensely. "Time is money."

He led Eden over to an oak tree next to the small clearing—which she now realized, for the first time since she'd moved in last month, was a kids' playground. She'd seen the area in passing as she went to her car, but had never explored further. A swing set, slide, and teeter-totter stood, unoccupied, a dozen feet away, shielded by a thatch of tall trees. Darrak stood with his arms crossed tightly in front of him.

"What?" Eden asked, and it actually came out sounding a lot harsher than she'd meant it to.

"I want you to know I didn't mean for this to happen." His handsome face was oddly expressionless.

The flat statement delivered in a monotone—was this supposed to be some sort of apology?—fell on the cool, late afternoon air. And it took that strange emotion inside of her and hardened it. In other words, he'd managed to officially piss her off.

"Oh?" she said. "And what exactly do you refer to? The original possession, throwing my life out of control? Or maybe draining me of energy on a regular basis and putting my life in danger? Scaring off a man who I really liked spending time with? Or was it neglecting to mention your sexual history and the fact that a meaningless roll in the hay with you might destroy my entire life?"

She was happy to see him wince a bit, and something resembling an emotion flickered in those currently flat blue eyes of his. "Meaningless, huh?"

Strange he'd pick up on that particular word in her rant. "Let's just end this now, Darrak, and not try to pretend it was anything more important. After all, being an ex-incubus I'm sure you've got so many notches in your bedpost it's . . . well, you probably needed to work at a bedpost factory to keep up with your past conquests."

"No, you're right. Of course. Meaningless." He nodded with a firm motion of his head. "You need to make me a promise, though."

She stifled an unpleasantly bitter laugh at that. "A promise? What might that be?"

"Don't use any black magic in the future. Ever."

"I wasn't planning on it." Eden's jaw tensed and she looked away.

He drew closer, touched her chin and made her look up at him. "I can still see your soul if I concentrate hard enough. And it's still as bright and shiny as the first time I saw you. I don't want you to risk that by dipping into the magic inside you."

"What if it's really, really important?"

"Even then."

The heat from his hand seared into her. It was hard not to remember how good those hands had felt on her body.

Meaningless.

She wished she really felt that way about it. About him. It would make everything way easier.

She batted his hand away and stepped back. "Well, that's no thanks to you, is it?"

"No, it's not."

"Let's not waste any more time with this. Time to finally say good-bye. You're going to be gone soon. Back to Salem, or wherever."

"Right. I . . . wanted to thank you, though."

Her eyebrows raised. "Thank me?"

"For not exorcising me. For trusting me despite the things you've seen or heard." He moved toward her again and took her face between his hands. "You'll be better off without me. Just like Selina says."

She looked into his eyes and hated to admit even to herself what she was feeling inside. She'd miss this demon. Even after everything she knew about him, everything she'd seen, and everything he'd done to her.

She'd miss him horribly.

No way, she thought, angry with herself. She wasn't letting herself feel like this. She forced herself to step away from him, and his hand dropped back to his side.

"You're right," she said as evenly and coolly as she could. "I will be better off without you."

"Eden—"

"Selina showed me the real truth about you. You're a monster. You've ruined my life. I should have exorcised you when I had the chance, but I was too stupid. I regret everything that's happened between us. Now, I just want you gone."

She twisted the words into him like a knife. Darrak's previously steady, unreadable gaze flickered as he looked away from her. Had she hurt his feelings?

Did an archdemon really have feelings? He'd claimed he now felt human emotions all too intensely. But she had no idea if that was really the truth or just more lies.

"Then let's not waste another minute," he said after a moment.

"Fine with me."

"Good-bye, Eden." He turned and walked back to Selina and the two of them entered the tree-shrouded playground.

⇒ TWENTY-TWO ⇐

Out of the corner of her eye, Eden spotted an uninvited guest lurking under a nearby car in the parking lot. A black cat that was trying to appear incognito.

Leena.

She ignored the shapeshifter, but couldn't help but find it vaguely amusing. The cat wanted nothing to do with her or Darrak, but she was curious enough to stick around to see how things played out?

Selina led them into the small wooded area until they found a bare patch covered with fallen leaves.

"White witches practice nature magic," she said wistfully. "I dabbled with that in the beginning, but now it's not even an option for me. Black magic will destroy nature."

"Vengeance isn't gained very well with rosebuds and peach nectar," Darrak said. "So what do I need to do?"

She eyed him. "Just stand there."

"At your mercy, you mean."

She smiled. "Just like old times."

Darrak looked at Eden, but she didn't meet his eyes. It was

better that he thought she was mad at him, hated him, and wanted nothing to do with him.

Better for *her*, that is. It made it easier.

The sun was low in the sky. It wouldn't be long before sunset. If this worked, Darrak wouldn't have to possess her tonight.

His curse would be broken.

The thought was a relief, of course. Her feelings for the demon might be a total conflicting mess, but she didn't want to be possessed by him. By anyone. Ever again.

"Are you ready?" Selina asked Darrak.

"I am."

"Have to warn you, it's not going to be a pleasure trip. For you, this is going to sting. A lot."

"I can take it."

"Then let's do this." She closed her eyes and held her arms up at her sides.

A moment later, Eden felt the energy begin to swirl in the open area they stood in, and small electric sparks flickered off the edges of the playground equipment. In response, her own magic began to wake up—a tingling inside, a growing power that was very difficult to ignore.

But she did ignore it.

She shivered, and it wasn't just from the temperature; she drew her thin coat closer to her body, crossing her arms as she stood and watched the witch and the demon.

Selina opened her eyes. "*Darrakayiis*, I use your true name to bind you where you stand."

Darrak went rigid in place.

Tensely, Eden noticed Selina's amulet darken a shade of gray as she began to channel her black magic for a specific purpose. It wasn't until that moment, and the witch's use of his full name, that she realized how much was currently at stake. Having it exist in theory to having it play out right in front of her were two separate things.

Selina now had the power to break Darrak's curse or destroy him where he stood.

She then understood how much trust Darrak had put into the witch. He was now at her mercy much as he'd been three hundred years ago. The only difference was she was much more powerful now. Did Selina still hold a grudge? Would Eden really blame her if she did? Had she been lying before by saying she'd help?

Eden felt a sliver of panic at the thought. Maybe the witch had lied for a chance to finish what she'd started with the demon. Eden had believed her completely. Darrak wasn't so naïve, of course. She could see in his eyes right now, that hope mixing with distrust. He'd willingly opened himself up to the pain that would either lead to his ultimate freedom or complete destruction.

She watched, warily, her hands clenched into fists at her sides, and she could feel her own magic now at her fingertips—just as Selina said it would be. So easy to use she didn't even need a training manual. Would it really be that simple? No more difficult than throwing a thought?

It was. That's why it was so dangerous.

"Do it." The pain in Darrak's voice was already noticeable. "Finish this one way or the other."

Selina smiled at Eden. "I know what you're thinking."

"You do?"

The witch nodded. "But don't worry. I won't hurt him more than I have to. And I will release him from this curse and the other spell I put on him. It'll be a new beginning for all of us."

She was telling the truth. Through their strange new bond, Eden knew it, and it was a huge relief. Despite being a black witch, Selina wasn't evil. She'd fought against it. She tried to help others with her books—man-hating diatribes that they were. Eden knew the witch would be able to help her with her strange new magical ability—a molten lava pool of power it was disturbingly tempting to jump into headfirst.

"Now, let me finish this," Selina said firmly.

That pesky lump of emotion came back to take up residence

in Eden's throat. The demon's pain-filled gaze was heavy on her as the energy swept through the playground and around her and she knew any moment he would disappear completely.

Good-bye, Darrak, she thought.

There was an interruption in the flicker of energy around Eden. She felt it. The witch's eyes were open again and her attention had shifted.

"Who the hell are you?" Selina asked sharply.

Eden turned to see that Malcolm was watching the proceedings, leaning his shoulder against a tree.

"Sorry. Am I interrupting something?" he asked.

Cold fear shot through her at the sight of him.

"Interrupting something?" Eden asked, forcing herself to laugh lightly at that. "Just three good friends hanging out in a children's playground. Nothing strange about that, is there?"

Malcolm approached slowly and Eden's gaze flicked to his hand where he held a palm-sized piece of rock salt. "I consulted with my mentor about what we discussed last night and I'm now ready to finish this."

"You know where I live?"

"I'm here, aren't I? Haven't you been expecting me?" Malcolm looked confused. Of course, he would be. The last time he'd seen Eden she'd agree to have Darrak exorcised without further argument.

She tentatively approached the college-kid-turned-secret-society-demon-hunter. "Malcolm, no. I've changed my mind. Please go."

"I can't do that."

"Eden," Darrak said with warning. "Be careful."

"That's him, isn't it?" Malcolm said, the tremor in his voice impossible to hide. "The *archdemon*. He's powerful enough to take solid form."

She swallowed nervously. "You need to go home. I spoke to your mother a little while ago. She says you have a scholarship. You need to go back to school. Have a real life."

"I don't care what my mother says. This is my life." His

gaze shifted over to Selina and he inhaled sharply. "She's a witch. I can sense her power."

Selina glared back at him. "Come any closer, kid, and I'll give you something else to sense."

His eyes returned to meet Eden's and they widened a fraction. "You're a witch now, too?"

She cringed. "I've been called many things in my life. That's now on the list."

Disappointment flooded his expression. "I wanted to help you. I failed. The darkness has claimed you."

She took a step toward him but he staggered back a little, clutching his solid crystal of salt. He looked very young, uncertain, and suddenly in over his head. "There are exceptions to what you've been taught by the Malleus. There are demons and witches who don't want to hurt anyone. And you can't kill them."

He shook his head, confused. "But my training, everything I've learned . . ."

"You're smart enough to see what I'm saying is true. I know you're afraid right now, but you don't have to be. And I think you're so brave for coming here and trying to do this on your own, but it's not necessary. We're here trying to fix this by ourselves and you need to go now so we can finish. Will you do that for me?"

The calm, soothing tone of her voice was not exactly what she was feeling inside, but she knew she had to keep her emotions in check. He could be made to see reason. It wasn't too late.

"I can kill him," Selina suggested.

"You're not helping," Eden said, shooting the witch a sharp look. "I thought you were a nice witch."

"Why does everyone think I'm nice? I do what I must to survive. And I'm not risking my *Oprah* appearance for anyone."

"He won't tell anyone," Eden said, even though she wasn't positive that was true. She exchanged a concerned glance with

Darrak, who otherwise kept very quiet, still bound to the spot where he stood by Selina's use of his true name. His expression, however, was no longer pain-filled or even emotionless. His brow was furrowed with concern. Was it for himself or for Eden?

Malcolm's hand curled around the piece of salt. "I can save you."

She couldn't help but smile at that. "I thought you'd want to kill me now, as well."

"You're not lost yet. We can help you. The Malleus—"

"They're the same bastards who killed my innocent human sister," Selina snapped. "Don't let them anywhere near you."

"Eden, be careful," Darrak warned.

Malcolm swallowed, his expression registering shock from what Selina said. "I need to think."

That was a very good sign. Eden felt she'd gotten through to him, even if it was just a little. The kid wanted to do the right thing, after all. Despite everything, that was his goal.

She heard a car pull into the parking lot only a few dozen feet away.

Selina sighed with annoyance. "I think we would have had more privacy at the coffee shop. I should have taken that fangirl up on the blueberry scone offer when I had the chance."

"Release me, Selina," Darrak said.

"Fine," she replied absently and flicked her wrist in his direction. "I release you."

The demon moved from the spot he had been frozen in and came immediately to Eden's side. "We'll do this another time. It's too dangerous right now."

The thought was a surprising relief. He was right. This wasn't a good time. Even if they had to wait a day, it would be worth it.

Malcolm's gaze snapped to the demon and his grip increased on the salt. "It's my duty to destroy you, demon."

Darrak looked directly at him. "I respect your dedication to a job, but you're a bit of a pain in the ass, you know that, kid?"

"Don't call me kid."

"Then stop acting like a spoiled child who thinks he knows what's right in the world. You have no idea what's really out there, do you? You've stamped out some nasties and consider yourself an expert. Your mind has been corrupted by this group you're in. You need to learn to think for yourself."

"I am thinking for myself. And it's my duty to destroy evil things that enter this world."

"Is that right?" Darrak's eyes narrowed and flickered with an inner fire. "If I was truly as bad as you think I am, the only thing left of you right now would be your shoes."

"Darrak, please," Eden hissed. He wasn't helping matters by baiting the kid. She'd seen Malcolm easily destroy the drifter the previous day. She didn't know if he'd also be able to trap an archdemon in that piece of salt, but she didn't want to find out.

"Please what?" he said.

"Don't set yourself up to get hurt."

He looked at her. "I didn't think you cared one way or the other what happens to me."

"I don't," she lied.

"You shouldn't."

"Then that's why I don't. But that doesn't mean I want you exorcised."

His jaw was tense. "I just want this over with."

"Me, too."

"Then let me help you," Malcolm said. "I can end this."

"Say another word"—Selina's fingertips sparked with visible magic—"and it will be your last."

Her amulet darkened another shade.

Eden grabbed Malcolm's hand that held the salt. She looked into his eyes. "Please don't do anything. I don't want you hurt, either."

He frowned at her. "Really?"

She nodded. "Really."

"Malcolm! There you are!" Rosa entered the clearing, hobbling along on her walking cane. Eden's heart sank. It must have been her car she heard pull up.

She should have considered selling tickets to Darrak's curse breaking. Maybe gotten some balloons and fruit punch. It was turning into a big party full of unwelcome guests.

Malcolm tensed. "Mother, please. I can handle this."

"Sweetie, you shouldn't be here right now, bothering these people. I told you to leave them alone."

She did? Eden's eyebrows went up.

But maybe this was a good thing. Having his mommy here might help to rein Malcolm in a bit. And Rosa had been very helpful earlier, both with the apology and the refund of the exorcism money.

Rosa moved closer, shaking her head. "I apologize for my son. He's very . . . overzealous. He has much to learn still."

Malcolm scowled at her and jerked away when she went to touch him.

"It's fine," Eden said tightly. "No harm done."

"I can't work like this," Selina said with frustration. "We'll have to do it another day. Eden, you have my phone number, right?"

"I do. But . . . Selina, please—"

"No," Selina held up a hand. "I'm all stressed out now. I'm going to call myself a taxi and go back to my hotel. Besides, I have a phone interview scheduled in an hour that I don't want to miss. I'll have to meditate before it to calm myself down. We'll talk later, okay?"

Eden didn't answer because she was now studying Rosa. Something had caught her eye. The harmless-looking short, fat exorcist had the sleeves of her coat pushed up so a strange pinkish mark on her left forearm was visible.

Strange, but familiar.

"I remembered what they call you," Rosa said as Selina was about to pass her on her way out of the playground. "It's the Love Witch."

"That's right."

"Your books are very popular."

"Over five million in print."

"Amazing what black magic will net you, isn't it?"

Selina's eyes narrowed. "I don't use black magic to help my writing."

"Sure you don't."

The mark. Eden blinked rapidly. It was the same as what Malcolm had shown her. The brand given to members of the Malleus. Only Rosa's was much older, less red and raw and new.

"Selina, wait a minute . . ." she began, feeling suddenly very nervous.

Selina brushed past the woman. "Excuse me."

"Oh, one last thing, dear," Rosa said.

"What?" Selina turned, annoyance plain on her face, and Rosa plunged the sharp tip of a dagger—previously sheathed at the end of her walking cane—through the witch's chest so quickly it was barely noticeable.

Selina gasped, her eyes widening. Magic crackled erratically through the clearing as the cool breeze blew some fall leaves from the trees. The witch touched her chest, only a small mark of red on her expensive white suit to show that she'd been injured.

"I . . ." she began, but then fell to her knees and collapsed. The magic that could be felt around them disappeared.

Eden's eyes widened and she staggered back from where Selina now lay on the ground.

Witches were still essentially human, Eden remembered Darrak telling her. They could be hurt. They could easily be killed.

Selina was dead. Easy as that.

⇒ TWENTY-THREE ⇐

"You *bitch*," Darrak moved forward, fury etched on his face. "Do you have any idea what you've done?"

"I killed a witch," Rosa said matter-of-factly. "It's part of my job. And don't take another step closer, *Darrakayiis*."

Darrak froze in place.

Eden turned to the woman and the pale shock must have been evident on her face.

"Yes," Rosa said. "I found out his true name. Extensive research will net you many facts."

"Mother—" Malcolm looked down at Selina with a strange expression on his face. It wasn't joy. "She was leaving. You didn't have to kill her."

"Of course I did. She was a witch."

Malcolm's normally smooth forehead was furrowed. "Of course, you're right."

"I am. Now we must deal with the demon."

Eden moved to stand in front of Darrak—currently frozen in place—and she held up her hands. She tried not to look at Selina's unmoving body lying there on the ground. It had happened so fast it still hadn't sunk in. She'd never seen anyone killed before. No, that wasn't true, was it? The serial killer the other day. Ben had shot him dead. But he'd deserved it. He was going to kill her.

Selina was going to help her. And now she was gone.

"You have the mark of the Malleus," Darrak observed tensely. He could speak but not move.

Rosa touched her arm. "I do, indeed."

"I thought that group was men-only."

Rosa snorted. "My, you've been out of the loop for quite some time, haven't you, archdemon? No, around the same time as women were granted the vote, we were also permitted to join the Malleus. By invitation only, of course."

"It's the same group who persecuted innocent women and burned them at the stake."

"There were some true witches who were destroyed then as well. The collateral damage is to be expected."

Darrak laughed humorlessly. "It's nice that you can differentiate the evil that humans are responsible for from other types."

"Yes it is, isn't it?" She wiped the tip of her cane on the grass and put the wooden sheath over it again before turning it crystal side up again.

Eden took a shaky breath. "Let me guess, Malcolm. This is your Malleus elder? The one you had to speak to about Darrak?"

Malcolm nodded stiffly. "My mother has been with the Malleus for many years. She knows what to do with an archdemon." He went to Rosa's side. "I have the rock salt, Mother. We will exorcise his essence, trap it, and then smash it to send him to the void."

She shook her head and leaned on her cane. "We won't be needing that today."

"What do you mean?"

Eden pressed back until she could feel Darrak's tense body behind her. She turned to look at him.

"Go," he whispered.

She shook her head. "I'm not leaving you. Besides, I can't go that far away from you, remember?"

"Selina's dead, and not by my hand. The curse can't be broken, not by her, anyhow. Let them do whatever it is they want to do with me, but save yourself."

She didn't budge. Her brain was working overtime. She could talk to them. Convince them that Darrak wasn't evil anymore. She'd seen something on Malcolm's face earlier. He was ready to believe her. Just a little more time was all it would take. He hadn't expected Rosa to kill Selina without any warning at all. Did he know what his mother was capable of before this? She seemed, on the surface, so harmless. But she wasn't.

"Please, Eden," Darrak said again.

"Just shut up, will you?"

"No, I won't shut up. Why won't you just let yourself hate me once and for all? It will make this easier."

"Easier for you or for me?"

"For both of us."

"I don't hate you," she said.

"Could have fooled me."

"Yeah, that's what I was trying to do."

"Exorcise me," he said loud enough to get Rosa's attention. She'd been speaking quietly with her son over by the swing set. "Let Malcolm do it. I won't resist."

Eden glared at him and felt tears burn at her eyes. So much for being all self-protective. Now that Selina was gone, it was the only way she could be rid of him for sure. She'd seen what he'd been capable of as an archdemon. And if he wasn't exorcised, she'd be putting her own life at risk even more.

Rosa turned to Eden. "I can feel your power. It's so fresh and untapped. Being a member of the Malleus gives one the ability to sense such things. But your power is not yet as vast as this creature's." She nudged Selina's body with her shoe. "You see she's already starting to disintegrate? That's what happens to black witches when they die."

And she was. Eden watched in shock as the witch's body disappeared little by little, leaving only her clothes and accessories behind.

"We have some witches who have offered their services to the Malleus in return for their lives," Rosa continued. "You may be an excellent candidate for this."

"That's real generous," Eden replied tightly.

"Yes, it is. Everyone is prone to make mistakes in their lives. Offer up their souls to evil demons for vast power as you've done." She shook her head. "It's very sad, but not all that unheard of."

She seemed so sure of herself and everything she said. How many years had she been a member of this group, killing witches and demons as easily as swatting flies?

"Darrak's not evil," Eden said and she sounded incredibly sure of that. More sure than she even thought she was.

Rosa pursed her lips as if she'd tasted something sour. "Step away from the demon and save yourself, dear."

Eden shook her head. "Is this how you find your targets? You wait for people possessed or dealing with other supernatural issues to call you and you come out like glorified ghost busters?"

Rosa smiled. "All for the price of an ad in the Yellow Pages. Isn't it great? However, it's very rare I've come face-to-face with an archdemon. I don't let opportunities like that pass me by, believe me."

"As soon as you exorcise Darrak, you'll kill me, won't you?"

"No," Malcolm said. "We won't. I swear it on my own soul."

Eden took a deep breath and let it out slowly. "You, I believe. But your mother is another story. She wants to.exorcise Darrak and then kill me. She won't be happy until she does that."

"You're wrong," Rosa said. "I don't want to exorcise him."

Well, that was a surprise. And a relief. Eden must have been even more convincing than she'd thought she was.

"You don't?" Darrak's voice was skeptical. "Then what the hell is this?"

"Like I said, it's very rare I've encountered an archdemon. You're the third I've ever faced." She walked a slow circle around his prone form. He eyed her suspiciously. "So much power, although currently diluted, but you'll do. Not quite as fearsome as you once were, are you?"

"I've been feeling a bit drained lately," he admitted. "Perhaps I need a nice long vacation somewhere tropical. I'll be sure to send you a postcard."

She smiled as her gaze moved to Eden. "And you've become a black witch through sex magic since I first saw you. Very powerful and very potent."

Honestly. Was Eden wearing a T-shirt that told the world that she and Darrak had been together? If she wasn't currently frozen with fear and worry, she'd be embarrassed.

Rosa's attention returned to the demon and she raised an eyebrow. "I would give a great deal to have that kind of magic at my fingertips."

Darrak's eyes narrowed. "Sorry, Rosa. You're not exactly my type."

She laughed. "Maybe twenty years ago."

"No, not even then. Much as I seem to have a thing for crazy redheads, you're the exception to the rule. So let me get this straight. You're an upstanding, youth-mentoring member of the Malleus with a little bit of a lust for power, are you?"

"Lust is a deadly sin," she said.

"No shit. So, you want me to make you into a black witch?"

"No, demon." She smiled. "I want to put you into my diamond."

She raised her cane and Eden's eyes went to the two-inch-wide crystal on the top of it. Now that she was paying attention, Eden realized that it wasn't totally clear. There was something inside of it. A barely noticeable thin swirling of . . . black smoke?

"What is that?" she asked, although she already had a good idea what it was.

She looked at the diamond affectionately. "These are the two other archdemons I mentioned a minute ago."

What had Malcolm told her last night? That using salt was best to trap a demon, because they could be destroyed when the salt was smashed by whomever did the trapping. But a diamond . . .

It was next to impossible to break—the hardest substance on earth. And the demon couldn't escape from it, either.

"Mother!" Malcolm sounded shocked. "I had no idea. You trapped them in the diamond? And that's a real diamond? It's huge."

"Yes." She brushed her fingers over it. "One hundred and eighty carats. Priceless. It was a present from a former mentor. He, too, had a similar diamond to this. But it takes three arch-demons inside of it to do anything worthwhile—three is that very special magic number—a triad. And once I have the es-sence of Darrakayiis in here . . ." She shook her head and smiled widely. "There will be no other woman on earth as powerful as I will be."

"Mother—"

"The magic I will be able to yield at my will." Her voice turned excited. "I'll be able to heal my frailties, become young again in body and mind. I will use this power to defeat the darkness, of course. And with it, I can walk between worlds— here, the Netherworld, and the Heavens—it will be as easy as walking into another room of a house. I will be a very powerful sorceress."

"Just like a witch?" Malcolm breathed.

"No, of course not. Better than that. *Purer* than that. My magic will help others."

"Help others?" Eden repeated, disgusted at what she was hearing. "You're going to help others by using the power from three trapped archdemons? That doesn't sound all that white and sparkly to me."

Rosa turned a concerned gaze to her. "Sometimes it takes evil to defeat evil."

"Then take me," Darrak said firmly. "But leave Eden alone."

"I would if I could." Rosa exhaled. "But unfortunately, you're still bound to her."

Eden's panicked gaze moved to the cane again. Two arch-demons were in there swirling about. She'd seen Darrak in Selina's vision. He was dangerous and deadly. How had Rosa managed to trap them?

She looked at Malcolm. "Help us."

Even though the inner struggle he was feeling was plain on his face, he shook his head and took a step backward. "I can't do that. My mother . . . she knows what she's doing. I have to trust her judgment. There's no other way."

"Darrakayiis," Rosa said in a commanding tone. "I need you to break your bonds with this witch. Show me your demon visage and kill her. Now."

He changed form in an instant and he curled his amber-fire-covered hand around Eden's throat before she had a chance to take even a step away from him. His sharp talons scratched dangerously against her jugular.

"Darra—" she tried to say his name in hopes of transferring the power back to her, but her air was cut off.

Probably should have thought about that a few minutes ago, actually. It might have helped.

She expected the fire covering him to burn her this time, but it was as dry and warm as it had been the last time. She clutched at his arm, clawing against it, but he was too strong. It was like fighting against a brick wall.

"I'm trying to resist," his dark raspy voice said as his grip tightened painfully, cutting off her air. "But . . . it's too hard. My true name . . ."

Now she knew why he didn't have his true name printed up on business cards to hand out to everyone he met. Because anyone who knew his name and had a little bit of power—as Eden had from her psychic energy and as Rosa had from her connection to the Malleus—could make him their puppet of death and destruction.

"He's killing her," Malcolm said, and he sounded upset.

"That's the general idea," Rosa replied calmly.

Darrak's eyes hadn't changed. She could see them past the flames. Still blue and human as his grip increased, cutting off the rest of her breath.

"Eden, I'm sorry for all of this. I . . . love you."

Archdemons didn't love. They couldn't love. Darrak had told that to Selina just before she'd cursed him. Had he lied? Was he lying now? Why would he tell her this when he was about to end her life?

She gasped for breath but there was no breath to gasp. He'd saved her life before, but now, despite the fact he was trying to fight it, he was squeezing it out of her.

Suddenly something small, black, and furry leapt through the air and attached itself to Darrak's arm, hissing and scratching. It was Leena. Eden had seen her in the parking lot earlier. She hadn't left.

"I can help protect you," she'd told Eden. *"Demons are repelled by shapeshifters."*

Darrak grabbed the cat by the scruff of her neck and threw her back from him. She hit a tree hard and fell to the ground. It knocked the cat out cold, but Eden could see her furry chest still moved, indicating she was still alive.

Darrak then released Eden, who fell to the ground in a heap. She closed her eyes and pretended to be dead.

"It is done," Darrak said. "And there are only moments before my host's remaining power fades and I will lose my form."

But it wasn't done. She wasn't dead, and he had to know that. Rosa didn't have complete control over him. In Selina's flashback, the witch had had a white circle of salt going for her as well as a black witch's level of power. All Rosa really had was his name. That meant he was able to fight this, even if just a little.

Eden pried one eye partially open. The sun was low in the sky but it hadn't set yet. It cast a golden glow over the clearing they were in.

"Very good," Rosa said, and Eden heard her approach closer. "My goodness, you're impressive, aren't you?"

"Goodness has nothing to do with it," Darrak replied.

"No, of course it doesn't. My, I shall enjoy using you, demon."

"You won't be the first."

"Mother, stop this right now," Malcolm protested, and he sounded on the verge of tears. "You've done enough! Eden's dead!"

"Please, Malcolm. Be quiet."

From her vantage point, Eden could narrowly see that Malcolm looked very upset with the show so far. His world had been rocked. His mother, whom he thought was a good upstanding exorcist had turned out to be a power-hungry sorceress wannabe, now greedily eyeing the seven-foot-tall horned archdemon from Hell she wanted to add to her growing collection.

Darrak didn't look down at her. His eyes were fixed on Rosa, who turned to him again.

She smiled. "It's time."

Then she began to chant something—but it wasn't Latin. It sounded older and rougher around the edges.

"Where did you learn that?" Darrak asked.

Rosa broke off. "This little ancient Sumerian ritual? From the mentor who gave me my diamond. Unfortunately, he's in a coma and his full-powered diamond is missing. If I'd had that, it would have saved me a lot of work over the years, don't you think?"

"Let me guess. You're responsible for his coma?"

She smiled thinly. "I'll never tell. Now silence, demon. No more interruptions." She began again.

After a minute, Darrak gasped. The flames that coated his body disappeared and he shifted back into human form in the blink of an eye. For a second, part of him turned to black smoke, before flickering back to his solid form.

He convulsed in pain, and clutched at his stomach.

"Why isn't it working?" Rosa asked, frowning. She repeated a couple words, which made Darrak gasp in agony again, flickering to smoke for a moment longer this time before regaining form.

"What in the world?" Rosa pondered, then clarity came into her eyes. "Foolish, demon. You didn't really kill her after all, did you?"

She unsheathed her dagger and moved toward Eden, who wasn't going to do an impression of an immobile pincushion any longer. Her eyes snapped all the way open and she scooted back a few feet.

"I guess I'll have to kill you myself," Rosa said.

"Don't touch her," Darrak growled.

"No, Mother." Malcolm grabbed her arm. "This has gone on long enough. I can't stand here and watch you do this."

"Get back from me, stupid boy." She struck Malcolm hard with her cane and he yelped in pain and fell back from her.

Eden scrambled to her feet. "*Darrakayiis*," she said, and Darrak immediately turned to face her as the power to control him shifted. There was sweat on his brow and a multitude of very human-looking emotions moving through his eyes.

"Command me to kill her," he managed. "I'll do it."

She shook her head. "Nobody else is dying here tonight."

"Mother, no!" Malcolm cried. She turned to see Rosa coming toward her with the dagger end of her cane exposed and aimed at her heart.

She didn't think. She didn't have to. The magic flared inside of her in an instant and it was enough to knock Rosa backward. The woman stumbled and fell to the ground.

"Leave us alone, you bitch," Eden warned. "I'm serious."

"I can help you," Rosa said.

"You just tried to stab me with the pointy end of your cane. How exactly is that helping me?"

"Let's forget about what's happened in the past and move on from here with a fresh slate."

"I want you to go now and never bother us again." The magic Eden had promised never to use crackled down her hands into her fingertips. She shot a look over at Malcolm. "Both of you."

"Then I won't trap him. I'll exorcise him. You wanted him gone," Rosa reasoned. "You called me in a panic, remember? You paid me money to get rid of him for you."

Eden clenched her hand into a fist at her side. "It's a woman's prerogative to change her mind."

Rosa had the audacity to look concerned for her. "He'll destroy you. Let us destroy him for you."

"No." It was such a simple word for something Eden felt so strongly about.

Rosa's lips thinned. "Then I'll have to destroy both of you." She held her cane up, muttered something indiscernible in that dead language under her breath, and the diamond on the top began to glow. "I need three for full power, but the archdemons I already have are enough to give me the magic I need right now."

"Eden—" Darrak's voice was strained. "Run!"

Rosa's eyes lit with fire, similar to Darrak's. She honestly thought she was channeling a pure power? She was either deceiving herself or lying to everyone else. Eden was willing to bet on the latter.

Eden felt powerful magic emanating from the diamond. It trapped her in place and it was like moving through taffy just to turn her head. It was too late to run. She watched, as if in slow motion, as Rosa turned the cane, blade side up, and moved toward her again.

"I will have him," she said firmly. "The archdemon is mine."

"No," Eden replied, struggling to speak. "He's *mine*."

And again, the magic was at her fingertips. She focused everything she had on Rosa's cane.

It was as though a shock wave emanated out from her

and focused directly around the diamond. A moment later it shattered as if it were no more than a lightbulb. The next moment, the heavy weight of Rosa's demon magic disappeared completely from the air.

The older woman's eyes were as wide as saucers. "You bitch! You broke my diamond!"

Eden staggered back into Darrak's arms. "Sorry. Was it expensive?"

How much was the average one hundred eighty carat diamond these days? She suddenly wished that Rosa didn't currently have her MasterCard number on file.

Magic continued to crackle at her fingertips. It would be so easy to finish this off. Just breaking a diamond seemed so anticlimactic.

But the next moment she felt Darrak's hands come around her waist from behind and he pulled her backward toward the teeter-totter.

"What are you doing?" she asked shakily.

"Preventative measures."

"From what?"

"Just trust me."

Rosa looked supremely pissed off. "Come Malcolm. We need to go back to the Malleus and report that . . ." She frowned. "What are you looking at, boy? Let's go!" She reached for him but her son staggered back from her.

Then Eden saw it and a chill ran down her spine.

There were two swirling clouds of black smoke on the ground near Rosa's feet.

By breaking the diamond, she'd destroyed the prison in which Rosa's archdemons were trapped. To destroy the archdemons, Rosa would have had to smash it by herself.

Eden had freed them.

"Darrak . . ." she began.

"Shh. Don't speak," he whispered in her ear, his arms still around her waist, holding her tightly in place. "Be very quiet."

Rosa looked down, finally seeing the black smoke just as it began to move up her legs. Her eyes widened in shock.

"Wait," she said, holding her hands out. "No. We can talk about this."

The incorporeal archdemons didn't seem in much of a mood to chat. They began moving quicker and quicker, swirling and twisting around Rosa's body like synchronized tornadoes.

"Malcolm!" she yelled. "Do something! You're a member of the Malleus! Exorcise them!"

Cradling his arm, Malcolm moved farther back from Rosa. "I'm sorry, Mother. But I've decided to take a leave of absence from the organization."

"You what?"

"I'm going back to college." His jaw set. "Just like you wanted, remember?"

Rosa glared at him. Before she could say another word the smoke moved to cover her completely.

And the moment after that, the blackness dissipated completely, leaving nothing behind.

⇒ TWENTY-FOUR ⇐

The first thing Eden did after Rosa disappeared with the archdemons was run over to check on Leena. The shapeshifter, still in cat form, was unconscious but breathing and her heartbeat was regular. Eden was no doctor—or veterinarian—but that seemed like a good sign.

She was ready for Malcolm to storm at her, furious at what happened to his mother, and wanting revenge. But he leaned against the trunk of a tall tree, his mouth still gaping open in shock at what had just happened. Even though the playground had grown darker with the setting sun, his face was very pale. He suddenly made eye contact with Eden and started slowly walking toward her.

Darrak stepped into his path. "Don't even think about it."

"No," Malcolm managed. "I—I wasn't thinking about hurting her. I had no idea what my mother was involved with all these years. I'm so sorry. If I'd known . . ." He shook his head. "The Malleus would never have approved something like this."

He looked so incredibly disillusioned. His worldview had

been shattered in thirty minutes or less. Quicker than ordering a pizza.

"Well, she did say it was to fight evil, right?" Eden said.

It was a shot in the dark. Eden didn't know why she was trying to defend the woman who'd tried to kill her and trap Darrak other than as an attempt to soften the blow to Malcolm.

And it actually earned a small snort of laughter from Malcolm. "From what I've seen tonight, my mother was more evil than the two of you put together. I'm sorry this had to happen."

"Which part?" Eden asked.

"All of it." He looked back to where his mother had been standing before the archdemons had covered her body like a black blanket from Hell. "Now I know why she wanted me to go back to school. I was going to major in Archaeology. She probably wanted me to learn how to dig up more magical artifacts for her to use in the future like that diamond of hers. She was so insistent that I go."

"And are you going to?" Eden asked.

He nodded. "I need time to think. After what I've seen . . ." He looked at both Eden and Darrak in turn. "I have a lot to think about."

Eden stood up and went over to him to give him a hug. Out of the corner of her eye she saw Darrak tense, ready to spring if Malcolm did anything. But she knew he wouldn't hurt her.

"Good-bye, Eden," he whispered. "And good luck to you."

"I'm going to need it, right?"

He smiled and flicked another glance at the demon. "You will. No doubt about it."

He didn't hug Darrak. Eden wasn't terribly surprised about that. He turned, without another word, and went to his car. A few moments later, gravel crunched as he drove away.

Eden turned to Darrak, surprised to see that he looked pissed off at her.

"What?"

He shook his head. "You weren't supposed to use your new

magic and now you've already used it as if it was a present you couldn't wait until Christmas to unwrap."

She put a hand on her hip. "I didn't exactly have a choice."

"There's always a choice. How do you feel?"

She thought about it. "I feel fine. Considering that a mini-apocalypse just went down in this playground of death and destruction." She glanced with regret and more than a little grief at the empty pile of clothes marking the place where Selina had been killed.

"And when you channeled the magic—?"

"Like I said, I feel just fine. Maybe Selina was wrong. Maybe I can do it without anything bad happening."

He pursed his lips and walked over to Selina's clothes, reaching down to retrieve her gray-stoned necklace—which had turned snow white. Now that Selina was gone Eden figured that was its default setting. He brought it over and fastened the chain around her neck. The heavy pendant fell to her chest.

"Look." His expression was grim.

She looked down to see the stone was slowly changing from unblemished white to a darker shade. Not as dark as Selina's had been, though. Eden's was a very light gray with some darker, marblelike veins running through it.

The current state of her compromised soul was now a lovely fashion accessory.

"Okay," Eden said after a moment. "Maybe channeling the black magic did do a little something after all."

"How can you sound so calm about this?"

"I don't exactly have any choice here, do I?"

His lips thinned. "There's still a choice, of course. We'll contact someone with the Malleus directly and arrange an official exorcism by someone who—"

She slapped him.

"Ow!" He held a hand to his cheek, frowning. "What the hell was that for?"

"Sorry. Couldn't help myself. I guess I react with violence

now when somebody says something outwardly stupid. I'll try something different next time to mix it up."

"It's not stupid. It's the only way."

"No it's not. We'll find another way to break your curse."

"Selina's dead."

"I know that."

"You have less than a year to live if I'm possessing you."

"I know that, too."

"Then why won't you consider exorcising—"

This time she kissed him. A bit less violent than slapping but no less dangerous. When she pulled away to see his shocked face, she poked a finger at him.

"I didn't just tap into my nasty black cesspool of magic tonight so I could call up 1-800-Exorcist tomorrow."

"Yeah, but—"

Another kiss. Longer this time. Eden grabbed hold of his plain black T-shirt to pull him closer. The night was cold and he felt very warm, despite the fact he wasn't wearing a coat.

"Then why did you do it?" he asked gruffly when they parted again.

"Because I need you."

He raised a dark eyebrow. "You need me for what?"

"You're my resident expert on the supernatural. And Andy's got a stack of cases involving werewolves and other . . . well, *Others*."

He nodded. "Good reason. I can definitely help with that. It's the least I can do."

"And . . . and I also need you to help me deal with this." She touched the grayish stone. "Selina promised to help me but now she's gone." Her voice caught. "She was a black witch but she wasn't all bad. She could control it. Maybe there's still hope for me."

"There's always hope."

"You think so?"

He nodded. "If you'd asked me that a couple weeks ago I would have said no, but now I think there might be."

"Even for a humanity-infused archdemon and a newly black witch?"

"Even for a couple of losers like that." He exhaled. "I'll figure out a way to break this curse."

"Well, that would be good. I'm kind of counting on it."

He touched her throat, stroking his thumb gently over where he'd nearly choked the life out of her. "I almost killed you."

"But you didn't. You were able to resist her even though she knew your true name."

"Only because my bond to you is stronger than that. It was still a struggle, though. Thankfully, Pussy Galore arrived to save the day."

"Our bond," she repeated. "That growing addiction to each other you mentioned the other day."

He nodded and stroked the long hair off her face. "For many reasons, it's going to be difficult. Being with you all the time until we figure out a solution to our problem."

She swallowed. "I know you wish it hadn't happened—"

He kissed her this time. Just a quick one. "You really haven't been paying attention."

She was confused. "But you said—"

"I said nothing good had ever come of being with someone for me before. And I was right—you're a black witch because of me."

"You didn't know."

"No, I didn't." He exhaled, then met her eyes. "But it can never happen again between us."

She was about to ask why, but then remembered what Selina had said. The spell she'd put on Darrak hadn't been removed. If they ever made love again, Eden would lose more of her soul as her black magic increased.

"Oh," she said after it sunk in. "So I guess we're really going to be like brother and sister now, aren't we?"

Darrak nodded, but drew his thumb over her bottom lip. "If the brother had incredibly inappropriate thoughts about his sister every minute of the day." He managed a small smile. "It's not going to be easy, but I won't hurt you again no matter how hard it gets." He cleared his throat. "You know. *Literally*."

"You're so noble."

"Totally."

She touched his hand. "And kissing?"

"Kissing is dangerous on many levels for us. It leads to other things."

"Good point." She forced herself to pull away from him and looked at the horizon to see the sun was slipping behind it as they spoke. A glance at Darrak's now shadowed face confirmed he was beginning to show the strain of losing form. But as usual he was fighting it.

"It's almost time," he warned her.

She held up her hands. "We need some rules."

He covered his stomach and hunched over a little. "Such as?"

"I'm going to dampen you when I need bathroom time."

"Fine."

"And no taking over my body to trip, slap, or punch people. And if I'm in danger of having another experience like what happened with the foamy salt mouth, you'll give me a better warning."

"Understood. Anything else?"

She couldn't think at the moment. "I'll make up an alphabetized list."

"I look forward to reading it."

She frowned. "And one more thing—"

He kissed her again, hard on her lips. When he pulled away she touched her mouth, feeling passion swell inside her for him even though she really wished she didn't feel that way. She forgot what she was going to say. "What was that for?"

"Just for the hell of it."

He grinned, before the pain of fighting against losing form swept that expression away. The next moment he turned to black smoke before her very eyes, swirling around for a moment before he disappeared inside of her. She braced a hand against the nearest tree to support herself after the wave of pleasure weakened her knees.

"Damn," she managed.

"You are both so screwed," Leena commented from a dozen feet away. She had returned to human form and shakily pushed up from the ground.

"Oh, I know that," Eden said. "And your point?"

"Just stating the obvious."

"Thought you were leaving."

"I thought so, too. But here I am."

Eden swallowed. "Thanks for helping out."

"I guess I'm in this up to my ass now. Maybe I'll stay after all."

Eden looked at her skeptically. "Let me guess. Nowhere else to go?"

Leena shrugged. "Sad, isn't it?"

"Very." She crossed her arms. "Well, I have to say you were right about one thing."

"What's that?"

"You make a kick-ass lasagna."

Leena grinned. "I knew you'd like it."

"Do you know how to cook anything else?"

"Are you asking me to move back in with you so I can feed you and protect you from that demon of yours?"

Eden touched her chest. She felt Darrak's presence as he settled in for the night. "He's not going to hurt me."

"Sure he won't." She rolled her eyes. "But actually I was thinking more along the lines of a chaperone. No more hanky-panky or you get more evil. Is that right?"

Maybe she should take out an ad in the daily newspaper. That way she could make sure everyone in the city knew about her magical sex issues.

"It's not going to be a problem," she said as firmly as she could.

Leena laughed out loud at that as she rubbed her hand against her head. She probably had a bump from hitting the tree earlier. "I heard the demon say that he loves you. So, yeah, it's going to be a problem. A big one."

Eden bit her bottom lip and waited for Darrak to respond to that, but all was quiet for the moment, other than the warm presence that let her know he was fully conscious and listening in.

Okay, so she was still possessed by an archdemon and former incubus. She'd been turned into a black witch who had to keep a rein on the magic now at her very fingertips for fear of losing her soul completely. The private investigation agency she owned 49 percent of had been inundated with supernatural clientele.

Was Darrak's newfound humanity a permanent change? Or would the fiery, horned archdemon return in all his nasty, evil glory someday when she least expected it? And would they find a way to break the curse before it killed her in a year?

Would they be able to control their passion for each other, regrettable or not, so she didn't lose another piece of her soul?

And . . . when he said he loved her, had he really meant it?

"One problem at a time, okay?" Eden said, a bit shakily, after a long moment passed.

"Yes," Darrak replied from inside of her. "One problem at a time."

⇒ TWENTY-FIVE ⇐

"This is all the information I have on her." Ben pushed the folder marked "Eden Riley" he'd taken from the precinct across the table.

"Thank you. Are you ready?"

Yes, he was. He was more ready than he'd ever been for anything in his life. He rolled up his sleeve and placed his arm down on the table, palm up.

A moment later the brand was pressed into his skin.

Scratch that. He wasn't ready. Nobody could be ready for pain like this without any anesthetic. But he gritted his teeth and didn't cry out. That wouldn't have made a very good impression, would it?

He smelled something burning and he knew it was his own flesh. Instead of trying to push the pain away he embraced it. This was his christening into a new world—a world he'd never even imagined before today. He felt the power enter him along with the pain, imbuing him with the ability to sense the Otherworldly.

He'd seen a demon with his own eyes. It wasn't something

he'd ever forget. That demon had taken someone he cared about. He thought he might be able to love Eden. Despite his past and the troubles he'd had, he was willing to open his heart to her.

She was in danger. It was obvious. And he'd do anything it took to save her from that . . . monster.

He wasn't able to save his fiancée—a woman he'd loved more than life itself. This would help to finally make up for that failure.

The brand was pulled away. He looked down at his charred flesh to see the circle enclosing the fleur-de-lis.

"Welcome to the Malleus," the white-haired man across the table said. "We welcome you as a brother. All that we have is yours. And all that you have is ours. We together will defeat the evil that permeates this world, protecting the citizens who don't realize what lurks in the shadows. Do you agree to this?"

"Yes," Ben said firmly. He was concerned with protecting this world and the people who lived in it. Of course he was. But he was mostly concerned with Eden. He feared for her safety. For her very soul. "You told me that you had information about Eden, other than what's in my files."

"Yes. Eden shows signs of psychic ability, correct?"

He nodded. "I dismissed it originally, but I think it might be very real. And after what I've seen I know it's possible."

"It is. She gets that from her father."

"Her father." His arm hurt so much it made it hard to think. "She doesn't know anything about her father. There's nothing about him in her file."

"No, there wouldn't be. Her mother never told her anything. As far as Caroline Riley was concerned he was a brief fling. A man with no past or future."

"Who is he?"

The white-haired man studied him as if gauging how ready Ben was to hear the truth. He was ready. No matter what it was.

"He's an angel."

Okay. He'd been wrong. He hadn't been ready for that.

"An . . . an *angel*? Eden's father is an angel? You've got to be kidding, right?"

The Malleus elder shook his head. "Eden Riley's psychic abilities and her closeness to the magical world are due entirely to the fact that she is half human and half angel, making her what is termed a *nephilim*. It's very rare, but not unheard of."

"A . . . nephilim?"

"This is the power Eden has deep inside of her—mostly dormant until now—from which the demon draws his energy. It's the reason he's able to take corporeal form."

Ben was stunned. "This is hard to believe."

"But do you?"

He nodded firmly and brushed his fingers against the gold cross he wore around his neck. "Yes, I do. I believe."

"Her involvement with this archdemon is very dangerous."

Ben clutched the side of the table, the pain from his fresh brand forgotten. "I need to save her."

"You will. But in the meantime, it won't be long before the news of his daughter's current situation will likely reach her father's ears. And to know that she has been corrupted by an archdemon . . . well . . ."

"Well what?" Ben asked.

The Malleus elder smiled thinly. "There is going to be serious hell to pay."

Turn the page for a special preview
of the next Living in Eden novel
by Michelle Rowen

SOMETHING WICKED

Coming soon from Berkley Sensation!

⇒ ONE ⇐

"Would you look at this place? Equal parts lust and desperation. It's fantastic."

Eden grimaced. She'd been trying to pay as little attention to Darrak as possible, but it wasn't easy. The demon was very hard to ignore.

"It's a single's club," she replied. "What did you expect?"

"This, of course. But it's even better than I thought it would be."

"You have a strange sense of what *better* is."

A tall man holding a bottle of Corona tapped Eden on her shoulder. When she turned to look at him he leered approvingly at her. "Who are you talking to, sexy lady?"

She cleared her throat. "Nobody. Just talking to myself. I do that frequently now that I've stopped taking my medication."

"Uh . . . *okay*." He slowly backed away from her and went to hit on someone else. Someone *sane*.

Darrak snorted. "Busted."

She felt her face redden. She had to remember that no one but her could see or hear Darrak at the moment. He was her demon. Her *inner* demon. After all, Eden Riley was the current cover girl for demonic possession.

This time she spoke under her breath so no one would hear. "I thought you said you were going to keep quiet once we got in here?"

"I lied. Besides, you need me to coach you through this, don't you? I thought you said you're a bit out of your element."

He was right about that.

"Okay, so coach me. Now what should I do?"

"Walk over to the bar, order a drink, and scan the room. I know he's around here somewhere. I just have to spot him."

"You still haven't told me how you found this guy. How were you able to contact anyone in your, uh, current condition?"

"I have my ways."

Well, that was cryptic. But instead of grilling him about it, Eden walked across the floor of the dark nightclub, Luxuria. It was very upscale with gleaming black floors and an indigo interior. A cascade of pretty sparkling light moved slowly across the hundreds of faces and bodies in attendance. But the lust and desperation Darrak mentioned seemed to permeate the entire building, giving it a distinctly unpleasant ambiance Eden was able to pick up with her subtle sixth sense.

As she walked, she tried not to twist her ankle in the four-inch stiletto heels Darrak strongly suggested she wear tonight. Her legs felt cold in her short skirt. She normally didn't like to show off so much skin, especially this late in October. However, a quick scan of the club made her feel that she was practically in casual wear compared to the other women-on-the-prowl. They, however, didn't share her inner accessory.

No one could see the demon, but that didn't mean he wasn't very much there, currently sharing her scantily-clad body.

Why wasn't Eden freaking out over the fact that she was possessed by a demon? She had. Many times. She'd since realized that no matter how much freaking out she did, it didn't do much to change the situation.

Three hundred years ago, Darrak had barely survived a

witch's death curse. It had destroyed his physical form, leaving only his essence behind. He'd existed for three centuries unseen and mostly unheard by the hosts he'd been forced to possess.

That is, until he'd possessed Eden.

For some reason—and it was probably because she was a little bit psychic and had been for as long as she could remember—he was able to feed off of that energy to communicate with her at night in her head and take physical form during daylight hours.

Until they found a way to break his curse and return him to full power so he could re-form a permanent body, they were stuck like this. And screaming about it wasn't going to do anything except make her throat hurt.

There was someone in this club tonight who could help them. A specialist in the affairs of Others—aka the Otherworldly—who would know where they'd need to go for curse removal. Whether this person was human or not was something the demon hadn't yet shared with her.

Demons, witches, fairies, and werewolves, Eden thought as she scanned the crowd of seemingly normal mingling singles. *Welcome to my new life. I definitely need a drink.*

The bartender eyed her when she slid onto a tall stool. "What's your pleasure?"

"Uh . . . I'll have a white wine. Thanks."

"That's so boring," Darrak commented internally. "A white wine? Could you order a more generic drink?"

She cleared her throat and tried to keep the smile fixed on her face.

"Sure thing," the bartender said, quickly uncapping a bottle of house white and pouring her a glass.

"Let me guess. You're not a fancy cocktail kind of girl," Darrak continued even though she wished he'd just shut up for a moment. The demon hadn't had much conversation in three centuries so now he was a regular chat factory. It was a good thing he had such a nice voice—deep, warm, and usually filled with wry amusement at the human world he witnessed through Eden's eyes.

"Not particularly," she replied dryly, when the bartender moved farther down the bar and out of earshot. "The little paper umbrellas can be so intimidating."

"It's all fun and games till someone pokes their eye out. So you've found something you like, and you stick with it."

"Makes things very simple."

"But how will you ever know if there's a drink out there that might be the best thing you've ever tasted?"

She shrugged a shoulder. "I'm perfectly content with my white wine."

"*Content*," he repeated and the one word sounded like a pronouncement on Eden's boring life. At least, up until she got possessed. Things now were difficult, awkward, and frequently dangerous, but they couldn't exactly be described as "boring." Too bad, really.

There was a wall-length mirror behind the bar that allowed her to see both herself and the club behind her. Her gaze didn't go to her long, bone-straight auburn hair, her green eyes lined with smoky liner, or her plunging neckline that showed off too much cleavage to be considered remotely modest, but instead to the necklace she wore. The pendant was light gray with darker veins running through it. It looked like a two inch oval piece of polished marble. She absently ran her fingertips over its cool surface.

"Don't worry." The previous amused and mocking edge to Darrak's voice was gone and replaced by a serious tone. "It's still practically white."

She tried to smile at her reflection. "You're a very good liar, you know that?"

"I have been told that once or twice before."

The amulet showed how damaged her soul was after she recently came into some . . . *powers*. *Dark* powers. She was now officially a "black witch"—a woman who had black magic at her fingertips to use whenever she wanted.

Using this kind of magic destroyed a soul piece by piece, little by little, eating away at one's ability to tell good from evil. The best solution—the *only* solution—was not to use the magic at all. Eden had used it just once and her soul was damaged from it. Just a shade darker, but it would never be completely pure again.

Eden could feel it now, only a short mental reach away—a bottomless ocean of power that itched to be used. It was like doing heroin. She'd heard that when you did that drug the first time, you were an immediate junkie.

Ditto black magic.

She hadn't told Darrak about this constant urge she now had to dip into the dark well of power. He was adamant that she never use it again, no matter what—it was too dangerous for her. He felt a great deal of guilt about her current gray-stoned predicament, which was understandable. After all, it was his fault she was now officially a black witch.

Having sex with the demon had—*hocus-pocus*—accidentally turned her into one.

She chewed her bottom lip and tasted her red lip gloss as the memory slid through her mind of what had happened between them.

Well . . . Darrak *did* have solid form during the day. And that form was a *mighty fine* one.

What could she say? It had happened. Once.

But it could never happen again. *Ever.* Not unless she wanted to put more of her soul at risk. And she didn't. She was very fond of her soul, even in its current, slightly dingy state.

"Do you see him yet?" she asked, taking her mind off other hazardous, horizontal subjects. She turned away from her reflection to look at the faces in the crowd, slowly scanning the width of the room.

"Not yet. This place is packed. I think every desperate single person in the city is here tonight."

Eden took a shaky sip of her wine. It tasted bland and, to be honest, a bit boring. Not that she'd ever admit it.

"I don't believe it," a voice said to her left. "Eden Riley. Long time no see."

She turned and her eyes widened with surprise. "You're kidding me. Graham . . . Graham Davis?"

The attractive dark-haired man grinned at her. "You remember me."

A matching smile blossomed on her face. "High school was only, oh, a dozen years ago."

"Seems like two dozen sometimes."

Darrak sighed internally. "Eden, you need to keep your attention on the room so I can spot my contact. Priorities, remember?"

Obviously the demon didn't realize how long it had been since she'd seen Graham. It felt like forever. She had no idea why they hadn't stayed in touch. After high school, Graham had gone backpacking in Europe, she'd gone off to university, and time had simply passed. Too bad, really. Graham had been one of her very best friends.

Graham's gaze moved down the front of her. "You're looking fantastic. Just as gorgeous as you were back in grade twelve."

She grinned. "Right back at you. And that's a great suit."

Graham looked down at his gray Armani suit. "I dress to impress."

"Eden . . ." Darrak said tightly. "I know we're in a lustful, desperate singles club, but that's no reason to let this guy hit on you."

Darrak thought Graham was hitting on her? She tried not to smile at the thought. As attractive as Graham Davis was, and as good friends as they'd been back when they were teenagers, she and Graham had never hooked up and never would. It could have had a little something to do with Graham being gay.

But Darrak didn't know that. Which would explain the jealous edge to his words.

The thought that another man's potential interest would

make Darrak immediately jealous, despite their mutually-agreed-to platonic partnership was . . . interesting.

But it only made things more complicated.

"You really shouldn't be here, Eden," Graham said.

That got her full attention. Maybe she misheard him. "I shouldn't?"

He shook his head, taking a moment to scan their surroundings. "If you're looking to meet someone new, there are better places than this to find someone. It's dangerous here."

She hadn't expected that statement to come out of his mouth. "Doesn't look all that dangerous to me. Besides, what are *you* doing here?" She raised an eyebrow. "Doesn't seem like your kind of singles club."

His mouth curled up on one side. "No? You don't think I can meet my future bride here?"

She smiled back at him. "Somehow, I doubt it."

Graham's grin widened. "I don't know. Maybe it's fate, us seeing each other again. Maybe I should leave my old life behind and you should marry me and we'll have lots of gorgeous babies together."

"I hate this guy," Darrak said. "Eden, letting this blast from your past drool on you is not productive to our goal tonight. Let's carry on, shall we?"

"Sounds like a perfect life," she said to Graham. "Shall we set a date?"

Graham held the smile a moment longer before it faded at the edges. "Seriously though, I think you should take off. This place . . . I don't know what's going on, but something's very wrong here."

She frowned. "Which means what?"

"I'm doing a story on this club for the *Toronto Star*."

"You're a journalist? That's so great. It's what you wanted to be back in the day."

He nodded. "Investigative journalist. And I've been investigating this club. There have been six women who've gone missing in the area, all of whom were regulars here since Luxuria opened for business last month. I feel like there might be a predator at work, and"—he shook his head—"I just have this strange hunch that it's directly related to the club itself. Like somebody on the inside is choosing victims from those who come here looking for love."

The thought made a chill run down her spine. "I haven't heard anything about this. Are the police investigating, too?"

"The disappearances, yes. The club itself, no. The missing women are only loosely connected to this place and they don't see the connection as keenly as I do. There's nothing yet that ties it directly to the club aside from a gut feeling on my part. If I find anything to substantiate my hunch, this place will be shut down in a heartbeat."

"So you're telling me to be careful."

"That's exactly what I'm telling you." Graham touched her arm. "Consider it a request from an old friend. Stay safe. Even though it's a big, lonely city and it's nice to find someone to be with, I figure it's way better to be alone and alive than alone and dead."

A chill went down Eden's spine. "You think the women are dead?"

"That's what I'm here to figure out and I'm not leaving until I do." He cocked an eyebrow. "And, you know, if I win a journalism award along the way, then it's all the better. It's going to be a great story."

Eden reached into her purse and pulled out a business card. "Here. Take this."

He did and looked at it. "You're a private investigator?"

"I . . . well, I own half of Triple-A Investigations. It's just a small office on the outskirts of the city. I assist someone else, mostly, but what I'm saying is if you need some help, I'd be happy to pitch in any way I can."

Graham smiled and tucked the card into the inner chest pocket of his jacket. "I'll definitely keep that in mind. It was good seeing you again, Eden."

"You, too. Good luck with the story."

"I'll take all the luck I can get." He touched her face and shook his head. "Twelve years."

"I know. And yet we still have that youthful glow."

"I turned thirty last week. The glow is starting to fade a bit." He laughed. "Let's not make it so long next time, okay? Good friends—people you can really trust—they're hard to find."

"You have my card. We'll do coffee and catch up?"

"Sounds like a plan."

Graham leaned over and gave Eden a quick kiss. She felt Darrak's presence tense inside of her, even though the kiss was only one of friendship.

However . . . something else happened with the contact. A sensation of dread, of fear, of darkness swept over her. As soon as it was there, before she could grab hold of it and analyze what she'd just seen and felt, it was gone. That was how her psychic abilities usually were. Totally useless.

"I'll give you a call tomorrow, Eden. Promise," Graham said before moving off into the crowd, which seemed to swallow him whole in a scattering of light and mingling bodies.

"I hate that guy," Darrak said. "Loathe him. And I can't believe you let him kiss you. I almost made you slap him, but lucky for him he didn't try to slip you the tongue. It's obvious to me that he's only after one thing from you and—"

"He's gay," Eden said simply.

"Oh." There was a pause. "I totally knew that."

"No, you didn't."

"No, actually I didn't. Huh."

"What do you think about the six missing women?" Eden asked quietly as she sipped on her glass of white wine and scanned the crowd looking for Darrak's contact. She felt disturbed by what Graham had told her and from her strange psychic flash.

"All I know is it has nothing to do with us. But he's right . . . sometimes people looking for love will find more than they bargain for. Places like this leave certain people exposed, willing victims driven by lust and desperation. Which, of course, is the vibe I feel here."

"Which you approve of."

"My incubus days are long behind me, but I still find it interesting how many of them are so quick to mistake lust for love in a desperate attempt not to be alone."

She didn't particularly like the reminder that Darrak had once been an incubus, a demon who fed off the sexual energy of humans. However, he'd been promoted to "archdemon," which, actually, was much scarier. Luckily for her, he'd changed a lot since being cursed.

"I liked being alone," she said. "I was perfectly content being alone before you arrived."

"Were you?" Darrak's tone turned amused again. "Or maybe I was the answer to your silent wish to have somebody in your bleak, lonely life. You're much too attractive to be a spinster."

"I think there's a big difference between having a live-in boyfriend and being possessed by a demon who will slowly but surely drain me of all of my energy until I'm dead."

She hadn't meant for it to sound quite so blunt, but the fact was, if they didn't find a solution to their problem, Darrak's demonic presence would eventually kill her. She knew in the three-hundred-plus years he'd been cursed, he'd been responsible for the deaths of hundreds of people he'd possessed. He told her because of this he'd tried his best to chose hosts that deserved death—murderers and other vile humans. But, still. Knowing she was possessed with someone who was essentially a metaphysical leech—even though he was a very attractive leech during daylight hours—didn't help her rest easy at night.

"We'll find a solution," Darrak said firmly. "I swear we will."

Eden downed the rest of her wine in one gulp, then dug into her purse to pay for it. "If you say so."

"I do." There was a pause. "And speaking of our solution, there he is."

Darrak's voice now held a thread of anxiety. This was important, after all. If they didn't find an answer to their mutual problem . . . well, she may as well invest in a nice gravesite with a view and he'd be forced to find his next unwilling victim.

"Where?"

"Over by the dance floor. To the right. There's a table with three blond women and the bald man staring at their breasts is the one we're looking for."

"Charming," she said, keeping her voice low. "He's human?"

"I think so. He's the personal assistant to the local wizard master. He's the one we really need to get to."

"Wizard master?" she repeated skeptically. "What is this, Dungeons & Dragons?"

"That's a game, right?"

"Yes."

"This isn't a game."

No, it definitely wasn't. Wizard master it was, then. "So what do I do?"

"Go over and say I sent you. He'll know who I am and what you're here for. The dress you're wearing is just for him. He's very fond of the ladies, as you can see, but he has a special place in his libido for redheads just like you. We're golden. But if that little pervert touches you, I'll probably rip his head off. Just an FYI. We'll have to see how it goes."

"Try to restrain yourself."

"This is it, Eden. We're close. I feel like this is going to be the solution to our mutual problem."

"I sure hope you're right." Because otherwise they were out of options.

She slid off the chair and adjusted her skirt that had crept up higher on her thighs. Then she forced herself to be brave and cross the floor, keeping the average-looking human in sight just in case he tried to magically disappear. It could happen.

Only fifteen feet away now. Twelve. Ten.

"Wait a second," Darrak said suddenly. "Eden, stop walking."

She froze in place. "What is it?"

"I'm not sure. I thought I saw someone I recognized."

"Who?"

"Look over toward the left, just a quick glance so I can check."

She did what he asked, sweeping her eyes slowly across a sea of faces. "Who is it?"

The demon swore.

Eden waited, every muscle in her body now tense.

"We need to get out of here right now," Darrak said tightly.

"But I thought you said we need to talk to the wizard master's assistant." She looked over at him laughing with the three women, oblivious to her. Only ten feet away. They were so close.

"No. This isn't the right time. Leave, Eden. Now, before I make you."

"But why are you—?"

The next moment, she found herself forcibly turned around toward the exit. If motivated enough, the demon was able to control her body—or parts of it, anyhow. Since Eden didn't enjoy losing control of her bodily functions, so to speak, she'd set up rules that prohibited him from ever doing that. At the moment, though, instead of anger she felt panic well inside her at his unexpected reaction.

"Darrak—"

"I'm serious," Darrak said. "You need to get us the hell out of here right now."

There was something in his voice that made her decide not to argue any further. Eden began walking toward the door. She exited and put one foot in front of the other on her way to her car.

"Are you going to tell me what that was about?" she asked.

"I saw someone I used to know. Someone I haven't seen for over three hundred years, since before I was cursed."

"Who was it?" Her hand shook as she tried to get her key into the lock of her rusted Toyota.

"He's an archdemon like me."

Eden inhaled sharply. "Does he know you're here?"

"I don't know. But coincidences are usually fate giving us a kick in the ass. All I know is he's dangerous. He wouldn't know what happened to me with the curse. And he wouldn't understand that I'm . . . well, I'm different than I used to be."

This was shorthand for saying Darrak used to be demonically evil and now—thanks to being infused with humanity after possessing humans for hundreds of years—he wasn't.

Which meant this other demon would be everything Darrak once was—powerful, destructive, scary, without conscience or empathy. Something she'd want to avoid in every way possible. "What would this demon do if he found out what happened to you?"

"I'm not sure."

She shivered as she got in the car and turned the key in the ignition. "So this demon . . . he's an old enemy of yours?"

"No," Darrak said wryly. "Actually, he was my best friend."

Penguin Group (USA) Online

What will you be reading tomorrow?

Patricia Cornwell, Nora Roberts, Catherine Coulter,
Ken Follett, John Sandford, Clive Cussler,
Tom Clancy, Laurell K. Hamilton, Charlaine Harris,
J. R. Ward, W.E.B. Griffin, William Gibson,
Robin Cook, Brian Jacques, Stephen King,
Dean Koontz, Eric Jerome Dickey, Terry McMillan,
Sue Monk Kidd, Amy Tan, Jayne Ann Krentz,
Daniel Silva, Kate Jacobs...

You'll find them all at
penguin.com

*Read excerpts and newsletters,
find tour schedules and reading group guides,
and enter contests.*

Subscribe to Penguin Group (USA) newsletters
and get an exclusive inside look
at exciting new titles and the authors you love
long before everyone else does.

PENGUIN GROUP (USA)
penguin.com